Great Irish Short Stories

Edited, with an Introduction, by Vivian Mercier

Tim :
may you enjoy these short stories. Some of them I heard from my Grand ma when I was a child.
God love you and bless you,
Earl G

BARNES
&NOBLE
B O O K S
NEW YORK

Contents

Introduction

This anthology has been planned with a dual purpose: to show that Irishmen do have a special gift for the short story, and to offer some reasons why they have developed this special talent. Why should Ireland—whose population is only four million, which has never had a period of great material wealth like Holland's or Portugal's or Sweden's, whose cultural influence on Europe even in the great period, say from 600 to 850 A.D., was relatively small and scattered—be ranked with the Great Powers of literature in even one restricted genre? My first answer must be that Ireland—except for a possible injustice to the Greeks, who have been in the short story business since Herodotus at least—has lawfully earned her rank. It would be impossible to compile a representative anthology of the world's short stories without including at least a couple of Irish writers: perhaps James Joyce and Frank O'Connor, or George Moore and Liam O'Flaherty.

But again, why? How did the materially underprivileged Irish attain their culturally privileged position? Partly against their will, one has to admit, for they were conquered by the English and eventually compelled to learn the conqueror's tongue. On the average, an Irish writer does not have to struggle so hard for world recognition as a Danish or a Dutch one, let alone a Hungarian or a Lithuanian. His visibility is high, so to speak. Three Irishmen, Shaw, Yeats and Beckett, have won the Nobel Prize for Literature; if Joyce had lived a few years longer, the prejudices aroused by his flouting of both literary and social taboos would have abated enough to permit his winning a Nobel award too. Nevertheless, Irish literature never would have been more than a province of English literature if, in learning English, the Irish had completely forgotten their original tongue. Gaelic, now the native language of no more than 50,000 Irishmen and Irishwomen though known to hundreds of thousands more, was the first European tongue after Latin to develop its own literature. When the Irish took enthusiastically to Christianity in the fifth century, they also acquired the Roman alphabet and could at last write down the lore that their druids and other learned men had preserved by word of mouth. Under the influence of Latin literature—and perhaps even of Greek—Gaelic developed a number of sophisticated poetic techniques and an expository prose that could deal with abstract ideas in theology and philosophy.

Early Gaelic narrative prose, which has survived in considerable quantity and is often vivid and exciting, nevertheless seems primitive beside the poetry and nonnarrative prose. The reason for this is, I believe, simple enough: in the words of the late Gerard Murphy, "there can be little doubt that Irish narrative tradition has on the whole been essentially oral." Many ancient Irish stories have survived only in manuscript form, but they usually show the characteristic strengths and weaknesses of word-of-mouth narration. They begin well and then tail off badly. Before the days of tape recorders, both storytellers and folklore collectors used to grow weary well before the end of a long story had been written down. If this happened in the nineteenth and early twentieth centuries, we can well imagine the same thing occurring in, say, the twelfth century. Often, the written story seems no more than a series of notes to aid a reciter's memory. The manuscripts themselves tell us that a learned Gaelic poet was supposed to know some 350 of these prose tales by heart.

But perhaps the strongest argument in favor of the oral folklore origin of the prose narratives is the fact that, in sharp contrast to the poems in the manuscripts, only a handful of stories, almost all dating from later than 1600, are attributed to particular authors. Comparisons between earlier and later manuscripts will often suggest that a man of letters has taken an early story and tinkered with it, usually spoiling it in the process, but it is hard to accept Professor James Carney's view that the old stories were literary products from the start. The fact that many of the old stories, particularly those dealing with the hero Finn MacCool (Fionn Mac Cumhail), have been recorded in Gaelic from the lips of illiterate farmers and fishermen or their wives does not settle the argument—since literate people could have taught the stories at some time in the past to those who could not read—but it does weigh heavily in favor of Murphy's view and against Carney's.

Because the Irish custom of oral storytelling seems so closely related to the growth of the Irish literary short story, I want to sketch briefly its chief social and esthetic features. Literacy, electricity, improved transportation, radio and television have virtually put an end to the custom, so that the following description refers chiefly to the past.

In the dark winter nights from Hallowe'en to St. Patrick's Day (17 March), an audience consisting mainly of older people would gather in some hospitable house around a turf fire to listen until bedtime to one or more storytellers. This gathering was usually called a *céilidhe*.[1] The ideal storyteller could entertain his listeners every night for 4½ months without repeating a single story. Professor James H. Delargy cites the names of some storytellers who could have accomplished this seemingly impossible feat without difficulty. One made a series of Ediphone recordings that ran to a total of over half a million words, or the equivalent of half a dozen average-length novels. Another recorded 120 *long* stories, besides other material. Others, whose repertory consisted mainly of shorter items, equalled or surpassed the traditional figure of 350 separate stories. Although most of these remarkable storytellers were men, a woman supplied 375 tales, of which forty were long. Éamonn Búrc of Carna recorded a story 34,000 words long, or about three times the length of the longest story in the present collection.

[1] Pronounced "kaylee."

Gaelic distinguishes between the long story (*sean-sgéal,*[2] literally "old story") and the short story (*eachtra*[3] or *seanchas*[4]). The *sean-sgéal* is either a tale of a legendary hero or what the professional folklorist calls a *märchen*— in layman's language, a fairy tale. The *eachtra* or *seanchas,* besides being shorter, stresses realistic detail even though it usually deals with the supernatural. Of the two stories collected by Synge that are reprinted here, "The Lady O'Conor" is the bare bones of a *sean-sgéal* while the other is definitely an *eachtra. A* storyteller who specialized in the shorter tales would be known as a "shanachie" (Gaelic *seanchaí*) whereas one who had mastered many a *sean-sgéal* would be given the nobler title of *sgéalaí.*[5] Although the Gaelic tradition has been emphasized here, storytelling continued for many years in districts that had become English-speaking. The Irish folklorists usually insist that the English versions are inferior to the Gaelic ones, but Patrick Kennedy's setting-down of "Cauth Morrisy Looking for Service," for example, shows that the English renderings had their own vigor.

Part I, entitled "Tales from the Ancient Literature and from Folklore," gives a broad sampling both of the old tradition and of the varied ways in which it became available in English. The first five pieces, some very short, are literal translations by scholars from Gaelic or Latin manuscripts: three concern the legendary adventures of favorite saints, while the other two are utterly pagan and primitive in both their tragedy and their comedy. All but one of these, though their translators, with the exception of that astonishing German Kuno Meyer, are hardly great literary artists, show something of the talent for lifelike and dramatic dialogue that came to be one of the hallmarks of the Irish short story.

[2] Pronounced "shan shgayl."

[3] Pronounced "achthrah."

[4] Pronounced "shanahus."

[5] Pronounced "shgaylee."

Lady Gregory also draws on the manuscript material, though she adapts it rather than gives a literal translation, rendering it into a stylized version of the English spoken by her neighbors in the village of Kiltartan, County Galway. The remaining five items in Part I translate, adapt or record folktales. Patrick Kennedy recorded in English what he had heard in English—or at any rate in the Irish-English then often called "the brogue." As for Gerald Griffin, nobody seems to know whether he heard "The Brown Man" in Gaelic or English or whether somebody else took it down for him, but he made no claim to have invented it himself (Irish fiction writers of the nineteenth century were not always so scrupulous, though perhaps less prone to pass off folk material as their own than to present their own work as folklore). Douglas Hyde's translation of a Gaelic folktale, "Leeam O'Rooney's Burial," shows how a wildly incredible story can still be given a carefully realistic setting. The selections from Synge's Aran Islands journal offer us not only the two stories but a picture of the storyteller and his audience. In telling Synge the shorter tale, Pat Dirane sought greater realism by pretending that everything in it had formed part of his personal experience (as did Cauth Morrisy in the Kennedy selection). Although the supposed widow's fickleness links this story with Hyde's, Dirane's tale contains nothing supernatural and could therefore easily be expanded into a modern realistic short story; Synge in fact made an Abbey Theatre play from it.

This is not to suggest that the development of the modern Irish short story from the oral folktale is unique. On the contrary, the same development has taken place all over the world. We can see it most clearly in Boccaccio's *Decameron*, where the transformation of folklore into sophisticated fiction occurs before our eyes as we read. All I would maintain is that the Irish short story has stayed closer to its folk roots than any other national or ethnic school of fiction except the Jewish: nothing so close to folk tradition as Isaac Bashevis Singer's "Gimpel the Fool" has been created by an Irishman since Yeats's *Stories of Red Hanrahan*. When we start searching for the origins of the worldwide short-story form of today, we soon find that short fiction did not become popular with educated readers until about 1800–1850. Inspired by Rousseau, readers and writers alike were seeking the natural, the primitive, the irrational, and they found what they wanted in folklore—recorded, adapted, or manufactured. The brothers Grimm collected folktales with scientific scholarship, but the Romantic creative writers—E. T. A. Hoffmann, for example—deliberately exploited the grotesque and supernatural aspects of folklore. These in turn led Hoffmann and, later, Poe and many others to quite profound studies in abnormal psychology. Eventually, an interest in more normal psychology developed, but most modern short stories center on a psychological crisis, which may vary from slight and transitory to permanently traumatic. Even today, the supernatural is regarded as a valid subject for short-story treatment—as in the work of Shirley Jackson or John Collier. Science fiction also deals with the supernatural, of course, merely giving it a pseudo-scientific basis.

Contemporary Irish writers have taken a violent dislike to the supernatural because leprechauns, banshees, and "the little people" in general were overexploited in nineteenth-century and early twentieth-century Irish (and pseudo-Irish) fiction. It is to the form rather than to the content of oral narrative that they remain faithful. Frank O'Connor in particular has striven hard, he tells us, to put back into the short story "the tone of a man's voice, speaking." In every one of his later stories we are conscious that *someone* is telling the story, even if we are not sure just who he is. Many years before O'Connor, however, George Moore tackled the same problem in his short stories about Irish life. In the first volume of them, *The Untilled Field* (1903), he tested a wide variety of narrative techniques, nearly all calculated to preserve the tone and vocabulary of the speaking voice. Later, in *A Story-Teller's Holiday* (1918), he adopted the device of a storytelling contest between himself and an imaginary Irish shanachie with the most un-Gaelic name of Alec Trusselby; here the narrator's presence and personality can never be lost sight of.

Frank O'Connor complained, in the preface to his paperback *Stories* already quoted, that James Joyce was one of the "skillful stylists" who had robbed the short story of the speaking voice; yet in many of the *Dubliners* stories Joyce used so much realistically colloquial dialogue that the reader almost overlooks the "mandarin" style of the narrative and descriptive passages; furthermore, "Clay," the story from that volume included here, though told in the third person, uses almost exactly the words that Maria would have chosen to tell her own story.

As already remarked, dialogue is one of the strong points of Irish short fiction from the very earliest times. In the nineteenth century, it is often the dialogue alone that makes Irish short stories readable, since the narrative and descriptive passages—unless the whole story is supposed to be told by a peasant—are couched in the most stilted hedge schoolmaster's or journalist's English. William Carleton, almost the first native Irishman to write significant fiction in English about his own country, was the son of a rural shanachie fluent in English as well as Gaelic; except for the dialogue, his writing is as stiltedly middle-class as anyone's. Before about 1850, it seems that one had to be educated at Trinity College, Dublin, in order to write fairly decent standard English. Without such an education, English-speaking Irishmen could write vigorously only in the colloquial language.

One quality indispensable to the oral storyteller is a sense of his audience. After all, they are right there under his nose. The greatest Gaelic storytellers were and are—for I have seen a couple of them at work—consummate actors, many of whom could not tell their stories to a recording machine without longing to make the appropriate gestures and facial movements. Delargy gives an account of a storyteller who, to keep in practice, would tell his stories—gestures and all—while facing a stone wall or the back of a cart. It was not until Frank O'Connor began to read his own stories aloud over the radio that he became conscious of "how the written word had robbed the story of its narrative impulse." What he meant, I think, was that the short story had lost its dramatic quality, its spontaneity, the sense of a man telling a story to other men. It must be remembered that the traditional storyteller was allowed some scope for spontaneity and individuality; as Delargy writes, "The tale must be passed on as it has been received, unaltered, not in regard to language, but in form and plot." O'Connor took similar liberties:

> When I was on the air I would drop whole passages or depart altogether from the script because those carefully arranged scenes and balanced sentences failed to get me beyond the microphone to listeners at the other side.

Because most modern Irish writers possess this awareness of audience, this sense of dramatic rapport between writer and reader, the typical Irish short story is more likely to be a *story*, not a prose poem, than its counterpart in other literatures. To a considerable extent, the short story in our time has usurped the territory of lyric poetry, so that symbolism tends to outweigh plot. But although I have tried to make an unbiased selection, most of the modern stories in this book are relatively long on plot and short on symbolism. Joyce was much closer to the present international norm fifty years ago than are many of his Irish successors: compare "Clay" with O'Connor's "Peasants" or Mary Lavin's "Brigid." The two latter stories appear very "busy" beside Joyce's.

When choosing a story I certainly have not insisted that it have a plot or even structural unity: if an author called something unclassifiable a short story and if I happened to admire it, in it went. Daniel Corkery's "Children," Seumas O'Kelly's "The Shoemaker," and James Stephens' "Three Women Who Wept" indicate how permissive I have been. On the other hand, my definitions of "Irish" and "short" were perhaps unnecessarily strict. With the exception of Carleton's "The Donagh," I haven't included any story over 10,000 words long. Since most of my selections were originally written in English, I have deliberately confined myself not merely to authors of Irish birth but to stories with an Irish background and/or characters. Although I haven't lost many authors by this decision, I can think of stories by Goldsmith, Wilde, Shaw, and Elizabeth Bowen that I should have liked to include.

One word in my title remains undefined, the most difficult of all. What is a "great" short story? How many stories in this collection really deserve that formidable adjective? Perhaps I should have used the one chosen by my greatest predecessor among Irish anthologists, W. B. Yeats. He gave the name *Representative Irish Tales* to a collection of which he was the editor, published in 1890. All the stories gathered here are in my estimation good of their kind, but not all of them are great. That warmhearted humorist Lynn Doyle might well have been shocked to hear any of his skillful tales described as "great," but I'm not yet enough of a culture snob to pass over a writer whose Ballygullion stories have given me so much pleasure, especially when read aloud with a North of Ireland accent. As for Somerville and Ross, so many important writers have praised their lighthearted "Irish R. M." stories that, like Rudyard Kipling, they are disapproved of only by middlebrows.

To be great for me, a short story has to echo in the reader's mind long after he has closed the book:

> The music in my heart I bore,
> Long after it was heard no more.

It must compel him to pursue all its implications—whether these be psychological, moral, social, or purely narrative—including "What happened next?" A novel can afford to spell out everything and tie up all its loose ends, but a short story must say little yet imply everything. Look at Joyce's "Clay," for instance: a whole life—past, present, and *future*—is laid bare in a few paragraphs, not Maria's life only but that of the two brothers. Lennox Robinson's "Education" performs a similar miracle for the life of a more complex and self-aware protagonist. George Moore's "So On He Fares"—its author's favorite—penetrates deeper than anything else of his, novel or autobiography, that I have read. The plot derives from folklore, yet the story reads like a confession far more sincere than anything in *Confessions of a Young Man*. In O'Connor's "The Man of the World," as the wife kneels in prayer and Larry looks at

Jimmy "in dismay," we suddenly realize that the boys are treating fellow human beings in an inhuman way (we do not need the explicit statement of Larry's reaction in the third paragraph from the end, and O'Connor should never have allowed himself to write it). The instantaneous illumination that leaps from this moment in O'Connor's story flashes from an image, a gesture, or a phrase in story after story among those reprinted here.

It is not altogether fanciful to perceive something of the same quality in the traditional stories—when St. Patrick says, "*Gratzacham*, take it," or when Mis, in lustier vein, says, "Don't mind the harp . . . but do the feat." In those old stories the more or less legendary protagonists define their personalities by word or deed with greater simplicity and more dazzling clarity than do the protagonists of the best modern short stories. Two lines of Yeats from a different context may sum up the essence of a great short story, Irish or not:

> Character isolated by a deed
> To engross the present and dominate memory.

I hope that the reader will find many stories here to "dominate memory."

—VIVIAN MERCER

TALES FROM THE ANCIENT LITERATURE AND FROM FOLKLORE

MUIRCHÚ MACCU MACTHENI
About A.D. *700*

All books about Irish literature should begin with St. Patrick or try to invoke his name as early as possible, for it was he, or other Christian missionaries like him, who brought the Roman alphabet to Ireland and thus made Gaelic literature possible. The traditional date of his arrival in Ireland as a missionary is 432, so that Muirchú's life of the saint, the earliest complete one that survives, was written more than two centuries after the events it claims to describe. The brief excerpt from it given here makes a complete short story, with characterization, suspense, and humor in full measure. A less talented storyteller might have ended with Dairi's gift of the hill, but the seemingly irrelevant anecdote of the doe and the fawn makes a charming, lifelike ending.

How St. Patrick Obtained Armagh

There was a certain wealthy and noble man in the country of the Oirghialla, whose name was Dairi. But Patrick besought him to bestow upon him some spot for religious uses. And the rich man said to the Saint: "What place do you want?"

"I beg you," said the Saint, "to give me that high land which is called Druim Sailech, and I will build there."

He, however, was unwilling to give that hill to the Saint, but he gave another place on lower ground, where the Fort of the Martyrs is now, near Ard Macha [Armagh]. And Saint Patrick dwelt there with his companions. But soon afterwards the groom of Dairi came, leading his horse to feed in the meadow of the Christians. And this bringing of the horse into his land annoyed Patrick, and he said: "Dairi has done foolishly in sending brute beasts to disturb the small spot which he gave to God."

But the groom, indeed, as if deaf, did not hear, and, as if dumb, not opening his mouth, said nothing, but leaving the horse there that night went away. Coming, however, the next morning to see his horse, he found him already dead, and returning home sorrowfully, he said to his master: "See, that Christian has killed your horse, for the trespass on his land annoyed him."

And Dairi said: "Let him be killed; go now and slay him."

But as they were going out, death swifter than words fell upon Dairi. And his wife said: "This is on account of the Christian; let someone go quickly and bring his blessings to us, and you will be saved; and let those who have gone to slay him be stopped and called back."

And two men went to the Christian, and hiding what had happened, said to him: "And behold Dairi is sick; let something be brought to him from you, if, perhaps, he may recover."

But Saint Patrick, knowing what had happened, said: "Certainly," and he blessed water, and he gave it to him, saying: "Go sprinkle your horse with this water, and take it with you."

And they did so, and the horse revived, and they took it with them, and Dairi was healed by the sprinkling of the water. And Dairi forthwith went to pay honor to Saint Patrick, bringing with him a wonderful over-sea brazen cauldron, holding three measures. And Dairi said to the

Saint: "Behold, let this cauldron be with you."

And Saint Patrick said "Gratzacham."[1]

And Dairi, having returned to his own house, said: "This is a foolish man, who said nothing good save 'Gratzacham' in return for the wonderful cauldron of three measures." And Dairi added, speaking to his servants: "Go, bring back our cauldron to us."

And they went and said to Patrick: "We will take back the cauldron."

Saint Patrick, however, said this time also, "Gratzacham, take it."

And they carried it away; and Dairi asked his followers, saying: "What did the Christian say when you took the cauldron?"

But they answered: "He said 'Gratzacham.'"

Dairi, answering, said: "'Gratzacham' at receiving, 'Gratzacham' at losing; his saying is good; his cauldron shall be brought back again to him with 'Gratzacham.'"

And Dairi himself went this time and brought back the cauldron to Patrick, saying to him: "Let your cauldron be with you, for you are a steadfast and immovable man. And, moreover, I give you that portion of the field, as much as I have, which you asked for before, and dwell there."

And that is the city which is now called Ard Macha.

And they both, Patrick and Dairi, went forth to look at the wonderful offering and friendly gift. And they went up to that hill and found a doe with its little fawn lying in the place where the altar of the church, to the left, at Ard Macha, is now. And the companions of Patrick wished to seize and slay the fawn, but the Saint was unwilling, and withheld them. Nay, more, he himself took the fawn and bore it on his shoulders, and the doe followed him like a

---

[1] *Gratias agamus*, Latin for "Let us give thanks"; although Muirchú wrote St. Patrick's life in Latin, his use of the peculiar spelling suggests that the story of Dairi was handed down by people who spoke no Latin.

pet sheep until he had laid down the fawn in another field at the north side of Ard Macha, where, as the learned say, some signs of his power remain to the present day.

Translated from the Latin by
Rev. Albert Barry, C.SS.R.

ANONYMOUS

Tenth Century

St. Brénainn or Brendan of Clonfert (not to be confused with his namesake, St. Brendan of Birr), a native of County Kerry, was a sixth-century Irish abbot
around whom a huge body of legend has accumulated.
Much of it deals with his supposed adventures on a
voyage far into the Atlantic, where he is said to have
visited many fabulous islands. To this day some people list him among the early discoverers of America.
The beautiful legend printed here does not form part
of any of the saint's "lives" but is found separately in
the manuscript known as the *Book of Lismore*. It gives
poignant expression to a theme familiar in both pagan
and Christian Irish literature—the disillusionment
with this world felt by one who has had a vision of
some ideal other world.

St. Brendan and the Harper

Once when Brénainn of the race of Altae was at Clonfert,
on Easter Day seven years before his death, he celebrated
Mass in the church, and preached and made the offering.
But when midday came, the monks went to their refectory;
there was a student inside with a harp in his hand, and he
began to play for them, and they gave him their blessing.
"I should be delighted, now," said the clerk, "if Brénainn
were in, so that I might play him three tunes." "He would
not allow you to come to him," said the monks, "for Brénainn has been for seven years without smiling and without hearing any of the music of the world; but he has two
balls of wax with a thread joining them, on the book be-

fore him, and when he hears music he puts the balls in his ears." "I shall go, nevertheless, to play to him," said the student.

He went away, with his harp tuned. "Open," said the clerk. "Who is this?" said Brénainn. "A student come to play the harp for you." "Play outside," said Brénainn. "If you would not think it troublesome," said the clerk, "I should be glad to be allowed inside the church to play awhile." "Very well," said Brénainn. "Open the door for me," said the student. Brénainn opened for him. The clerk brought his harp along; Brénainn put the two balls of wax in his ears. "I do not like playing to you unless you take the wax out of your ears," said the student. "It shall be done, then," said Brénainn; he put them on the book. He played him three tunes. "A blessing upon you, student," said he, "with your music, and may you get Heaven for it!"

Brénainn put the balls in his ears afterwards, for he did not wish to listen to it any more. "Why do you not listen to the music?" said the student. "Is it because you think it bad?" "Not for that," said Brénainn, "but like this. One day when I was in this church, seven years ago to this very day, after preaching here and after Mass, the priests went to the refectory; I was left here alone, and a great longing for my Lord seized me, when I had gone up to the Body of Christ. As I was there, trembling and terror came upon me; I saw a shining bird at the window, and it sat on the altar. I was unable to look at it because of the rays which surrounded it, like those of the sun. 'A blessing upon you, and do you bless me, priest,' it said. 'May God bless you,' said Brénainn;[1] 'who are you?' said Brénainn. 'The angel Michael,' it said, 'come to speak with you.' 'I give thanks to God for speaking with you,' said Brénainn, 'and why have you come?' 'To bless you and to make music for you from your Lord,' said the bird. 'You are welcome to me,' said Brénainn. The bird set its beak on the side of its wing, and

---

[1] Here Brendan's story drops temporarily into the third person.

I was listening to it from that hour to the same hour the next day; and then it bade me farewell."

Brénainn put his stole round the neck of the harp. "Do you think this sweet, student?" he said; "I give my word before God," said Brénainn, "that after *that* music, no music of the world seems any sweeter to me than does this stole round the neck, and to hear it I take to be but little profit. Take a blessing, student, and you shall have Heaven for that playing," said Brénainn.

Translated from Middle Irish
by Kenneth Hurlstone Jackson

ANONYMOUS
Eleventh Century?

This magical story of love requited after death attracted William Butler Yeats so much that he made it into one of his longer poems, "Baile and Aillinn." Although basically the same brief story is found in three different manuscripts, it seems to be no more than an outline. Anything that might be forgotten easily, like the genealogy at the beginning, is set down in detail, but the beauty of the heroine and the prowess of the hero are not described for us at all; no doubt a skillful storyteller could go on for five minutes about either topic without once repeating himself. Where repeats are called for in the manuscript, such as the details of Aillinn's funeral or of what was written on her tablet, they are either dismissed with an "etc." or completely ignored; note, too, that a passage has to be supplied in brackets at the end of the next to the last paragraph if the story is to make sense at all. This 750-word "scenario" would doubtless have been expanded to ten times the length as an oral narrative. Nevertheless, the modern reader may prefer the terseness of the story as written. I have adapted Kuno Meyer's literal translation of 1892, adding as few words to it as possible.

Baile the Sweetspoken, Son of Buan

Three grandsons of Caba son of Cinga son of Ros son of Rudraige—namely, Monach and Buan and Fercorb, from whom are descended the Tribe of Buan and the Tribe of

Corb and the Monachs of Ara. Buan's only son was Baile. He was the true love of Aillinn, daughter of Lugaid son of Fergus of the Sea (or else she was the daughter of Eogan son of Dathi); indeed, he was loved by everyone who saw him or heard of him, both men and women, on account of the famous stories about him. So he and Aillinn agreed to meet in dalliance at Rosnaree, at the house of Maeldub, on the brink of the Boyne in Bregia.

The man came from the north to meet her, from Emain Macha across the Fews Mountains, over the plain of Muirthemne, to Baile's Strand. His party unyoked their chariots, put their horses out to graze, and made merry.

While they were there, they saw a horrible apparition coming toward them from the south, all alone. His route and progress were irregular. He sped over the earth like the darting of a hawk from a cliff or the wind from the green sea. His left side was landward.

"Meet him," said Baile, "and ask him where is he going or where is he coming from or why is he in a hurry."

"Back up north to Bann Mouth I am going now from Mount Leinster, and I have no news except that the daughter of Lugaid son of Fergus had fallen in love with Baile, son of Buan, and was coming to meet him when the warriors of Leinster overtook her and killed her, as druids and great seers foretold about them—that they would not meet in life, but they would meet after their deaths, never to part. That is my news." He left them then, and they were not able to stop him.

When Baile heard that, he fell dead and lifeless. His grave and *ráth*[1] were dug, his stone was set up, and his funeral games were held by the men of Ulster. A yew tree grew up through his grave, and at its top the form and shape of Baile's head were to be seen. Hence the name "Baile's Strand."

Meanwhile the same uncanny man went south to where Aillinn was and entered the sun parlor. "Where does the man we don't know come from?" asked the girl.

---

[1] Gaelic for a circular earth fortification; here, a burial mound.

"From the north of Ireland, from Bann Mouth, and I am going beyond this place to Mount Leinster."

"Have you news?" asked the girl.

"I have no news worth keening here, but beside Baile's Strand I saw the men of Ulster at funeral games, digging a *ráth* and setting up a stone and writing the name of Baile, son of Buan, the royal heir of Ulster, who was coming to meet a sweetheart with whom he had fallen in love; for it is not their fate to meet in life nor to see each other alive." He darted out when he had finished telling his bad news. Aillinn fell dead and lifeless, and her grave was dug, etc.

An apple tree grew through her grave and was a large tree at the end of the seventh year, and the shape of Aillinn's head was at its top. At the end of seven years, princes and seers and prophets cut down the tree which was over Baile and made a poet's tablet of it; and the visions and feasts and loves and wooings of Ulster are written in it. In the same way the wooings of Leinster are written in the tablet [made of the tree that grew on Aillinn's grave].

Then came the *Samhain* (Hallowe'en), and its feast was celebrated by Art, son of Conn. Poets and men of every art came to that feast, as was the custom, and brought their tablets with them. Art saw the tablets, and when he saw them, he asked for them. The two tablets were brought to him and he held them in his hands face to face. One tablet leaped toward the other, and they twined together as a honeysuckle twines around a branch. It was impossible to separate them, and they were kept, like any other jewel, in the treasury at Tara until Dunlang, son of Enda, burned it when he killed the maids in waiting.

Translated from Middle Irish by Kuno Meyer
and Vivian Mercier

ANONYMOUS
Eleventh Century?

Irish short-story writers of today usually show skill in dialogue, some of their tales consisting of that and very little else. We have already seen examples of what Irish writers could do with dialogue more than ten centuries ago, but this is our first example of a story made up almost entirely of talk. St. Moling (who gave his name to St. Mullins in County Carlow) belongs to the seventh century. Note how politely the saint and the devil converse together and what sympathy is shown for the Prince of Darkness. This isolated legend forms part of the later annotations to *The Martyrology of Oengus*, a poem on the Irish saints written about A.D. 800.

St. Moling and the Devil

Once as he was praying in his church, he saw a youth coming in to him. Purple raiment he wore and a distinguished form had he.

"That is well, O cleric," says he.

"Amen," says Moling.

"Why dost thou not salute me?" says the youth.

"Who art thou?" says Moling.

"I am Christ the Son of God," he answers.

"I know not that," says Moling. "When Christ used to go to converse with God's servants, not in purple, nor royally, used he to go, but in the shapes of the wretched, to wit, of the sick and of the leper, Christ was wont to be."

"Is it unbelief thou hast in me?" says the youth; "whom dost thou suppose to be here?"

"I suppose," says Moling, "that it is the Devil for my hurt."

"Ill for thee is the unbelief," says the youth.

"Well," says Moling, "here is thy successor, the Gospel of Christ," raising the gospel.

"Do not raise it, O cleric," saith the Devil: "likelier it is I whom thou thinkest. I am the man of tribulations."

"Wherefore hast thou come?" says Moling.

"That thou mayst bestow thy blessing upon me."

"I will not bestow it," says Moling, "for thou dost not deserve it. Not the better wouldst thou be. What good would it be to thee?" asks Moling.

"If," says the Devil, "thou shouldst go into a tub of honey and bathe therein with thy raiment on, its odor would remain upon Thee unless thy raiment should be washen."

"Why does that seem good to thee?" asks Moling.

"Because, though thy blessing do naught else to me, its good luck and its goodness and its blossom will be on me eternally."

"Thou shalt not have it," says Moling, "for thou deservest it not."

"Well," says the Devil, "bestow the full of a curse upon me."

"What good were that to thee?" asks Moling.

"Easy to say, O cleric," he answers: "the mouth from which the curse on me shall come, its venom and its hurt will be against thee."

"Go," says Moling, "thou hast no right to a blessing."

"Better were it for me," says he, "that I had. How shall I earn it?"

"By service to God," says Moling.

"Woe is me," says the Devil; "I cannot bring it."

"Even a trifle of study."

"Thy study is not greater than mine, and it helps me not."

"Fasting then," says Moling.

"I am fasting since the beginning of the world, and not the better am I."

"To make genuflexion," says Moling.

"I cannot bend down forward, for backwards are my knees."[1]

"Go forth," says Moling; "I am unable to teach thee or to save thee."

Translated from Middle Irish
by Whitley Stokes

---

[1] The Devil is obviously pictured as having legs like a goat's.

ANONYMOUS
Eighteenth Century?

The Library of St. Patrick's College, Maynooth, the premier ecclesiastical seminary in Ireland, has yielded up this extraordinary tale—or summary of a tale. In the manuscript, the story serves as introduction to a verse elegy supposedly chanted over Dubh Ruis's body by his wife, Mis (Pronounce their names "Duv Rish" or "Doo Rish," and "Mish"). Dated 1769 and written in modern Gaelic, the story nevertheless reaches back to very primitive tradition. Although some of the sly humor may be of 18th-century origin, Brian Ó Cuív, who first edited the Gaelic text, thinks that the use of sexual intercourse as a cure for insanity formed part of the story from the very beginning—possibly in pre-historic times. Professor Ó Cuív amusingly describes the anonymous author as "an Irish forerunner of Freud."

The Romance of Mis and Dubh Ruis

Mis, the daughter of Dáire Dóidgheal, sang this, lamenting her mate and companion Dubh Ruis, the sweet harper of Feidhlim the son of Criomthann, the king of Munster. For the soldiers of Clanmaurice killed this Dubh Ruis when he went to levy on them the tribute that King Feidhlim had given him for subduing Mis the daughter of Dáire and re-storing her to her senses. For she was a *geilt* [lunatic] for seven score years (or according to others for three hun-dred years) on Slieve Mish[1] in the barony of Clanmaurice,

---

[1] Mis's Mountain.

near Tralee in County Kerry, from the day her father Dáire the Great was killed, when he came to conquer Ireland in the battle of Ventry. For he brought her with him, since she was his only daughter, and, when the battle was over, she came with many others to look for her father's body amongst the slaughter, and when she found the body with its many wounds, she began to suck and drink the blood from the wounds, so that she flew away in the end in a fever of madness to Slieve Mish, and remained there for the aforesaid time, so that fur and hair grew on her, so long that it trailed on the ground behind. And the nails of her feet and hands grew so excessively that there was no beast or person she would meet but she would tear apart immediately.

And the flight of her madness gave her such a speed of movement that she would run like the wind and overtake in running anything she pleased, and there was no animal or person she killed but she would eat and drink whatever she wished of its flesh and blood, so that a desert stripped of people and cattle was created for fear of her in that part of the country which is called the barony of Clanmaurice, for King Feidhlim issued a general proclamation that she should not be killed for any reason. However, he offered and promised great rewards, together with the tributes of the same barony, to the man who would take or capture her alive.

Many journeyed to attempt her one after the other, so that the majority perished by her in the venture. However, Dubh Ruis, the harper, said at last to Feidhlim the king that he himself would attempt her with his harp; and the king laughed at him, but Dubh Ruis asked for a handful of gold and a handful of silver, which were necessary for the venture, to be given to him and he would go to attempt her. The king gave him the gold and the silver and he made no stay until he reached Slieve Mish. And when he reached the mountain, he sat down in the place where he thought she might be found, spread his cloak or mantle under him, and scattered the gold and the silver on the edges of the cloak. He lay on his back. He put the harp on his body. He opened his trousers or his breeches and bared himself, for he thought that if he could lie with her and know her, it would be a good means and device for bringing her to her sense or her natural reason. He was not long thus before she came to the spot, having heard the music, and she stood looking savagely at him and listening to the music. "Aren't you a man?" said she. "I am," said he. "What is this?" said she, putting her hand on the harp. "A harp," said he. "Ho, ho!" said she, "I remember the harp; my father had one like it. Play it for me." "I will," said he, "but don't do me any damage or harm." "I won't," said she. Then she looked at the gold and silver and said, "What are these?" "Gold and silver," said he. "I remember," said she, "my father had gold. Och, ochone!"

As she looked at him, she caught sight of his nakedness and his members of pleasure. "What are those?" she said, pointing to his bag or his eggs—and he told her. "What is this?" said she, about the other thing that she saw. "That is the wand of the feat," said he. "I do not remember that," said she, "my father hadn't anything like that. The wand of the feat; what is the feat?" "Sit beside me," said he, "and I will do the feat of the wand for you." "I will," said she, "and stay you with me." "I will," said he, and lay with her and knew her, and she said, "Ha, ba, ba, that was a good feat; do it again." "I will," said he; "however, I will play the harp for you first." "Don't mind the harp," said she, "but do the feat." "I wish to partake of food," said he, "for I am hungry." "I will get you a stag," said she. "Do, and I have bread myself." "Where is it?" said she. "Here it is," said he. "Ha, ha, I remember the bread; my father used to have it. Don't go away," said she. "I will not," said he.

It was not long before she returned with a strangled stag under her arm, and she was going to tear it apart to eat it as it was, when Dubh Ruis said to her, "Wait, and I will bleed the stag and cook the flesh." Then he cut the stag's throat and skinned it. And he made a great fire of the forest brushwood and gathered a heap of granite stones and put them in the fire. He made a wide round hole in the ground and filled it with water. He cut up the meat and wrapped it in a bundle of sedge, and wrapped a straw rope round it, and put it into the hole, and kept feeding and sinking those thoroughly heated, red-hot stones into the water, and kept it boiling all the time until the meat was cooked. He took it out of the hole and put the fat of the stag into the boiling water so that it melted, Then he spread out on the stag's hide his meat and bread and told her to come and eat her meal, for she had been watching him peacefully and wonderingly all this time. "I remember," said she, "that it is cooked meat my father used to have, and I know that it is best that way, and not the way I had it." With that, Dubh Ruis broke the bread and carved the meat for her, and made her eat her fill quietly and contentedly, so that she said that she would do whatever he told her if only he would stay with her. Then he brought her fresh water in his cloak or his helmet, and she drank her fill of it.

Then he brought her to the hole in which the lukewarm broth and the melted fat of the stag was, and put her standing in it, and took the hide of the deer and rubbed and kneaded the joints of her body and her bones, and began to scrub and scour and polish her with the fat of the stag and with the broth, until he cleaned her a great deal and brought streams of sweat from her. He collected foliage and moss and green rushes and made a bed for her; he spread the hide of the stag under her and his cloak over her. He lay down beside her, and knew her, and so they slept till morning. However, he could not waken her in the morning, so he arose and dressed himself and built a hut or shelter of the tops and branches of trees over her, and she did not wake till evening, and when she did not find him with her, she began to lament (and he was secretly listening to her) and to say, amongst other things:

> It is not the gold I weep for, the sweet harp
> or the eggs,
> But the wand of the feat which Dubh Ruis,
> son of Raghnall, had.

He remained thus with her on the mountain for two months, and at the end of that time the hair had all fallen from her, from the continual scrubbing and cleaning that we have described, and her mind and memory, her sense and natural reason returned to her, and Dubh Ruis put suitable clothes on her before bringing her home. And it is written that she remained in the same form and shape and in the same age as she was the day she went mad on the mountain; and Dubh Ruis married her, and she bore him four children, and she was amongst the fairest and most talented women of Munster in her time.

Translated from Modern Irish by
Professor David Greene of Trinity College, Dublin

PATRICK KENNEDY
1801–1873

A County Wexford man, Patrick Kennedy was born of peasant stock. The Carew family, local landowners, recognized his intelligence and paid for his secondary education. He became a teacher in Dublin but afterwards set up in business there for himself as a bookseller. Late in his life, he began to publish the folklore he had heard as a country boy, along with translations from Gaelic literature and shrewd critical comments on the Irish tradition generally, in a series of magazine articles that later were gathered into books. The folktale here reprinted comes from his best-known book, *Legendary Fictions of the Irish Celts* (1866). Kennedy tells us that "the narrator of the following travelling sketch was a half-witted woman, who, although she had heard it from someone else, was under the impression that she had undergone part of the adventures in some form or other." Undoubtedly she told the tale in the kind of English here set down, since Gaelic had disappeared from Wexford even in Kennedy's youth.

Cauth Morrisy Looking for Service

Well, neighbours, when I was a *thuckeen*[1] about fifteen years of age, and it was time to be doing something for myself, I set off one fine day in spring along the yalla high-

[1] Young girl.

road; and if anybody axed me where I was goin', I'd make a joke of it, and say I was going out of Ireland to live in the Roer. Well, I travelled all day, and dickens a bit o' me was the nearer to get a service; and when the dark hour come, I got a lodging in a little house by the side of the road, where they were drying flax over a roaring turf fire. I'll never belie the *vanithee*[2] her goodness. She give me a good quarter of well-baked barley bread, with butter on it, and made me sit on the big griddle over the ash pit in the corner; but what would you have of it? I held the bread to the fire to melt the butter, and bedad the butter fell on the lighted turf, and there it blazed up like vengeance, and set the flax afire, and the flax set the t'atch afire, and maybe they didn't get a fright.

"Oh, musha, vanithee," says they, "wasn't it the divel bewitched you to let that *omadhawn*[3] of a girl burn us out of house and home this way? Be off, you torment, and purshuin' to you!"

Well, if they didn't hunt me out, and throw potsticks and tongses and sods o' fire after me, lave it till again—and I run and I run till I run head foremost into a cabin by the side of the road.

The woman o' the house was sitting at the fire, and she got frightened to see me run in that way. "Oh, musha, ma'am," says I, "will you give me shelter?" and so I up and told her my misfortunes.

"Poor colleen," says she, "my husband is out, and if he catches a stranger here, he'll go mad and break things. But I'll let you get up on the hurdle over the room, and for your life don't budge."

"I won't," says I, "and thank you, ma'am." Well, I was hardly in bed when her crooked disciple of a man kem in with a sheep on his back he was after stealing.

"Is everything ready?" says he.

"It is," says she.

So with that he skinned the sheep, and popped a piece

[2] Woman of the house.

[3] Fool.

down into the boiling pot, and went out and hid the skin, and buried the rest o' the mate in a hole in the flure, and covered it with the griddle, and covered the griddle again with some o' the clay he removed from the flure.

Well, when he made his supper on the mutton, he says to his wife, "I hope no one got lodging while I was away."

"Arrah, who'd get it?" says she.

"That's not the answer I want," says he. "Who did you give shelter to?"

"Och, it was only to a little slip of a girl that's as fast as the knocker of Newgate since eleven o'clock, on the hurdle."

"Molly," says he, "I'll hang for you someday, so I will. But first and foremost I'll put the stranger out o' pain."

When I hear him talk, I slip down, and was out o' the door in a jiffy; but he was as stiff as I was stout, and he fling the hatchet after me and cut off a piece of my heel.

"Them is the tricks of a clown," says I to myself, and I making away at the ling of my life; but as luck would have it, I got shelter in another cabin, where a nice old man was sitting over the fire, reading a book.

"What's the matter, poor girl?" says he, and I up and told him what happened me.

"Never fear," says he; "the man o' the mutton won't follow you here. I suppose you'd like your supper."

Well, sure enough, the fright, and the run, and the cut heel, and that, made me hungry, and I didn't refuse a good plate o' stirabout.

"Colleen," says the man, "I can't go to sleep early in the night; maybe you'd tell a body a story."

"Musha, an' the dickens a story meself has," says I.

"That's bad," says he; "the fire is getting low: take that *booran*[4] out to the clamp, and bring in the full of it of turf."

"I will, sir," says I. But when I took a turf out of the end of the clamp, five hundred sods tumbled down on me, head and pluck; and I thought the breath was squeezed out of me. "If that's the way," says I, "let the old gentleman him-

---

[4] Chamber pot.

self come out and bring in his firing." So I went in, and had like to faint when I came to the fire.

"What ails you, little girl?" says he.

"The clamp that fell on me," says I.

"Oh, but it's meself that's sorry," says he. "Did you think of e'er another story while you were at the clamp?"

"Indeed an' I didn't."

"Well, it can't be helped. I suppose you're tired. Take that rushlight into the barn, but don't set it on fire. You'll find plenty of dry straw for a bed, and come in to your breakfast early."

Well, I bade him goodnight, and when I came into the barn, sure enough, there was no scarcity of straw. I said my prayers, but the first bundle I took out of the heap, I thought all the straw in the barn was down on my poor bones. "Oh vuya, vuya, Cauth," says I to myself, "if your poor father and mother knew the state you're in, wouldn't they have the heart-scald." But I crept out and sat down on a bundle and began to cry.

I wasn't after cryin' a second *dhrass*[5] when I heard steps outside the door, and I hid myself again under the straw, leaving a little peephole. In came three as ugly-looking fellows as you'd find in a *kish o' brogues*[6] with a coffin on their shoulders. They wondered at the candle, but they said nothing till they put the coffin down and began to play cards on it with the dirtiest deck I ever see before or since. Well, they cheated and scolded and whacked one another, and in two minutes they were as great as pickpockets again.

At last says one, "It's time to be goin'; lift the corpse."

"It's easy say 'lift,'" says another. "You two have the front, and I must bear up all the hind part—I won't put a hand to it."

"Won't you?" says the others; "sure, there's little Cauth Morrisy under the straw to help you."

"Oh, Lord, gentlemen, I'm not in it at all," says myself; but it was all no use. I had to get under one corner, and

---

[5] Fit.

[6] Basketful of shoes.

there we trudged on in the dark, through *knocs*[7] and ploughed fields and bogs, till I thought the life would leave me.

At last, at the flight of night, one of them says, "Stop here, and Cauth Morrisy will mind the corpse till we come back. Cauth, if you let anything happen to the honest man inside, you'll sup sorrow—mind what I say."

So they left me, and lonesome and frightened I was, you may depend. But wasn't I frightened in earnest when I heard the corpse's knuckles tapping inside o' the led. "Oh, sir, honey," says I, "what's troubling you?"

"It's air I want," says he; "lift up the led a little."

I lifted up a corner.

"That won't do," says he; "I'm stifling. Throw off the led, body and bones."

I did so, and there was a wicked-looking fellow inside, with a beard on him a week old. "Thankee, ma'am," says he; "I think I'll be the easier for that. This is a lonesome place them thieves left me in. Would you please to join me in a game of spoil-five?"

"Oh, musha, sir," says I, "isn't it thinking of making your soul you ought to be?"

"I don't want your advice," says he; "maybe I haven't a soul at all. There's the cards. I deal—you cut."

Well, I was so afeard that I took a hand with him; but the dirty divel, he done nothing the whole time but cursin', and swearin', and cheatin'. At last, says I to myself, "I can't be safe in such company." So I threw down the cards, though I was within three of the game, and walked off.

"Come back and finish the game, Cauth Morrisy," says he, shouting out, "or I'll make it the bad game for you."

But I didn't let on to hear him, and walked away.

"Won't you come back, Cauth?" says he. "Then here goes."

Well, the life had like to leave me, for I heard him tearing after me in his coffin, every bounce it gave striking terror into my heart. I run, and I bawled, and he bawling after me, and the coffin smashing against the stones. At

[7] Hills.

last, where did I find myself but at the old gentleman's door, and if I didn't spring in and fasten the bolt, lave it till again.

"Ah, is that you, my little colleen? I thought you were asleep. Maybe you have a story for me now."

"Indeed an' I have, sir," says I, an' I told him all that happen me since I saw him last.

"You suffered a good deal," says he. "If you told me that story before, all your trouble'd be spared to you."

"But how could I tell it, sir," says I, "before it happened?"

"That's true," says he, and he began to scratch his wig. I was getting drowsy, and I didn't remember anything more till I woke next morning in the dry gripe of a ditch with a *bochyeen*[8] under my head. So—

> *There was a tree at the end of the house,*
> *and it was bending, bending,*
> *And my story is ending, ending.*

---

[8] Dried cow dung.

GERALD GRIFFIN
1803–1840

Born in the town of Limerick and educated there, Gerald Griffin spent the years 1823–26 in London as a hack writer. After suffering a nervous breakdown, he returned to Limerick and there wrote a number of poems, short stories, novels and plays—most of which, however, were published in London. The novel *The Collegians* (later dramatized by Dion Boucicault as *The Colleen Bawn*) proved by far the most popular work by this prolific young author. Griffin's ill-starred love for a married woman, a Quaker, doubtless helped him reach his decision to join the Irish Christian Brothers in 1838. Two years later, while a teaching brother at the North Monastery in Cork, he died of typhus during an epidemic. Griffin either knew Gaelic himself or drew on the knowledge of others who did, for many of his short stories are based on Gaelic folklore and literature. "The Brown Man," from his first book, *Holland-Tide* (1827), may have been brought to Limerick by the Vikings, for it seems to be an example of Aarne-Thompson Folktale Type 363, "a story almost entirely confined to the shores of the Baltic and to Norway." With his facetious tone and phonetic spelling of Irish English, Griffin almost ruined a terrifying vampire tale.

The Brown Man

The common Irish expression of "the seven devils," does not, it would appear, owe its origin to the supernatural influences ascribed to that numeral, from its frequent association with the greatest and most solemn occasions of theological history. If one were disposed to be fancifully metaphysical upon the subject, it might not be amiss to compare credulity to a sort of mental prism, by which the great volume of the light of speculative superstition is refracted in a manner precisely similar to that of the material, everyday sun, the great refractor thus showing only *blue* devils to the dwellers in the good city of London, *orange* and *green* devils to the inhabitants of the sister (or rather stepdaughter), island, and so forward until the seven component hues are made out, through the other nations of the earth. But what has this to do with the story? In order to answer that question, the story must be told.

In a lonely cabin, in a lonely glen, on the shores of a lonely lough, in one of the most lonesome districts of west Munster, lived a lone woman named Guare. She had a beautiful daughter named Nora. Their cabin was the only one within three miles round them every way. As to their mode of living, it was simple enough, for all they had was one little garden of white cabbage, and they had eaten that down to a few heads between them, a sorry prospect in a place where even a handful of *prishoc* weed was not to be had without sowing it.

It was a very fine morning in those parts, for it was only snowing and hailing, when Nora and her mother were sitting at the door of their little cottage, and laying out plans for the next day's dinner. On a sudden, a strange horseman rode up to the door. He was strange in more ways than one. He was dressed in brown, his hair was brown, his eyes were brown, his boots were brown, he rode a brown horse, and he was followed by a brown dog.

"I'm come to marry you, Nora Guare," said the Brown Man.

"Ax my mother fusht, if you plaise, sir," said Nora, dropping him a curtsy.

"You'll not refuse, ma'am," said the Brown Man to the old mother. "I have money enough, and I'll make your daughter a lady, with servants at her call, and all manner of fine doings about her." And so saying, he flung a purse of gold into the widow's lap.

"Why then, the heavens speed you and her together; take her away with you, and make much of her," said the old mother, quite bewildered with all the money.

"Agh, agh," said the Brown Man, as he placed her on his horse behind him without more ado. "Are you all ready now?"

"I am!" said the bride. The horse snorted, and the dog barked, and almost before the word was out of her mouth, they were all whisked away out of sight. After travelling a day and a night, faster than the wind itself, the Brown Man pulled up his horse in the middle of the Mangerton mountain, in one of the most lonesome places that eye ever looked on.

"Here is my estate," said the Brown Man.

"A'then, is it this wild bog you call an estate?" said the bride.

"Come in, wife, this is my palace," said the bridegroom.

"What! a clay-hovel, worse than my mother's!"

They dismounted, and the horse and the dog disappeared in an instant, with a horrible noise, which the girl did not know whether to call snorting, barking, or laughing.

"Are you hungry?" said the Brown Man. "If so, there is your dinner."

"A handful of raw white-eyes,[1] and a grain of salt!"

"And when you are sleepy, here is your bed," he continued, pointing to a little straw in a corner, at sight of which Nora's limbs shivered and trembled again. It may be easily supposed that she did not make a very hearty dinner that evening, nor did her husband neither.

In the dead of the night, when the clock of Mucruss Abbey had just tolled one, a low neighing at the door, and a soft barking at the window were heard. Nora feigned sleep. The Brown Man passed his hand over her eyes and face. She snored. "I'm coming," said he, and he arose gently from her side. In half an hour after she felt him by her side again. He was cold as ice.

[1] A kind of potato.

The next night the same summons came. The Brown Man rose. The wife feigned sleep. He returned cold. The morning came.

The next night came. The bell tolled at Mucruss, and was heard across the lakes. The Brown Man rose again, and passed a light before the eyes of the feigning sleeper. None slumber so sound as they who *will* not wake. Her heart trembled, but her frame was quiet and firm. A voice at the door summoned the husband.

"You are very long coming. The earth is tossed up, and I am hungry. Hurry! Hurry! Hurry! if you would not lose all."

"I'm coming!" said the Brown Man. Nora rose and followed instantly. She beheld him at a distance winding through a lane of frost-nipt sallow trees. He often paused and looked back, and once or twice retraced his steps to within a few yards of the tree behind which she had shrunk. The moonlight, cutting the shadow close and dark about her, afforded the best concealment. He again proceeded, and she followed. In a few minutes they reached the old Abbey of Mucruss. With a sickening heart she saw him enter the churchyard. The wind rushed through the huge yew tree and startled her. She mustered courage enough, however, to reach the gate of the churchyard and look in. The Brown Man, the horse, and the dog were there seated by an open grave, eating something, and glancing their brown, fiery eyes about in every direction. The moonlight shone full on them and her. Looking down towards her shadow on the earth, she started with horror to observe it move, although she was herself perfectly still. It waved its black arms and motioned her back. What the feasters said, she understood not, but she seemed still fixed in the spot. She looked once more on her shadow; it raised one hand, and pointed the way to the lane; then slowly rising from the ground, and confronting her, it walked rapidly off in that direction. She followed as quickly as might be.

She was scarcely in her straw, when the door creaked behind, and her husband entered. He lay down by her side, and started.

"Uf! Uf!" said she, pretending to be just awakened, "how cold you are, my love!"

"Cold, inagh? Indeed you're not very warm yourself, my dear, I'm thinking."

"Little admiration I shouldn't be warm, and you laving me alone this way at night, till my blood is snow broth, no less."

"Umph!" said the Brown Man, as he passed his arm round her waist. "Ha! your heart is beating fast?"

"Little admiration it should. I am not well, indeed. Them pzaties and salt don't agree with me at all."

"Umph!" said the Brown Man.

The next morning as they were sitting at the breakfast table together, Nora plucked up a heart and asked leave to go to see her mother. The Brown Man, who ate nothing, looked at her in a way that made her think he knew all. She felt her spirit die away within her.

"If you only want to see your mother," said he, "there is no occasion for your going home. I will bring her to you here. I didn't marry you to be keeping you gadding."

The Brown Man then went out and whistled for his dog and his horse. They both came; and in a very few minutes they pulled up at the old widow's cabin door.

The poor woman was very glad to see her son-in-law, though she did not know what could bring him so soon.

"Your daughter sends her love to you, Mother," says the Brown Man, the villain, "and she'd be obliged to you for a *loand* of a *shoot* of your best clothes, as she's going to give a grand party, and the dressmaker has disappointed her."

"To be sure and welcome," said the mother; and making up a bundle of the clothes, she put them into his hands.

"Whogh! whogh!" said the horse as they drove off, "that was well done. Are we to have a mail[2] of her?"

"Easy, ma-coppuleen,[3] and you'll get your 'nough before night," said the Brown Man, "and you likewise, my little dog."

[2] Meal.

[3] My little horse.

"Boh!" cried the dog, "I'm in no hurry—I hunted down a doe this morning that was fed with milk from the horns of the moon."

Often in the course of that day did Nora Guare go to the door and cast her eye over the weary flat before it, to discern, if possible, the distant figures of her bridegroom and mother. The dusk of the second evening found her alone in the desolate cot. She listened to every sound. At length the door opened, and an old woman, dressed in a new *jock*, and leaning on a staff, entered the hut. "O Mother, are you come?" said Nora, and was about to rush into her arms, when the old woman stopped her.

"Whisht! whisht! my child!—I only stepped in before the man to know how you like him? Speak softly, in dread he'd hear you—he's turning the horse loose in the swamp abroad over."

"O Mother, Mother! such a story!"

"Whisht! easy again—how does he use you?"

"Sarrow worse. That straw my bed, and them white-eyes —and bad ones they are—all my diet. And 'tisn't that same, only—"

"Whisht! easy, again! He'll hear you, may be—Well?"

"I'd be easy enough only for his own doings. Listen, mother. The fusht night, I came about twelve o'clock—"

"Easy, speak easy, eroo!"

"He got up at the call of the horse and the dog, and staid out a good hour. He ate nothing next day. The second night, and the second day, it was the same story. The third—"

"Husht! husht! Well, the third night?"

"The third night I said I'd watch him. Mother, don't hold my hand so hard—He got up, and I got up after him— Oh, don't laugh, Mother, for 'tis frightful—I followed him to Mucruss churchyard—Mother, Mother, you hurt my hand—I looked in at the gate—there was great moonlight there, and I could see everything as plain as day."

"Well, darling—husht! softly! What did you see?"

"My husband by the grave, and the horse,—Turn your head aside, Mother, for your breath is very hot—and the dog and they eating.—Ah, you are not my mother!"

shrieked the miserable girl, as the Brown Man flung off his disguise and stood before her, grinning worse than a blacksmith's face through a horse collar. He just looked at her one moment, and then darted his long fingers into her bosom, from which the red blood spouted in so many streams. She was very soon out of all pain, and a merry supper the horse, the dog, and the Brown Man had that night, by all accounts.

ISABELLA AUGUSTA, LADY GREGORY
1852–1932

The widow of a distinguished British colonial admin-
istrator, Lady Gregory learned Gaelic and collected
folklore in the bilingual Barony of Kiltartan, near her
County Galway estate, Coole Park. Her friendship with
the poet W. B. Yeats, to whom she lent money and gave
hospitality at Coole, has become almost legendary. With
him she founded the Abbey Theatre, of which she
remained a director until her death; she also collaborated
on a number of his plays and wrote many of her own.
In her old age, her friendship, encouragement, and advice
were valued by Sean O'Casey. Among her most
important works stand the two volumes *Cuchulain
of Muirthemne* (1902) and *Gods and Fighting Men*
(1904), in which she retold the classic tales of Early
Irish literature, using the Irish English of the Kiltartan folk.
The present story, one of the best-known in
the Cuchulain (Ulster) cycle, supplied the basis for
Yeats' verse tragedy, *On Baile's Strand*. (Pronounce
"Conchubar" as "Connor," "Aoife" as "Eefa," and
"Cuchulain" as "Coo Hullin"; the other names can be
pronounced as spelled without causing serious pain to a
Celtic scholar.)

The Only Son of Aoife

The time Cuchulain came back from Alban, after he had
learned the use of arms under Scathach, he left Aoife, the
queen he had overcome in battle, with child.

And when he was leaving her, he told her what name to
give the child, and he gave her a gold ring and bade her

keep it safe till the child grew to be a lad, and till his thumb would fill it; and he bade her to give it to him then, and to send him to Ireland, and he would know he was his son by that token. She promised to do so, and with that Cuchulain went back to Ireland.

It was not long after the child was born, word came to Aoife that Cuchulain had taken Emer to be his wife in Ireland. When she heard that, great jealousy came on her, and great anger, and her love for Cuchulain was turned to hatred; and she remembered her three champions that he had killed, and how he had overcome herself, and she determined in her mind that when her son would come to have the strength of a man, she would get her revenge through him. She told Conlaoch, her son, nothing of this, but brought him up like any king's son; and when he was come to sensible years, she put him under the teaching of Scathach, to be taught the use of arms and the art of war. He turned out as apt a scholar as his father, and it was not long before he had learnt all Scathach had to teach.

Then Aoife gave him the arms of a champion, and bade him go to Ireland, but first she laid three commands on him: the first never to give way to any living person, but to die sooner than be made turn back; the second, not to refuse a challenge from the greatest champion alive, but to fight him at all risks, even if he was sure to lose his life; the third, not to tell his name on any account, though he might be threatened with death for hiding it. She put him under *geasa*, that is, under bonds, not to do these things.

Then the young man, Conlaoch, set out, and it was not long before his ship brought him to Ireland, and the place he landed at was Baile's Strand, near Dundealgan.

It chanced that at that time Conchubar, the High King, was holding his court there, for it was a convenient gathering place for his chief men, and they were settling some business that belonged to the government of that district.

When word was brought to Conchubar that there was a ship come to the strand, and a young lad in it armed as if for fighting, and armed men with him, he sent one of the chief men of his household to ask his name, and on what business he was come.

The messenger's name was Cunaire, and he went down to the strand, and when he saw the young man he said: "A welcome to you, young hero from the east, with the merry face. It is likely, seeing you come armed as if for fighting, you are gone astray on your journey; but as you are come to Ireland, tell me your name and what your deeds have been, and your victories in the eastern bounds of the world."

"As to my name," said Conlaoch, "it is of no great account; but whatever it is, I am under bonds not to tell it to the stoutest man living."

"It is best for you to tell it at the king's desire," said Cunaire, "before you get your death through refusing it, as many a champion from Alban and from Britain has done before now." "If that is the order you put on us when we land here, it is I will break it," said Conlaoch, "and no one will obey it any longer from this out."

So Cunaire went back and told the king what the young lad had said. Then Conchubar said to his people: "Who will go out into the field, and drag the name and the story out of this young man?" "I will go," said Conall, for his hand was never slow in fighting. And he went out, and found the lad angry and destroying, handling his arms, and they attacked one another with a great noise of swords and shouts, and they were gripped together, and fought for a while, and then Conall was overcome, and the great name and the praise that was on Conall, it was on the head of Conlaoch it was now.

Word was sent then to where Cuchulain was, in pleasant, bright-faced Dundealgan. And the messenger told him the whole story, and he said: "Conall is lying humbled, and it is slow the help is in coming, it is a welcome there would be before the Hound."

Cuchulain rose up then and went to where Conlaoch was, and he still handling his arms. And Cuchulain asked him his name and said: "It would be well for you, young hero of unknown name, to loosen yourself from this knot, and not to bring down my hand upon you, for it will be hard for you to escape death." But Conlaoch said: "If I put you down in the fight, the way I put down your comrade, there will be a great name on me; but if I draw back now, there will be mockery on me, and it will be said I was afraid of the fight. I will never give in to any man to tell the name, or to give an account of myself. But if I was not held with a command," he said, "there is no man in the world I would sooner give it to than to yourself, since I saw your face. But do not think, brave champion of Ireland, that I will let you take away the fame I have won, for nothing."

With that they fought together, and it is seldom such a battle was seen, and all wondered that the young lad could stand so well against Cuchulain.

So they fought a long while, neither getting the better of the other, but at last Cuchulain was charged so hotly by the lad that he was forced to give way, and although he had fought so many good fights, and killed so many great champions, and understood the use of arms better than any man living, he was pressed very hard.

And he called for the Gae Bulg, and his anger came on him, and the flames of the hero-light began to shine about his head, and by that sign Conlaoch knew him to be Cuchulain, his father. And just at that time he was aiming his spear at him, and when he knew it was Cuchulain, he threw his spear crooked that it might pass beside him. But Cuchulain threw his spear, the Gae Bulg, at him with all his might, and it struck the lad in the side and went into his body, so that he fell to the ground.

And Cuchulain said: "Now, boy, tell your name and what you are, for it is short your life will be, for you will not live after that wound."

And Conlaoch showed the ring that was on his hand, and he said: "Come here where I am lying on the field, let my men from the east come round me. I am suffering for revenge. I am Conlaoch, son of the Hound, heir of dear Dundealgan; I was bound to this secret in Dun Scathach, the secret in which I have found my grief."

And Cuchulain said: "It is a pity your mother not to be here to see you brought down. She might have stretched out her hand to stop the spear that wounded you." And Conlaoch said: "My curse be on my mother, for it was she put me under bonds; it was she sent me here to try my strength against yours." And Cuchulain said: "My curse be on your mother, the woman that is full of treachery; it is through her harmful thoughts these tears have been brought on us." And Conlaoch said: "My name was never forced from my mouth till now; I never gave an account of myself to any man under the sun. But, O Cuchulain of the sharp sword, it was a pity you not to know me the time I threw the slanting spear behind you in the fight."

And then the sorrow of death came upon Conlaoch, and Cuchulain took his sword and put it through him, sooner than leave him in the pain and the punishment he was in.

And then great trouble and anguish came on Cuchulain, and he made this complaint:

"It is a pity it is, O son of Aoife, that ever you came into the province of Ulster, that you ever met with the Hound of Cuailgne.

"If I and my fair Conlaoch were doing feats of war on the one side, the men of Ireland from sea to sea would not be equal to us together. It is no wonder I to be under grief when I see the shield and the arms of Conlaoch. A pity it is there is no one at all, a pity there are not hundreds of men on whom I could get satisfaction for his death.

"If it was the king himself had hurt your fair body, it is I would have shortened his days.

"It is well for the House of the Red Branch, and for the heads of its fair army of heroes, it was not they that killed my only son.

"It is well for Laegaire of Victories it is not from him you got your heavy pain.

"It is well for the heroes of Conall they did not join in the killing of you; it is well that travelling across the plain of Macha they did not fall in with me after such a fight.

"It is well for the tall, well-shaped Forbuide; well for Dubthach, your Black Beetle of Ulster.

"It is well for you, Cormac Conloingeas, your share of arms gave no help, that it is not from your weapons he got his wound, the hard-skinned shield or the blade.

"It is a pity it was not one on the plains of Munster, or in Leinster of the sharp blades, or at Cruachan of the rough fighters, that struck down my comely Conlaoch.

"It is a pity it was not in the country of the Cruithne, of the fierce Fians, you fell in a heavy quarrel, or in the country of the Greeks, or in some other place of the world, you died, and I could avenge you.

"Or in Spain, or in Sorcha, or in the country of the Saxons of the free armies; there would not then be this death in my heart.

"It is very well for the men of Alban it was not they that destroyed your fame; and it is well for the men of the Gall.

"Och! It is bad that it happened; my grief! it is on me is the misfortune, O Conlaoch of the Red Spear, I myself to have spilled your blood.

"I to be under defeat, without strength. It is a pity Aoife never taught you to know the power of my strength in the fight.

"It is no wonder I to be blinded after such a fight and such a defeat.

"It is no wonder I to be tired out, and without the sons of Usnach beside me.

"Without a son, without a brother, with none to come after me; without Conlaoch, without a name to keep my strength.

"To be without Naoise, without Ainnle, without Ardan; is it not with me is my fill of trouble?

"I am the father that killed his son, the fine green branch; there is no hand or shelter to help me.

"I am a raven that has no home; I am a boat going from wave to wave; I am a ship that has lost its rudder; I am the apple left on the tree; it is little I thought of falling from it; grief and sorrow will be with me from this time."

Then Cuchulain stood up and faced all the men of Ulster. "There is trouble on Cuchulain," said Conchubar; "he is after killing his own son, and if I and all my men were to go against him, by the end of the day he would destroy every man of us. Go now," he said to Cathbad, the Druid, "and bind him to go down to Baile's Strand, and to give three days fighting against the waves of the sea, rather than to kill us all."

So Cathbad put an enchantment on him, and bound him

to go down. And when he came to the strand, there was a great white stone before him, and he took his sword in his right hand, and he said: "If I had the head of the woman that sent her son to his death, I would split it as I split this stone." And he made four quarters of the stone.

Then he fought with the waves three days and three nights, till he fell from hunger and weakness, so that some men said he got his death there. But it was not there he got his death, but on the plain of Muirthemne.

DOUGLAS HYDE

1862–1949

Born at French Park, County Roscommon, Douglas Hyde was the third son of the Rev. Arthur Hyde, himself descended from three successive generations of Anglican clergymen. Young Hyde learned Latin and Greek from his father and Gaelic from his poorer Roscommon neighbors. (He once said, "I dream in Irish.") After taking his B.A. and Doctor of Laws degrees at Trinity College, Dublin, he founded the Gaelic League (1893) to encourage the teaching of Gaelic and the revival of Gaelic culture. He remained President of the League until 1915 and during an American lecture tour in 1905–6 collected over $60,000 for it. He was Professor of Modern Irish at University College, Dublin, until his retirement in 1932. In May, 1938, he was elected unopposed as the first President of Ireland under the Constitution of 1937. After serving the full seven-year term, he retired once more to French Park, where he died. Most of Hyde's writings are in Gaelic, and include original poetry and plays as well as editions of folktales and folk poetry. Many of his Gaelic editions include on facing pages vigorous translations into Irish English, like the one included here from *Beside the Fire* (1890). The Gaelic was written down for Hyde by a Mr. Lynch Blake, who had collected the story from an old "travelling man" or tramp, named William Grady, originally from Clare-Galway, County Galway; it forms a comic counterpart to the near-tragic story collected by J. M. Synge that follows it here.

Leeam O'Rooney's Burial

In the olden time there was once a man named William O'Rooney, living near Clare-Galway. He was a farmer. One day the landlord came to him and said: "I have three years' rent on you, and unless you have it for me within a week, I'll throw you out on the side of the road."

"I'm going to Galway with a load of wheat tomorrow, said Leeam (William), "and when I get the price of it I'll pay you."

Next morning he put a load of wheat on the cart, and was going to Galway with it. When he was gone a couple of miles from the house, a gentleman met him and asked him: "Is it wheat you've got on the cart?"

"It is," says Leeam; "I'm going to sell it to pay my rent."

"How much is there in it?" said the gentleman.

"There's a ton, honest, in it," said Leeam.

"I'll buy it from you," said the gentleman, "and I'll give you the biggest price that's going in the market. When you'll go as far as the cart *boreen* (little road) that's on your left hand, turn down, and be going till you come to a big house in the valley. I'll be before you there to give you your money."

When Leeam came to the *boreen* he turned in, and was going until he came as far as the big house. Leeam wondered when he came as far as the big house, for he was born and raised (*i.e.*, reared) in the neighbourhood, and yet he had never seen the big house before, though he thought he knew every house within five miles of him.

When Leeam came near the barn that was close to the big house, a little lad came out and said: "A hundred thousand welcomes to you, William O'Rooney," put a sack on his back and went in with it. Another little lad came out and welcomed Leeam, put a sack on his back, and went in with it. Lads were coming welcoming Leeam, and putting the sacks on their backs and carrying them in, until the ton of wheat was all gone. Then the whole of the lads came round him, and Leeam said; "Ye all know me, and I don't know ye!" Then they said to him: "Go in and eat your dinner; the master's waiting for you."

Leeam went in and sat down at table; but he had not the second mouthful taken till a heavy sleep came on him, and he fell down under the table. Then the enchanter made a false man like William, and sent him home to William's wife with the horse and cart. When the false man came to Leeam's house, he went into the room, lay down on the bed and died.

It was not long till the cry went out that Leeam O'Rooney was dead. The wife put down water, and when it was hot, she washed the body and put it over the board (*i.e.*, laid it out). The neighbours came, and they keened sorrowfully over the body, and there was great pity for the poor wife, but there was not much grief on herself, for Leeam was old and she was young. The day on the morrow the body was buried, and there was no more remembrance of Leeam.

Leeam's wife had a servant boy, and she said to him: "You ought to marry me and to take Leeam's place."

"It's too early yet, after there being a death in the house," said the boy; "wait till Leeam is a week buried."

When Leeam was seven days and seven nights asleep, a little boy came to him and awoke him, and said: "You've been asleep for a week; but we sent your horse and cart home. Here's your money, and go."

Leeam came home, and as it was late at night nobody saw him. On the morning of that same day Leeam's wife and the servant lad went to the priest and asked him to marry them.

"Have you the marriage money?" said the priest.

"No," said the wife; "but I have a *sturk* of a pig at home, and you can have her in place of money."

The priest married them, and said: "I'll send for the pig tomorrow."

When Leeam came to his own door, he struck a blow on it. The wife and the servant boy were going to bed, and they asked: "Who's there?"

"It's I," said Leeam; "open the door for me."

When they heard the voice, they knew that it was Leeam who was in it, and the wife said: "I can't let you in, and it's a great shame, you to be coming back again, after being seven days in your grave."

"Is it mad you are?" said Leeam.

"I'm not mad," said the wife; "doesn't every person in the parish know that you are dead, and that I buried you decently. Go back to your grave, and I'll have a mass read for your poor soul tomorrow."

"Wait till daylight comes," said Leeam, "and I'll give you the price of your joking!"

Then he went into the stable, where his horse and the pig were, stretched himself in the straw, and fell asleep.

Early on the morning of the next day, the priest said to a little lad that he had: "Get up, and go to Leeam O'Rooney's house, and the woman that I married yesterday will give you a pig to bring home with you."

The boy came to the door of the house, and began knocking at it with a stick. The wife was afraid to open the door, but she asked: "Who's there?"

"I," said the boy; "the priest sent me to get a pig from you."

"She's out in the stable," said the wife; "you can get her for yourself, and drive her back with you."

The lad went into the stable, and began driving out the pig, when Leeam rose up and said: "Where are you going with my pig?"

When the boy saw Leeam, he never stopped to look again, but out with him as hard as he could, and he never stopped till he came back to the priest, and his heart coming out of his mouth with terror.

"What's on you?" says the priest.

The lad told him that Leeam O'Rooney was in the stable, and would not let him drive out the pig.

"Hold your tongue, you liar!" said the priest; "Leeam O'Rooney's dead and in the grave this week."

"If he was in the grave this seven years, I saw him in the stable two moments ago; and if you don't believe me, come yourself, and you'll see him."

The priest and the boy then went together to the door

of the stable, and the priest said: "Go in and turn me out that pig."

"I wouldn't go in for all ever you're worth," said the boy.

The priest went in, and began driving out the pig, when Leeam rose up out of the straw and said: "Where are you going with my pig, Father Patrick?"

When the priest saw Leeam, off and away with him, and he crying out: "In the name of God, I order you back to your grave, William O'Rooney."

Leeam began running after the priest, and saying, "Father Patrick, Father Patrick, are you mad? Wait and speak to me."

The priest would not wait for him, but made off home as fast as his feet could carry him, and when he got into the house, he shut the door. Leeam was knocking at the door till he was tired, but the priest would not let him in. At last, he put his head out of a window in the top of the house, and said: "William O'Rooney, go back to your grave."

"You're mad, Father Patrick! I'm not dead, and never was in a grave since I was born," said Leeam.

"I saw you dead," said the priest; "you died suddenly, and I was present when you were put into the grave, and made a fine sermon over you."

"The devil from me, but, as sure as I'm alive, you're mad!" said Leeam.

"Go out of my sight now," said the priest, "and I'll read a mass for you, tomorrow."

Leeam went home then, and knocked at his own door, but his wife would not let him in. Then he said to himself: "I may as well go and pay my rent now." On his way to the landlord's house, everyone who saw Leeam was running before him, for they thought he was dead. When the landlord heard that Leeam O'Rooney was coming, he shut the doors and would not let him in. Leeam began knocking at the hall door till the lord thought he'd break it in. He came to a window in the top of the house, put out his head, and asked: "What are you wanting?"

"I'm come to pay my rent like an honest man," said Leeam.

"Go back to your grave, and I'll forgive you your rent," said the lord.

"I won't leave this," said Leeam, "till I get a writing from you that I'm paid up clean till next May."

The lord gave him the writing, and he came home and knocked at his own door, but the wife would not let him in. She said that Leeam O'Rooney was dead and buried, and that the man at the door was only a deceiver.

"I'm no deceiver," said William; "I'm after paying my master three years' rent, and I'll have possession of my own house, or else I'll know why."

He went to the barn and got a big bar of iron, and it wasn't long till he broke in the door. There was great fear on the wife, and the newly married husband. They thought they were in the time of the General Resurrection, and that the end of the world was coming.

"Why did you think I was dead?" said Leeam.

"Doesn't everybody in the parish know you're dead?" said the wife.

"Your body from the devil," said Leeam, "you're humbugging me long enough, and get me something to eat."

The poor woman was greatly afraid, and she dressed him some meat, and when she saw him eating and drinking, she said: "It's a miracle."

Then Leeam told her his story from first to last, and she told him each thing that happened, and then he said: "I'll go to the grave tomorrow, till I see the *behoonuch*[1] ye buried in my place."

The day on the morrow Leeam brought a lot of men with him to the churchyard, and they dug open the grave, and were lifting up the coffin, when a big black dog jumped out of it, and made off, and Leeam and the men after it. They were following it till they saw it going into the house in which Leeam had been asleep, and then the ground opened, and the house went down, and nobody ever saw it from that out; but the big hole is to be seen till this day.

When Leeam and the men went home, they told everything to the priest of the parish, and he dissolved the mar-

[1] Gaelic *bitheamhnach*, "thief, rascal."

riage that was between Leeam's wife and the servant boy.

Leeam lived for years after that, and he left great wealth behind him, and they remember him in Clare-Galway still, and will remember him if this story goes down from the old people to the young.

Translated from Modern Irish
by Douglas Hyde

J. M. SYNGE
1871–1909

John Millington Synge once intended to become a concert violinist but realized that, even if he reached a satisfactory level of performance, he would be too shy to face an audience. He then tried writing, with very little success. In 1898, acting on a suggestion that W. B. Yeats had made to him in Paris two years before, Synge visited the Aran Islands off the west coast of Ireland. At once his creative powers were stimulated by the primitive life and colorful speech of the islanders, though his first play was not to be performed until five years later. He visited the islands five times in all, steadily improving his knowledge of Gaelic, which he had first studied as an undergraduate at Trinity College, Dublin, and deepening his understanding of the island people. Before his untimely death of cancer, he had written six plays, of which *Riders to the Sea*, *The Well of the Saints*, and *The Playboy of the Western World* are masterpieces. Synge published no original fiction; the two folktales given here were recorded by him during his first Aran Islands visit. In the case of the longer story, I have included Synge's comments on the teller, the setting, and the tale; the double plot is very similar to that of *The Merchant of Venice* (combining Aarne-Thompson Folktale Types 882 and 890). The shorter story, told by the same old man, provided the plot for Synge's first play, *In the Shadow of the Glen*. Although it is a folktale, the storyteller pretends that it is a real experience of his own; we have seen the same pretence in Kennedy's "Cauth Morrisy Looking for Service."

The Lady O'Conor

When I was going out this morning to walk round the island with Michael, the boy who is teaching me Irish, I met an old man making his way down to the cottage. He was dressed in miserable black clothes which seemed to have come from the mainland, and was so bent with rheumatism that, at a little distance, he looked more like a spider than a human being.

Michael told me it was Pat Dirane, the storyteller old Mourteen had spoken of on the other island. I wished to turn back, as he appeared to be on his way to visit me, but Michael would not hear of it.

'He will be sitting by the fire when we come in,' he said; 'let you not be afraid, there will be time enough to be talking to him by and by.'

He was right. As I came down into the kitchen some hours later, old Pat was still in the chimney corner, blinking with the turf smoke.

He spoke English with remarkable aptness and fluency, due, I believe, to the months he spent in the English provinces working at the harvest when he was a young man.

After a few formal compliments, he told me how he had been crippled by an attack of the 'old hin' (*i.e.* the influenza), and had been complaining ever since in addition to his rheumatism.

While the old woman was cooking my dinner, he asked me if I liked stories, and offered to tell one in English, though he added, it would be much better if I could follow the Gaelic. Then he began:—

There were two farmers in County Clare. One had a son, and the other, a fine rich man, had a daughter.

The young man was wishing to marry the girl, and his father told him to try and get her if he thought well, though a power of gold would be wanting to get the like of her.

'I will try,' said the young man.

He put all his gold into a bag. Then he went over to the other farm, and threw in the gold in front of him.

'Is that all gold?' said the father of the girl.

'All gold,' said O'Conor (the young man's name was O'Conor).

'It will not weigh down my daughter,' said the father.

'We'll see that,' said O'Conor.

Then they put them in the scales, the daughter in one side and the gold in the other. The girl went down against the ground, so O'Conor took his bag and went out on the road.

As he was going along, he came to where there was a little man, and he standing with his back against the wall.

'Where are you going with the bag?' said the little man.

'Going home,' said O'Conor.

'Is it gold you might be wanting?' said the man.

'It is, surely,' said O'Conor.

'I'll give you what you are wanting,' said the man, 'and we can bargain in this way—you'll pay me back in a year the gold I give you, or you'll pay me with five pounds cut off your own flesh.'

That bargain was made between them. The man gave a bag of gold to O'Conor, and he went back with it, and was married to the young woman.

They were rich people, and he built her a grand castle on the cliffs of Clare, with a window that looked out straight over the wild ocean.

One day when he went up with his wife to look out over the wild ocean, he saw a ship coming in on the rocks, and no sails on her at all. She was wrecked on the rocks, and it was tea that was in her, and fine silk.

O'Conor and his wife went down to look at the wreck, and when the lady O'Conor saw the silk, she said she wished a dress of it.

They got the silk from the sailors, and when the Captain came up to get the money for it, O'Conor asked him to come again and take his dinner with them. They had a grand dinner, and they drank after it, and the Captain was tipsy. While they were still drinking, a letter came to

O'Conor, and it was in the letter that a friend of his was dead, and that he would have to go away on a long journey. As he was getting ready, the Captain came to him.

'Are you fond of your wife?' said the Captain.

'I am fond of her,' said O'Conor.

'Will you make me a bet of twenty guineas no man comes near her while you'll be away on the journey?' said the Captain.

'I will bet it,' said O'Conor; and he went away.

There was an old hag who sold small things on the road near the castle, and the lady O'Conor allowed her to sleep up in her room in a big box. The Captain went down on the road to the old hag.

'For how much will you let me sleep one night in your box?' said the Captain.

'For no money at all would I do such a thing,' said the hag.

'For ten guineas?' said the Captain.

'Not for ten guineas,' said the hag.

'For twelve guineas?' said the Captain.

'Not for twelve guineas,' said the hag.

'For fifteen guineas?' said the Captain.

'For fifteen I will do it,' said the hag.

Then she took him up and hid him in the box. When night came the lady O'Conor walked up into her room, and the Captain watched her through a hole that was in the box. He saw her take off her two rings and put them on a kind of a board that was over her head like a chimney piece, and take off her clothes, except her shift, and go up into her bed.

As soon as she was asleep, the Captain came out of his box, and he had some means of making a light, for he lit the candle. He went over to the bed where she was sleeping without disturbing her at all, or doing any bad thing, and he took the two rings off the board, and blew out the light, and went down again into the box.

He paused for a moment, and a deep sigh of relief rose from the men and women who had crowded in while the story was going on, till the kitchen was filled with people.

As the Captain was coming out of his box, the girls, who had appeared to know no English, stopped their spinning and held their breath with expectation.

The old man went on—

When O'Conor came back, the Captain met him and told him that he had been a night in his wife's room, and gave him the two rings.

O'Conor gave him the twenty guineas of the bet. Then he went up into the castle, and he took his wife up to look out of the window over the wild ocean. While she was looking he pushed her from behind, and she fell down over the cliff into the sea.

An old woman was on the shore, and she saw her falling. She went down then to the surf and pulled her out all wet and in great disorder, and she took the wet clothes off her, and put on some old rags belonging to herself.

When O'Conor had pushed his wife from the window, he went away into the land.

After a while the lady O'Conor went out searching for him, and when she had gone here and there a long time in the country, she heard that he was reaping in a field with sixty men.

She came to the field and she wanted to go in, but the gateman would not open the gate for her. Then the owner came by, and she told him her story. He brought her in, and her husband was there, reaping, but he never gave any sign of knowing her. She showed him to the owner, and he made the man come out and go with his wife.

Then the lady O'Conor took him out on the road where there were horses, and they rode away.

When they came to the place where O'Conor had met the little man, he was there on the road before them.

'Have you my gold on you?' said the man.

'I have not,' said O'Conor.

'Then you'll pay me the flesh off your body,' said the man.

They went into a house, and a knife was brought, and a

clean white cloth was put on the table, and O'Conor was put upon the cloth.

Then the little man was going to strike the lancet into him, when says lady O'Conor—

'Have you bargained for five pounds of flesh?'

'For five pounds of flesh,' said the man.

'Have you bargained for any drop of his blood?' said lady O'Conor.

'For no blood,' said the man.

'Cut out the flesh,' said lady O'Conor, 'but if you spill one drop of his blood, I'll put that through you.' And she put a pistol to his head.

The little man went away and they saw no more of him.

When they got home to their castle, they made a great supper, and they invited the Captain and the old hag, and the old woman that had pulled the lady O'Conor out of the sea.

After they had eaten well, the lady O'Conor began, and she said they would all tell their stories. Then she told how she had been saved from the sea, and how she had found her husband.

Then the old woman told her story, the way she had found the lady O'Conor wet, and in great disorder, and had brought her in and put on her some old rags of her own.

The lady O'Conor asked the Captain for his story, but he said they would get no story from him. Then she took her pistol out of her pocket, and she put it on the edge of the table, and she said that any one that would not tell his story would get a bullet into him.

Then the Captain told the way he had got into the box, and come over to her bed without touching her at all, and had taken away the rings.

Then the lady O'Conor took the pistol and shot the hag through the body, and they threw her over the cliff into the sea.

That is my story.

It gave me a strange feeling of wonder to hear this illiterate native of a wet rock in the Atlantic telling a story that is so full of European associations.

The incident of the faithful wife takes us beyond Cymbeline to the sunshine on the Arno, and the gay company who went out from Florence to tell narratives of love. It takes us again to the low vineyards of Würzburg on the Main, where the same tale was told in the middle ages, of the 'Two Merchants and the Faithful Wife of Ruprecht von Würzburg.'

The other portion, dealing with the pound of flesh, has a still wider distribution, reaching from Persia and Egypt to the *Gesta Romanorum*, and the *Pecorone* of Ser Giovanni, a Florentine notary.

The present union of the two tales has already been found among the Gaels, and there is a somewhat similar version in Campbell's *Popular Tales of the Western Highlands*.

He That's Dead Can Do No Hurt

One day I was travelling on foot from Galway to Dublin, and the darkness came on me and I ten miles from the town I was wanting to pass the night in. Then a hard rain began to fall and I was tired walking, so when I saw a sort of a house with no roof on it up against the road, I got in the way the walls would give me shelter.

As I was looking round I saw a light in some trees two perches off, and thinking any sort of a house would be better than where I was, I got over a wall and went up to the house to look in at the window.

I saw a dead man laid on a table, and candles lighted, and a woman watching him. I was frightened when I saw him, but it was raining hard, and I said to myself, if he was dead he couldn't hurt me. Then I knocked on the door and the woman came and opened it.

"Good evening, ma'am," says I.

"Good evening kindly, stranger," says she. "Come in out of the rain."

Then she took me in and told me her husband was after dying on her, and she was watching him that night.

"But it's thirsty you'll be, stranger," says she. "Come into the parlor."

Then she took me into the parlor—and it was a fine clean house—and she put a cup, with a saucer under it, on the table before me with fine sugar and bread.

When I'd had a cup of tea, I went back into the kitchen where the dead man was lying, and she gave me a fine new pipe off the table with a drop of spirits.

"Stranger," says she, "would you be afeard to be alone with himself?"

"Not a bit in the world, ma'am," says I; "he that's dead can do no hurt."

Then she said she wanted to go over and tell the neighbors the way her husband was after dying on her, and she went out and locked the door behind her.

I smoked one pipe, and I leaned out and took another off the table. I was smoking it with my hand on the back of my chair—the way you are yourself this minute, God bless you—and I looking on the dead man, when he opened his eyes as wide as myself and looked at me.

"Don't be afraid, stranger," said the dead man; "I'm not dead at all in the world. Come here and help me up and I'll tell you all about it."

Well, I went up and took the sheet off of him, and I saw that he had a fine clean shirt on his body, and fine flannel drawers.

He sat up then, and says he—

"I've got a bad wife, stranger, and I let on to be dead the way I'd catch her goings on."

Then he got two fine sticks he had to keep down his wife, and he put them at each side of his body, and he laid himself out again as if he was dead.

In half an hour his wife came back and a young man along with her. Well, she gave him his tea, and she told him he was tired, and he would do right to go and lie down in the bedroom.

The young man went in and the woman sat down to watch by the dead man. A while after she got up and "Stranger," says she, "I'm going in to get the candle out of the room; I'm thinking the young man will be asleep by this time." She went into the bedroom, but the divil a bit of her came back.

Then the dead man got up, and he took one stick, and he gave the other to myself. We went in and saw them lying together with her head on his arm.

The dead man hit him a blow with the stick so that the blood out of him leapt up and hit the gallery.

That is my story.

SHORT STORIES

WILLIAM CARLETON
1794–1869

William Carleton (the family name was originally
O'Carolan) grew up in a family of fourteen, being the
youngest son of an impoverished farmer in a Gaelic-
speaking area near the town of Clogher, County Ty-
rone. He picked up an education, at various "hedge
schools" and then from a priest who was a distant relative, fully intending to become a Roman Catholic priest
himself. Carleton gave up this plan after a disil-
lusioning experience of what he felt to be superstition,
the pilgrimage to St. Patrick's Purgatory in Lough
Derg. At one time he belonged to the Ribbonmen, a
secret society sworn to fight landlords; at another time
he worked as a private tutor. Finally, he went to Dublin, became a Protestant, took a teaching post at a
Protestant school, and married a Protestant wife. His
first stories were satirical caricatures of Irish Catholicism, published in 1828–29, though he later mellowed
toward the faith of his fathers. The two series of short
stories and novellas that made him famous were published under the general title of *Traits and Stories of
the Irish Peasantry* in 1830 and 1834. He continued to
write novels and short fiction until his death, the best
of his novels being *Fardorougha the Miser* and *The
Black Prophet*. "The Donagh," from *Traits and Stories*, Second Series, is easily the longest story in this
anthology because Carleton, like most writers of the
Romantic period, needs plenty of elbowroom. At heart

he was a moralist or a sociologist rather than a literary artist, but his thorough knowledge of the peasant life he describes keeps us constantly fascinated. The "donagh" or shrine that gives this story both its title and its central symbol can now be viewed in the National Museum in Dublin. Known as the *Domhnach Airgid* (Silver Shrine), it used to contain an eighth- or ninth-century manuscript of the Gospels. Its inner bronze-plated box of yew wood possibly dates from the seventh century, while the elaborate outer case of precious metal was made in 1350.

The Donagh; or, The Horse-Stealers

Carnmore, one of those small villages that are to be found in the outskirts of many parishes in Ireland, whose distinct boundaries are lost in the contiguous mountain wastes, was situated at the foot of a deep gorge, or pass, overhung by two bleak hills, from the naked sides of which the storm swept over it without discomposing the peaceful little nook of cabins that stood below. About a furlong farther down were two or three farmhouses, inhabited by a family named Cassidy, men of simple, inoffensive manners and considerable wealth. They were, however, acute and wise in their generation; intelligent cattle dealers, on whom it would have been a matter of some difficulty to impose an unsound horse, or a cow older than was intimated by her horn-rings, even when conscientiously dressed up for sale by the ingenious aid of the file or burning-iron. Between their houses and the hamlet rose a conical pile of rocks, loosely heaped together, from which the place took its name of Carnmore.

About three years before the time of this story there came two men with their families to reside in the upper village, and the house which they chose as a residence was one at some distance from those which composed the little group we have just been describing. They said their name was Meehan, although the general report went that this was not true; that the name was an assumed one, and that some dark mystery, which none could penetrate, shrouded their history and character. They were certainly remarkable men. The elder, named Anthony, was a dark, black-browed person, stern in his manner, and atrociously cruel in his disposition. His form was herculean, his bones strong and hard as iron, and his sinews stood out in undeniable evidence of a life hitherto spent in severe toil and exertion, to bear which he appeared to an amazing degree capable. His brother Denis was a small man, less savage and daring in his character, and consequently more vacillating and cautious than Anthony; for the points in which he resembled him were superinduced upon his natural disposition by the close connection that subsisted between them, and by the identity of their former pursuits in life, which, beyond doubt, had been such as could not bear investigation.

The old proverb of "birds of a feather flock together" is certainly a true one, and in this case it was once more verified. Before the arrival of these men in the village there had been five or six bad characters in the neighborhood, whose delinquencies were pretty well-known. With these persons the strangers, by that sympathy which assimilates with congenial good or evil, soon became acquainted; and although their intimacy was as secret and cautious as possible, still it had been observed and was known; for they had frequently been seen skulking together at daybreak or in the dusk of evening.

It is unnecessary to say that Meehan and his brother did not mingle much in the society of Carnmore. In fact, the villagers and they mutually avoided each other. A mere return of the common phrases of salutation was generally the most that passed between them: they never entered into that familiarity which leads to mutual intercourse and justifies one neighbour in freely entering the cabin of another, to spend a winter's night or a summer's evening in amusing conversation. Few had ever been in the house of the Meehans since it became theirs. Nor were the means of their subsistence known. They led an idle life, had no scarcity of food, were decently clothed, and never wanted money—circumstances which occasioned no small degree of conjecture in Carnmore and its vicinity.

Some said they lived by theft; others, that they were coiners; and there were many who imagined, from the diabolical countenance of the elder brother, that he had sold himself to the devil, who, they affirmed, set his mark upon him, and was his paymaster. Upon this hypothesis several were ready to prove that he had neither breath nor shadow: they had seen him, they said, standing under a hedgerow of elder—that unholy tree which furnished wood for the cross, and on which Judas hanged himself—yet, although it was noonday in the month of July, his person threw out no shadow. Worthy souls! because the man stood in the shade at the time. But with these simple explanations Superstition had nothing to do, although we are bound, in justice to the reverend old lady, to affirm that she was kept exceedingly busy in Carnmore. If a man had a sick cow, she was elf-shot; if his child became consumptive, it had been overlooked, or received a blast from the fairies; if the whooping cough was rife, all the afflicted children were put three times under an ass; or when they happened to have the "mumps," were led before sunrise to a south-running stream, with a halter hanging about their necks, under an obligation of silence during the ceremony. In short, there could not possibly be a more superstitious spot than that which these men of mystery had selected for their residence. Another circumstance which caused the people to look upon them with additional dread was their neglect of mass on Sundays and holidays, though they avowed themselves Roman Catholics. They did not, it is true, join in the dances, drinking matches, football, and other sports with which the Carnmore folk celebrated the Lord's Day; but they scrupled not, on the other hand, to mend their garden ditch or mold a row of cabbages on the Sabbath— a circumstance for which two or three of the Carnmore boys were, one Sunday evening when tipsy, well-nigh chastising them. Their usual manner, however, of spending that day was by sauntering lazily about the fields, or stretching themselves supinely on the sunny side of the hedges, their arms folded into their bosoms, and their hats lying over their faces to keep off the sun.

In the meantime, loss of property was becoming quite

common in the neighborhood. Sheep were stolen from the farmers, and cows and horses from the more extensive graziers in the parish. The complaints against the authors of these depredations were loud and incessant. Watches were set, combinations for mutual security formed, and subscriptions to a considerable amount entered into, with a hope of being able, by the temptation of a large reward, to work upon the weakness or cupidity of some accomplice to betray the gang of villains who infested the neighborhood. All, however, was in vain: every week brought some new act of plunder to light, perpetrated upon such unsuspecting persons as had hitherto escaped the notice of the robbers; but no trace could be discovered of the perpetrators. Although theft had from time to time been committed upon a small scale before the arrival of the Meehans in the village, yet it was undeniable that since that period the instances not only multiplied, but became of a more daring and extensive description. They arose in a gradual scale from the hen-roost to the stable; and with such ability were they planned and executed, that the people, who in every instance identified Meehan and his brother with them, began to believe and hint that, in consequence of their compact with the devil, they had power to render themselves invisible. Common fame, who can best treat such subjects, took up this and never laid it aside until, by narrating several exploits which Meehan the elder was said to have performed in other parts of the kingdom, she wound it up by roundly informing the Carnmorians that having been once taken prisoner for murder, he was caught by the leg when half through a hedge, but that being most wickedly determined to save his neck, he left the leg with the officer who took him, shouting out that it was a new species of leg-bail; and yet he moved away with surprising speed upon two of as good legs as any man in his Majesty's dominions might wish to walk off upon from the insinuating advances of a bailiff or a constable!

The family of the Meehans consisted of their wives, and three children, two boys and a girl—the former were the offspring of the younger brother, and the latter of Anthony. It has been observed, with truth and justice, that there is no man, how hardened and diabolical soever in his natural temper, who does not exhibit to some particular object a peculiar species of affection. Such a man was Anthony Meehan. That sullen hatred which he bore to human society, and that inherent depravity of heart which left the trail of vice and crime upon his footsteps, were flung off his character when he addressed his daughter Anne. To him her voice was like music. To her he was not the reckless villain, treacherous and cruel, which the helpless and unsuspecting found him, but a parent kind and indulgent as ever pressed an only and beloved daughter to his bosom. Anne was handsome: had she been born and educated in an elevated rank in society, she would have been softened by the polish and luxury of life into perfect beauty; she was, however, utterly without education. As Anne experienced from her father no unnatural cruelty, no harshness, nor even indifference, she consequently loved him in return; for she knew that tenderness from such a man was a proof of parental love rarely to be found in life. Perhaps she loved not her father the less on perceiving that he was proscribed by the world—a circumstance which might also have enhanced in his eyes the affection she bore him. When Meehan came to Carnmore she was sixteen; and as that was three years before the incident occurred on which we have founded this narrative, the reader may now suppose her to be about nineteen; an interesting country girl as to person, but with a mind completely neglected, yet remarkable for an uncommon stock of good nature and credulity.

About the hour of eleven o'clock one winter's night in the beginning of December, Meehan and his brother sat moodily at their hearth. The fire was of peat which had recently been put down, and from between the turf the ruddy blaze was shooting out in those little tongues and gusts of sober light which throw around the rural hearth one of those charms which make up the felicity of domestic life. The night was stormy, and the wind moaned and howled along the dark hills beneath which the cottage stood. Every object in the house was shrouded in a mellow shade, which afforded to the eye no clear outline, except around the hearth alone, where the light brightened into a

golden hue, giving the idea of calmness and peace. Anthony
Meehan sat on one side of it, and his daughter opposite
him, knitting. Before the fire sat Denis, drawing shapes in
the ashes for his own amusement.

"Bless me," said he, "how sthrange it is!"

"What is?" inquired Anthony, in his deep and grating
tones.

"Why, thin, it is sthrange!" continued the other, who,
despite of the severity of his brother, was remarkably superstitious—"a coffin I made in the ashes three times runnin'! Isn't it very quare, Anne?" he added, addressing the
niece.

"Sthrange enough, of a sartinty," she replied, being unwilling to express before her father the alarm which the
incident, slight as it was, created in her mind; for she, like
the uncle, was subject to such ridiculous influences. "How
did it happen, uncle?"

"Why, thin, no way in life, Anne; only, as I was thryin'
to make a shoe, it turned out a coffin on my hands. I thin
smoothed the ashes, and began agin, an' sorra bit of it but
was a coffin still. Well, says I, I'll give you another chance
—here goes once more; an', as sure as a gun's iron, it was
a coffin the third time! Heaven be about us, it's odd
enough!"

"It would be little matther you were nailed down in a
coffin," replied Anthony fiercely; "the world would have
little loss. What a pitiful, cowardly rascal you are—afraid
o' your own shadow afther the sun goes down, except I'm
at your elbow! Can't you dhrive all them palavers out o'
your head? Didn't the sargint tell us, an' prove to us, the
time we broke the guardhouse, an' took Frinch lave o' the
ridgment for good, that the whole o' that, an' more along
wid it, is all priestcraft?"

"I remimber he did, sure enough. I dunna where the
same sargint is now, Tony? About no good, anyway, I'll
be bail. Howsomever, in regard o' that, why doesn't yourself give up fastin' from the mate of a Friday?"

"Do you want me to sthretch you on the hearth?" replied the savage, whilst his eyes kindled into fury, and his
grim visage darkened into a Satanic expression. "I'll tache

you to be puttin' me through my catechiz about atin' mate. I may manage that as I plase; it comes at first cost, anyhow; but no cross-questions to me about it, if you regard your health!"

"I must say for you," replied Denis reproachfully, "that you're a good warrant to put the health astray upon us of an odd start: we're not come to this time o' day widout carryin' somethin' to remember you by. For my own part, Tony, I don't like such tokens; an' moreover, I wish you had resaved a thrifle o' larnin', espishily in the writin' line; for whenever we have any difference you're so ready to prove your opinion by settin' your mark upon me, that I'd rather, fifty times over, you could write it with pen an' ink."

"My father will give that up, uncle," said the niece. "It's bad for anybody to be fightin', but worst of all for brothers, that ought to live in peace and kindness. Won't you, father?"

"Maybe I will, dear, some o' these days, on your account, Anne; but you must get this creature of an uncle of yours to let me alone, an' not be aggravatin' me with his folly. As for your mother, she's worse; her tongue's sharp enough to skin a flint, and a batin' a day has little effect on her."

Anne sighed, for she knew how low an irreligious life, and the infamous society with which, as her father's wife, her mother was compelled to mingle, had degraded her.

"Well, but, Father, you don't set her a good example yourself," said Anne; "and if she scolds and drinks now, you know she was a different woman when you got her. You allow this yourself; and the crathur, the dhrunkest time she is, doesn't she cry bitterly, remimberin' what she has been. Instead of one batin' a day, Father, thry no batin' a day, an' maybe it'll turn out betther than thumpin' an' smashin' her, as you do."

"Why, thin, there's thruth an' sinse in what the girl says, Tony," observed Denis.

"Come," replied Anthony, "whatever she may say, I'll suffer none of your interference. Go an' get us the black bottle from the place: it'll soon be time to move. I hope they won't stay too long."

Denis obeyed this command with great readiness, for whisky in some degree blunted the fierce passions of his brother and deadened his cruelty, or, rather, diverted it from minor objects to those which occurred in the lawless perpetration of his villainy.

The bottle was got; and in the meantime the fire blazed up brightly. The storm without, however, did not abate, nor did Meehan and his brother wish that it should. As the elder of them took the glass from the hands of the other, an air of savage pleasure blazed in his eyes, on reflecting that the tempest of the night was favorable to the execution of the villainous deed on which they were bent.

"More power to you!" said Anthony, impiously personifying the storm. "Sure, that's one proof that God doesn't throuble His head about what we do, or we would not get such a murtherin' fine night as is in it, anyhow. That's it! blow an' tundher away, an' keep yourself an' us as black as hell, sooner than we should fail in what we intind! Anne, your health, *acushla*[1]*!*—Yours, Dinny! If you keep your tongue off o' me, I'll neither make nor meddle in regard o' the batin' o' you."

"I hope you'll stick to that, anyhow," replied Denis. "For my part, I'm sick and sore o' you everyday in the year. Many another man would put salt wather between himself and yourself, sooner nor become a batin'-stone for you, as I have been. Few would bear it when they could mend themselves."

"What's that you say?" replied Anthony, suddenly laying down his glass, catching his brother by the collar, and looking him, with a murderous scowl, in the face. "Is it thrachery you hint at?—eh? sarpent, is it thrachery you mane?" and as he spoke he compressed Denis's neck between his powerful hands until the other was black in the face.

Anne flew to her uncle's assistance, and with much difficulty succeeded in rescuing him from the deadly grip of her father, who exclaimed, as he loosed his hold, "You may thank the girl, or you'd not spake, nor dare to spake, about crossin' the salt wather or lavin' me in a desateful way

---

[1] Gaelic *a chuisle*, "O pulse [of my heart]."

agin. If I ever suspect that a thought of thrachery comes into your heart, I'll do for you; and you may carry your story to the world I'll send you to."

"Father, dear, why are you so suspicious of my uncle?" said Anne. "Sure, he's a long time livin' with you, an' goin' step for step in all the danger you meet with. If he had a mind to turn out a Judas agin you, he might a done it long agone; not to mintion the throuble it would bring on his own head, seein' he's as deep in everything as you are."

"If that's all that's throubling you," replied Denis, trembling, "you may make yourself asy on the head of it. But well I know 'tisn't that that's on your mind; 'tis your own conscience; but, sure, it's not fair nor rasonable for you to vent your evil thoughts on me!"

"Well, he won't," said Anne; "he'll quit it, his mind's throubled, an', dear knows, it's no wondher it should. Och, I'd give the world wide that his conscience was lightened of the load that's upon it! My mother's lameness is nothin'; but the child, poor thing! An' it was only widin three days of her lyin'-in. Och, it was a cruel sthroke, father! An' when I seen its little innocent face, dead, an' me widout a brother, I thought my heart would break, thinkin' upon who did it!" The tears fell in showers from her eyes, as she added, "Father, I don't want to vex you, but I wish you to feel sorry for that at laste. Oh, if you'd bring the priest, an' give up sich coorses, father dear, how happy we'd be, an' how happy yourself ud be!"

Conscience for a moment started from her sleep, and uttered a cry of guilt in his spirit; his face became ghastly, and his eyes full of horror; his lips quivered, and he was about to upbraid his daughter with more harshness than usual, when a low whistle, resembling that of a curlew, was heard at a chink of the door. In a moment he gulped down another glass of spirits, and was on his feet: "Go, Denis, an' get the arms," said he, "while I let them in."

On opening the door, three men entered, having their greatcoats muffled about them, and their hats slouched. One of them, named Kenny, was a short villain, but of a thick-set, hairy frame. The other was known as "the Big Mower," in consequence of his following that employment every season, and of his great skill in performing it. He had a deep-rooted objection against permitting the palm of his hand to be seen; a reluctance which common fame attributed to the fact of his having received on that part the impress of a hot iron, in the shape of the letter T, not forgetting to add that T was the hieroglyphic for Thief. The villain himself affirmed it was simply the mark of a cross, burned into it by a blessed friar, as a charm against St. Vitus's dance, to which he had been subject. The people, however, were rather sceptical, not of the friar's power to cure that malady, but of the fact of his ever having moved a limb under it; and they concluded with telling him, good-humoredly enough, that, notwithstanding the charm, he was destined to die "wid the threble of it in his toe." The third was a noted pedlar called Martin, who, under pretense of selling tape, pins, scissors, &c., was very useful in "setting" such premises as this virtuous fraternity might, without much risk, make a descent upon.

"I thought yees would outstay your time," said the elder Meehan, relapsing into his determined hardihood of character; "we're ready, hours agone. Dick Rice gave me two curlew an' two patrich[2] calls today. Now pass the glass among yees while Denny brings the arms. I know there's danger in this business, in regard of the Cassidys livin' so near us. If I see anybody afut, I'll use the curlew call; an' if not, I'll whistle twice on the patrich one, an' yees may come an. The horse is worth aighty guineas if he's worth a shillin'; an' we'll make sixty of him ourselves."

For some time they chatted about the plan in contemplation, and drank freely of the spirits, until at length the impatience of the elder Meehan at the delay of his brother became ungovernable. His voice deepened into tones of savage passion as he uttered a series of blasphemous curses against this unfortunate butt of his indignation and malignity. At length he rushed out furiously to know why he did not return; but on reaching a secret excavation in the mound against which the house was built, he found, to his utter dismay, that Denis had made his escape by an artifi-

---

[2] Partridge.

cial passage scooped out of it to secure themselves a retreat
in case of surprise or detection. It opened behind the house
among a clump of blackthorn and brushwood, and was
covered with green turf in such a manner as to escape the
notice of all who were not acquainted with the secret. Meehan's face, on his return, was worked up into an expression
truly awful.

"We're sold!" said he; "but stop, I'll tache the thraithur
what revinge is!"

In a moment he awoke his brother's two sons, and
dragged them by the neck, one in each hand, to the hearth.

"Your villain of a father's off," said he, "to betray us. Go
an' folly him—bring him back, an' he'll be safe from me;
but let him become a stag agin us, an' if I should hunt you
both into the bowels of the airth, I'll send yees to a short
account. I don't care that," and he snapped his fingers—
"ha, ha!—no, I don't care that for the law; I know how to
dale with it when it comes! An' what's the stuff about the
other world but priestcraft and lies!"

"Maybe," said the Big Mower, "Denis is gone to get the
foreway of us, an' to take the horse himself. Our best plan
is to lose no time, at all events; so let us hurry, for fraid the
night might happen to clear up."

"He!" said Meehan, "he go alone! No; the miserable
wretch is afeard of his own shadow. I only wondher he
stuck to me so long; but, sure, he wouldn't, only I bate the
courage in, and the fear out of him. You're right, Brian,"
said he, upon reflection; "let us lose no time, but be off. Do
yees mind?" he added to, his nephews; "did yees hear me?
If you see him, let him come back, an' all will be berrid;
but if he doesn't, you know your fate;" saying which, he
and his accomplices departed amid the howling of the
storm.

The next morning Carnmore, and indeed the whole parish, was in an uproar; a horse, worth eighty guineas, had
been stolen in the most daring manner from the Cassidys,
and the hue-and-cry was up after the thief or thieves who
took him. For several days the search was closely maintained, but without success: not the slightest trace could be
found of him or them. The Cassidys could very well bear

to lose him; but there were many struggling farmers, on whose property serious depredations had been committed, who could not sustain their loss so easily. It was natural, under these circumstances, that suspicion should attach to many persons, some of whom had but indifferent characters before, as well as to several who certainly had never deserved suspicion. When a fortnight or so had elapsed, and no circumstances transpired that might lead to discovery, the neighbors, including those who had principally suffered by the robberies, determined to assemble upon a certain day at Cassidy's house, for the purpose of clearing themselves, on oath, of the imputations thrown out against some of them as accomplices in the thefts. In order, however, that the ceremony should be performed as solemnly as possible, they determined to send for Father Farrell and Mr. Nicholson, a magistrate, both of whom they requested to undertake the task of jointly presiding upon this occasion; and that the circumstance should have every publicity, it was announced from the altar by the priest on the preceding Sabbath, and published on the church gate in large legible characters, ingeniously printed with a pen by the village schoolmaster.

In fact, the intended meeting and the object of it were already notorious; and much conversation was held upon its probable result, and the measures which might be taken against those who should refuse to swear. Of the latter description there was but one opinion, which was that their refusal in such a case would be tantamount to guilt. The innocent were anxious to vindicate themselves from suspicion; and as the suspected did not amount to more than a dozen, of course the whole body of the people, including the thieves themselves, who applauded it as loudly as the others, all expressed their satisfaction at the measures about to be adopted. A day was therefore appointed on which the inhabitants of the neighborhood, particularly the suspected persons, should come to assemble at Cassidy's house, in order to have the characters of the innocent cleared up, and the guilty made known.

On the evening before this took place were assembled in Meehan's cottage the elder Meehan and the rest of the gang, including Denis, who had absconded on the night of the theft.

"Well, well, Denny," said Anthony who forced his rugged nature into an appearance of better temper that he might strengthen the timid spirit of his brother against the scrutiny about to take place on the morrow—perhaps, too, he dreaded him—"Well, well, Denny, I thought, sure enough, that it was some new piece of cowardice came over you. Just think of him," he added, "shabbin' off, only because he made, with a bit of a rod, three strokes in the ashes that he thought resembled a coffin!—ha, ha, ha!"

This produced a peal of derision at Denis's pusillanimous terror.

"Ay!" said the Big Mower, "he was makin' a coffin, was he? I wondher it wasn't a rope you drew, Denny. If any here dies in the coil, it will be the greatest coward, an' that's yourself."

"You may all laugh," replied Denis, "but I know such things to have a manin'. When my mother died, didn't my father—the heavens be his bed—see a black coach about a week before it? an' sure, from the first day she tuck ill, the dead-watch was heard in the house every night. And what was more nor that, she kept warm until she went into her grave; an' accordingly didn't my sisther Shibby die within a year afther?"

"It's no matther about thim things," replied Anthony; "it's thruth about the dead-watch, my mother keepin' warm, an' Shibby's death, anyway. But on the night we tuck Cassidy's horse I thought you were goin' to betray us; I was surely in a murdherin' passion, an' would have done harm, only things turned out as they did."

"Why," said Denis, "the thruth is, I was afeard some of us would be shot, an' that the lot would fall on myself; for the coffin, thinks I, was sent as a warnin'. How-and-ever, I spied about Cassidy's stable till I seen that the coast was clear; so whin I heard the low cry of the patrich that Anthony and I agreed on, I joined yees."

"Well, about tomorrow," observed Kenny—"ha, ha, ha! —there'll be lots o' swearin'. Why, the whole parish is to switch the primer; many a thumb and coat cuff will be kissed in spite of priest or magistrate. I remimber once, whin I was swearin' an *alibi* for long Paddy Murray, that suffered for the M'Gees, I kissed my thumb, I thought, so smoothly that no one would notish it; but I had a keen one to dale with, so says he, 'You know, for the matther o' that, my good fellow, that you have your thumb to kiss every-day in the week,' says he; 'but you might salute the book out o' decency and good manners—not,' says he, 'that you an' it are strangers either; for, if I don't mistake, you're an ould hand at swearin' *alibis.*' At all evints, I had to smack the book itself, and it's I and Barney Green and Tim Casserly that did swear stiffly for Paddy; but the thing was too clear agin him; so he suffered, poor fellow, an' died right game, for he said over his dhrop—ha, ha, ha!—that he was as innocent o' the murdher as a child unborn; and so he was in one sinse, bein' afther gettin' absolution."

"As to thumb-kissin'," observed the elder Meehan, "let there be none of it among us tomorrow; if we're caught at it, 'twould be as bad as stayin' away altogether. For my part, I'll give it a smack like a pistol shot—ha, ha, ha!"

"I hope they won't bring the priest's book," said Denis. "I haven't the laste objection agin payin' my respects to the magistrate's paper, but somehow I don't like tastin' the priest's in a falsity."

"Don't you know," said the Big Mower, "that whin a magistrate's present it's ever an' always only the Tistament by law that's used. I myself wouldn't kiss the mass-book in a falsity."

"There's none of us sayin' we'd do it in a lie," said the elder Meehan; "an' it's well for thousands that the law doesn't use the priest's book; though, afther all, aren't there books that say religion's all a sham? I think myself it is; for if what they talk about justice an' Providence is thrue, would Tom Dillon be transported for the robbery we committed at Bantry? Tom, it's true, was an ould offender; but he was innocent of that, anyway. The world's all chance, boys, as Sargint Eustace used to say, and whin we die there's no more about us; so that I don't see why a man mightn't was well switch the priest's book as any other, only that somehow a body can't shake the terror of it off o' them."

"I dunna, Anthony, but you an' I ought to curse that sargint; only for him we mightn't be as we are, sore in our conscience, an' afeard of every fut we hear passin'," observed Denis.

"Spake for your own cowardly heart, man alive," replied Anthony; "for my part, I'm afeard o' nothin'. Put round the glass, and don't be nursin' it there all night. Sure, we're not so bad as the rot among the sheep, nor the black leg among the bullocks, nor the staggers among the horses, anyhow; an' yet they'd hang us up only for bein' fond of a bit o' mate—ha, ha, ha!"

"Thrue enough," said the Big Mower, philosophizing. "God made the beef and the mutton, and the grass to feed it; but it was man made the ditches. Now we're only bringin' things back to the right way that Providence made them in, when ould times were in it, manin' before ditches war invinted—ha, ha, ha!"

" 'Tis a good argument," observed Kenny, "only that judge and jury would be a little delicate in actin' up to it; an' the more's the pity. Howsomever, as Providence made the mutton, sure it's no harm for us to take what He sends."

"Ay, but," said Denis—

"God made man, an' man made money;
God made bees, an' bees made honey;
God made Satan, an' Satan made sin;
An' God made a hell to put Satan in.

Let nobody say there's not a hell; isn't it there plain from Scripthur?"

"I wish you had Scripthur tied about your neck!" replied Anthony. "How fond of it one o' the greatest thieves that ever missed the rope is! Why, the fellow could plan a roguery with any man that ever danced the hangman's hornpipe, an' yit he be's repatin' bits an' scraps of ould prayers, an' charms, an' stuff. Ay, indeed! Sure, he has a varse out

o' the Bible that he thinks can prevint a man from bein'
hung up any day!"

While Denny, the Big Mower, and the two Meehans
were thus engaged in giving expression to their peculiar
opinions, the pedlar held a conversation of a different kind
with Anne.

With the secrets of the family in his keeping, he commenced a rather penitent review of his own life, and expressed his intention of abandoning so dangerous a mode
of accumulating wealth. He said he thanked Heaven that
he had already laid up sufficient for the wants of a reasonable man; that he understood farming and the management of sheep particularly well; that it was his intention to
remove to a different part of the kingdom and take a farm;
and that nothing prevented him from having done this before but the want of a helpmate to take care of his establishment. He added that his present wife was of an intoler-
able temper and a greater villain by fifty degrees than himself. He concluded by saying that his conscience twitched
him night and day for living with her, and that, by abandoning her immediately, becoming truly religious, and taking Anne in her place, he hoped, he said, to atone in some
measure for his few errors.

Anthony, however, having noticed the earnestness which
marked the pedlar's manner, suspected him of attempting
to corrupt the principles of his daughter, having forgotten
the influence which his own opinions were calculated to
produce upon her heart.

"Martin," said he, " 'twould be as well you ped attintion
to what we're sayin' in regard o' the trial tomorrow, as to
be palaverin' talk into the girl's ear that can't be good
comin' from your lips. Quit it, I say, quit it! *Corp an
duowol*[3]—I won't allow such proceedings!"

"Swear till you blister your lips, Anthony," replied Martin; "as for me, bein' no residenthur, I'm not bound to it;
an' what's more, I'm not suspected. 'Tis settin' some other
bit o' work for yees I'll be, while you're all clearin' your-

[3] Would-be phonetic Gaelic for "Devil take you" or "Devil take
me."

selves from stealin' honest Cassidy's horse. I wish we had him safely disposed of in the manetime, an' the money for him an' the other beasts in our pockets."

Much more conversation of a similar kind passed between them upon various topics connected with their profligacy and crimes. At length they separated for the night, after having concerted their plan of action for the ensuing scrutiny.

The next morning, before the hour appointed arrived, the parish, particularly the neighborhood of Carnmore, was struck with deep consternation. Labor became suspended, mirth disappeared, and every face was marked with paleness, anxiety, and apprehension. If two men met, one shook his head mysteriously, and inquired from the other, "Did you hear the news?"

"Ay! ay! the Lord be about us all! I did; an' I pray God it may lave the counthry as it came to it!"

"Oh, an' that it may, I humbly make supplication this day!"

If two women met, it was with similar mystery and fear. "Vread, do you know what's at the Cassidys'?"

"Whisht, *ahagur!* I do; but let what will happen, sure it's best for us to say nothin'."

"Say!—the blessed Virgin forbid! I'd cut my hand off o' me afore I'd spake a word about it; only that—"

"Whisht, woman!—for mercy's sake—don't—"

And so they would separate, each crossing herself devoutly.

The meeting at Cassidy's was to take place that day at twelve o'clock; but about two hours before the appointed time, Anne, who had been in some of the other houses, came into her father's, quite pale, breathless, and trembling.

"Oh!" she exclaimed, with clasped hands, whilst the tears fell fast from her eyes, "we'll be lost—ruined! Did yees hear what's in the neighborhood wid the Cassidys?"

"Girl," said the father, with more severity than he had ever manifested to her before, "I never yit ris my hand to you, but *ma corp an duowol,* if you open your lips, I'll fell you where you stand. Do you want that cowardly uncle

o' yours to be the manes o' hangin' your father? Maybe
that was one o' the lessons Martin gave you last night?"
And as he spoke he knit his brows at her with that murderous scowl which was habitual to him. The girl trembled,
and began to think that since her father's temper deepened
in domestic outrage and violence as his crimes multiplied,
the sooner she left the family the better. Every day indeed
diminished that species of instinctive affection which she
had entertained towards him, and this in proportion as her
reason ripened into a capacity for comprehending the dark
materials of which his character was composed.

"What's the matter now?" inquired Denis, with alarm.
"Is it anything about us, Anthony?"

"No, 'tisn't," replied the other, "anything about us!
What ud it be about us for? 'Tis a lyin' report that some
cunnin' knave spread, hopin' to find out the guilty. But hear
me, Denis, once for all: we're going to clear ourselves—
now listen, an' let my words sink deep into your heart—if
you refuse to swear this day, no matther what's put into
your hand, you'll do harm—that's all—have courage, man;
but should you cow, you're coorse will be short; an' mark,
even if *you* escape me, your sons won't. I have it all
planned; an' *corp an duowol!* thim you won't know from
Adam will revinge me if I'm taken up through your un-
manliness."

"Twould be betther for us to lave the counthry," said
Anne. "We might slip away as it is."

"Ay," said the father, "an' be taken by the neck afore
we'd get two miles from the place! No, no, *girsha*[4]; it's the
safest way to brazen thim out. Did you hear me, Denis?"

Denis started, for he had been evidently pondering on
the mysterious words of Anne, to which his brother's anxiety to conceal them gave additional mystery. The coffin,
too, recurred to him; and he feared that the death shad-
owed out by it would in some manner or other occur in the
family. He was, in fact, one of those miserable villains with
but half a conscience—that is to say, as much as makes
them the slaves of the fear which results from crime, with-

---

[4] Gaelic *geirrseach*, "girl."

out being the slightest impediment to their committing it. It was no wonder he started at the deep, pervading tones of his brother's voice, for the question was put with ferocious energy.

On starting, he looked with vague terror on his brother, fearing, but not comprehending, his question.

"What is it, Anthony?" he inquired.

"Oh, for that matther," replied the other, "nothin' at all. Think of what I said to you, anyhow: swear through thick an' thin, if you have a regard for your own health or for your childher. Maybe I had betther repate it agin for you," he continued, eyeing him with mingled hatred and suspicion. "Denis, as a friend I bid you mind yourself this day, an' see you don't bring aither of us into throuble."

There lay before the Cassidys' houses a small flat of common, trodden into rings by the young horses they were in the habit of training. On this level space were assembled those who came, either to clear their own character from suspicion, or to witness the ceremony. The day was dark and lowering, and heavy clouds rolled slowly across the peaks of the surrounding mountains; scarcely a breath of air could be felt; and as the country people silently approached, such was the closeness of the day, their haste to arrive in time, and their general anxiety, either for themselves or their friends, that almost every man on reaching the spot might be seen taking up the skirts of his *cotha-more*, or "big coat" (the peasant's handkerchief), to wipe the sweat from his brow; and as he took off his dingy woollen hat, or *caubeen*, the perspiration rose in strong exhalations from his head.

"Michael, am I in time?" might be heard from such persons as they arrived. "Did this business begin yit?"

"Full time, Larry; myself's here an hour ago, but no appearance of anything as yit. Father Farrell an' Squire Nicholson are both in Cassidy's, waitin' till they're all gother, whin they'll begin to put thim through their facins. You hard about what they've got?"

"No; for I'm only on my way home from the berril of a

*cleaveen*⁵ of mine, that we put down this mornin' in Tully-ard. What is it?"

"Why, man alive, it's through the whole parish inready!" He then went on, lowering his voice to a whisper, and speaking in a tone bordering on dismay.

The other crossed himself, and betrayed symptoms of awe and astonishment, not unmingled with fear.

"Well," he replied, "I dunna whether I'd come here if I'd known that; for, innocent or guilty, I wouldn't wish to be near it. Och, may God pity thim that's to come acrass it, espishly if they dare to do it in a lie!"

"They needn't, I can tell yees both," observed a third person, "be a hair afeard of it, for the best rason livin', that there's no thruth at all in the report, nor the Cassidys never thought of sindin' for anything o' the kind. I have it from Larry Cassidy's own lips, an' he ought to know best."

The truth is that two reports were current among the crowd: one, that the oath was to be simply on the Bible; and the other, that a more awful means of expurgation was to be resorted to by the Cassidys. The people, consequently, not knowing which to credit, felt the most painful of all sensations—uncertainty.

During the period which intervened between their assembling and the commencement of the ceremony, a spectator, interested in contemplating the workings of human nature in circumstances of deep interest, would have had ample scope for observation. The occasion was to them a solemn one. There was little conversation among them; for when a man is wound up to a pitch of great interest, he is seldom disposed to relish discourse. Every brow was anxious, every cheek blanched, and every arm folded: they scarcely stirred, or when they did, only with slow, abstracted movements, rather mechanical than voluntary. If an individual made his appearance about Cassidy's door, a sluggish stir among them was visible, and a low murmur of a peculiar character might be heard; but on perceiving that it was only some ordinary person, all subsided again into a brood-

⁵ Gaelic *cliamhain,* "a relative by marriage."

ing stillness that was equally singular and impressive.

Under this peculiar feeling was the multitude when Meehan and his brother were seen approaching it from their own house. The elder, with folded arms, and hat pulled over his brows, stalked grimly forward, having that remarkable scowl upon his face which had contributed to establish for him so diabolical a character. Denis walked by his side, with his countenance strained to inflation—a miserable parody of that sullen effrontery which marked the unshrinking miscreant beside him. He had not heard of the ordeal, owing to the caution of Anthony, but notwithstanding his effort at indifference, a keen eye might have observed the latent anxiety of a man who was habitually villainous and naturally timid.

When this pair entered the crowd, a few secret glances, too rapid to be noticed by the people, passed between them and their accomplices. Denis, on seeing them present, took fresh courage, and looked with the heroism of a blusterer upon those who stood about him, especially whenever he found himself under the scrutinizing eye of his brother. Such was the horror and detestation in which they were held, that on advancing into the assembly the persons on each side turned away and openly avoided them; eyes full of fierce hatred were bent on them vindictively; and "curses, not loud, but deep," were muttered with an indignation which nothing but a divided state of feeling could repress within due limits. Every glance, however, was paid back by Anthony with interest from eyes and black shaggy brows tremendously ferocious; and his curses, as they rolled up half-smothered from his huge chest, were deeper and more diabolical by far than their own. He even jeered at them; but there was something truly appalling in the dark gleam of his scoff which threw them at an immeasurable distance behind him in the power of displaying on the countenance the worst of human passions.

At length Mr. Nicholson, Father Farrell, and his curate, attended by the Cassidys and their friends, issued from the house; two or three servants preceded them, bearing a table and chairs for the magistrate and priests, who, however, stood during the ceremony. When they entered one of the rings before alluded to, the table and chairs were placed in the center of it, and Father Farrell, as possessing most influence over the people, addressed them very impressively.

"There are," said he, in conclusion, "persons in this crowd whom we know to be guilty; but we will have an opportunity of now witnessing the lengths to which crime, long indulged in, can carry them. To such people I would say, beware! for they know not the situation in which they are placed."

During all this time there was not the slightest allusion made to the mysterious ordeal which had excited so much awe and apprehension among them—a circumstance which occasioned many a pale, downcast face to clear up, and reassume its usual cheerful expression. The crowd now were assembled around the ring, and every man on whom an imputation had been fastened came forward, when called upon, to the table at which the priests and magistrate stood uncovered. The form of the oath was framed by the two clergymen, who, as they knew the reservations and evasions commonest among such characters, had ingeniously contrived not to leave a single loophole through which the consciences of those who belonged to this worthy fraternity might escape.

To those acquainted with Irish courts of justice there was nothing particularly remarkable in the swearing. Indeed, one who stood among the crowd might hear from those who were stationed at the greatest distance from the table such questions as the following:—

"Is the *thing* in it, Art?"

"No; 'tis nothin' but the law Bible, the magistrate's own one."

To this the querist would reply, with a satisfied nod of the head, "Oh, is that all? I heard they war to have *it*." On which he would push himself through the crowd until he reached the table, where he took his oath as readily as another.

"Jem Hartigan," said the magistrate to one of those persons, "are you to swear?"

"Faix, myself doesn't know, your honor: only that I hard them say that the Cassidys mintioned our names along wid many other honest people; an' one wouldn't, in that case, lie under a false report, your honor, from any one, when we're as clear as them that never saw the light of anything of the kind."

The magistrate then put the book into his hand, and Jem, in return, fixed his eye, with much apparent innocence, on his face. "Now, Jem Hartigan," &c., &c., and the oath was accordingly administered. Jem put the book to his mouth, with his thumb raised to an acute angle on the back of it; nor was the smack by any means a silent one which he gave it (his thumb).

The magistrate set his ear with the air of a man who had experience in discriminating such sounds. "Hartigan," said he, "you'll condescend to kiss the book, sir, if you please; there's a hollowness in that smack, my good fellow, that can't escape me."

"Not kiss it, your honour? Why, by this staff in my hand, if ever a man kissed—"

"Silence, you impostor," said the curate; "I watched you closely, and am confident your lips never touched the book."

"My lips never touched the book! Why, you know I'd be sarry to conthradict either o' yees; but I was jist goin' to observe, wid simmission, that my own lips ought to know best; an' don't you hear them tellin' you that they did kiss it?" and he grinned with confidence in their faces.

"You double-dealing reprobate," said the parish priest, "I'll lay my whip across your jaws. I saw you, too, an' you did not kiss the book."

"By dad, an' maybe I did not, sure enough," he replied. "Any man may make a mistake unknownst to himself; but I'd give my oath, an' be the five crasses, I kissed it as sure as—however, a good thing's never the worse o' bein' twice done, gintlemen; so here goes, jist to satisfy yees," and placing the book near his mouth, and altering his position a little, he appeared to comply, though, on the contrary, he touched neither it nor his thumb. "It's the same thing to me," he continued, laying down the book with an air of confident assurance—"it's the same thing to me if I kissed it fifty times over, which I'm ready to do if that doesn't satisfy yees."

As every man acquitted himself of the charges brought against him, the curate immediately took down his name. Indeed, before the "clearing" commenced, he requested that such as were to swear would stand together within the ring, that after having sworn, he might hand each of them a certificate of the fact, which they appeared to think might be serviceable to them, should they happen to be subsequently indicted for the same crime in a court of justice. This, however, was only a plan to keep them together for what was soon to take place.

The detections of thumb-kissing were received by those who had already sworn, and by several in the outward crowd, with much mirth. It is but justice, however, to many of those assembled, to state that they appeared to entertain a serious opinion of the nature of the ceremony, and no small degree of abhorrence against those who seemed to trifle with the solemnity of an oath.

Standing on the edge of the circle, in the innermost row, were Meehan and his brother. The former eyed, with all the hardness of a stoic, the successive individuals as they passed up to the table. His accomplices had gone forward, and to the surprise of many who strongly suspected them, in the most indifferent manner "cleared" themselves, in the trying words of the oath, of all knowledge of and participation in the thefts that had taken place.

The grim visage of the elder Meehan was marked by a dark smile, scarcely perceptible; but his brother, whose nerves were not so firm, appeared somewhat confused and distracted by the imperturbable villainy of the perjurers.

At length they were called up. Anthony advanced slowly but collectedly to the table, only turning his eye slightly about to observe if his brother accompanied him. "Denis," said he, "which of us will swear first? You may." For as he doubted his brother's firmness, he was prudent enough, should he fail, to guard against having the sin of perjury to answer for, along with those demands which his country had to make for his other crimes. Denis took the book, and cast a slight glance at his brother, as if for encouragement. Their eyes met, and the darkened brow of Anthony hinted at the danger of flinching in this crisis. The tremor of his hand was not, perhaps, visible to any but Anthony, who, however, did not overlook this circumstance. He held the book, but raised not his eye to meet the looks of either the magistrate or the priests; the color also left his face as with shrinking lips he touched the Word of God in deliberate falsehood. Having then laid it down, Anthony received it with a firm grasp, and whilst his eye turned boldly in contemptuous mockery upon those who presented it, he impressed it with the kiss of a man whose depraved conscience seemed to goad him only to evil. After "clearing" himself he laid the Bible upon the table with the affected air of a person who felt hurt at the imputation of theft, and joined the rest with a frown upon his countenance and a smothered curse upon his lips.

Just at this moment a person from Cassidy's house laid upon the table a small box covered with black cloth; and our readers will be surprised to hear that if fire had come down visibly from heaven, greater awe and fear could not have been struck into their hearts or depicted upon their countenances. The casual conversation, and the commentaries upon the ceremony they had witnessed, instantly settled into a most profound silence, and every eye was turned towards it with an interest absolutely fearful.

"Let," said the curate, "none of those who have sworn depart from within the ring until they once more clear themselves upon this," and as he spoke he held it up. "Behold!" said he, "and tremble—behold THE DONAGH!!!"

A low murmur of awe and astonishment burst from the people in general, whilst those within the ring, who, with few exceptions, were the worst characters in the parish, appeared ready to sink into the earth. Their countenances, for the most part, paled into the condemned hue of guilt; many of them became almost unable to stand; and altogether, the state of trepidation and terror in which they stood was strikingly wild and extraordinary.

The curate proceeded: "Let him now who is guilty depart; or if he wishes, advance and challenge the awful penalty annexed to perjury upon THIS! Who has ever been known to swear falsely upon the Donagh without being visited by a tremendous punishment, either on the spot, or in twenty-four hours after his perjury? If we ourselves have not seen such instances with our own eyes, it is because none liveth who dare incur such a dreadful penalty; but we have heard of those who did, and of their awful punishment afterwards. Sudden death, madness, paralysis, self-destruction, or the murder of someone dear to them, are the marks by which perjury on the Donagh is known and visited. Advance now, ye who are innocent; but let the guilty withdraw, for we do not desire to witness the terrible vengeance which would attend a false oath upon the DONAGH. Pause, therefore, and be cautious! for if this grievous sin be committed, a heavy punishment will fall, not only upon you, but upon the parish in which it occurs!"

The words of the priest sounded to the guilty like the death sentence of a judge. Before he had concluded, all, except Meehan and his brother and a few who were really innocent, had slunk back out of the circle into the crowd. Denis, however, became pale as a corpse, and from time to time wiped the large drops from his haggard brow. Even Anthony's cheek, despite of his natural callousness, was less red; his eyes became disturbed; but by their influence he contrived to keep Denis in sufficient dread to prevent him from mingling, like the rest, among the people. The few who remained along with them advanced, and notwithstanding their innocence, when the Donagh was presented, and the figure of Christ and the Twelve Apostles displayed in the solemn tracery of its rude carving, they exhibited symptoms of fear. With trembling hands they touched the Donagh, and with trembling lips kissed the crucifix, in attestation of their guiltlessness of the charge of which they had been accused.

"Anthony and Denis Meehan, come forward," said the curate, "and declare your innocence of the crimes with which you are charged by the Cassidys and others."

Anthony advanced; but Denis stood rooted to the ground; on perceiving which the former sternly returned a step or two, and catching him by the arm with an admonitory grip that could not easily be misunderstood, compelled him to proceed with himself step by step to the table. Denis, however, could feel the strong man tremble, and perceive that although he strove to lash himself into the energy of despair, and the utter disbelief of all religious sanction, yet the trial before him called every slumbering prejudice and apprehension of his mind into active power. This was a death blow to his own resolution, or, rather, it confirmed him in his previous determination not to swear on the Donagh, except to acknowledge his guilt, which he could scarcely prevent himself from doing, such was the vacillating state of mind to which he felt himself reduced.

When Anthony reached the table, his huge form seemed to dilate by his effort at maintaining the firmness necessary to support him in this awful struggle between conscience and superstition on the one hand, and guilt, habit, and infidelity on the other. He fixed his deep, dilated eyes upon the Donagh in a manner that betokened somewhat of irresolution; his countenance fell; his color came and went, but eventually settled in a flushed red; his powerful hands and arms trembled so much that he folded them to prevent his agitation from being noticed; the grimness of his face ceased to be stern, while it retained the blank expression of guilt; his temples swelled out with the terrible play of their blood vessels; his chest, too, heaved up and down with the united pressure of guilt and the tempest which shook him within. At length he saw Denis's eye upon him, and his passions took a new direction: he knit his brows at him with more than usual fierceness, ground his teeth, and with a step and action of suppressed fury he placed his foot at the edge of the table, and bowing down under the eye of God and man, took the awful oath on the mysterious Donagh in a falsehood! When it was finished a feeble groan broke from his brother's lips. Anthony bent his eye on him with a deadly glare; but Denis saw it not. The shock was beyond his courage—he had become insensible.

Those who stood at the outskirts of the crowd, seeing Denis apparently lifeless, thought he must have sworn falsely on the Donagh, and exclaimed, "He's dead! Gracious God! Denis Meehan's struck dead by the Donagh! He swore in a lie, and is now a corpse!" Anthony paused, and calmly surveyed him as he lay with his head resting upon the hands of those who supported him. At this moment a silent breeze came over where they stood, and as the Donagh lay upon the table, the black ribbons with which it was ornamented fluttered with a melancholy appearance that deepened the sensations of the people into something peculiarly solemn and preternatural. Denis at length revived, and stared wildly and vacantly about him. When composed sufficiently to distinguish and recognize individual objects, he looked upon the gloomy visage and threatening eye of his brother, and shrunk back with a terror almost epileptical. "Oh!" he exclaimed, "save me!—save me from that man, and I'll discover all!"

Anthony calmly folded one arm into his bosom, and his lip quivered with the united influence of hatred and despair.

"Hould him!" shrieked a voice, which proceeded from his daughter—"hould my father, or he'll murdher him! Oh! oh! merciful Heaven!"

Ere the words were uttered she had made an attempt to clasp the arms of her parent, whose motions she understood; but only in time to receive from the pistol, which he had concealed in his breast, the bullet aimed at her uncle! She tottered; and the blood spouted out of her neck upon her father's brows, who hastily put up his hand and wiped it away, for it had actually blinded him.

The elder Meehan was a tall man, and as he stood elevated nearly a head above the crowd, his grim brows red with his daughter's blood—which, in attempting to wipe away, he had deeply streaked across his face—his eyes shooting fiery gleams of his late resentment, mingled with the wildness of unexpected horror—as he thus stood, it would be impossible to contemplate a more revolting picture of that state to which the principles that had regulated his life must ultimately lead, even in this world.

On perceiving what he had done, the deep working of his powerful frame was struck into sudden stillness, and he turned his eyes on his bleeding daughter with a fearful perception of her situation. Now was the harvest of his creed and crimes reaped in blood; and he felt that the stroke which had fallen upon him was one of those by which God will sometimes bare His arm and vindicate His justice. The reflection, however, shook him not; the reality of his misery was too intense and pervading, and grappled too strongly with his hardened and unbending spirit, to waste its power upon a nerve or a muscle. It was abstracted, and beyond the reach of bodily suffering. From the moment his daughter fell he moved not; his lips were half open with the conviction produced by the blasting truth of her death, effected prematurely by his own hand.

Those parts of his face which had not been stained with her blood assumed an ashy paleness, and rendered his countenance more terrific by the contrast. Tall, powerful, and motionless, he appeared, to the crowd, glaring at the girl, like a tiger anxious to join his offspring, yet stunned with the shock of the bullet which has touched a vital part. His iron-grey hair, as it fell in thick masses about his neck was moved slightly by the blast, and a lock which fell over his temple was blown back with a motion rendered more distinct by his statue-like attitude, immovable as death.

A silent and awful gathering of the people around this impressive scene intimated their knowledge of what they considered to be a judicial punishment annexed to perjury upon the Donagh. This relic lay on the table, and the eyes of those who stood within view of it, turned from Anthony's countenance to it, and again back to his bloodstained visage, with all the overwhelming influence of superstitious fear. Shudderings, tremblings, crossings, and ejaculations marked their conduct and feeling; for though the incident in itself was simply a fatal and uncommon one, yet they considered it supernatural and miraculous.

At length a loud and agonising cry burst from the lips of Meehan—"Oh, God!—God of heaven an' earth!—have I murdhered my daughter?" and he cast down the fatal weapon with a force which buried it some inches into the wet clay.

The crowd had closed upon Anne; but with the strength of a giant he flung them aside, caught the girl in his arms, and pressed her bleeding to his bosom. He gasped for breath. "Anne," said he,—"Anne, I am without hope, an' there's none to forgive me except you—none at all: from God to the poorest of His creatures, I am hated an' cursed by all except you! Don't curse me, Anne—don't curse me. Oh, isn't it enough, darlin', that my sowl is now stained with your blood, along with my other crimes? Oh, think, darlin', of my broken heart! In hell, on earth, an' in heaven, there's none to forgive your father but yourself!—NONE! NONE! Oh, what's comin' over me! I'm dizzy an' shiverin'! How cowld the day's got of a sudden! Hould up, *avourneen machree*[6]! *I* was a bad man; but to you, Anne, I was not as I was to every one! Darlin', oh, look at me with forgiveness in your eye; or, anyway, don't curse me! Oh! I'm far cowlder now! Tell me that you forgive me, *acushla oge machree!*[7]—*Manim asthee hu,*[8] darlin', say it. I DARN'T LOOK TO GOD! but oh! do you say the forgivin' word to your father before you die!"

"Father," said she, "I deserve this—it's only just. I had plotted with that divilish Martin to betray them all, except yourself, an' to get the reward; an' then we intended to go —an'—live at a distance—an' in wickedness—where we— might not be known. He's at our house—let him be—secured. Forgive me, father; you said so often that there was no thruth in religion—that I began to—think so. Oh! —God! have mercy upon me!" and with these words she expired.

Meehan's countenance, on hearing this, was overspread with a ghastly look of the most desolating agony; he staggered back, and the body of his daughter, which he strove to hold, would have fallen from his arms, had it not been caught by the bystanders. His eye sought out his brother, but not in resentment. "Oh! she died, but didn't say, 'I FORGIVE YOU!' Denis, bring me home—I'm sick—very sick— oh, but it's cowld—everything's reeling—cowld—cowld it is!" and as he uttered the last words he shuddered, fell

---

[6] Darling of my heart.

[7] Young pulse of my heart.

[8] My life is in you.

down in a fit of apoplexy, never to rise again; and the bodies of his daughter and himself were both waked and buried together.

The result is brief. The rest of the gang were secured; Denis became approver, by whose evidence they suffered that punishment decreed by law to the crimes of which they had been guilty. The two events which we have just related of course added to the supernatural fear and reverence previously entertained for this terrible relic. It is still used as an ordeal of expurgation in cases of stolen property; and we are not wrong in asserting that many of those misguided creatures, who too frequently hesitate not to swear falsely on the Word of God, would suffer death itself sooner than commit a perjury on the Donagh.

GEORGE MOORE
1852–1933

The eldest son of an Irish landowner who kept a racing stable, George Augustus Moore was educated at Oscott, a Roman Catholic boarding school in England. Aspiring to become a painter, he went to Paris to study after inheriting his father's estate. Later he turned to writing and began to introduce the techniques and subject matter of Flaubert, Maupassant, and Zola into English fiction. *Esther Waters* (1894) was his most successful realistic novel. He also wrote criticism of art and literature and a series of self-dramatizing autobiographies, the best being *Hail and Farewell* (1911–14), an amusing account of his share in the Irish literary revival. Late in life he turned to historical and legendary fiction, including *A Story-Teller's Holiday* (1918), which exploits the Irish middle ages for pathos, eroticism, and humor. The modern Irish short story begins with Moore's *The Untilled Field* (1903), written, he says, "in the hope of furnishing the young Irish of the future with models." Some of the stories were translated and first published in Gaelic. "Julia Cahill's Curse," though available elsewhere, has been included here as a prototype of all those Irish stories that try to deal artistically with social conflicts. Moore lets the story convey its own moral—that the curse is not Julia's but the puritanical priest's. "So On He Fares" is utterly different: a story of sibling rivalry (Moore had a younger brother who bore one of his own names, Augustus), it seems to probe a private wound in a way quite uncharacteristic of Moore.

Julia Cahill's Curse

"And what has become of Margaret?"

"Ah, didn't her mother send her to America as soon as the baby was born? Once a woman is wake here she has to go. Hadn't Julia to go in the end, and she the only one that ever said she didn't mind the priest?"

"Julia who?" said I.

"Julia Cahill."

The name struck my fancy, and I asked the driver to tell me her story.

"Wasn't it Father Madden who had her put out of the parish, but she put her curse on it, and it's on it to this day."

"Do you believe in curses?"

"Bedad I do, sir. It's a terrible thing to put a curse on a man, and the curse that Julia put on Father Madden's parish was a bad one, the divil a worse. The sun was up at the time, and she on the hilltop raising both her hands. And the curse she put on the parish was that every year a roof must fall in and a family go to America. That was the curse, your honor, and every word of it has come true. You'll see for yourself as soon as we cross the mearing."[1]

"And what became of Julia's baby?"

"I never heard she had one, sir."

He flicked his horse pensively with his whip, and it seemed to me that the disbelief I had expressed in the power of the curse disinclined him for further conversation.

"But," I said, "who is Julia Cahill, and how did she get the power to put a curse upon the village?"

"Didn't she go into the mountains every night to meet the fairies, and who else could 've given her the power to put a curse on the village?"

"But she couldn't walk so far in one evening."

"Them that's in league with the fairies can walk that far and as much farther in an evening, your honor. A shepherd saw her; and you'll see the ruins of the cabins for yourself

[1] boundary line.

as soon as we cross the mearing, and I'll show you the cabin of the blind woman that Julia lived with before she went away."

"And how long is it since she went?"

"About twenty year, and there hasn't been a girl the like of her in these parts since. I was only a gossoon[2] at the time, but I've heard tell she was as tall as I'm myself, and as straight as a poplar. She walked with a little swing in her walk, so that all the boys used to be looking after her, and she had fine black eyes, sir, and she was nearly always laughing. Father Madden had just come to the parish; and there was courting in these parts then, for aren't we the same as other people—we'd like to go out with a girl well enough if it was the custom of the country. Father Madden put down the ball alley because he said the boys stayed there instead of going into Mass, and he put down the crossroad dances because he said dancing was the cause of many a bastard, and he wanted none in his parish. Now there was no dancer like Julia; the boys used to gather about to see her dance, and who ever walked with her under the hedges in the summer could never think about another woman. The village was cracked about her. There was fighting, so I suppose the priest was right: he had to get rid of her. But I think he mightn't have been as hard on her as he was.

"One evening he went down to the house. Julia's people were well-to-do people, they kept a grocery store in the village; and when he came into the shop who should be there but the richest farmer in the country, Michael Moran by name, trying to get Julia for his wife. He didn't go straight to Julia, and that's what swept him. There are two counters in that shop, and Julia was at the one on the left hand as you go in. And many's the pound she had made for her parents at that counter. Michael Moran says to the father, 'Now, what fortune are you going to give with Julia?' And the father says there was many a man who would take her without any; and that's how they spoke, and Julia listening quietly all the while at the opposite counter. For Michael

[2] Gaelic *garsún,* "boy."

didn't know what a spirited girl she was, but went on arguing till he got the father to say fifty pounds, and thinking he
had got him so far he said, 'I'll never drop a flap to her unless you give the two heifers.' Julia never said a word, she
just sat listening. It was then that the priest came in. And
over he goes to Julia; 'And now,' says he, 'aren't you proud
to hear that you'll have such a fine fortune, and it's I that'll
be glad to see you married, for I can't have any more of
your goings-on in my parish. You're the encouragement of
the dancing and courting here; but I'm going to put an end
to it.' Julia didn't answer a word, and he went over to them
that were arguing about the sixty pounds. 'Now why not
make it fifty-five?' says he. So the father agreed to that
since the priest had said it. And all three of them thought
the marriage was settled. 'Now what will you be taking,
Father Tom?' says Cahill, 'and you, Michael?' Sorra one of
them thought of asking her if she was pleased with Michael;
but little did they know what was passing in her mind, and
when they came over to the counter to tell her what they
had settled, she said, 'Well, I've just been listening to you,
and 'tis well for you to be wasting your time talking about
me,' and she tossed her head, saying she would just pick the
boy out of the parish that pleased her best. And what angered the priest most of all was her way of saying it—that
the boy that would marry her would be marrying herself
and not the money that would be paid when the book was
signed or when the first baby was born. Now it was agin
girls marrying according to their fancy that Father Madden
had set himself. He had said in his sermon the Sunday before that young people shouldn't be allowed out by themselves at all, but that the parents should make up the mar-
riages for them. And he went fairly wild when Julia told
him the example she was going to set. He tried to keep his
temper, sir, but it was getting the better of him all the
while, and Julia said, 'My boy isn't in the parish now, but
maybe he is on his way here, and he may be here tomorrow
or the next day.' And when Julia's father heard her speak
like that he knew that no one would turn her from what
she was saying, and he said, 'Michael Moran, my good
man, you may go your way: you'll never get her.' Then he

went back to hear what Julia was saying to the priest, but it was the priest that was talking. 'Do you think,' says he, 'I am going to let you go on turning the head of every boy in the parish? Do you think,' says he, 'I'm going to see you gallivanting with one and then with the other? Do you think I'm going to see fighting and quarrelling for your like? Do you think I'm going to hear stories like I heard last week about poor Patsy Carey, who has gone out of his mind, they say, on account of your treatment? No,' says he, 'I'll have no more of that. I'll have you out of my parish, or I'll have you married.' Julia didn't answer the priest; she tossed her head, and went on making up parcels of tea and sugar and getting the steps and taking down candles, though she didn't want them, just to show the priest that she didn't mind what he was saying. And all the while her father trembling, not knowing what would happen, for the priest had a big stick, and there was no saying that he wouldn't strike her. Cahill tried to quiet the priest, he promising him that Julia shouldn't go out any more in the evenings, and bedad, sir, she was out the same evening with a young man and the priest saw them, and the next evening she was out with another and the priest saw them, nor was she minded at the end of the month to marry any of them. Then the priest went down to the shop to speak to her a second time, and he went down again a third time, though what he said the third time no one knows, no one being there at the time. And next Sunday he spoke out, saying that a disobedient daughter would have the worst devil in hell to attend on her. I've heard tell that he called her the evil spirit that set men mad. But most of the people that were there are dead or gone to America, and no one rightly knows what he did say, only that the words came pouring out of his mouth, and the people when they saw Julia crossed themselves, and even the boys who were most mad after Julia were afraid to speak to her. Cahill had to put her out."

"Do you mean to say that the father put his daughter out?"

"Sure, didn't the priest threaten to turn him into a rabbit if he didn't, and no one in the parish would speak to

Julia, they were so afraid of Father Madden, and if it hadn't been for the blind woman that I was speaking about a while ago, sir, it is to the poorhouse she'd have to go. The blind woman has a little cabin at the edge of the bog—I'll point it out to you, sir; we do be passing it by—and she was with the blind woman for nearly two years disowned by her own father. Her clothes wore out, but she was as beautiful without them as with them. The boys were told not to look back, but sure they couldn't help it.

"Ah, it was a long while before Father Madden could get shut of her. The blind woman said she wouldn't see Julia thrown out on the roadside, and she was as good as her word for well-nigh two years, till Julia went to America, so some do be saying, sir, whilst others do be saying she joined the fairies. But 'tis for sure, sir, that the day she left the parish, Pat Quinn heard a knocking at his window and somebody asking if he would lend his cart to go to the railway station. Pat was a heavy sleeper and he didn't get up, and it is thought that it was Julia who wanted Pat's cart to take her to the station; it's a good ten mile; but she got there all the same!"

"You said something about a curse?"

"Yes, sir. You'll see the hill presently. A man who was taking some sheep to the fair saw her there. The sun was just getting up and he saw her cursing the village, raising both her hands, sir, up to the sun, and since that curse was spoken, every year a roof has fallen in, sometimes two or three."

I could see he believed the story, and for the moment I, too, believed in an outcast Venus becoming the evil spirit of a village that would not accept her as divine.

"Look, sir, the woman coming down the road is Bridget Coyne. And that's her house," he said, and we passed a house built of loose stones without mortar, but a little better than the mud cabins I had seen in Father MacTurnan's parish.

"And now, sir, you will see the loneliest parish in Ireland."

And I noticed that though the land was good, there seemed to be few people on it, and what was more signifi-

cant than the untilled fields were the ruins, for they were
not the cold ruins of twenty, or thirty, or forty years ago
when the people were evicted and their tillage turned into
pasture—the ruins I saw were the ruins of cabins that had
been lately abandoned, and I said:

"It wasn't the landlord who evicted these people."

"Ah, it's the landlord who would be glad to have them
back, but there's no getting them back. Everyone here will
have to go, and 'tis said that the priest will say Mass in an
empty chapel, sorra a one will be there but Bridget, and
she'll be the last he'll give communion to. It's said, your
honor, that Julia has been seen in America, and I'm going
there this autumn. You may be sure I'll keep a lookout for
her."

"But all this is twenty years ago. You won't know her.
A woman changes a good deal in twenty years."

"There will be no change in her, your honor. Sure hasn't
she been with the fairies?"

So On He Fares

His mother had forbidden him to stray about the roads
and, standing at the garden gate, little Ulick Burke often
thought he would like to run down to the canal and watch
the boats passing. His father used to take him for walks
along the towing path, but his father had gone away to
the wars two years ago, and standing by the garden gate
he remembered how his father used to stop to talk to the
lock-keepers. Their talk turned often upon the canal and
its business, and Ulick remembered that the canal ended in
the Shannon, and that the barges met ships coming up from
the sea.

He was a pretty child with bright blue eyes, soft curls,
and a shy winning manner, and he stood at the garden
gate thinking how the boats rose up in the locks, how the
gate opened and let the boats free, and he wondered if his
father had gone away to the war in one of the barges. He
felt sure if he were going away to the war he would go in
a barge. And he wondered if the barge went as far as the

war or only as far as the Shannon. He would like to ask his mother, but she would say he was troubling her with foolish questions, or she would begin to think again that he wanted to run away from home. He wondered if he were to hide himself in one of the barges whether it would take him to a battlefield where he would meet his father walking about with a gun upon his shoulder.

And leaning against the gatepost, he swung one foot across the other, though he had been told by his mother that he was like one of the village children when he did it. But his mother was always telling him not to do something, and he could not remember everything he must not do. He had been told not to go to the canal lest he should fall in, nor into the field lest he should tear his trousers. He had been told he must not run about in the garden lest he should tread on the flowers, and his mother was always telling him he was not to talk to the school children as they came back from school, though he did not want to talk to them. There was a time when he would have liked to talk to them: now he ran to the other side of the garden when they were coming home from school; but there was no place in the garden where he could hide himself from them, unless he got into the dry ditch. The school children were very naughty children; they climbed up the bank, and, holding on to the paling, they mocked at him; and their mockery was to ask him the way to "Hill Cottage"; for his mother had had the name painted on the gate, and no one else in the parish had given their cottage a name.

However, he liked the dry ditch, and under the branches, where the wren had built her nest, Ulick was out of his mother's way, and out of the way of the boys; and lying among the dead leaves he could think of the barges floating away, and of his tall father who wore a red coat and let him pull his moustache. He was content to lie in the ditch for hours, thinking he was a bargeman and that he would like to use a sail. His father had told him that the boats had sails on the Shannon—if so it would be easy to sail to the war; and, breaking off in the middle of some wonderful war adventure, some tale about his father and his father's soldiers, he would grow interested in the life of the ditch, in the coming and going of the wren, in the chirrup of a bird in the tall larches that grew beyond the paling.

Beyond the paling there was a wood full of moss-grown stones and trees overgrown with ivy, and Ulick thought that if he only dared to get over the paling and face the darkness of the hollow on the other side of the paling, he could run across the meadow and call from the bank to a steersman. The steersman might take him away! But he was afraid his mother might follow him on the next barge, and he dreamed a story of barges drawn by the swiftest horses in Ireland.

But dreams are but a makeshift life. He was very unhappy, and though he knew it was wrong he could not help laying plans for escape. Sometimes he thought that the best plan would be to set fire to the house; for while his mother was carrying pails of water from the backyard, he would run away; but he did not dare to think out his plan of setting fire to the house, lest one of the spirits which dwelt in the hollow beyond the paling should come and drag him down a hole.

One day he forgot to hide himself in the ditch, and the big boy climbed up the bank, and asked him to give him some gooseberries, and though Ulick would have feared to gather gooseberries for himself, he did not like to refuse the boy, and he gave him some, hoping that the big boy would not laugh at him again. And they became friends, and very soon he was friends with them all, and they had many talks clustered in the corner, the children holding on to the palings, and Ulick hiding behind the hollyhocks ready to warn them.

"It's all right, she's gone to the village," Ulick said. One day the big boy asked him to come with them; they were going to spear eels in the brook, and he was emboldened to get over the fence, and to follow across the meadow, through the hazels, and very soon it seemed to him that they had wandered to the world's end. At last they came to the brook and the big boy turned up his trousers, and Ulick saw him lifting the stones with his left hand and plunging a fork into the water with his right. When he brought up a struggling eel at the end of the fork, Ulick clapped his hands and laughed, and he had never been so happy in his life before.

After a time there were no more stones to raise, and sitting on the bank they began to tell stories. His companions asked him when his father was coming back from the wars, and he told them how his father used to take him for walks up the canal, and how they used to meet a man who had a tame rat in his pocket. Suddenly the boys and girls started up, crying, "Here's the farmer," and they ran wildly across the fields. However, they got to the highroad long before the farmer could catch them, and his escape enchanted Ulick. Then the children went their different ways, the big boy staying with Ulick, who thought he must offer him some gooseberries. So they crossed the fence together and crouched under the bushes, and ate the gooseberries till they wearied of them. Afterwards they went to look at the bees, and while looking at the insects crawling in and out of their little door, Ulick caught sight of his mother, and she coming towards them. Ulick cried out, but the big boy was caught before he could reach the fence, and Ulick saw that, big as the boy was, he could not save himself from a slapping. He kicked out, and then blubbered, and at last got away. In a moment it would be Ulick's turn, and he feared she would beat him more than she had beaten the boy, for she hated him, whereas she was only vexed with the boy; she would give him bread and water; he had often had a beating and bread and water for lesser wickedness than the bringing of one of the village boys into the garden to eat gooseberries.

He put up his right hand and saved his right cheek, and then she tried to slap him on the left, but he put up his left hand, and this went on until she grew so angry that Ulick thought he had better allow her to slap him, for if she did not slap him at once she might kill him.

"Down with your hands, sir, down with your hands, sir," she cried, but before he had time to let her slap him, she said, "I will give you enough of bees," and she caught one that had just rested on a flower and put it down his neck. The bee stung him in the neck where the flesh is softest, and he ran away screaming, unable to rid himself of the bee. He broke through the hedges of sweet pea, and he dashed through the poppies, trampling through the flower beds, until he reached the dry ditch.

There is something frightful in feeling a stinging insect in one's back, and Ulick lay in the dry ditch, rolling among the leaves in anguish. He thought he was stung all over; he heard his mother laughing and she called him a coward through an opening in the bushes, but he knew she could not follow him down the ditch. His neck had already begun to swell, but he forgot the pain of the sting in hatred. He felt he must hate his mother, however wicked it might be to do so. His mother had often slapped him; he had heard of boys being slapped, but no one had ever put a bee down a boy's back before; he felt he must always hate her, and creeping up through the brambles to where he could get a view of the garden, he waited until he saw her walk up the path into the house; and then, stealing back to the bottom of the ditch, he resolved to get over the paling. A few minutes after he heard her calling him, and then he climbed the paling, and he crossed the dreaded hollow, stumbling over the old stones.

As he crossed the meadow he caught sight of a boat coming through the lock, but the lock-keeper knew him by sight, and would tell the bargeman where he came from, and he would be sent home to his mother. He ran on, trying to get ahead of the boat, creeping through hedges, frightened lest he should not be able to find the canal! Now he stopped, sure that he had lost it; his brain seemed to be giving way, and he ran like a mad child up the bank. Oh, what joy! The canal flowed underneath the bank. The horse had just passed, the barge was coming, and Ulick ran down the bank calling to the bargeman. He plunged into the water, getting through the bulrushes. Half of the barge had passed him, and he held out his hands. The ground gave way and he went under the water; green light took the place of day, and when he struggled to the surface he saw the rudder moving. He went under again, and remembered no more until he opened his eyes and saw the bargeman leaning over him.

"Now, what ails you to be throwing yourself into the

water in that way?"

Ulick closed his eyes; he had no strength for answering him, and a little while after he heard someone come on board the barge, and he guessed it must be the man who drove the horse. He lay with his eyes closed, hearing the men talking of what they should do with him. He heard a third voice, and guessed it must be a man come up from the cabin. This man said it would be better to take him back to the last lock, and they began to argue about who should carry him. Ulick was terribly frightened, and he was just going to beg of them not to bring him back when he heard one of them say, "It will be easier to leave him at the next lock." Soon after, he felt the boat start again, and when Ulick opened his eyes, he saw hedges gliding past, and he hoped the next lock was a long way off.

"Now," said the steersman, "since you are awaking out of your faint, you'll be telling us where you come from, because we want to send you home again."

"Oh," he said, "from a long way off, the Shannon."

"The Shannon!" said the bargeman. "Why, that is more than seventy miles away. How did you come up here?"

It was a dreadful moment. Ulick knew he must give some good answer or he would find himself in his mother's keeping very soon. But what answer was he to give? It was half accident, half cunning that made him speak of the Shannon. The steersman said again, "The Shannon is seventy miles away, how did you get up here?" and by this time Ulick was aware that he must make the bargemen believe he had hidden himself on one of the boats coming up from the Shannon, and that he had given the bargeman some money, and then he burst into tears and told them he had been very unhappy at home; and when they asked him why he had been unhappy, he did not answer, but he promised he would not be a naughty boy any more if they would take him back to the Shannon. He would be a good boy and not run away again. His pretty face and speech persuaded the bargemen to bring him back to the Shannon; it was decided to say nothing about him to the lock-keeper, and he was carried down to the cabin. He had often asked his father if he might see the bargeman's cabin; and his father had promised him that the next time they went to the canal he should go on board a barge and see the cabin; but his father had gone away to the wars. Now he was in the bargeman's cabin, and he wondered if they were going to give him supper and if he would be a bargeman himself when he grew up to be a man.

Some miles farther the boat bumped the edge of the bridge, and on the other side of the bridge there was the lock, and he heard the lock gate shut behind the boat and the water pour into the lock; the lock seemed a long time filling, and he was frightened lest the lockman might come down to the cabin, for there was no place where he could hide.

After passing through the lock one of the men came down to see him, and he was taken on deck, and in the calm of the evening Ulick came to look upon the bargemen as his good angels. They gave him some of their supper, and when they arrived at the next lock they made their beds on the deck, the night being so warm. It seemed to Ulick that he had never seen the night before, and he watched the sunset fading streak by streak, and imagined he was the captain of a ship sailing in the Shannon. The stars were so bright that he could not sleep, and it amused him to make up a long story about the bargemen snoring by his side. The story ended with the sunset and then the night was blue all over, and raising himself out of his blanket he watched the moonlight rippling down the canal. Then the night grew grey. He began to feel very cold, and wrapped himself in his blanket tightly, and the world got so white that Ulick grew afraid, and he was not certain whether it would not be better to escape from the boat and run away while everybody slept.

He lay awake maturing his little plan, seeing the greyness pass away and the sky fill up with pink and fleecy clouds.

One of the men roused, and, without saying a word, went to fetch a horse from the stables, and another went to boil the kettle in the cabin, and Ulick asked if he might help him; and while he blew the fire he heard the water running into the lock, and thought what a fool they were

making of the lock-keeper, and when the boat was well on
its way towards the next lock the steersman called him to
come up, and they breakfasted together. Ulick would have
wished this life to go on for ever, but the following day
the steersman said:

"There is only one lock more between this and our last
stopping place. Keep a lookout for your mother's cottage."

He promised he would, and he beguiled them all the
evening with pretended discoveries. That cabin was his
mother's cabin. No, it was farther on, he remembered those
willow trees. Ulick's object was to get as far away from his
home as possible; to get as near to the Shannon as he could.

"There's not a mile between us and the Shannon now,"
said the steersman. "I believe you've been telling us a lot of
lies, my young man."

Ulick said his mother lived just outside the town, they
would see the house when they passed through the last
lock, and he planned to escape that night, and about an
hour before the dawn he got up, and, glancing at the sleeping men, he stepped ashore and ran until he felt very tired.
And when he could go no farther, he lay down in the hay
in an outhouse.

A woman found him in the hay some hours after, and
he told her his story, and as the woman seemed very kind
he laid some stress on his mother's cruelty. He mentioned
that his mother had put a bee down his neck, and bending
down his head he showed her where the bee had stung him.
She stroked his pretty curls and looked into his blue eyes,
and she said that anyone who could put a bee down a boy's
neck must be a she-devil.

She was a lone widow longing for someone to look after,
and in a very short time Ulick was as much loved by his
chance mother as he had been hated by his real mother.

Three years afterwards she died, and Ulick had to leave
the cottage.

He was now a little over thirteen, and knew the ships
and their sailors, and he went away in one of the ships that
came up the river, and sailed many times round the coast
of Ireland, and up all the harbors of Ireland. He led a wild,
rough life, and his flight from home was remembered like

a tale heard in infancy, until one day, as he was steering his ship up the Shannon, a desire to see what they were doing at home came over him. The ship dropped anchor, and he went to the canal to watch the boats going home. And it was not long before he was asking one of the bargemen if he would take him on board. He knew what the rules were, and he knew they could be broken, and how, and he said if they would take him he would be careful the lockmen did not see him, and the journey began.

The month was July, so the days were as endless and the country was as green and as full of grass as they were when he had come down the canal, and the horse strained along the path, sticking his toes into it just as he had done ten years ago; and when they came to a dangerous place Ulick saw the man who was driving the horse take hold of his tail, just as he had seen him do ten years ago.

"I think those are the rushes, only there are no trees, and the bank doesn't seem so high." And then he said as the bargeman was going to stop his horse, "No, I am wrong. It isn't there."

They went on a few miles farther, and the same thing happened again. At last he said, "Now I am sure it is there."

And the bargeman called to the man who was driving the horse and stopped him, and Ulick jumped from the boat to the bank.

"That was a big leap you took," said a small boy who was standing on the bank. "It is well you didn't fall in."

"Why did you say that?" said Ulick, "is your mother telling you not to go down to the canal?"

"Look at the frog! He's going to jump into the water," said the little boy.

He was the same age as Ulick was when Ulick ran away, and he was dressed in the same little trousers and little boots and socks, and he had a little grey cap. Ulick's hair had grown darker now, but it had been as fair and as curly as this little boy's, and he asked him if his mother forbade him to go down to the canal.

"Are you a bargeman? Do you steer the barge or do you drive the horse?"

"I'll tell you about the barge if you'll tell me about your mother. Does she tell you not to come down to the canal?"

The boy turned away his head and nodded it.

"Does she beat you if she catches you here?"

"Oh, no, mother never beats me."

"Is she kind to you?"

"Yes, she's very kind, she lives up there, and there's a garden to our cottage, and the name 'Hill Cottage' is painted up on the gate post."

"Now," said Ulick, "tell me your name."

"My name is Ulick."

"Ulick! And what's your other name?"

"Ulick Burke."

"Ulick Burke!" said the big Ulick. "Well, my name is the same. And I used to live at Hill Cottage, too."

The boy did not answer.

"Whom do you live with?"

"I live with mother."

"And what's her name?"

"Well, Burke is her name," said the boy.

"But her front name?"

"Catherine."

"And where's your father?"

"Oh, father's a soldier; he's away."

"But my father was a soldier too, and I used to live in that cottage."

"And where have you been ever since?"

"Oh," he said, "I've been a sailor. I think I will go in the cottage with you."

"Yes," said little Ulick, "come up and see mother, and you'll tell me where you've been sailing," and he put his hand into the seafarer's.

And now the seafarer began to lose his reckoning; the compass no longer pointed north. He had been away for ten years, and coming back he had found his own self, the self that had jumped into the water at this place ten years ago. Why had not the little boy done as he had done, and been pulled into the barge and gone away? If this had happened Ulick would have believed he was dreaming or that he was mad. But the little boy was leading him, yes, he remembered the way, there was the cottage, and its paling, and its hollyhocks. And there was his mother coming out of the house, and very little changed.

"Ulick, where have you been? Oh, you naughty boy," and she caught the little boy up and kissed him. And so engrossed was her attention in her little son that she had not noticed the man he had brought home with him.

"Now, who is this?" she said.

"Oh, Mother, he jumped from the boat to the bank, and he will tell you, Mother, that I was not near the bank."

"Yes, Mother, he was ten yards from the bank; and now tell me, do you think you ever saw me before?—"

She looked at him.

"Oh, it's you! Why we thought you were drowned."

"I was picked up by a bargeman."

"Well, come into the house and tell us what you've been doing."

"I've been seafaring," he said, taking a chair. "But what about this Ulick?"

"He's your brother, that's all."

His mother asked him of what he was thinking, and Ulick told her how greatly astonished he had been to find a little boy exactly like himself, waiting at the same place.

"And father?"

"Your father is away."

"So," he said, "this little boy is my brother. I should like to see father. When is he coming back?"

"Oh," she said, "he won't be back for another three years. He enlisted again."

"Mother," said Ulick, "you don't seem very glad to see me."

"I shall never forget the evening we spent when you threw yourself into the canal. You were a wicked child."

"And why did you think I was drowned?"

"Well, your cap was picked up in the bulrushes."

He thought that whatever wickedness he had been guilty of might have been forgiven, and he began to feel that if he had known how his mother would receive him he would not have come home.

"Well, the dinner is nearly ready. You'll stay and have

some with us, and we can make you up a bed in the kitch-
en."

He could see that his mother wished to welcome him,
but her heart was set against him now as it had always
been. Her dislike had survived ten years of absence. He
had gone away and had met with a mother who loved him,
and had done ten years' hard seafaring. He had forgotten
his real mother—forgotten everything except the bee and
the hatred that gathered in her eyes when she put it down
his back; and that same ugly look he could now see gathering in her eyes, and it grew deeper every hour he remained
in the cottage. His little brother asked him to tell him tales
about the sailing ships, and he wanted to go down to the
canal with Ulick, but their mother said he was to bide here
with her. The day had begun to decline, his brother was
crying, and he had to tell him a sea story to stop his crying.
"But Mother hates to hear my voice," he said to himself,
and he went out in the garden when the story was done.
It would be better to go away, and he took one turn round
the garden and got over the paling at the end of the dry
ditch, at the place he had got over it before, and he walked
through the old wood, where the trees were overgrown with
ivy, and the stones with moss. In this second experience
there was neither terror nor mystery—only bitterness. It
seemed to him a pity that he had ever been taken out of
the canal, and he thought how easy it would be to throw
himself in again, but only children drown themselves because their mothers do not love them; life had taken a hold
upon him, and he stood watching the canal, though not
waiting for a boat. But when a boat appeared, he called to
the man who was driving the horse to stop, for it was the
same boat that had brought him from the Shannon.

"Well, was it all right?" the steersman said. "Did you find
the house? How were they at home?"

"They're all right at home," he said; "but father is still
away. I am going back. Can you take me?"

The evening sky opened calm and benedictive, and the
green country flowed on, the boat passed by ruins, castles,
and churches, and every day was alike until they reached
the Shannon.

E. Œ. SOMERVILLE AND MARTIN ROSS
1858–1949 and 1862–1915

Edith Anna Œnone Somerville (1858–1949) and Violet Florence Martin (1862–1915) were first cousins and members of the Anglo-Irish country gentry. They loved fox-hunting, dogs, and horses. A riding accident in 1898 probably shortened Miss Martin's life, but Miss Somerville became a Master of Foxhounds in 1903— apparently the first woman ever to do so. The two cousins did not meet until 1886 but very soon became inseparable. They lived together at the Somerville home in Drishane, County Cork, though Violet took her pen name from her family's home, Ross House, County Galway. Their first book, *An Irish Cousin*, appeared in 1889, and their most ambitious work, a realistic novel entitled *The Real Charlotte*, in 1895. *Some Experiences of an Irish R. M.* (1899), a series of short stories, relates the Irish adventures of Major Sinclair Yeates, an Englishman "of Irish extraction" who holds the post of Resident Magistrate in the West of Ireland. This book proved immensely popular and was followed by two sequels. After Miss Martin's death, Miss Somerville continued to write under their joint pseudonym. "Oweneen the Sprat," from *Further Experiences of an Irish R. M.* (1908), exploits the favorite Somerville and Ross theme of English forthrightness at grips with the subtlety and deviousness of the Irish. Major Yeates, Philippa, Slipper, and Flurry Knox were old-established figures in the series by the time this story was written, so that their characterization is taken pretty much for granted, but this need not put off readers who have not met them before. More confusing is the casual, "impressionistic" way in which the story develops. Somerville and Ross maintain the attitudes and subject matter of nineteenth-century fiction, but their narrative technique is sometimes very "advanced." Their mastery of the English spoken by Irish people who are bilingual or only a generation removed from Gaelic has been equalled but never surpassed.

Oweneen the Sprat

I was laboring in the slough of Christmas letters and bills, when my wife came in and asked me if I would take her to the Workhouse.

"My dear," I replied, ponderously, but, I think, excusably, "you have, as usual, anticipated my intention, but I think we can hold out until after Christmas."

Philippa declined to pay the jest the respect to which its age entitled it, and replied inconsequently that I knew perfectly well that she could not drive the outside car with the children and the Christmas tree. I assented that they would make an awkward team, and offered, as a substitute for my services, those of Denis, the stopgap.

Those who live in Ireland best know the staying powers of stopgaps. Denis, uncle of Michael Leary the whip, had been imported into the kennels during my ministry, to bridge a hiatus in the long dynasty of the kennel-boys, and had remained for eighteen months, a notable instance of the survival of what might primarily have been considered the unfittest. That Denis should so long have endured his nephew's rule was due not so much to the tie of blood, as to the privileged irresponsibility of a stopgap. Nothing was expected of him, and he pursued an unmolested course, until the return of Flurry Knox from South Africa changed the general conditions. He then remained submerged until he drifted into the gap formed in my own establishment by Mr. Peter Cadogan's elopement.

Philippa's Workhouse tea took place on Christmas Eve. We were still hurrying through an early luncheon when the nodding crest of the Christmas tree passed the dining-room windows. My youngest son immediately upset his pudding into his lap; and Philippa hustled forth to put on her hat, an operation which, like the making of an omelette, can apparently only be successfully performed at the last moment. With feelings of mingled apprehension and relief I saw the party drive from the door, the Christmas tree seated on one side of the car, Philippa on the other, clutching her offspring, Denis on the box, embosomed, like a wood pigeon, in the boughs of the spruce fir. I congratulated myself that the Quaker, now white with the snows of many winters, was in the shafts. Had I not been too deeply engaged in so arranging the rug that it should not trail in the mud all the way to Skebawn, I might have noticed that the lamps had been forgotten.

It was, as I have said, Christmas Eve, and as the afternoon wore on I began to reflect upon what the road from Skebawn would be in another hour, full of drunken people, and, what was worse, of carts steered by drunken people. I had assured Philippa (with what I believe she describes as masculine *esprit de corps*) of Denis's adequacy as a driver, but that did not alter the fact that in the last rays of the setting sun, I got out my bicycle and set forth for the Workhouse. When I reached the town it was dark, but the Christmas shoppers showed no tendency to curtail their operations on that account, and the streets were filled with an intricate and variously moving tide of people and carts. The paraffin lamps in the shops did their best, behind bunches of holly, oranges, and monstrous Christmas candles, and partially illumined the press of dark-cloaked women, and more or less drunken men, who swayed and shoved and held vast conversations on the narrow pavements. The red glare of the chemist's globe transformed the leading female beggar of the town into a being from the Brocken; her usual Christmas family, contributed for the festival by the neighbors, as to a Christmas number, were grouped in fortunate ghastliness in the green light. She extracted from me her recognized tribute, and pursued by her assurance that she would forgive me now till Easter (*i.e.*, that further alms would not be exacted for at least a fortnight), I made my way onward into the outer darkness, beyond the uttermost link in the chain of public houses.

The road that led to the Workhouse led also to the railway station; a quarter of a mile away the green light of a signal post stood high in the darkness, like an emerald. As I neared the Workhouse I recognized the deliberate footfall of the Quaker, and presently his long pale face entered the circle illuminated by my bicycle lamp. My family were not at all moved by my solicitude for their safety, but, being in want of an audience, were pleased to suggest that I should drive home with them. The road was disgustingly muddy; I tied my bicycle to the back of the car with the rope that is found in the wells of all outside cars. It was not till I had put out the bicycle lamp that I noticed that the car lamps had been forgotten, but Denis, true to the convention of his tribe, asseverated that he could see better without lights. I took the place vacated by the Christmas tree, the Quaker pounded on at his usual stone-breaking trot, and my off-spring, in strenuous and entangled duet, declaimed to me the events of the afternoon.

It was without voice or warning that a row of men was materialized out of the darkness, under the Quaker's nose; they fell away to right and left, but one, as if stupefied, held on his way in the middle of the road. It is not easy to divert the Quaker from his course; we swung to the right, but the wing of the car, on my side, struck the man full in the chest. He fell as instantly and solidly as if he were a stone pillar, and, like a stone, he lay in the mud. Loud and inebriate howls rose from the others, and, as if in answer, came a long and distant shriek from an incoming train. Upon this, without bestowing an instant's further heed to their fallen comrade, the party took to their heels and ran to the station. It was all done in a dozen seconds; by the time the Quaker was pulled up we were alone with our victim, and Denis was hoarsely suggesting to me that it would be better to drive away at once. I have often since then regretted that I did not take his advice.

The victim was a very small man; Denis and I dragged him to the side of the road, and propped him up against the wall. He was of an alarming limpness, but there was a something reassuring in the reek of whisky that arose as I leaned over him, trying to diagnose his injuries by the aid of a succession of lighted matches. His head lay crookedly on his chest; he breathed heavily but peacefully, and his limbs seemed uninjured. Denis at my elbow, did not cease to assure me, tremulously, that there was nothing ailed the man, that he was a stranger, and that it would be as good for us to go home. Philippa, on the car, strove as best she might with the unappeasable curiosity of her sons and with the pigheaded anxiety of the Quaker to get home to his dinner. At this juncture a voice, fifty yards away in the darkness, uplifted itself in song: "Heaven's refle-hex! Kill-ar-ney!" it bawled hideously.

It fell as balm upon my ear, in its assurance of the proximity of Slipper.

"Sure I know the man well," he said, shielding the flame of a match in his hand with practised skill. "Wake up, me *bouchaleen!*" He shook him unmercifully. "Open your eyes, darlin'!"

The invalid here showed signs of animation by uttering an incoherent but, as it seemed, a threatening roar. It lifted Denis as a feather is lifted by a wind, and wafted him to the Quaker's head, where he remained in strict attention to his duties. It also lifted Philippa.

"Is he very bad, do you think?" she murmured at my elbow. "Shall I drive for the doctor?"

"Arrah, what docthor?" said Slipper magnificently. "Give me a half-crown, Major, and I'll get him what meddyceen will answer him as good as any docthor! Lave him to me!" He shook him again. "I'll regulate him!"

The victim here sat up, and shouted something about going home. He was undoubtedly very drunk. It seemed to me that Slipper's ministrations would be more suitable to the situation than mine, certainly than Philippa's. I administered the solatium; then I placed Denis on the box of the car with the bicycle lamp in his hand, and drove my family home.

After church next day we met Flurry Knox. He ap-

proached us with the green glint in his eye that told that
game was on foot, whatever that game might be.

"Who bailed you out, Mrs. Yeates?" he said solicitously.
"I heard you and the Major and Denis Leary were all in
the lock-up for furious driving and killing a man! I'm told
he was anointed last night."

Philippa directed what she believed to be a searching
glance at Flurry's face of friendly concern.

"I don't believe a word of it!" she said dauntlessly, while
a very becoming warmth in her complexion betrayed an in-
ward qualm. "Who told you?"

"The servants heard it at first Mass this morning; and
Slipper had me late for church telling me about it. The fel-
low says if he lives he's going to take an action against the
Major."

I listened with, I hope, outward serenity. In dealings with
Flurry Knox the possibility that he might be speaking the
truth could never be safely lost sight of. It was also well to
remember that he generally knew what the truth was.

I said loftily, that there had been nothing the matter with
the man but Christmas Eve, and inquired if Flurry knew his
name and address.

"Of course I do," said Flurry, "he's one of those mountainy men that live up in the hill behind Aussolas. Oweneen
the Sprat is the name he goes by, and he's the crossest little
thief in the Barony. Never mind, Mrs. Yeats, I'll see you
get fair play in the dock!"

"How silly you are!" said Philippa; but I could see that
she was shaken.

Whatever Flurry's servants may have heard at first Mass
was apparently equalled, if not excelled, by what Denis
heard at second. He asked me next morning, with a gallant
attempt at indifference, if I had had any word of "the man-
een."

" 'Twas what the people were saying on the roads last
night that he could have the law on us, and there was more
was saying that he'd never do a day's good. Sure they say
the backbone is cracked where the wheel of the car went
over him! But didn't yourself and the misthress swear black

and blue that the wheel never went next or nigh him? And
didn't Michael say that there wasn't a Christmas this ten
years that that one hadn't a head on him the size of a bulla-
wawn with the len'th o' dhrink?"

In spite of the contributory negligence that might be assumed in the case of anyone with this singular infirmity, I
was not without a secret uneasiness. Two days afterwards
I received a letter, written on copybook paper in a clerkly
hand. It had the Aussolas postmark, in addition to the im-
print of various thumbs, and set forth the injuries inflicted
by me and my driver on Owen Twohig on Christmas Eve,
and finally, it demanded a compensation of twenty pounds
for the same. Failing this satisfaction the law was threatened, but a hope was finally expressed that the honorable
gentleman would not see a poor man wronged; it was, in
fact, the familiar mixture of bluff and whine, and, as I said
to Philippa, the Man-een (under which title he had passed
into the domestic vocabulary) had of course got hold of a
letter writer to do the trick for him.

In the next day or so I met Flurry twice, and found him
so rationally interested, and even concerned, about fresh
versions of the accident that had cropped up, that I was
moved to tell him of the incident of the letter. He looked
serious, and said he would go up himself to see what was
wrong with Oweneen. He advised me to keep out of it for
the present, as they might open their mouths too big.

The moon was high as I returned from this interview;
when I wheeled my bicycle into the yard I found that the
coach house in which I was wont to stable it was locked;
so also was the harness room. Attempting to enter the
house by the kitchen door I found it also was locked; a
gabble of conversation prevailed within, and with the
mounting indignation of one who hears but cannot make
himself heard, I banged ferociously on the door. Silence
fell, and Mrs. Cadogan's voice implored heaven's protection.

"Open the door!" I roared.

A windlike rush of petticoats followed, through which
came sibilantly the words, "Glory be to goodness! 'Tis the
masther!"

The door opened, I found myself facing the entire strength of my establishment, including Denis, and augmented by Slipper.

"They told me you were asking afther me, Major," began Slipper, descending respectfully from the kitchen table, on which he had been seated.

I noticed that Mrs. Cadogan was ostentatiously holding her heart, and that Denis was shaking like the conventional aspen.

"What's all this about?" said I, looking round upon them. "Why is the whole place locked up?"

"It was a little unaisy they were," said Slipper, snatching the explanation from Mrs. Cadogan with the determination of the skilled leader of conversation; "I was telling them I seen two men below in the plantation, like they'd be watching out for someone, and poor Mr. Leary here got a reeling in his head after I telling it—"

"Indeed the crayture was as white, now, as white as a masheroon!" broke in Mrs. Cadogan, "and we dhrew him in here to the fire till your Honor came home."

"Nonsense!" I said angrily, "a couple of boys poaching rabbits! Upon my word, Slipper, you have very little to do coming here and frightening people for nothing."

"What did I say," demanded Slipper, dramatically facing his audience, "only that I seen two men in the plantation. How would I know what business they had in it?"

"Ye said ye heard them whishling to each other like curlews through the wood," faltered Denis, "and sure that's the whishle them Twohigs has always—"

"Maybe it's whistling to the girls they were!" suggested Slipper, with an unabashed eye at Hannah.

I told him to come up with me to my office, and stalked from the kitchen, full of the comfortless wrath that has failed to find a suitable victim.

The interview in the office did not last long, nor was it in any way reassuring. Slipper, with the manner of the confederate who had waded shoulder to shoulder with me through gore, could only tell me that though he believed that there was nothing ailed the Man-een, he wouldn't say but what he might be sevarely hurted. That I wasn't gone five minutes before near a score of the Twohigs come leathering down out of the town in two ass-butts (this term indicates donkey-carts of the usual dimensions), and when Oweneen felt them coming, he let the most unmerciful screech, upon which Slipper, in just fear of the Twohigs, got over the wall, and executed a strategic retreat upon the railway station, leaving the Twohigs to carry away their wounded to the mountains. That for himself he had been going in dread of them ever since, and for no one else in the wide world would he have put a hand to one of them.

I preserved an unshaken front towards Slipper, and I was subsequently sarcastic and epigrammatic to Philippa on the subject of the curlews who were rabbiting in the plantation, but something that I justified to myself as a fear of Philippa's insatiable conscientiousness, made me resolve that I would, without delay, go "back in the mountain," and interview Oweneen the Sprat.

New Year's Day favored my purpose, bringing with it clear frost and iron roads, a day when even the misanthropic soul of a bicycle awakens into sympathy and geniality. I started in the sunny vigor of the early afternoon, I sailed up the hills with the effortless speed of a seagull, I free-wheeled down them with the dive of a swallow, and, as it seemed to me, with a good deal of its grace. Had Oweneen the Sprat had the luck to have met me when, at the seventh milestone from Shreelane, I realized that I had beaten my own best time by seven minutes, he could practically have made his own terms. At that point, however, I had to leave the high road, and the mountain lane that ensued restored to me the judicial frame of mind. In the first twenty yards my bicycle was transformed from a swallow to an opinionated and semi-paralyzed wheelbarrow; struggling in a species of dry watercourse I shoved it up the steep gradients of a large and brown country of heather and bog, silent save for the contending voices of the streams. A family of goats, regarding me from a rocky mound, was the first hint of civilization; a more reliable symptom presently advanced in the shape of a lean and hump-backed sow, who bestowed on me a side glance of tepid interest as she squeezed past.

The bohereen dropped, with a sudden twist to the right, and revealed a fold in the hillside, containing a half-dozen or so of little fields, crooked, and heavily walled, and nearly as many thatched cabins, flung about in the hollows as indiscriminately as the boulders upon the wastes outside. A group of children rose in front of me like a flight of starlings, and scudded with barefooted nimbleness to the shelter of the houses, in a pattering, fluttering stampede. I descended upon the nearest cabin of the colony. The door was shut; a heavy padlock linking two staples said Not at Home, and the nose of a dog showed in a hole above the sill, sniffing deeply and suspiciously. I remembered that the first of January was a holy day, and that every man in the colony had doubtless betaken himself to the nearest village. The next cottage was some fifty yards away, and the faces of a couple of children peered at me round the corner of it. As I approached they vanished, but the door of the cabin was open, and blue turf smoke breathed placidly outwards from it. The merciful frost had glazed the inevitable dirty pool in front of the door, and had made practicable the path beside it; I propped my bicycle against a rock, and projected into the dark interior an inquiry as to whether there was anyone in.

I had to repeat it twice before a small old woman with white hair and a lemon-colored face appeared; I asked her if she could tell me where Owen Twohig lived.

"Your Honor's welcome," she replied, tying the strings of her cap under her chin with wiry fingers, and eyeing me with concentrated shrewdness. I repeated the question.

She responded by begging me to come in and rest myself, for this was a cross place and a backwards place, and I should be famished with the cold—"sure them little wheels dhraws the wind."

I ignored this peculiarity of bicycles, and, not without exasperation, again asked for Owen Twohig.

"Are you Major Yeates, I beg your pardon?"

I assented to what she knew as well as I did.

"Why then 'tis here he lives indeed, in this little house, and a poor place he have to live in. Sure he's my son, the crayture—" her voice at once ascended to the key of lamentation—"faith, he didn't rise till to-day. Since Christmas Eve I didn't quinch light in the house with him stretched in the bed always, and not a bit passed his lips night or day, only one suppeen of whisky in its purity. Ye'd think the tongue would light out of his mouth with the heat, and ye'd see the blaze of darkness in his face! I hadn't as much life in me this morning as that I could wash my face!"

I replied that I wanted to speak to her son, and was in a hurry.

"He's not within, asthore, he's not within at all. He got the lend of a little donkey, and he went back the mountain to the bonesetter, to try could he straighten the leg with him."

"Did Dr. Hickey see him?" I demanded.

"Sure a wise woman came in from Finnaun, a' Stephen's Day," pursued Mrs. Twohig swiftly, "and she bet three spits down on him, and she said it's what ailed him he had the Fallen Palate, with the dint o' the blow the car bet him in the poll, and that anyone that have the Fallen Palate might be speechless for three months with it. She took three ribs of his hair then, and she was pulling them till she was in a passpiration, and in the latther end she pulled up the palate." She paused and wiped her eyes with her apron. "But the leg is what has him destroyed altogether; she told us we should keep sheep's butter rubbed to it in the place where the thrack o' the wheel is down in it."

The blush of a frosty sunset was already in the sky, and the children who had fled before me had returned, reinforced by many others, to cluster in a whispering swarm round my bicycle, and to group themselves attentively in the rear of the conversation.

"Look here, Mrs. Twohig," I said, not as yet angry, but in useful proximity to it, "I've had a letter from your son, and he and his friends have been trying to frighten my man, Denis Leary; he can come down and see me if he has anything to say, but you can tell him from me that I'm not going to stand this sort of thing!"

If the Widow Twohig had been voluble before, this pronouncement had the effect of bringing her down in spate. She instantly, and at the top of her voice, called heaven to witness her innocence, and the innocence of her "little boy"; still at full cry, she sketched her blameless career, and the unmerited suffering that had ever pursued her and hers; how, during the past thirty years, she had been drooping over her little orphans, and how Oweneen, that was the only one she bad left to do a hand's turn for her, would be "under clutches" the longest day that he'd live. It was at about this point that I gave her five shillings. It was a thoroughly illogical act, but at the moment it seemed inevitable, and Mrs. Twohig was good enough to accept it in the same spirit. I told her that I would send Dr. Hickey to see her son (which had, it struck me, a somewhat stemming effect upon her eloquence), and I withdrew, still in magisterial displeasure. I must have been half-way down the lane before it was revealed to me that a future on crutches was what Mrs. Twohig anticipated for her son.

By that nights's post I wrote to Hickey, a strictly impartial letter, stating the position, and asking him to see Owen Twohig, and to let me have his professional opinion upon him. Philippa added a postscript, asking for a nerve tonic for the parlormaid, a Dublin girl, who, since the affair of the curlews in the plantation, had lost all color and appetite, and persisted in locking the hall door day and night, to the infinite annoyance of the dogs.

Next morning, while hurrying through an early breakfast, preparatory to starting for a distant Petty Sessions, I was told that Denis wished to speak to me at the hall door. This, as I before have had occasion to point out, boded affairs of the first importance. I proceeded to the hall door, and there found Denis, pale as the Lily Maid of Astolat, with three small fishes in his hand.

"There was one of thim before me in my bed lasht night!" he said in a hoarse and shaken whisper, "and there was one in the windy in the harness room, down on top o' me razor, and there was another nelt to the stable door with the nail of a horse's shoe."

I made the natural suggestion that someone had done it for a joke.

"Thim's no joke, sir," replied Denis, portentously, "thim's Sprats!"

"Well, I'm quite aware of that," I said, unmoved by what appeared to be the crushing significance of the statement.

"Oweneen the *Sprat!*" murmured Philippa, illuminatingly, emerging from the dining-room door with her cup of tea in her hand, "it's Hannah, trying to frighten him!"

Hannah, the housemaid, was known to be the humorist of the household.

"He have a brother a smith, back in the mountain," continued Denis, wrapping up the sprats and the nail in his handkerchief; " 'twas for a token he put the nail in it. If he dhraws thim mountainy men down on me, I may as well go under the sod. It isn't yourself or the misthress they'll folly; it's meself." He crept down the steps as deplorably as the Jackdaw of Rheims, "and it's what Michael's after telling me, they have it all through the country that I said you should throw Twohig in the ditch, and it was good enough for the likes of him, and I said to Michael 'twas a lie for them, and that we cared him as tender as if he was our mother itself, and we'd have given the night to him only for the misthress that was roaring on the car, and no blame to her; sure the world knows the mother o' children has no courage!"

This drastic generality was unfortunately lost to my wife, as she had retired to hold a court of inquiry in the kitchen.

The inquiry elicited nothing beyond the fact that since Christmas Day Denis was "using no food," and that the kitchen, so far from indulging in practical jokes at his expense, had been instant throughout in sympathy, and in cups of strong tea, administered for the fortification of the nerves. All were obviously deeply moved by the incident of the sprats, the parlormaid indeed having already locked herself into the pantry, through the door of which, on Philippa's approach, she gave warning hysterically.

The matter remained unexplained, and was not altogether to my liking. As I drove down the avenue, and saw Denis carefully close the yard gates after me, I determined that I would give Murray, the District Inspector of Police, a brief sketch of the state of affairs. I did not meet Murray, but, as it happened, this made no difference. Things were already advancing smoothly and inexorably towards their preordained conclusion.

I have since heard that none of the servants went to bed that night. They, including Denis, sat in the kitchen, with locked doors, drinking tea and reciting religious exercises; Maria, as a further precaution, being chained to the leg of the table. Their fears were in no degree allayed by the fact that nothing whatever occurred, and the most immediate result of the vigil was that my bath next morning boiled as it stood in the can, and dimmed the room with clouds of steam—a circumstance sufficiently rare in itself, and absolutely without precedent on Sunday morning. The next feature of the case was a letter at breakfast time from a gentleman signing himself "Jas. Fitzmaurice." He said that Dr. Hickey having gone away for a fortnight's holiday, he (Fitzmaurice) was acting as his locum tenens. In that capacity he had opened my letter, and would go and see Twohig as soon as possible. He enclosed prescription for tonic as requested.

It was a threatening morning, and we did not go to church. I noticed that my wife's housekeeping *séance* was unusually prolonged, and even while I smoked and read the papers, I was travelling in my meditations to the point of determining that I would have a talk with the priest about all this infernal nonsense. When Philippa at length rejoined me, I found that she also had arrived at a conclusion, impelled thereto by the counsels of Mrs. Cadogan, abetted by her own conscience.

Its result was that immediately after lunch, long before the Sunday roast beef had been slept off, I found myself carting precarious parcels—a jug, a bottle, a pudding dish —to the inside car, in which Philippa had already placed herself, with a pair of blankets and various articles culled from my wardrobe (including a pair of boots to which I was sincerely attached). Denis, pale yellow in complexion and shrouded in gloom, was on the box, the Quaker was in the shafts. There was no rain, but the clouds hung black and low.

It was an expedition of purest charity; so Philippa explained to me over again as we drove away. She said nothing of propitiation or diplomacy. For my part I said nothing at all, but I reflected on the peculiar gifts of the Dublin parlormaid in valeting me, and decided that it might be better to allow Philippa to run the show on her own lines, while I maintained an attitude of large-minded disapproval.

The blankets took up as much room in the car as a man; I had to hold in my hand a jug of partly jellified beef tea. A sourer Lady Bountiful never set forth upon an errand of mercy. To complete establishment—in the words of the *Gazette*—Maria and Minx, on the floor of the car, wrought and strove in ceaseless and objectless agitation, an infliction due to the ferocity of a female rival, who terrorized the high road within hail of my gates. I thanked heaven that I had at least been firm about not taking the children; for the dogs, at all events, the moment of summary ejectment would arrive sooner or later.

Seven miles in an inside car are seven miles indeed. The hills that had run to meet my bicycle and glided away behind it, now sat in their places to be crawled up and lumbered down, at such a pace as seemed good to the Quaker, whose appetite for the expedition was, if possible, less than that of his driver. Appetite was, indeed, the last thing suggested by the aspect of Denis. His drooping shoulders and deplorable countenance proclaimed apology and deprecation to the mountain tops, and more especially to the mountainy men. Looking back on it now, I recognize the greatness of the tribute to my valour and omnipotence that he should have consented thus to drive us into the heart of the enemy's country.

A steep slope, ending with a sharp turn through a cutting, reminded me that we were near the mountain bohereen that was our goal. I got out and walked up the hill, stiffly, because the cramp of the covered car was in my legs. Stiff though I was, I had outpaced the Quaker, and was near the top of the hill, when something that was apparently a brown croquet ball rolled swiftly round the bend above me, charged into the rock wall of the cutting with a clang, and came on down the hill with a weight and venom unknown to croquet balls. It sped past me, missed the Quaker by an uncommonly near shave, and went on its way, hotly pursued by the two dogs, who, in the next twenty yards, discovered with horror that it was made of iron, a fact of which I was already aware.

I have always been as lenient as the law and other circumstances would allow towards the illegal game of "bowling." It consists in bowling an iron ball along a road, the object being to cover the greatest possible distance in a given number of bowls. It demands considerable strength and skill, and it is played with a zest much enhanced by its illegality and by its facilities as a medium for betting. The law forbids it, on account of its danger to the unsuspecting wayfarer, in consideration of which a scout is usually posted ahead to signal the approach of the police, and to give warning to passers-by. The mountainy men, trusting to their isolation, had neglected this precaution, with results that came near being serious to the Quaker, and filled with wrath, both personal and official, I took the hill at a vengeful run, so as to catch the bowler red-handed. At the turn in the cutting I met him face to face. As a matter of fact he nearly ran into my arms, and the yelp of agony with which he dodged my impending embrace is a lifelong possession. He was a very small man; he doubled like a rabbit, and bolted back towards a swarm of men who were following the fortunes of the game. He flitted over the wall by the roadside, and was away over the rocky hillside at a speed that even in my best days would have left me nowhere.

The swarm on the road melted; a good part of it was quietly absorbed by the lane up which I had dragged my bicycle two days before, the remainder, elaborately uninterested and respectable, in their dark blue Sunday clothes, strolled gravely in the opposite direction. A man on a bicycle met them, and dismounted to speak to the leaders. I wondered if he were a policeman in plain clothes on the prowl. He came on to meet me, leading his bicycle, and I perceived that a small black leather bag was strapped to the carrier. He was young, and apparently very hot.

"I beg your pardon," he said in the accents of Dublin,

"I understand you're Major Yeates. I'm Dr. Hickey's 'locum,' and I've come out to see the man you wrote to me about. From what you said I thought it better to lose no time."

I was rather out of breath, but I expressed my sense of indebtedness.

"I think there must be some mistake," went on the 'locum.' "I've just asked these men on the road where Owen Twohig lives, and one of them—the fellow they call Skipper, or some such name—said Owen Twohig was the little chap that's just after sprinting up the mountain. He seemed to think it was a great joke. I suppose you're sure Owen was the name?"

"Perfectly sure," I said heavily.

The eyes of Dr. Fitzmaurice had travelled past me, and were regarding with professional alertness something farther down the road. I followed their direction, dreamily, because in spirit I was far away, tracking Flurry Knox through deep places.

On the hither side of the rock cutting, the covered car had come to a standstill. The reins had fallen from Denis's hands; he was obviously having the "wakeness" appropriate to the crisis. Philippa, on the step below him, was proffering to him the jug of beef tea and the bottle of port. He accepted the latter.

"He knows what's what!" said the "locum."

W. B. YEATS

1865–1939

William Butler Yeats, who won the Nobel Prize for literature in 1923, was almost certainly the greatest poet that Ireland has produced in either language. Many critics regard him as the greatest lyric poet who has written in English in this century. His *Collected Poems* and *Collected Plays* are already classics. The Abbey Theatre and the whole Irish theatre movement might never have existed without his inspiration and guidance; while not Ireland's greatest playwright, he ranks high on the list. His *Autobiography* and several important biographies of him tell the story of his public and private life in copious detail. Yeats' work in prose fiction is of minor significance, but besides editing several anthologies of short stories and folktales he published one short novel, *John Sherman* (1891), and three small volumes of short stories—the latter now collected in *Mythologies*. "The Tables of the Law" is a beautiful, haunting story in its own right, in spite of its rather dated prose style, and it is full of Yeats' lifelong preoccupation with the occult. It gains further importance from its effect upon James Joyce, who devotes a whole page of *Stephen Hero* to this story and its companion piece, "The Adoration of the Magi." Young Stephen Daedalus is represented as repeating both stories to himself and being fondest of the passage beginning "Why do you fly from our torches . . . ?" at the end of "The Tables of the Law." Echoes of this tale recur in the third episode of *Ulysses*. To extract the maximum pleasure from this mannered story, one should take a hint from Joyce and read it aloud.

The Tables of the Law

I. "Will you permit me, Aherne," I said, "to ask you a question, which I have wanted to ask you for years, and have not asked because we have grown nearly strangers? Why did you refuse the biretta, and almost at the last moment? When you and I lived together, you cared neither for wine, women, nor money, and had thoughts for nothing but theology and mysticism." I had watched through dinner for a moment to put my question, and ventured now, because he had thrown off a little of the reserve and indifference which, ever since his last return from Italy, had taken the place of our once close friendship. He had just questioned me, too, about certain private and almost sacred things, and my frankness had earned, I thought, a like frankness from him.

When I began to speak he was lifting a glass of that wine which he could choose so well and valued so little; and while I spoke, he set it slowly and meditatively upon the table and held it there, its deep red light dyeing his long delicate fingers. The impression of his face and form, as they were then, is still vivid with me, and is inseparable from another and fanciful impression: the impression of a man holding a flame in his naked hand. He was to me, at that moment, the supreme type of our race, which, when it has risen above, or is sunken below, the formalisms of half-education and the rationalisms of conventional affirmation and denial, turns away, unless my hopes for the world and for the Church have made me blind, from practicable desires and intuitions towards desires so unbounded that no human vessel can contain them, intuitions so immaterial that their sudden and far-off fire leaves heavy darkness about hand and foot. He had the nature, which is half monk, half soldier of fortune, and must needs turn action into dreaming, and dreaming into action; and for such there is no order, no finality, no contentment in this world. When he and I had been students in Paris, we had belonged to a little group which devoted itself to speculations about

alchemy and mysticism. More orthodox in most of his beliefs than Michael Robartes, he had surpassed him in a
fanciful hatred of all life, and this hatred had found expression in the curious paradox—half borrowed from some
fanatical monk, half invented by himself—that the beautiful arts were sent into the world to overthrow nations, and
finally life herself, by sowing everywhere unlimited desires,
like torches thrown into a burning city. This idea was not
at the time, I believe, more than a paradox, a plume of the
pride of youth; and it was only after his return to Ireland
that he endured the fermentation of belief which is coming
upon our people with the reawakening of their imaginative
life.

Presently he stood up, saying, "Come, and I will show
you why; you at any rate will understand," and taking
candles from the table, he lit the way into the long paved
passage that led to his private chapel. We passed between
the portraits of the Jesuits and priests—some of no little
fame—his family had given to the Church; and engravings
and photographs of pictures that had especially moved him;
and the few paintings his small fortune, eked out by an almost penurious abstinence from the things most men desire, had enabled him to buy in his travels. The photographs
and engravings were from the masterpieces of many
schools; but in all the beauty, whether it was a beauty of
religion, of love, or of some fantastical vision of mountain
and wood, was the beauty achieved by temperaments which
seek always an absolute emotion, and which have their
most continual, though not most perfect, expression in the
legends and vigils and music of the Celtic peoples. The
certitude of a fierce or gracious fervor in the enraptured
faces of the angels of Francesca, and in the august faces of
the sibyls of Michaelangelo; and the incertitude, as of souls
trembling between the excitement of the spirit and the excitement of the flesh, in wavering faces from frescoes in the
churches of Siena, and in the faces like thin flames, imagined by the modern symbolists and Pre-Raphaelites, had
often made that long, grey, dim, empty, echoing passage
become to my eyes a vestibule of eternity.

Almost every detail of the chapel, which we entered by

a narrow Gothic door, whose threshold had been worn smooth by the secret worshippers of the penal times, was vivid in my memory; for it was in this chapel that I had first, and when but a boy, been moved by the mediaevalism which is now, I think, the governing influence in my life. The only thing that seemed new was a square bronze box which stood upon the altar before the six unlighted candles and the ebony crucifix, and was like those made in ancient times of more precious substances to hold the sacred books. Aherne made me sit down on an oak bench, and having bowed very low before the crucifix, took the bronze box from the altar, and sat down beside me with the box upon his knees.

"You will perhaps have forgotten," he said, "most of what you have read about Joachim of Flora, for he is little more than a name to even the well-read. He was an abbot in Cortale in the twelfth century, and is best known for his prophecy, in a book called *Expositio in Apocalypsin,* that the Kingdom of the Father was past, the Kingdom of the Son passing, the Kingdom of the Spirit yet to come. The Kingdom of the Spirit was to be a complete triumph of the Spirit, the *spiritualis intelligentia* he called it, over the dead letter. He had many followers among the more extreme Franciscans, and these were accused of possessing a secret book of his called the *Liber inducens in Evangelium aeternum.* Again and again groups of visionaries were accused of possessing this terrible book, in which the freedom of the Renaissance lay hidden, until at last Pope Alexander IV had it found and cast into the flames. I have here the greatest treasure the world contains. I have a copy of that book; and see what great artists have made the robes in which it is wrapped. This bronze box was made by Benvenuto Cellini, who covered it with gods and demons, whose eyes are closed to signify an absorption in the inner light." He lifted the lid and took out a book bound in leather, covered with filigree work of tarnished silver. "And this cover was bound by one of the binders that bound for Canevari; while Giulio Clovio, an artist of the later Renaissance, whose work is soft and gentle, took out the beginning page of every chapter of the old copy, and set in its place a page surmounted by an elaborate letter and a miniature of some one of the great whose example was cited in the chapter; and wherever the writing left a little space elsewhere, he put some delicate emblem or intricate pattern."

I took the book in my hands and began turning over the gilded, many-colored pages, holding it close to the candle to discover the texture of the paper.

"Where did you get this amazing book?" I said. "If genuine, and I cannot judge by this light, you have discovered one of the most precious things in the world."

"It is certainly genuine," he replied. "When the original was destroyed, one copy alone remained, and was in the hands of a lute player of Florence, and from him it passed to his son, and so from generation to generation until it came to the lute player who was father to Benvenuto Cellini, and from him it passed to Giulio Clovio, and from Giulio Clovio to a Roman engraver; and then from generation to generation, the story of its wandering passing on with it, until it came into the possession of the family of Aretino, and to Giulio Aretino, an artist and worker in metals, and student of the cabbalistic reveries of Pico della Mirandola. He spent many nights with me at Rome, discussing philosophy; and at last I won his confidence so perfectly that he showed me this, his greatest treasure; and, finding how much I valued it, and feeling that he himself was growing old and beyond the help of its teaching, he sold it to me for no great sum, considering its great preciousness."

"What is the doctrine?" I said. "Some mediaeval strawsplitting about the nature of the Trinity, which is only useful today to show how many things are unimportant to us, which once shook the world?"

"I could never make you understand," he said with a sigh, "that nothing is unimportant in belief, but even you will admit that this book goes to the heart. Do you see the tables on which the commandments were written in Latin?" I looked to the end of the room, opposite to the altar, and saw that the two marble tablets were gone, and that two large empty tablets of ivory, like large copies of the little tablets we set over our desks, had taken their place. "It has swept the commandments of the Father away," he went on, "and displaced the commandments of the Son by the commandments of the Holy Spirit. The first book is called *Fractura Tabularum*. In the first chapter it mentions the names of the great artists who made them graven things and the likeness of many things, and adored them and served them; and the second the names of the great wits who took the name of the Lord their God in vain; and that long third chapter, set with the emblems of sanctified faces, and having wings upon its borders, is the praise of breakers of the seventh day and wasters of the six days, who yet lived comely and pleasant days. Those two chapters tell of men and women who railed upon their parents, remembering that their god was older than the god of their parents; and that which has the sword of Michael for an emblem commends the kings that wrought secret murder and so won for their people a peace that was *amore somnoque gravata et vestibus versicoloribus*, "heavy with love and sleep and many-colored raiment"; and that with the pale star at the closing has the lives of the noble youths who loved the wives of others and were transformed into memories, which have transformed many poorer hearts into sweet flames; and that with the winged head is the history of the robbers who lived upon the sea or in the desert, lives which it compares to the twittering of the string of a bow, *nervi stridentis instar*; and those two last, that are fire and gold, and devoted to the satirists who bore false witness against their neighbors and yet illustrated eternal wrath, and to those that have coveted more than other men wealth and women, and have thereby and therefore mastered and magnified great empires.

"The second book, which is called *Straminis Deflagratio*, recounts the conversations Joachim of Flora held in his monastery at Cortale, and afterwards in his monastery in the mountains of La Sila, with travellers and pilgrims, upon the laws of many countries; how chastity was a virtue and robbery a little thing in such a land, and robbery a crime and unchastity a little thing in such a land; and of the persons who had flung themselves upon these laws and become *decussa veste Dei sidera*, stars shaken out of the raiment of God.

"The third book, which is the close, is called *Lex Secreta*, and describes the true inspiration of action, the only Eternal Evangel; and ends with a vision, which he saw among the mountains of La Sila, of his disciples sitting throned in the blue deep of the air, and laughing aloud, with a laughter that was like the rustling of the wings of Time: *Coelis in coeruleis ridentes sedebant discipuli mei super thronos: talis erat risus, qualis temporis pennati susurrus.*"

"I know little of Joachim of Flora," I said, "except that Dante set him in Paradise among the great doctors. If he held a heresy so singular, I cannot understand how no rumors of it came to the ears of Dante; and Dante made no peace with the enemies of the Church."

"Joachim of Flora acknowledged openly the authority of the Church, and even asked that all his published writings, and those to be published by his desire after his death, should be submitted to the censorship of the Pope. He considered that those whose work was to live and not to reveal were children and that the Pope was their father; but he taught in secret that certain others, and in always increasing numbers, were elected, not to live, but to reveal that hidden substance of God which is color and music and softness and a sweet odor; and that these have no father but the Holy Spirit. Just as poets and painters and musicians labor at their works, building them with lawless and lawful things alike, so long as they embody the beauty that is beyond the grave, these children of the Holy Spirit labor at their moments with eyes upon the shining substance on which Time has heaped the refuse of creation; for the world only exists to be a tale in the ears of coming generations; and terror and content, birth and death, love and hatred, and the fruit of the Tree, are but instruments for that supreme art which is to win us from life and gather us into eternity like doves into their dovecots.

"I shall go away in a little while and travel into many lands, that I may know all accidents and destinies, and when I return, will write my secret law upon those ivory tablets, just as poets and romance-writers have written the principles of their art in prefaces; and will gather pupils about me that they may discover their law in the study of my law, and the Kingdom of the Holy Spirit be more widely and firmly established."

He was pacing up and down, and I listened to the fervor of his words and watched the excitement of his gestures with not a little concern. I had been accustomed to welcome the most singular speculations, and had always found them as harmless as the Persian cat, who half closes her meditative eyes and stretches out her long claws before my fire. But now I would battle in the interests of orthodoxy, even of the commonplace; and yet could find nothing better to say than: "It is not necessary to judge everyone by the law, for we have also Christ's commandment of love."

He turned and said, looking at me with shining eyes:

"Jonathan Swift made a soul for the gentlemen of this city by hating his neighbor as himself."

"At any rate, you cannot deny that to teach so dangerous a doctrine is to accept a terrible responsibility."

"Leonardo da Vinci," he replied, "has this noble sentence: 'The hope and desire of returning home to one's former state is like the moth's desire for the light; and the man who with constant longing awaits each new month and new year, deeming that the things he longs for are ever too late in coming, does not perceive that he is longing for his own destruction.' How then can the pathway which will lead us into the heart of God be other than dangerous? Why should you, who are no materialist, cherish the continuity and order of the world as those do who have only the world? You do not value the writers who will express nothing unless their reason understands how it will make what is called the right more easy; why, then, will you deny a like freedom to the supreme art, the art which is the foundation of all arts? Yes, I shall send out of this chapel saints, lovers, rebels, and prophets: souls that will surround themselves with peace, as with a nest made with grass; and others over whom I shall weep. The dust shall fall for many years over this little box; and then I shall open it; and the tumults which are, perhaps, the flames of the Last Day shall come from under the lid."

I did not reason with him that night, because his excitement was great and I feared to make him angry; and when I called at his house a few days later, he was gone and his house was locked up and empty. I have deeply regretted my failure both to combat his heresy and to test the genuineness of his strange book. Since my conversion I have indeed done penance for an error which I was only able to measure after some years.

II. I was walking along one of the Dublin quays, on the side nearest the river, about ten years after our conversation, stopping from time to time to turn over the works upon an old bookstall, and thinking, curiously enough, of the terrible destiny of Michael Robartes, and his brotherhood, when I saw a tall and bent man walking slowly along the other side of the quay. I recognized, with a start, in a lifeless mask with dim eyes, the once resolute and delicate face of Owen Aherne. I crossed the quay quickly, but had not gone many yards before he turned away, as though he had seen me, and hurried down a side street; I followed, but only to lose him among the intricate streets on the north side of the river. During the next few weeks I inquired of everybody who had once known him, but he had made himself known to nobody; and I knocked, without result, at the door of his old house; and had nearly persuaded myself that I was mistaken, when I saw him again in a narrow street behind the Four Courts, and followed him to the door of his house.

I laid my hand on his arm; he turned quite without surprise; and indeed it is possible that to him, whose inner life had soaked up the outer life, a parting of years was a parting from forenoon to afternoon. He stood holding the door half open, as though he would keep me from entering; and would perhaps have parted from me without further words had I not said: "Owen Aherne, you trusted me once, will you not trust me again, and tell me what has come of the ideas we discussed in this house ten years ago?—but perhaps you have already forgotten them."

"You have a right to hear," he said, "for since I have told you the ideas, I should tell you the extreme danger they contain, or rather the boundless wickedness they contain; but when you have heard this we must part, and part for ever, because I am lost, and must be hidden!"

I followed him through the paved passage, and saw that its corners were choked with dust and cobwebs; and that the pictures were grey with dust and shrouded with cobwebs; and that the dust and cobwebs which covered the ruby and sapphire of the saints on the window had made it very dim. He pointed to where the ivory tablets glimmered faintly in the dimness, and I saw that they were covered with small writing, and went up to them and began to read the writing. It was in Latin, and was an elaborate casuistry, illustrated with many examples, but whether from his own life or from the lives of others I do not know. I had read but a few sentences when I imagined that a faint perfume had begun to fill the room, and turning round asked Owen Aherne if he were lighting the incense.

"No," he replied, and pointed where the thurible lay rusty and empty on one of the benches; as he spoke the faint perfume seemed to vanish, and I was persuaded I had imagined it.

"Has the philosophy of the *Liber inducens in Evangelium aeternum* made you very unhappy?" I said.

"At first I was full of happiness," he replied, "for I felt a divine ecstasy, an immortal fire in every passion, in every hope, in every desire, in every dream; and I saw, in the shadows under leaves, in the hollow waters, in the eyes of men and women, its image, as in a mirror; and it was as though I was about to touch the Heart of God. Then all changed and I was full of misery; and in my misery it was revealed to me that man can only come to that Heart through the sense of separation from it which we call sin, and I understood that I could not sin, because I had discovered the law of my being, and could only express or fail to express my being, and I understood that God has made a simple and an arbitrary law that we may sin and repent!"

He had sat down on one of the wooden benches and now became silent, his bowed head and hanging arms and listless body having more of dejection than any image I have met

with in life or in any art. I went and stood leaning against
the altar, and watched him, not knowing what I should say;
and I noticed his black closely-buttoned coat, his short hair,
and shaven head, which preserved a memory of his priestly
ambition, and understood how Catholicism had seized him
in the midst of the vertigo he called philosophy; and I noticed his lightless eyes and his earth-colored complexion,
and understood how she had failed to do more than hold
him on the margin: and I was full of an anguish of pity.

"It may be," he went on, "that the angels who have
hearts of the Divine Ecstasy, and bodies of the Divine Intellect, need nothing but a thirst for the immortal element,
in hope, in desire, in dreams; but we whose hearts perish
every moment, and whose bodies melt away like a sigh,
must bow and obey!"

I went nearer to him and said, "Prayer and repentance
will make you like other men."

"No, no," he said, "I am not among those for whom
Christ died, and this is why I must be hidden. I have a
leprosy that even eternity cannot cure. I have seen the
whole, and how can I come again to believe that a part is
the whole? I have lost my soul because I have looked out
of the eyes of the angels."

Suddenly I saw, or imagined that I saw, the room dark-
en, and faint figures robed in purple, and lifting faint
torches with arms that gleamed like silver, bending above
Owen Aherne; and I saw, or imagined that I saw, drops, as
of burning gum, fall from the torches, and a heavy purple
smoke, as of incense, come pouring from the flames and
sweeping about us. Owen Aherne, more happy than I who
have been half initiated into the Order of the Alchemical
Rose, or protected perhaps by his great piety, had sunk
again into dejection and listlessness, and saw none of these
things; but my knees shook under me, for the purple-robed
figures were less faint every moment, and now I could
hear the hissing of the gum in the torches. They did not
appear to see me, for their eyes were upon Owen Aherne;
now and again I could hear them sigh as though with sorrow for his sorrow, and presently I heard words which I
could not understand except that they were words of sor-

row, and sweet as though immortal was talking to immortal. Then one of them waved her torch, and all the torches waved, and for a moment it was as though some great bird made of flames had fluttered its plumage, and a voice cried as from far up in the air, "He has charged even his angels with folly, and they also bow and obey; but let your heart mingle with our hearts, which are wrought of Divine Ecstasy, and your body with our bodies, which are wrought of Divine Intellect." And at that cry I understood that the Order of the Alchemical Rose was not of this earth, and that it was still seeking over this earth for whatever souls it could gather within its glittering net; and when all the faces turned towards me, and I saw the mild eyes and the unshaken eyelids, I was full of terror, and thought they were about to fling their torches upon me, so that all I held dear, all that bound me to spiritual and social order, would be burnt up, and my soul left naked and shivering among the winds that blow from beyond this world and from beyond the stars; and then a voice cried, "Why do you fly from our torches that were made out of the trees under which Christ wept in the Garden of Gethsemane? Why do you fly from our torches that were made out of sweet wood, after it had perished from the world?"

It was not until the door of the house had closed behind my flight, and the noise of the street was breaking on my ears, that I came back to myself and to a little of my courage; and I have never dared to pass the house of Owen Aherne from that day, even though I believe him to have been driven into some distant country by the spirits whose name is legion, and whose throne is in the indefinite abyss, and whom he obeys and cannot see.

LYNN DOYLE
1873–1961

Leslie A. Montgomery, who wrote under the pseudonym "Lynn Doyle," followed what seems at first sight an unlikely profession for a humorist—banking. But a bank clerk or the manager of a branch bank in a small Irish town meets a great many people and sees a good deal not only of the surface of life but of what goes on underneath. Montgomery, who was born in the North of Ireland, published his first book, *Ballygullion*, in 1908. This collection of short stories about a small town in, apparently, County Down was an immediate success. Two further volumes of stories about the town of Ballygullion appeared in later years. The narrator of all three volumes is supposed to be Pat Murphy, a Catholic small farmer with a taste for sport and whiskey—legal or illegal. Master MacDermott, the somewhat alcoholic schoolmaster of the Ballygullion elementary school, frequently appears in the stories. Lynn Doyle lived near Dublin after his retirement from banking and continued to write; during his long life he produced, besides short stories, novels, plays, verse, essays, and a charming book of Irish travels. "A Persian Tale" from *Lobster Salad* (1922) does not depend heavily on slapstick for its humor, as many of the other Ballygullion stories tend to do. The notion of a funeral pyre for the cat is a delightful invention. The cat's name, by the way, was probably not "Paddy Shaw" but "Padishah," an appropriate Persian title.

A Persian Tale

The wee schoolmaster, bein' inclined to a dhrop of whisky, an' not gettin' any great encouragement from the ould sister to take it in his own house, was in the habit of dhroppin' intil Michael Casshidy's pub most nights; an' to keep the sister from thinkin' long when he was away, he hit on the notion of gettin' her a pet of some kind.

Now, though it's mortial hard to explain why, there's a sthrong fellow feelin' between a cat an' an ould maid; an' afther goin' round as many bastes as would ha' filled a zoo she fixed her affections on a big cat with a coat on it like a sheep, that she called a Persian, a conceited useless baste that would sit washin' an polishin' at itself with the mice runnin' over it.

But ye never seen womankind yet that wasn't fond of some useless bein', cat or man; an' for many a long day Paddy Shaw, as she called him, was the comfort of her heart.

In the end, between the laziness an' him bein' a greedy gorb of an animal, Paddy grew to a most lamentable size, an' could hardly move about; an' Miss MacDermott got uneasy about him. The master said the only thing for him was whisky, an', troth, himself was well experienced in the same commodity.

"Whisky," sez the masther, "is the universal remedy for the male kind. The female sex seems to get on without it in a most remarkable way, but for their lords an' masters there's no medicine to be compared with it."

Now I may tell ye Miss MacDermott had no such notion of the virtues of whisky as the wee man had—an' small wondher; for it was him had all the fun out of what whisky was dhrunk in the MacDermott family, an' herself all the bother. But she got terrible fond of the cat, and would ha' done near anythin' to bring it to itself again, so she give in to the masther's notion, an' even went the length of promisin' to pay for any whisky he bought while the cure was goin' on.

The wee man was terribly pleased about it. He had been what you'd know off color for a while before; but he brightened up straight away. At first I thought it was on account of him gettin' his whisky on the cheap, an', mind ye, that meant somethin'; but all the same it didn't explain why he was takin' so much intherest in the cat. At last he let out the reason himself.

"Ye'll think it strange, Pat," sez he, "comin' from a man like myself that has been singin' the praises of whisky these twenty-five years an' more; but the truth is, a kind of a doubt about the virtues of the immortal liquor has been risin' in my mind this while past."

"In the name of goodness, masther," sez I, "what has put that notion in your head?"

"It was partly put there by the doctor, that has lattherly been usin' some very alarmin' classical terms in connection with my liver, an' partly by the parish priest, a man," sez the masther, blinkin' at me a bit droll, "for whose opinion I have a great deal of respect, not only from his sacred callin', but in his capacity as manager of the Ballygullion National School.

"Now I may tell ye, Pat," went on the wee man, "that till lately any misgivin' the pair of them was able to stir up was always scatthered like mornin' mist before the third half-glass of Michael's special. But what's worst of all," sez he, "for this while past there has been a thraitor in an' about the middle button of my waistcoat basely suggestin' that the effects of our national beverage is not just as beneficent on the system as has been supposed."

"Ye're never thinkin' of givin' up the whisky altogether, masther?" sez I.

"I've been meditatin' it seriously for some time, Pat," sez he, "without gettin' much further than that. But I see some chance of comin' to a decision now that I've hit on the great an' scientific notion of thryin' the effects of a dhrop on the cat."

"How in the name of goodness is that goin' to help ye?" sez I.

"It's as simple as two-times tables," sez he. "The only difficulty I had was in the adjustin' of what you might call the alcoholic values between me an' the animal."

"I don't quite follow ye there," sez I.

"Wait," sez he, "an' I'll explain. I suppose you're aware that the average life of a man is generally taken to be about seventy years?"

"I'm told they lived a deal longer in ould times, masther," sez I. "Did they take a sup then, do ye think?"

"It's undherstood, Pat," sez the masther, "that they took a deal of dhrink before the Flood; an' with all that they lived, some of them, to be near a thousand. It's a very consolin' bit of history, for if it proves anythin' at all it's that too much water is just as bad as too much whisky; an' the case of Noah, though he made his name by water, shows that he didn't think a heap of it as a dhrink. However, seventy years is our average these times, an' seventy years is all a reasonable bein' need aim at.

"Now, as ye know, I'm just fifty-five. If I can stand it another fifteen years I've had my share, an' barrin' maybe in the matther of whisky, I've never wanted more than my share. Well, the average life of a cat bein', say, fourteen years, it follows that the vitality of the beast is as five to one compared with a man. Ye got the length of proportion at school, Pat, didn't ye?"

"I did," sez I, "afther doin' a lot of damage among canes."

"Very well," sez the masther, "you'll see at once that if the cat can stand three years' whisky I can stand fifteen, an' that's all I want."

"How long is he at it now?" sez I, "an' how is he doin'?"

"He's only six or eight weeks at it yet," sez the masther, "an' except in the matther of hair, where the beast is undoubtedly losin' ground, he's doin' beyond my wildest dhreams. Instead of bein' what he used to be, an idle useless drone of a crather, he's skippin' about like a young one, an' killin' mice—aye, an' even rats—like a terrier. I've noticed the same thing with myself, many a time. There I'll be in the school as heavy as a dunce, with even vulgar fractions a bother to me; an' before I've been in Michael's half an hour, I can do repeatin' decimals in my head. I admit, mind ye, that the doctor had me a bit daunted a while back; but the outcome of this experiment has been very reassurin'. For anythin' plain an' straightforward like colic or the worms I'll agree with every old woman in the neighborhood that Dr. Dickson has his points; but when he takes it upon him to lay down how far alcohol is beneficial to the human system, the man goes clean beyond his depth."

An' away trots the wee man up the street with the tall hat cocked over his right eye, an' him whistlin'.

It was a month or more before I met the masther again, an' when I did he was very serious-lookin'.

"Ye find me very low in spirits, Pat," sez he, noticin' my look. "The truth is, I'm a bit bothered by the latest results of the investigations at present bein' conducted by myself an' that long-haired divil of a cat. I've been observin' lately that although he's bustlin' about fussy enough afther the mice, when ye look into results he's missin' a deal more than he's catchin'. An' when I came to apply this observation to my own case, an' put down on paper the sums I told you I could do so well in my head when I was sittin' in Michael's, I found out that though the decimals was repeatin' plenty the divil a very much of it was the truth. I'm still very far from bein' convinced that whisky isn't good for the brains, mind ye, Pat; but if the other notion should have come into the head of the P. P. it would be no great advantage to one MacDermott."

"How could it, masther," sez I, "an' you teachin' like a professor this half a lifetime?"

"There's a little circumstance that has given me some uneasiness on the subject all the same," sez the masther. "The sister at home there, though not perhaps in the same scientific way, takes near as much intherest in Paddy as I do myself, but that hasn't kept her from complainin' about the mice a good deal this last while; an' here about a week ago hasn't she installed a lump of a tortoiseshell kitten as what our friends the Presbyterians would call 'assistant an' successor.' I never thought anythin' of it till comin' down the road the next mornin' doesn't Father Richard stop me an' suggest that I should appoint big Danny Burke a monitor.

He put it to me that he was thinkin' about my health, an'
tryin' to make my work a bit easier; but do you know,
Pat," sez the wee man, with the ould comical cock of his
eyebrow, "I wouldn't be surprised if there was as Presby-
terian a kind of idea at the back of his head as a parish
priest could credibly be supposed to have.

"Come away on down to Michael's," sez he, "an' I'll do
a bit of experimentin' on myself; for I'm in poor heart this
minit."

About the third wee drop out of Michael's black bottle,
he begins to revive.

"Wine, Pat," sez he, "maketh glad the heart of man. We
have the word of a very wise one on that; an' ye may swear
he didn't learn it at second hand. An' I'll go bail if he'd
lived in the time of whisky he'd ha' said the same about
that too. If I was only sure it would keep on doin' it, it's a
short life an' a merry one I'd go in for, let the docthor say
what he likes. But a kind of a doubt is creepin' on me even
about the fun part of it. It's not lastin' with the cat."

"Ye told me he was very lively at the first," sez I.

"At the beginnin', Pat," sez the masther, "when I'd got
him to the right mixture the noble animal used to go about
the house with a smile playin' round his whiskers like the
sun on a row of pint bottles. But lattherly his spirits has
been goin' down in a way that's not at all encouragin', an'
this last week or two ye could hardly live in the house with
him."

"Ye should give him less, masther," sez I.

"I can't," sez he. "He's carnaptious enough as it is; an'
if I dock him of one spoonful of his allowance he gets
clean unbearable. He's stopped chasin' his tail, too," sez the
wee man, "the only bit of light-heartedness he had left.
I've been thryin' to persuade myself that it's through him
not takin' the same intherest in it now that most of the hair
is gone; but still it's a bad sign.

"In my opinion his intellect is failin'. He's beginnin' to
have delusions. Every now an' then he'll jump out intil the
middle of the kitchen floor as if he was killin' things. I believe it's mice he's seein'. It's only the other night he made

a wicked lepp at somethin' he thought he seen, an' near brained himself on the door of the oven.

"The wholly all of it is, Pat, the beast is rangin' himself most damnably on the side of the P. P. I'm beginnin' to see a melancholy prospect of spring water openin' before me. The divil take all cats," sez he, rappin' on the table for another dhrink; "for this long-haired curiosity is sthrikin' at the whole foundations of my existence."

"I'll tell you what I'll do, masther," sez I; "I'll dhrop round the morrow night an' have a look at him. Maybe I could find out somethin' else the matter with him than the dhrink."

"If ye can, Pat," sez the wee man, shakin' me by the hand, "I'll put the whole resources of Michael's bar at your disposal, an' carry ye home myself. But I misdoubt when ye clap eyes on the dirty brute ye'll come to the same dismal conclusion about him as myself. Good night, now, an' don't forget what ye said."

I was just dandherin' quietly home to shire my head a bit before encountherin' the wife, when who should come up behind me but Docthor Dickson. Divil a word of a good night or anythin' else he said, but just into me like a day's work.

"I seen ye comin' out of the public house with the masther, Murphy," sez he. "Do ye know that you're assistin' that decent foolish wee body to commit suicide?"

"Bless my soul, docthor," sez I, "ye don't mean to say it's as bad as that with him."

"I do then," sez he, very short, "the man's liver is nearly rotted away with the poison he's been puttin' into him these twenty years, with you an' the like of ye eggin' him on. Ye should be ashamed of yourself, Murphy. I thought betther of ye than that."

"Ye may think betther than that of me still, docthor," sez I. "I know he's been doin' himself harm this long time. But he's in the notion of quittin' it, an' I'm goin' up the morrow night to help him in the same direction."

For I may tell ye that was what was in my head when I offered to go up. An' with that I told him all about the cat.

The docthor turned away his head as I was tellin' him; but I could see the shouldhers of him shakin'.

"There's no doubt," sez he at the last, "whether it's the whisky does it for him or not, he's a comical wee crather. An' it would be doin' a kindness to the whole counthryside as well as himself if we could bring him round again."

"An' can it be done yet, docthor?" sez I.

"If he would only stop now," sez he, "I believe I could save the liver yet, or at any rate bits of it. Let me think a minit. Do you really believe, Pat," sez he, afther a bit, "he's in earnest over this business of the cat?"

"I do," sez I. "If the liquor kills the cat, I believe he'll make a big stagger at stoppin' it himself."

"Very well," sez the docthor, "would ye take a cat's life to save a man's?"

"If the wee masther is as bad as ye say—an' I don't doubt ye over it—short of a hangin' matther I'm on for anything," sez I.

"It's well said," sez the docthor. "Then come round by my surgery the morrow night an' I'll give ye a bottle of something to dhrop in the cat's dhrink that'll make a quick an' easy end of him. And if the wee man shows no sign of takin' a lesson by it ye might near as well give him the rest of the bottle himself; for to be plain with ye," sez the docthor, very serious-lookin', "if he doesn't soon alther his way of goin', he's likely to make a poor enough end of it."

When I looked at the cat the next night, the docthor's words came into my mind, an' troth they were true. The divil a more miserable anatomy of a bein' ye ever looked at in your life. From a big, lazy, sonsy-looking animal with a fleece on him like a Shrop ram he was gathered into a wee miserable dwinin' crather with not as much hair on him as would ha' made a shavin' brush. I don't mind tellin' ye that the look of him gave my own thoughts a twist in the direction of spring water. For it come into my head that bad an' all as it was for the cat himself, it would ha' been a deal worse if he'd had a wife an' family dependin' on him.

"If the whisky has done that on him, masther," sez I, "he's no great advertisement for it."

"There's no denyin' that he's gettin' to be a very uncomfortable-lookin' crony to take a dhrink along with," sez the masther, blinkin' at him very sober. "If ye can find nothin' else the matther with him, I misdoubt the takin's of Michael Casshidy's bar is goin' down one of these days with a wallop. But wait till ye see the change on him when he gets a sup. Here, Paddy, Paddy," sez he, an' reaches down a saucer.

Sure enough there was a wondherful change come on the brute the minit he seen it. Up went the ould motheaten tail over his back as if he was a kitten again; and though ye'd ha' thought by the look of him a minit before he wouldn't have budged from where he was lyin' if the house was on fire, he was at the saucer in two lepps, an' over the whiskers in it before it was well on the floor.

"It's a horrid pity, Pat," sez the masther, "that any doubt of the virtues of the stuff should be creepin' on the cowld stomachs of the present generation; for there's no denyin' it's the great medicine. Look at the poor benighted crather that hasn't near the intelligence an' none of the book learnin' of a man like me, an' even himself would hardly lift his head from the saucer if ye tould him the next minit was to be his last."

There was more truth in the wee man's words than he knowed. As he went into the panthry for two glasses, I emptied the doctor's bottle into the saucer. The cat took about three more laps at it, shook his head, give back a step, an' rolled on the floor.

"Masther," I shouts, "masther! come here quick. The cat's gone."

An' sure enough before the masther got the length of where he was lyin', poor Paddy was as dead as Hecthor.

The masther straightened himself up afther a long look at him, went over to the dhresser where he had a gallon jar sittin', an' poured himself out a rozener that if the cat had got it would ha' saved Doctor Dickson the expense of a bottle, I could hear the tumbler rattlin' again his teeth as the stuff went down. When he turned round he was very white an' washy lookin'.

"I'm sorry about the brute, Pat," sez he, afther a minit or

two. "Not because he's dead; for the way things was goin'
with him, it was in my mind to step down to the docthor's
one of these nights an' give him a speedy release; but it's at
the back of my head that maybe I didn't give him fair play.
Well, it's past prayin' for now, like many another thing, an'
we'll let it go. First of all, by way of carryin' out the funeral customs of this island, an' next, to celebrate his memory, we'll just have a thimbleful apiece."

"I'll put this stuff out of the road first," thinks I to myself, liftin' the saucer an' throwin' the contents of it in the
fire.

When I looked at the wee masther he was layin' down
his glass. There was just what ye'd know of color come into
his face, an' when he spoke it was the ould masther again.

"It's three months, Pat," sez he, "since the late lamented
an' myself embarked on this experiment, an' five times
three is fifteen. That gives me till October is a year. I'll
turn it over in my mind for a minit or two, an' in the meantime we'll carry out a great an' appropriate notion that
came into my head as I watched ye there pourin' that
saucerful of good dhrink on the fire.

"When I had made up my accounts to finish off my deceased unfortunate colleague I was greatly bothered about
the question of his last rites. To give him Christian burial
was clean out of the question; for as far as I could see there
was no hope of him dyin' in a state of grace. Then takin'
into account that the ould Egyptians considhered the cat a
sacred animal, I thought of thryin' their way of it; but the
divil a thing I knowed about embalmin'—which was the
way they done it—no more than my grandmother; an' to
pickle the beast would be to make a very scaresome-lookin'
corpse of him. But watchin' ye just now, as I said, it come
on me like a flash that we'd pay him our last respects in the
ancient Roman manner."

"An' what else would that be but Christian burial, masther?" sez I.

"It's another kind of Romans that's in my mind, Pat,"
sez he, "an older branch of the family. Away out to the
coal-hole an' bring a good armful of sticks an' shavin's to
the foot of the garden, an' I'll show ye how it's done.

"Now, Pat," sez the wee man, layin' the cat on the top of the sticks, "put a match to the shavin's, till I go back for the rest of the materials."

By the time I heard him behind me there was nothin' left of poor Paddy but the bones; an' when I looked round, the masther was comin' down the garden with the gallon jar in one hand an' two tumblers in the other.

"It was the practice of the same Romans, Pat," sez he, "when they had burned the corpse of the deceased, to put out the fire with a drop of the very best—or rather, Misther Murphy," sez he, blinkin' in the firelight, "with the best the poor benighted heathen knew about, havin' in those days nothin' more satisfactory to dhrink than a cowld splash of wine. An' though I don't find it in the books, there's no manner of doubt that, such as it was, they took a jorum at the same time just to dhrive away sorrow. So we'll do the full rites by poor Paddy." With that he sets the tumblers on the ground an' pours out two stiff ones.

"Stand back now, Pat," sez he; an' before I knowed what he was afther he had cowped the gallon jar on the fire. The flames went up with a woof! would ha' frightened ye, an' for a minit I thought the masther was desthroyed; but when I thrailed him back, barrin' the nap on his tall hat he wasn't a thraneen the worse.

"Didn't I tell ye," sez he. "The divil an ancient Roman ever seen a flame like that in his life. It's the great stuff—gimme my glass—an' here's Paddy Shaw's memory in the last dhrop—worse luck—I'll ever taste of it."

DANIEL CORKERY
1878–1964

Daniel Corkery was born in the city of Cork and spent his life in or near it. Educated by the Presentation Brothers, he became an elementary schoolteacher in 1898 and, after learning Gaelic, an enthusiastic voluntary worker for the Gaelic League. In 1909 he founded the Cork Dramatic Society, for which he wrote his first play. Soon afterwards he began his only novel, *The Threshold of Quiet*, published in 1917, just a year after his first volume of short stories, *A Munster Twilight*. Although his lameness prevented him from taking an active part in the fighting against the British, his second volume of short stories, *The Hounds of Banba* (1920), served as propaganda. Two fine volumes of literary history and criticism earned him the Professorship of English at University College, Cork, in 1931, a post that he held until his retirement in 1947. Besides two further volumes of short stories, his works include three plays performed at the Abbey Theatre. Frank O'Connor gives a vivid account of his debt to Corkery's teaching and personality in *An Only Child*. "The Stones," a powerful story of primitive superstition, is reprinted from *The Stormy Hills* (1929), while the impressionistic sketch "Children"—almost a prose poem—comes from *Earth Out of Earth* (1939).

The Stones

I. Though John Redney's house was far back in the glen, his straggling farm spread out into the river valley of which the glen itself was, as one might say, a side pocket, narrow and secret. In all its winding length there was no other house: it was even more lonely now than when long years before John Redney had played in it, a companionless child.

When the sudden downpour of rain towards the end of August swept his newly gathered cruach of turf from the inches,[1] leaving him without fuel for the coming year, he knew quite well that all down the valley, and on the heights as well, the farmers were shaking their heads over what had befallen him, were by adding this to that, proverb to proverb, memory to memory, strengthening one another's belief that such disasters did not overtake a man without cause. And the picture he made himself of them so grouped was a pain that almost overwhelmed the pain of his actual loss.

Only two days before, he had finished the ferrying over of the turf from the bogs on the other side of the river. He had thrown it out there loosely, not far from the bank, for, the very next day, he was going to cart it up the glen to the little rise where the Redneys had built their cruach as long as anyone remembered. That very evening he had sent his laboring boy over to Con Jer for the loan of his horse and man for the next day, for the one day only, to help him in drawing the turf from the inches to that traditional ground. Con Jer had answered the boy that he came at a most unfortunate time, that he had never been so busy, that he couldn't think of letting him have even the horse not to mind one of his men as well. He said he was surprised that John Redney would not have thought of that himself. Innocently enough the boy repeated the words as Con Jer had spoken them. And so it was that the next day John Redney hastened down the glen, mounted a hillock at the mouth of it, and scowled at the swirling waters rolling his turf along the valley—good black turf, as firm a sod as he had ever cut, and a whole year's supply of it, and more.

The morning after, as he gazed at the drenched fields

---

[1] *Cruach*, Gaelic for "stack" or "rick." "Turf" is peat. "Inches," low grassy ground by a river, from Gaelic *inis*, "an island."

from which the sudden mountain floods were rapidly disappearing, he could not help recalling the very words the boy had brought back in his mouth from Con Jer, nor how they had set him on fire, maddened him until he had told him angrily that it might be a good thing for Con Jer to go up to Carrigavawring and have a look at his own effigy there. No, the exact words he had used were: "Well, boy, Con Jer's effigy in stone, up there on Carrigavawring, if Con Jer went up and had a look at it—one look"—and there he had stopped. It had been in his mind to say that one glance at it would leave Con Jer with only very little thought indeed for crops or cattle or fences or anything else that concerned this world of living men. This, however, he had not said and perhaps it was better so. The boy had, he was certain, truly reported the words, only half aware of the threat in them; and repeated in that broken uncertain fashion, they had had, it might be, raised more confusion in Con Jer's mind than if they had been made into a frightful story. What did he care! Let them now come together, the farmers of the valley, stick their noses into one another's faces, make out that his turf had not been swept from him without reason—it was all one to him. Con Jer would toss and turn on his pillow for many a night to come, wondering if what the boy had reported was true and, if true, what would come of it.

More and more as he dully stared in front of him the river was reassuming its own true shape. Through the levels of the valley it curved from side to side with the light of the day, although it was a grey day, thick upon its surface, causing the pasture lands on either side to look dark and heavy. If the Nyhans had flung up a bit of a dam where the engineer had told them, there was an end to those sudden floodings; but no, the Nyhans hadn't it in them even to help themselves, when by doing so they would help another. The whole lot of them, the farmers on this side and the other, were against him.

II. It is a stony land. The name of it, Kilclaw, might mean either the Stone Church or the Stony Wood. Nobody now knows which. The woods were felled some hundreds of years ago; but felling the trees had not been sufficient, for, that done, even the roughest kind of tillage was not yet possible until the little patches first marked out for it had been cleared of the largest of the stones embedded in them. The roots of them were found to be tougher than those of the wild ash, the mountain fir, or the oak. Yet removed they were, dragged to the sides of the little fields, however they managed it, crop upon crop of them, year after year, decade after decade, century after century, until the stone mounds that now enclose the little patches of wheat or oats or potatoes take up as much, if not more, of the ground than the croppings within them. The boulders earliest removed were huge, huger than would now appear, for their bases once again are hidden deep in the ground. Halfway up their flanks, sometimes all the way, they are clothed with brown and silvery mosses, or with innumerable layers of the tiniest fern. On top of and around and between them, thousands and thousands of smaller stones have been piled or flung; and these, more exposed to the winds and rain and sunshine, have not clothed themselves at all, remain still unclad, may remain for ever unclad, unsoftened with verdure, bleached-looking, bare and stark. The people of the place fancy they see in them—those moss-clad boulders, those skull-like smaller stones that surmount them, effigies, images of their neighbors, never of themselves. A farmer using the *poirse*[2] of a neighbor as a shortcut for his turf or corn may suddenly behold in some place that he has already passed by some hundreds of times, the rough effigy of one of the dwellers in the valley: if however, he be wise and of good heart he will keep his discovery to himself, for it bodes no one any good, this unexpected revelation of one's image in the stones.

John Redney never had been either wise or of good heart. His mind dwelt too much on things that were abroad in the air, in the darkness, drifting hither and thither. He was a poor lonely creature, living there in that unvisited glen, his the only house within it. His children were scattered far from him, were not writing to him, it was said,

[2] Gaelic, "a narrow lane."

and his wife had become long since a poor sorry drudge to him. Having loosed that word effigy upon the wind, he went uselessly and restlessly strealing about his straggling fields more silent and gloomy than ever. He came to know that Con Jer had laughed at the threat, had said, "And John Redney wants me to mount up to Carrigavawring and have a look at myself! I won't then. I have something else to do." But Redney knew that if that laughter of Con Jer's was loud it was also hollow. He felt quite certain that Con Jer did not laugh in his heart when he laid his head on the pillow in the darkness.

III. At this time arrived one who had long since outgrown the beliefs of the hillsides—the ex-soldier, Jack Lambert, Miles Lambert's good-for-nothing son. He had slaved and tramped his way in England, had been in America, Canada, and Australia—and nowhere had done any good. He had found himself in the Great War, first in France, then in Gallipoli. Again and again he had come back to his father's house and again wandered off from it whither he would. He had been at home this time only a week or so when the news was abroad that he had been seen in Redney's company traversing the most hidden and ill-reputed places at unearthly hours. Even on nights that were stormy and wild and without a glimpse of either moonlight or starlight, the two of them were heard going by. On quieter nights the sounds of the footsteps of the two of them had wakened people from their sleep, had caused them to lift their heads to listen. Johneen Kelleher had been out in his fields before the dawn drawing the stooks together, making them ready for the help that was to come to him as soon as the sun had dried the corn—and those two misguided men he had seen coming down from the stony hills where there were neither houses nor tilled fields nor traffic, and they looked as if they had been abroad the livelong night! Over his story a dozen heads drew into a circle; and one and then another remarked how much Lambert was changing; how he had taken on strange airs, had been found staring intently into this man's haggard, and elsewhere, in a place where he could have had no business, had suddenly raised his head above a mound of stones. Besides they had all noticed how, whenever he chanced to meet them now upon the road, he would look through them as if he knew the very thoughts they were thinking. Yet it was not he they blamed. He they knew was but the empty book into which old Redney was writing all the perversity he had ever indulged in that crabbed brain of his. Larry Condon broke up their discussion with a free gesture. What was Lambert but a common bummer, sponging on Redney, who, fool that he was, God knows he was queer since the day he was born, had been glad to find anyone at all to strike up a friendship with, to drink with, to gossip with; and none of them could deny that Lambert was a man of fine discourse when he had swallowed down a glass or two of good whiskey. They all knew as well as he did, that Lambert gave no credence to those beliefs of theirs. Since they had often defended their beliefs against him, this they could not argue against, whereupon, silenced for the time, they broke the gathering and went through the darkness each to his lonely house. But by the next night some other tidings of the two secret men would have floated into some farmyard or other and another discussion would take place around the hearth. The faces of the two of them, the look of intentness in them, began now to abide in the memory of all who crossed them. Whatever had come to possess them! the people asked one another. Were the two of them determined not to cease their searching until they had discovered the effigies of all the farmers of Kilclaw? Fear spread from house to house along the valley. There was not now a dweller in it who, if he spied the two of them coming towards him along the road, would not turn aside into some farmer's *poirse* to escape the peering of their eyes.

IV. They were an ill-matched pair: Lambert, the ex-soldier brazen-eyed, straight-lipped, withered-skinned, impudent, and with a reckless way of striding along: old Redney, shy and tongue-tied, looking out from under his shaggy brows, his head down, his left hand clenched across the small of his back, his right hand tight and heavy upon the knob of his stick. With quick, uncertain steps, he made forwards as if his secret knowledge was no happy cargo. The neighbors would see him hobbling along with Lambert, always a little in the rear. They would see him stop up, his stick directed across a valley or along the flank of a mountain while Lambert's eyes searched the distance indicated; or Lambert they would find looking back over his shoulder waiting for the other as he clambered clumsily over those fences of loose stones. And the same anxiety arose again and again:

"Are they burying the whole countryside of us?"

"And what will they gain by it?"

"Nothing except the pacifying of their own wicked minds."

" 'Tis a frightful thing for a man to know that he is already in the stone, that he is there to be seen for all time. If you woke up in the dead of the night, a wild night or a night of hard frost, you wouldn't like to picture it. You'd feel the frost in your shoulder bones."

But those who gathered of a night time to Con Jer's were a quiet lot; Lambert and Redney might by dint of searching come on the images of the whole countryside and they would not lift an arm to prevent it. The younger men who met after the day in Dan Owen's were different. It was Pat Early, whose shoulder blow would fell a bullock, determined for that group what they should do.

The next day they loitered around the tumbledown cabin where their one smith kept his forge. Into its smoky background they retired, all of them except Pat Early himself, when they discovered that Lambert was coming along the road. From within they heard the approaching footsteps: they then heard Pat Early's voice: "Lambert," he said, with a rasping tone, "Come over here."

They heard the footsteps cease. Pat's voice they heard again:

"Come over here. I have a word to say to you."

They could now see Lambert in the brightness of the doorway, his back almost towards them:

"Well?" he said.

"Did you hear Pat Nyhan is after dying on them?"

"I didn't: where would I hear it?"

Though he answered glibly enough, those within thought they saw him start when Pat flung the unexpected question at him.

"If you knew he was going to meet his end, sudden, and without preparation, you might have warned him: 'twould be a neighborly act."

They expected Lambert to deny, if only for safety's sake, any foreknowledge of Pat Nyhan's death; but the words they heard were:

"Is this a place for neighborly acts?"

His next word then they felt would be either of old Redney's cruach of turf that the August flood had swept down the valley or else of the Nyhans' failure to build the rampart which would forever save the levels from the swollen river. Pat Early, however, gave him no time: he blazed out:

"Why don't you answer the question I put to you?"

"Question!"

"Did you know—did you know that something was in store for Pat Nyhan, some misfortune or other?"

"Two nights ago," he answered after a slight pause and quite in a low voice, "John Redney showed me him in the stone."

They grew cold to hear him. And he had said the words in a way that showed that himself was no longer a mocker. Pat Early cried out quickly and with great strength and warmth, to their great relief:

" 'Tis a lie!"

Lambert, however, who had turned to go, was not disturbed either by the words or the force in them; he looked back and said in the same low voice:

"If he showed—the sight to me he can show it to you, that is if you care to see it, now the man's dead. Some people mightn't like to."

The listeners gathered out noiselessly from the shelter of the forge, all of them; they feared that Pat Early was shaken, but again sturdily he answered:

"See what? A couple of stones! Do you think I believe old Redney has power over us?"

"But you'd face it?"

"I'd face a couple of stones anyhow."

"We'd all do that," John Morian added.

"By day or night?"

" 'Tis equal."

"Very well; I'll tell himself."

V. It was now the end of November. The night, it seemed, could not hold any more stars, nor the air any more cold. Con Jer's son, Tadhg, was one of the whispering group. Others were Pat Early, his brother-in-law, Michael Glynn, the smith's son, Larry Mehigan, and the teacher's son, Jim Carey, who had ventured without his father's knowledge. Morian was with them also. Larry Mehigan was delicate: the piercing cold had urged to rapid walking, and they had mounted Knockanuller at one spurt before they were suddenly aware of his gasping, of his effort to keep up with them:

"Are we going too fast?" Michael Glynn said.

"I'll be all right in a minute," Larry answered; but immediately he had to turn aside doubled up in a fit of coughing.

" 'Twas the cold made us hurry: 'twas a queer thing for us to do."

"But 'tisn't good to be stopping here; that's the devil of a wind for him."

"There's shelter beyond."

" 'Tis more than twenty years since I was up in these places."

"Who'd come up here? What business would you have?"

"We'll be going on now."

"How far up he came to find poor Pat Nyhan's image."

They thought of him rigid in his bed.

" 'Tis a frightful night to be dead on."

They did not laugh. Another time they would have done so at such awkward words, but dimly in the starlight they individually spied out shoulders of whitish rock and boulders that looked like massive, ancient, long-weathered skulls. The little narrow path they were on was bordered by some of those immemorial pilings of stones, large and small. The mounds kept the wind from them, but the open spaces of the bogland would have been more welcome to them. "Look, they're waiting for us."

Sitting in the shelter of an upright slab of rock they saw the two figures; Redney's rigid grasp of the knob of his stick they noticed especially.

"Are ye waiting long?" Pat Early said, casually, he hoped.

"Mind ye," old Redney answered, " 'tisn't by my wish ye're up here at all; far from it."

Pat Early thought he wished to put them off. "If you can show us what Lambert said, 'tis right you should."

"I can show ye that all right, since ye wish it."

They all began to move forward. In the dim light the round water-worn stones in the *poirse* began to roll under their feet. Pat Early said:

"I see we would have done right to have our spectacles with us to see it."

Only after a few moments the old man understood the words. He then said, calmly and coldly:

"There'll be light enough where 'tis. The moon's there already."

As he spoke he raised his stick towards the brow of the hill, which was gapped and rugged with boulders and rocks. There the sky was becoming more and more luminous and the stars were gone. The moon they understood to be away towards the right. When they pierced through among the boulders they saw it suddenly, rising in splendor. Slabs of blanched stone, pillar stones of shadow, gaps of darkness —sharp-edged, were all about them in confusion. They felt astray.

"There's Pat Nyhan. The Nyhans were up here always."

Even if, with his stick, he had not pointed out the particular group of stones in that long-deserted mountain farm ground they would have known it for Pat Nyhan. It was set up in a listening attitude, Pat Nyhan's attitude; just so he used to listen, his left ear advanced, for he had been for years a little hard of hearing. They recollected too having heard that the Nyhans had come from this place. As they looked they could swear they saw the stones stir. One or two of the men fidgeted, looking around. Others stared at the stones in a dull sort of way. They were conscious of a desire to strike old Redney or the ex-soldier, yet conscious also that that was not in the bargain. The ex-soldier stood a little apart from them, neither looking nor speaking. Suddenly Larry Mehigan with that burred and resonant consumptive's voice of his said:

"Up here too the Redneys were always. I heard tell of them."

Their eyes swept from the image and fastened on Redney. He turned his back on them as if he would set off for home. Indistinctly he grumbled at them over his shoulder:

"Ye're after seeing what ye came to see."

He put out his left hand and Lambert came and folded it in his arm, protectingly. They then began to move off, the two of them. The others hesitated. As soon as he had said the words, Mehigan had been taken with a fit of coughing. The stone desert was ringing with the sound of it, and the dogs in distant farm yards had awakened and were answering back. But the dogs' barking Larry heard no more than he heard his own coughing: his excited brain was working all the time; he would blurt out, not giving the spasm time to exhaust itself:

" 'Tis true what I say. Up here they were always, the Redneys."

"Somehow that's true. I heard it said; 'twas said," Morian gave his opinion earnestly.

They came closer together. They were thankful to Larry. His words excused them from looking around any more at the stone image, listening in the way that a tall deaf old man would listen.

Larry's cough had ceased, and they began to hasten after the two others. When they got within a short distance of them they saw old Redney stop up rather suddenly and raising his stick, point out something to Lambert. A word however he did not speak. The whole of them stopped up where they were. Individually fright fell on them. They did not want to know what the old man was pointing at. Lambert seemed vexed and impatient. They heard his whisper: "Come on, come on." But old Redney seemed not to be able to move nor to change his attitude. The moon poured its light on them all: old Redney with his stick stretched out, Lambert a little apart from him, waiting impatiently, and the other group still farther apart, puzzled and anxious. The cold was intense, and the sparkling earth was as silent as the starry heavens. The distant farm dogs had put their noses again upon the ground. It was their own stillness made the men aware of the benumbed stillness about them.

"Come on, come on," they again heard whispered very hoarsely, and Lambert made a stride towards the petrified figure of his friend. As he neared it they saw the stick fall clattering to the frozen ground, and the next moment they saw Redney fling himself helplessly into Lambert's arms, a thin whimpering wail breaking from him into the silence.

"Look!" the boy Jim Carey cried; and right beyond the two clutching figures they saw old Redney in stone! The image was dark against the sky and immensely larger than the poor stricken thing in the ex-soldier's arms. It seemed to mock him, the head of it stretched out in unrelenting eagerness. One glance they gave it and without a word broke from the place.

Jack Lambert a few days afterwards was seen driving from the place, no one knew whither. Old Redney was missed. His poor bedraggled wife they would see driving the cows of a night time to the inches. She kept her thoughts to herself. Only after weeks and weeks the men of the valley learned her husband had taken to his bed, awaiting his doom. In tongue-tied silence still he awaits it, his eyes staring out straight before him.

Children

"No, no; you'll not be the grandmother. I'll be the grandmother. Won't I, Pidgie?"

"Well, I'll be the woman with the green shawl so," Maggie said.

"That was his wife."

"Whose wife?"

"The man who was dead. Who else?"

"And what'll I be, Pidgie?"

"Do ye remember the old one was taking her snuff? 'The Will of God be done,' she was saying. Do you remember her?"

"But what about me? I have no one."

Pidgie settled that, too: "You'll be the old man who had his handkerchief in his hat—see now?"

"But what'll I be saying? I don't know what he was saying."

"That's always the way with you. Because you always have someone by the tail. You don't know nothing. You must be holding out the hat in your left hand and catching hold of everyone with the other hand, and saying: 'When is the funeral leaving, ma'am? Oh my!'"

"That's easy, anyway. 'When is the funeral—'"

"No, that's not it. Look up in their faces. Open your eyes and look up at them. Wider. Wider, can't you? Begging like. 'When is the funeral leaving—?'"

"And what about the one had her hair down, and her blouse all open? And her face! Did you see her face? All *white*!"

"That was his sister. You don't know nothing either."

"And what was she saying—the white one?"

"I know," said Mamie, "Um, um, blimely end."

"You fool!"

"That's what I heard, anyway."

"Um, um, blimely end."

They laughed at Pidgie's mimicry.

"What was it so? You don't know yourself and you're laughing at me."

"'Untimely end,' she was saying. What else?"

"And what's untimely end?"

"Because she starved him."

"Who?"

"His wife. The one with the green shawl."

"Oh!"

"And why didn't she answer her?"

"Didn't you see the old one with the snuff holding her back? Wasn't chalky-face only looking for fight? What else?"

"And what made her starve him?"

"She didn't starve him at all, you goose. Starve him, I'd like to see her. Sure they always say that."

"God, he was looking awful. I'll never go to a wake again."

"You said that the last time, too."

"Well, I won't. You'd think he was listening. Didn't I see him all night!"

" 'And hale and sound you left your mother's house.' "

"What's that?"

"That's what she was saying. 'Untimely end. Untimely end. And hale and sound—' "

"We'll begin now. I'll be the old granny."

"Well, fool about. 'Is it my poor man is dead or the little one? Is it my—' "

"You, now, Maggie."

" 'Untimely end. Untimely end; and safe and—' "

"Liz, you now."

"What is it? Oh, I know. 'When is the funeral leaving, ma'am? Oh my! When—' "

"Now, Andy; you stretch out."

"I won't."

"You'll have to. How can we have a wake without a corpse? Now, no laughing out of ye. No one is to laugh. Only very mournful. Mournful. You're to be crying. Begin now."

From the next room came their mother's voice: "Be quiet, I'm telling ye. Is it rouse up the child ye will?"

She was about to go in to them when she was aware that Mrs. Deeling from the floor above had entered. She had stolen in quietly, as if she had come from a quiet place. Mrs. Buttimer, speaking in a low voice, said:

"How is she today?"

"Grand then. Grand. As happy as Larry."

"You have your hands full with her. She can't hold out much longer. God knows they're a great trial when they're so old."

"Wisha, there's no one hastening her out. I'll miss her when she goes, for all her figaries."

"Sure you'd miss an old chair."

"I don't mind at all, only when I wake up in the night and not a stir in the house."

Mrs. Buttimer tapped at the door of the room where the chidren were having their wake. The voices quieted for the moment.

"In the middle of the night when there's not a stir, only herself gabbling away. To her little brother she do be speaking, and he dead this seventy years! 'Don't go near that one. She'll pick you.' "

"Who'd pick him?"

"Some old goose they had. And you know she says it like this: 'Johnny! Johnny! Keep away. Keep away, Johnny. She'll pick you.' God knows, Mrs. B., you'd take your oath she had him by the hand."

"My!"

"Listening to her and I trying not to listen—that's the way with me. And I after hearing it all a hundred times over. And the whole world asleep outside. And the whole house."

" 'Twould be worse if the poor old thing was in pain."

"That's true, too."

" 'Tis thankful to God you ought to be."

"And I am; but 'tis cruel lonesome, I'm telling you; and some night I'll break down."

"You won't then."

"What was she doing and I coming down, do you think? Picking flowers!"

"My!"

"To hear the little old voice of her! Like a little bird. 'Here's a lovely one, now. Wait, now, and I'll get them red primroses. Wait now.' "

"Isn't it good to have her so kind."

"Do you know what I said to her? 'If it's flowers you want, you'll have to travel a mile or two from Coley's Lane, ma'am.' She only looked at me. You'd think she never heard the name!"

"Wonderful. Do you know, Mrs. Deeling, I never spent a whole day in the country. Would you believe that? A real day: waking up, and eating, and lying down. Never."

"No? Oh, when I married himself first I used often go

down to the old woman's house in Caherlag. That's why I'm lonesome when she begins to ramble about it. It comes back to me: the little stream, the little donkey, the blue-bells—"

In spite of the closed door the children's voices came into the room. Mrs. Buttimer said:

"Wouldn't they annoy you. They'll rouse him on me."

"They won't, then. I'm watching him. Look, he's laughing. 'Tis something in his mind."

"I often see him laughing like that."

The voices in the other room were strengthening:

"Untimely end!" "Untimely end!" "When is the funeral leaving, ma'am? Oh my!" "You starved him."

Mrs. Buttimer rose and tapped a little viciously at the door; and again the wailing hubbub quieted. Mrs. Deeling was bending above the cradle; she said, raising her head:

"Laughing away for himself. And look at the fist of him! 'Tisn't picking flowers he is, I tell you. But I'd better go up and see what the child above is at."

She turned to Mrs. Buttimer.

"Do you know, 'tis queer, when you think of it. That poor child of mine—if ever a woman had to struggle and to fight her way through the trials and troubles of this world, 'twas that poor thing above in the bed. Sickness and sorrow and death and hunger. And there she is now, picking flowers for herself in the fields!"

" 'Tis blest you are. Do you hear them inside?"

Mrs. Deeling said:

"If she's after dropping off I'll come down again."

"Do then."

She went out quietly, as if going to a quiet place; and Mrs. Buttimer, her head a little on one side, looked down on the face of the child, sturdy-looking in his dreams. She looked down on it long and steadily, thinking of nothing, too happy to think of anything. In spite of the hubbub in the next room, the whole house, the whole world, to her seemed to be quite still.

SEUMAS O'KELLY
1881–1918

Seumas O'Kelly was born and educated in the small town of Loughrea, County Galway. After graduating from secondary school, he began to write for a local paper; at 22 he became editor of another in Skibbereen, County Cork. Soon he moved to an editorship nearer Dublin and made contact with writers and future revolutionaries in the capital. An attack of rheumatic fever in 1911 weakened his heart. After having to give up two editorial positions in Dublin because of poor health, he returned to his less demanding post with *The Leinster Leader*. In 1918 O'Kelly replaced the Irish leader Arthur Griffith, then in jail, as editor of the Sinn Fein newspaper *Nationality* in Dublin. British soldiers and their girls, celebrating the Armistice, staged a riot at the *Nationality* office, causing O'Kelly to have a fatal heart attack. Before his premature death, O'Kelly had had four plays performed at the Abbey Theatre, had published an impressive novel, *The Lady of Deerpark* (1917), and had written enough short stories to fill five volumes, three of them posthumous. His best story, "The Weaver's Grave," too long for this collection, is in *The Portable Irish Reader*. "The Shoemaker," reprinted from *Waysiders* (1917), is not, properly speaking, a short story but a series of anecdotes. The last and longest of these, about Gobstown—that "miserable place" which "lay under the blight of a good landlord"—shows the Irish gifts for paradox and tall tales at their best. Gentlest of satirists, gentlest of realists, O'Kelly possessed unique quality.

The Shoemaker

I. Obeying a domestic mandate, Padna wrapped a pair of boots in paper and took them to the shoemaker, who operated behind a window in a quiet street.

The shoemaker seemed to Padna a melancholy man. He wore great spectacles, had a white patch of forehead, and two great bumps upon it. Padna concluded that the bumps had been encouraged by the professional necessity of constantly hanging his head over his knees.

The shoemaker invited Padna to sit down in his workshop, which he did. Padna thought it must be very dreary to sit there all day among old and new boots, pieces of leather, boxes of brass eyelets, awls, knives, and punchers. No wonder the shoemaker was a melancholy-looking man.

Padna maintained a discreet silence while the shoemaker turned his critical glasses upon the boots he had brought him for repair. Suddenly the great glasses were turned upon Padna himself, and the shoemaker addressed him in a voice of amazing pleasantness.

"When did you hear the cuckoo?" he asked.

Padna, at first startled, pulled himself together. "Yesterday," he replied.

"Did you look at the sole of your boot when you heard him?" the shoemaker asked.

"No," said Padna.

"Well," said the shoemaker, "whenever you hear the cuckoo for the first time in the spring, always look at the sole of your right boot. There you will find a hair. And that hair win tell you the kind of a wife you will get."

The shoemaker picked a long hair from the sole of Padna's boot and held it up in the light of the window.

"You'll be married to a brown-haired woman," he said. Padna looked at the hair without fear, favor, or affection, and said nothing.

The shoemaker took his place on his bench, selected a half-made shoe, got it between his knees, and began to stitch with great gusto. Padna admired the skilful manner in which he made the holes with his awl and drew the wax-end with rapid strokes. Padna abandoned the impression that the shoemaker was a melancholy man. He thought he never sat near a man so optimistic, so mentally emancipated, so detached from the indignity of his occupation.

"These are very small shoes you are stitching," said Padna, making himself agreeable.

"They are," said the shoemaker. "But do you know who makes the smallest shoes in the world? You don't? Well, well!—The smallest shoes in the world are made by the clurichaun, a cousin of the leprechaun. If you creep up on the west side of a fairy fort after the sun has set and put your ear to the grass, you'll hear the tapping of his hammer. And do you know who the clurichaun makes shoes for? You don't? Well, well!—He makes shoes for the swallows. Oh, indeed they do, swallows wear shoes. Twice a year swallows wear shoes. They wear them in the spring, and again at the fall of the year. They wear them when they fly from one world to another. And they cross the Dead Sea. Did you ever hear tell of the Dead Sea? You did. Well, well!—No bird ever yet flew across the Dead Sea. Any of them that tried it dropped and sank like a stone. So the swallows, when they come to the Dead Sea, get down on the bank, and there the clurichauns have millions of shoes waiting for them. The swallows put on their shoes and walk across the Dead Sea, stepping on bright yellow and black stepping-stones that shine across the water like a lovely carpet. And do you know what the stepping-stones across the Dead Sea are? They are the backs of sleeping frogs. And when the swallows are all safe across, the frogs waken up and begin to sing, for then it is known the summer will come. Did you never hear that before? No? Well, well!"

A cat, friendly as the shoemaker himself, leapt on to Padna's lap. The shoemaker shifted the shoe he was stitching between his knees, putting the heel where the toe had been.

"Do you know where they first discovered electricity?" he asked.

"In America," Padna ventured.

"No. In the back of a cat. He was a big buck Chinese cat. Every hair on him was seven inches long, in color gold, and thick as copper wire. He was the only cat who ever looked on the face of the Empress of China without blinking, and when the Emperor saw that, he called him over and stroked him on the back. No sooner did the Emperor of China stroke the buck cat than back he fell on his plush throne, as dead as his ancestors. So they called in seven wise doctors from the seven wise countries of the East to find out what it was killed the Emperor. And after seven years they discovered electricity in the backbone of the cat, and signed a proclamation that it was from the shock of it the Emperor had died. When the Americans read the proclamation, they decided to do whatever killing had to be done as the cat had killed the Emperor of China. The Americans are like that—all for imitating royal families."

"Has this cat any electricity in her?" Padna asked.

"She has," said the shoemaker, drawing his wax-end. "But she's a civilized cat, not like the vulgar fellow in China, and civilized cats hide their electricity much as civilized people hide their feelings. But one day last summer I saw her showing her electricity. A monstrous black rat came prowling from the brewery, a bald patch on his head and a piece missing from his left haunch. To see that fellow coming up out of a gullet and stepping up the street, in the middle of the broad daylight, you'd imagine he was the county inspector of police."

"And did she fight the rat?" Padna asked.

The shoemaker put the shoe on a last and began to tap with his hammer. "She did fight him," he said. "She went out to him twirling her moustaches. He lay down on his back. She lay down on her side. They kept grinning and sparring at each other like that for half an hour. At last the monstrous rat got up in a fury and come at her, the fangs stripped. She swung round the yard, doubled in two, making circles like a Catherine wheel about him until the old blackguard was mesmerized. And if you were to see the bulk of her tail then, all her electricity gone into it! She caught him with a blow of it under the jowl, and he fell in a swoon. She stood over him, her back like the bend of a hoop, the tail beating about her, and a smile on the side of her face. And that was the end of the monstrous brewery rat."

Padna said nothing, but put the cat down on the floor. When she made some effort to regain his lap, he surreptitiously suggested, with the tip of his boot, that their entente was at an end.

A few drops of rain beat on the window, and the shoemaker looked up, his glasses shining, the bumps on his forehead gleaming. "Do you know the reason God makes it rain?" he asked.

Padna, who had been listening to the conversation of two farmers the evening before, replied, "I do. To make turnips grow."

"Nonsense!" said the shoemaker, reaching out for an awl. "God makes it rain to remind us of the Deluge. And I don't mean the Deluge that was at all at all. I mean the Deluge that is to come. The world will be drowned again. The belly-band of the sky will give, for that's what the rainbow is, and it only made of colors. Did you never know until now what the rainbow was? No? Well, well!—As I was saying, when the belly-band of the sky bursts the Deluge will come. In one minute all the valleys of the earth will be filled up. In the second minute the mountains will be topped. In the third minute the sky will be emptied and its skin gone, and the earth will be no more. There will be no ark, no Noah, and no dove. There will be nothing only one great waste of grey water and in the middle of it one green leaf. The green leaf will be a sign that God has gone to sleep, the trouble of the world banished from His mind. So whenever it rains remember my words."

Padna said he would, and then went home.

II. When Padna called on the shoemaker for the boots that had been left for repair, they were almost ready. The tips only remained to be put on the heels. Padna sat down in the little workshop, and under the agreeable influence of the place he made bold to ask the shoemaker if he had grown up to be a shoemaker as the geranium had grown up to be a geranium in its pot on the window.

"What!" exclaimed the shoemaker. "Did you never hear tell that I was found in the country under a head of cabbage? No! Well, well! What do they talk to you at home about at all?"

"The most thing they tell me," said Padna, "is to go to bed and get up in the morning. What is the name of the place in the country where they found you?"

"Gobstown," said the shoemaker. "It was the most miserable place within the ring of Ireland. It lay under the blight of a good landlord, no better. That was its misfortune, and especially my misfortune. If the Gobstown landlord was not such a good landlord it's driving on the box of an empire I would be today instead of whacking tips on the heels of your boots. How could that be? I'll tell you that.

"In Gobstown the tenants rose up and demanded a reduction of rent; the good landlord gave it to them. They rose up again and demanded another reduction of rent; he gave it to them. They went on rising up, asking reductions, and getting them, until there was no rent left for anyone to reduce. The landlord was as good and as poor as our best.

"And while all this was going on Gobstown was surrounded by estates where there were the most ferocious landlords—rack-renting, absentee, evicting landlords, landlords as wild as tigers. And these tiger landlords were leaping at their tenants and their tenants slashing back at them as best they could. Nothing, my dear, but blood and the music of grapeshot and shouts in the night from the jungle. In Gobstown we had to sit down and look on, pretending, moryah, that we were as happy as the day was long.

"Not a scalp was ever brought into Gobstown. No man of us ever went out on an adventure which might bring him home again through the mouth of the county jail. Not a secret enterprise that might become a great public excitement was ever hatched, not to speak of being launched. We had not as much as a fife-and-drum band. We did not know how to play a tin whistle or beat upon the tintinnabulum. We never waved a green flag. We had not a branch of any kind of a league. We had no men of skill to draft a resolution, indite a threatening letter, draw a coffin, skull, and crossbones, fight a policeman, or even make a speech. We were never a delegate at a convention, an envoy to America, a divisional executive, a deputation, or a demonstration. We were nothing. We wilted under the blight of our good landlord as the green stalk wilts under the frost of the black night—Hand me that knife. The one with the wooden handle.

"In desperation we used rouse ourselves and march into the demonstrations on other estates. We were a small and an unknown tribe. The Gobstown contingent always brought up the rear of the procession—a gawky, straggling, bad-stepping, hay-foot, straw-foot lot! The onlookers hardly glanced at us. We stood for nothing. We had no name. Once we rigged up a banner with the words on it, 'Gobstown to the Front!' but still we were put to the back, and when we walked through this town, the servant girls came out of their kitchens, laughed at us, and called out, 'Gobstown to the Back of the Front!'

"The fighting men came to us, took us aside, and asked us what we were doing in Gobstown. We had no case to make. We offered to bring forward our good landlord as a shining example, to lead our lamb forward in order that he might show up the man-eaters on the other estates. The organizers were all hostile. They would not allow us into the processions any more. If we could bring forward some sort of roaring black devil, we would be more than welcome. Shining examples were not in favor. We were sent home in disgrace and broke up. As the preachers say, our last state was worse than our first.

"We became sullen and drowsy and fat and dull. We got to hate the sight of each other, so much so that we began to pay our rents behind each other's backs, at first the reduced rents, then, gale day by gale day, we got back to the original rent, and kept on paying it. Our good landlord took his rents and said nothing. Gobstown became the most accursed place in all Ireland. Brother could not trust brother. And there were our neighbors going from one sensation to

another. They were as lively as trout, as enterprising as
goats, as intelligent as Corkmen. They were thin and eager
and good-tempered. They ate very little, drank water, slept
well, men with hard knuckles, clean bowels, and pale eyes.
Anything they hit went down. They were always ready to
go to the gallows for each other.

"I had a famous cousin on one of these estates, and I
suppose you heard of him? You didn't! What are they
teaching you at school at all? Latin grammar? Well, well!
—My cousin was a clumsy fellow with only a little of middling kind of brains, but a bit of fight in him. Yet look at
the way he got on, and look at me, shedding little boys like
yourself! I was born under a lucky star but my cousin was
born under a lucky landlord—a ferocious fellow who got
into a garret in London and kept roaring across at Ireland
for more and more blood. Every time I thought of that old
skin of a man howling in the London garret I said to myself, 'He'll be the making of my cousin.' And so, indeed,
he was. Three agents were brought down on my cousin's
estate. State trials were running like great plays in the
courthouse. Blood was always up. They had six fife-and-
drum bands and one brass band. They had green and gold
banners with harps and streamers, and mottoes in yellow
lettering, that took four hardy men to carry on a windy
day. The heads of the Peelers were hardly ever out of their
helmets. The resident magistrate rose one day in the bosom
of his family, his eyes closed, to say grace before meals,
and from dint of habit he was chanting the Riot Act over
the table until his wife flew at him with, 'How dare you,
George! The mutton is quite all right!' Little boys no bigger than yourself walking along the roads to school in that
splendid estate could jump up on the ditch and make good
speeches.

"My cousin's minute books—he was secretary of everything—would stock a bookshop, and were noted for beautiful expressions. He was the author of ten styles of resolution construction. An enemy christened him Resolving
Kavanagh. Every time he resolved to stand where he always stood he resolved. Everybody put up at his house. He
was seen in more torchlight processions than Bryan

O'Lynn. A room in his house was decorated in a beautiful scheme of illuminated addresses with border designs from the Book of Kells. The homes of the people were full of the stumps of burned-down candles, the remains of great illuminations for my cousin whenever he came out of prison. I tell you no lie when I say that that clumsy cousin of mine became clever and polished, all through pure practice. He had the best of tutors. The skin of a landlord in the London garret, his agents, their understrappers, removable magistrates, judges, Crown solicitors, county inspectors of police, sergeants, constables, secret service men—all drove him from fame to fame until in the end they chased him out the only gap that was left open to the like of him—the English Parliament. Think of the streak of that man's career! And there was I, a man of capacity and brains, born with the golden spoon of talent in my mouth, dead to the world in Gobstown! I was rotting like a turnip under the best and the most accursed of landlords. In the end I could not stand it—no man of spirit could.

"One day I took down my ashplant, spat on my fist, and set out for my cousin's place. He gave me no welcome. I informed him as to how the land lay in Gobstown. I said we must be allowed to make a name for ourselves as the producers of a shining example of a landlord. My cousin let his head lie over a little to one side and then said, 'In this country shining examples ought only be used with the greatest moderation.' He looked out through the window and after some time said, 'That Gobstown landlord is the most dangerous lunatic in all Ireland.' 'How is that?' said I. 'Because,' said my famous cousin, 'he has a perfect heart.' He put his head over to the other side, looked at me and said, 'If Gobstown does not do something, he may be the means of destroying us all.' 'How?' said I. 'He may become contagious,' said my cousin. 'Only think of his example being followed and Ireland turned into one vast tract of Gobstowns! Would not any fate at all be better than that?' I who knew said, 'God knows it would.'

"My cousin sighed heavily. He turned from me, leaving me standing there in the kitchen, and I saw him moving with a ladder to the loft overhead. This he mounted and disappeared in the black rafters. I could hear him fumbling somewhere under the thatch. Presently down he came the ladder, a gun in one hand, and a fistful of cartridges in the other. He spoke no word, and I spoke no word. He came to me and put the gun in my hand and the handful of cartridges in my pocket. He walked to the fire and stood there with his back turned. I stood where I was, a Gobstown mohawk, with the gun in my hand. At last I said, 'What is this for?' and grounded the gun a little on the floor. My cousin did not answer at once. At last he said without moving, 'It's for stirring your tea, what else?' I looked at him and he remained as he was and, the sweat breaking out on the back of my neck, I left the house and made across the fields for home, the cartridges rattling in my pocket every ditch I leapt, the feel of the gun in my hand becoming more familiar and more friendly.

"At last I came to the summit of a little green hill overlooking Gobstown, and there I sat me down. The sight of Gobstown rose the gorge in me. Nothing came out of it but weak puffs of turf smoke from the chimneys—little pallid thin streaks that wobbled in the wind. There, says I, is the height of Gobstown. And no sound came up out of it except the cackle of geese, and then the bawl of an old ass in the bog. There, says I, is the depth of Gobstown. And rising up from the green hill I made up my mind to save Ireland from Gobstown even if I lost my own soul. I would put a bullet in the perfect heart of our good landlord.

"That night I lay behind a certain ditch. The moon shone on the nape of my neck. The good landlord passed me by on the road, he and his good wife, chattering and happy as a pair of lovers. I groped for the gun. The queerest feeling came over me. I did not even raise it. I had no nerve. I quaked behind the ditch. His footsteps and her footsteps were like cracks of this hammer on my head. I knew, then, in that minute, that I was no good, and that Gobstown was for ever lost—What happened me? Who can say that for certain? Many a time have I wondered what came over me in that hour. I can only guess.—Nobody belonging to me had ever been rack-rented. I had never seen any of my own people evicted. No great judge of assize had ever looked down on me from his bench to the dock and addressed to me stern words. I had never heard the clang behind me of a prison door. No royal hand of an Irish constabularyman had ever brought a baton down on my head. No carbine had ever butted the soft places of my body. I had no scars that might redden with memories. The memories I had and that might give me courage were not memories of landlords. There was nothing of anger in my heart for the Gobstown landlord, and he went by. I dragged my legs out of the ditch and drowned my cousin's gun in a boghole. After it I dropped in the handful of cartridges. They made a little gurgle in the dark water like blood in a shot man's throat. And that same night I went home, put a few things in a red handkerchief, and stole out of Gobstown like a thief. I walked along the roads until I came to this town, learned my trade, became a respectable shoemaker, and—tell your mother I never use anything only the best leather. There are your boots, Padna, tips and all—half-a-crown. Thanks, and well wear!"

PÁDRAIC Ó CONAIRE

1881–1928

Pádraic Ó Conaire (Patrick Conroy) was born in Galway City and first educated at the Presentation Convent there. His parents were Gaelic speakers, and, when he was orphaned at the age of eleven, he went to live with an uncle who was a well-to-do shopkeeper at Garaffin, Rosmuc, County Galway, in the heart of a Gaelic-speaking area. Pádraic attended the local national school for four years. Thereafter he went as a boarder to Rockwell College, County Tipperary, and thence to Blackrock College, Dublin—both secondary schools. In 1899 he obtained a minor civil service post in London. Life in that city made him cosmopolitan in outlook and yet intensified his nationalism: he became a very successful teacher in Gaelic League classes and began to write in Gaelic about 1905. In 1914, soon after the outbreak of World War I, he resigned from the British Civil Service and returned to Ireland, traveling all over the country with a donkey and cart. He was a small man but physically very strong, a heavy drinker, a spendthrift, and doubtless attractive to women: at any rate a professor's wife left her husband for him. During his later years he taught Gaelic in Galway City, but died in Dublin while on a visit. In spite of his defiance of convention, his countrymen took him to their hearts, and a charmingly human statue of him stands—or rather, sits—in the principal square of his native city. Ó Conaire was perhaps the most prolific and certainly the most modern of Gaelic fiction writers in his time, well aware of what had been done in other countries by writers like Chekhov and Conrad. He wrote plays, novels, essays, critical articles, textbooks, children's stories, but above all he was a master of the short story. The one given here was first published in 1913, though the translation used is one that appeared in *Irish Writing, No. 33* (1955). Most of Ó Conaire still remains untranslated, for apparently only three of his books have yet found their way into English: *The Land of Wonders, The Woman at the Window,* and *Field and Fair: Travels with a Donkey in Ireland.*

The Woman on Whom God Laid His Hand

A neater boat than the *Little Brown Girl* wasn't to be seen in the bay of Galway, and since she was being offered for sale by the merchant who owned her, Patrick O'Nee thought she would be a good dowry for his daughter, if he could get her reasonably cheap. But Anthony O'Malley, the young man who was about to marry his daughter, said they ought to give the boat a trial before buying her, to see if she were as good as her report. The old man thought that that was good advice, and he himself, his son James, and O'Malley went out to spend a night on the waves fishing to test her.

Kate, the girl who was to be married, accompanied them to the quay to see them off, and she stood a long time on the hillock watching the fleet of fishing boats going west over the bay with a following wind. On her return home, it was already early evening, and her mother had supper prepared. The table was laid, a cake was cooling on the windowsill, and the kettle was singing merrily. The two women sat down at the table, and they looked out from time to time at the boats that were like a flock of nuns taking the air on the lawn of their convent.

It was very calm. The birds that had been lively and singing an hour before were becoming listless. Sleep was stealing over them. But the young woman remained at the window until the boats disappeared from her view in the darkness, until a fine star that had the light of a new moon rose in the west.

The old woman by the fireside gave a sigh.

"What ails you, Mother?" said Kate, going over to her.

"I'll be lonely without you, dear."

"Won't you have my father, not to mention James?"

"It's not long James will stay with us. The young people want nothing now but to be off."

"But isn't it often you set us laughing, telling us how you eloped with father despite your people," said Kate.

"And look at the life I've had since!"

It wasn't often that her mother complained, and it troubled the young woman that her thoughts were on such things. She knew well that her mother's people had opposed her marriage so strongly that they never spoke to her since! Her mother had been well brought up and educated, but she had accepted the life that her husband gave her.

"But I'm not slipping away from you," said Kate. "You'll see me often. I won't be more than twenty miles distant from you."

"I know that, asthore," said the mother, "but for some time now I've been thinking that the curse my father put on me has followed me. Look how they all left me—and you, yourself, now. It seems to me that they went off because I am a little strange from time to time—what do they say?—to the seventh generation!"

Kate took hold of her mother's hand and began to stroke it lovingly. She knew well what was in the old woman's mind. She knew that there had been scarcely a generation of her mother's people without someone that was a little strange, and some of them were so strange that they had to be put under lock and key. But the people of the place were not aware of that, for her mother belonged to another county, and if the person had heard of it, no mention had ever been made of it.

"You shouldn't say that," said Kate nervously.

"But it's the truth, Kate," said the old woman.

Night fell. Kate lit the lamp. She put a blind on the window.

"The wind is rising; there is danger on the sea tonight," said the old woman.

The daughter removed the blind from the window. The

moon was in the sky and the sea was still. You'd think that nobody would ever be drowned in it.

"Look out, Mother," said Kate, "there isn't a breath of wind. You're becoming sleepy."

They were not expecting the boat till dawn.

"I'll stay here till morning," said the old woman, musing.

"Isn't it a lot of people," said she, "that have been drowned from this place since I came to live here? Patrick Pat was drowned, and his crew, on a moonlight night like this last year, and Michileen Peig Beg was drowned, and his sister, the year before last, and the year before last—or was it three years ago?—the people from the island were drowned."

Her mother rambled on at the fire, but her talk did not upset her daughter. Two better boatmen than her father and O'Malley were not to be found in the port.

"Come over to me," said the old woman suddenly.

She went over to her. The old woman caught hold of her two hands, and looked into her eyes.

"Kate, tell me the truth," said she, "if one or two of the boat's company are to be drowned tonight, who would you prefer to be saved?" "For the love of God, Mother, stop talking like that," said Kate, in torment, and she loosened the tight grip her mother had of her, and the two of them sat in silence on either side of the fire. They fell asleep. It was morning when the two of them were wakened suddenly. Some heavy thing thudded against the closed door. The two women looked at each other.

"Open the door," said the old woman, "till I see which one of them came safe."

She had to open it herself, Kate was too terrified, and who should fall on a heap on the floor but O'Malley, dripping wet, and horror in his eyes.

But he managed to tell the story to the women. The boat had foundered on the Eagle's Rock. He had succeeded in bringing the old man ashore, but the life had gone out of him.

"Let us go out looking for the bodies," said the old woman, and they went out.

The body of the son was never found. The shore was

searched from Slyne Head to Galway, but it wasn't seen anywhere. A funeral was held for the father, but his wife shed not a tear.

At times she used to be seen in some corner, a neighbor woman talking to her, and if you were listening you would hear her say: "It was part of the old curse, this drowning. How could I cry? Isn't my heart too full. I always knew he would be drowned some day."

After the burial of her husband she became stranger than ever. She used to get up unknown to Kate, and slip out, and search the shore for her son. She used to be seen often at night on the beach, her hair streaming in the wind, with nothing on but her nightdress, moving on alone, searching every pool, and knocking her feet against the sharp stones.

She used to sing:

> "I walk out at night
>   In the wind and the rain,
>   Searching for my son, my treasure,
>   Where have you gone from me, James?"

And then another thought would come to her, and she would sing,

> "But when the child Jesus,
>   Was lying at the foot of the Tree,
>   You were there, Mary,
>   And He on your knee."

And she would say that her own sorrow was greater than Mary's sorrow, for the body of her son was brought back to her after the Crucifixion.

"Where have you strayed from me, James? Why aren't you on my knee?" she would say.

She was growing worse from day to day. Her memory left her. She remembered nothing since her marriage thirty years before. If someone spoke of her husband, she would say she had no husband, but that she would soon have despite her people. If someone referred to her family, she would say that she had no family. How could she have, when she was not married yet? But she could tell you about everything that happened to her during her youth. She used to talk to Kate about those days, imagining that Kate was her young sister—the young sister she loved long ago—and poor Kate had to listen to her, and to keep her in conversation far into the night, until her heart was broken.

The neighbors pitied them both. The old woman had been somewhat queer ever since she came to the place. Yet nobody thought that she had lost her mind forever, nobody thought that she was suffering from the same malady that had stricken so many of her people. The neighbors couldn't think that, knowing so little about her forebears, and if she had become a little bit queerer, that was no wonder, seeing what she had suffered.

But Kate recognized the infirmity, and she kept her secret to herself. She didn't reveal it even to O'Malley, and it wasn't long until she was sorry she hadn't. At first she had no desire to keep her secret from him, but one day he asked her if it was that infirmity her mother was suffering from, and she replied that she didn't think so. For she would have had to tell him all about her people, about her mother's two brothers who were in the lunatic asylum, and about the sister who had never left the house unaccompanied for twenty years.

About this time Kate said to herself that it would do her mother a lot of good if she could go on a long visit far away from the sea. It was on a rock at the mouth of the quay that her father had been drowned, and when the tide was out this rock was visible, and her mother could see it from the house. Wouldn't it be a great blessing if she were living far away from that accursed rock? Her eldest sister was married down in Mayo and the young woman thought that she couldn't do better than pay her a visit. They weren't as friendly as two sisters should be, and when Kate walked into her after the long journey, she received no great welcome.

Her sister and her husband had a public house, and since they were better off than the people at home, her sister thought that Kate had come to look for help, as she had come before. The man of the house was serving in the shop, and the two women were left alone, but since there was a little window between the shop and the room in which they were sitting, they could hear clearly the voices of the men who were drinking.

"Well, Kate, how is Mother?" said the woman of the house.

"Badly, Mary, badly!"

The married woman was knitting, but she would lift her eyes from time to time, and you could see the affection and greed warring in them.

"Is she worse?" she asked.

"She is far worse."

"Did she do anything strange of late?"

"She does something strange every day of the year, Mary."

Neither of them spoke for a little while. They heard a young man who was merry with drink singing in the shop.

"Every day that breaks a fear comes on me that she will do something dreadful," said Kate. "She only recognizes me an odd time. She thinks that I'm her sister, that I'm Bridget O'Donnell."

"God save us, and she hasn't seen Bridget O'Donnell for thirty-two years, since she married Father!"

The man of the house was heard speaking strongly.

"And Bridget and her husband are becoming very friendly with us," said the woman of the house thoughtfully. "They were here yesterday and they took tea with us nicely and mannerly, and the Captain said that he had never tasted such tea, except once in India."

"Bad cess to Bridget and to the Captain too," said Kate impatiently. "It wasn't to talk about them that I came here to you."

The woman in question was a sister of her mother's who was married to a captain in the army. The girls never called any of the mother's people "Aunt" or "Uncle." They were great ones and they would have no connection with the family. None of them even attended the funeral.

"Aren't you very impatient," said the woman of the house, "but is she bad every day?"

"Oh no, sometimes she is in her proper senses, but she's a greater object of pity then than at any other time."

Kate stood up. Swelling and energy came into her voice.

"Mary," she said, "the heart is being broken in my breast. God alone knows what I have suffered for the past year. I'm there in the kitchen with her, she sitting at the window looking out at the sea, and grief that you never saw the likes of in her face. She would like to go away but she can't, for she has her eyes fixed on that accursed rock at the mouth of the quay. And when the tide is ebbing, she remains in her chair at the window until the rock appears and when she sees it rising out of the sea, she begins to rave, until she loses her mind completely. It would be a great blessing from God if she could get away from the evil place for a long time. I'm certain, Mary, that she would be glad to pay you a long visit."

She became silent until she would hear what her sister would say.

"Seven and sixpence," said the man of the house, "take it or leave it."

The woman of the house did not speak for a long time. The scarf she was knitting was spread out on the table before her, and her spectacles beside it. At last she began to explain why she could not undertake the care of her mother. The house was narrow enough for themselves already; they would have no room for her, they would have to get a woman to attend her, and money was very scarce with all the debts they had, and they had a big family, and expected another soon. They'd have to send Thomas to school some place, and that would cost them thirty pounds a year.

And so on. Kate was becoming angry.

"And of course, Mary, it would be a great shame to you to have the likes of her in the house. Wouldn't the whole world know?" The other woman arose in a fury.

"The whole world would know here, perhaps," said she, "but that O'Malley fellow that is to marry you wouldn't know. To keep it from him you thought of banishing your poor mother—"

"I didn't!"

"Oh, but you did, I say, for fear that he would not marry

you at all, if he knew about the terrible disease that follows our family."

"You're a liar!"

"And you're a brazen liar to pretend that it was for
Mother's sake you came here."

The words went from mouth to mouth between them
like sharp poisoned knives till the two of them were severely wounded.

Kate left the house with hatred in her heart for her sister.
She made for the station, but the last train had gone and
she had to stay in the town until morning. She spent the
night in a hotel near the station and she remembered the
hotel, and the night she spent in it, for the rest of her life.

She didn't sleep, but lay on the bed without taking off a
stitch. For the sake of her mother she had made the journey, or at least she had believed that when setting out, but
as she lay thinking during the night she began to fear that
her sister was not altogether wrong. Would she have
thought of sending her mother away, if O'Malley were not
coming to town for the fishing? Wouldn't he be in and out
of the house every day. Wouldn't he soon notice what was
wrong with her mother? And when he would hear of the
affliction of her mother's people, what would he say about
her having concealed it. Wouldn't he hate and despise her,
considering how he used to tell her everything himself.

With the coming of morning she had no recollection of
the rock on which her father had been drowned, or of the
ocean at which her mother kept staring when she was well,
or of the terrible suffering in her eyes, or of her own pity
for her, or of the love they had for each other. The heavy
word that had been spoken to her lay on her heart. She
thought a worse woman than herself had never been born.

On reaching home she saw a little crowd of people outside the house of John O'Neill, the justice of the peace.
There was a car on the street, and a policeman holding the
horse. As she went past the house, she noticed all the people looking sharply at her, and that some of them seemed
to be about to speak to her, but that they were shy of doing so. She didn't go far till she was called from a house,
and she went in. Her mother was in there before her, sing-

ing a love song, her old wedding dress wet and dirty on her, and ribbons and lace that were bright once falling down from her. O'Malley was there, and he explained all to Kate. He told her that her mother had been arrested that morning. She had escaped from the old woman that had been watching her, had wounded a neighbor woman who had tried to take her home, and was to be sent to the lunatic asylum.

Kate spoke to her but she did not recognize her. She was talking foolishly and saying she was very thankful to these noble people—she meant the police—who were about to take her to the man she loved. When she mounted the car she recognized Kate, or at least she thought she was her sister.

"I trusted you," she said, "but you thought to keep me from him like everyone else. But you didn't succeed. These gentlemen came to help me. It was he that sent them to me—

> "O youth of the grey eyes
> To whom I gave my heart's love. . . ."

were the last words Kate heard from her as the car moved off down the road.

Kate and O'Malley went on to the house. They had two and a half miles to walk, and neither spoke a word until they were at the quay. The fishing fleet was going west out on the bay with sails set.

O'Malley wished to say something to the girl he loved, but what could he say? At last he had to speak.

"Take courage, Kate," he said.

"I will," said she.

"God laid a heavy hand on her," said he.

"But it is heavier by far the hand he laid on the people she left behind," said she, "but let us accept the will of God."

There's a stone beside the quay they call "The Big Stone," and as they were going past it, Kate said, "Let us sit down here a little while, Anthony."

They sat down. He held her by the hand, and she was looking straight out at the sea.

"It's often I thought for the past two years," and you would think from her that she was talking to herself, "it's often I thought when the bad turn came on her, that a person was the worse for having mind and understanding. She has a light heart tonight, and my heart is as black as coal, and as heavy as lead."

The young man did not understand her.

"It was the mind that ruined our lives."

"But listen to me, Kate, my treasure. Our lives have not been ruined. There is a beautiful life in store for us together with the help of God."

"There isn't. I'll never marry."

"You'll never marry? Why?"

"I deceived you Anthony; I never told you how my mother was afflicted."

"But I knew. People don't talk about such things," said the young man bewildered.

"But I concealed from you the affliction of my mother's people: I never told you that she had two brothers in the asylum, and a sister not much better."

"What misfortune has struck you, Kate—haven't I known that for years?" The girl was surprised but she did not question him. The tears came.

The sun was sinking into the sea when they parted.

"There's no use in talking to me," said she. "I'll never marry," were the last words she spoke to him that night.

And she did not marry. O'Malley came to her often and asked her, but she would not consent. She's living in the little house beside the quay yet, and you will see her often at the window, looking out at the sea, and at the rock where her people were drowned, waiting for the day she'll join her mother in heaven—or in the asylum.

Translated from Modern Irish
by Séamus O'Néill

JAMES STEPHENS
1882?–1950

James Stephens looked like a pixie or a leprechaun and, for all that is known about his early life, might as well have been one. His last name was perhaps an assumed one; his parents are thought to have abandoned him, and it is certain that he knew hunger, poverty, and homelessness as a child. He was educated in a Dublin orphanage, enough to become a typist in a Dublin lawyer's office about 1903. In 1907 he began contributing prose and verse to Arthur Griffith's weekly, *Sinn Féin*. George Russell ("AE") recognized his talent and got to know him the following year. *Insurrections* (1909), Stephen's first volume of poetry, was dedicated to "AE." In 1912 *The Crock of Gold*, a prose fantasy about leprechauns and philosophers, gods and policemen, made Stephens world famous; in 1913 came *Here Are Ladies*, his first volume of short stories. Like his birth, Stephens' marriage is surrounded by mystery: he married the widow of a former friend in 1918, but it has been hinted that they eloped while her husband was still alive. Stephens' later life was plagued by illness, which undoubtedly contributed to the decline in his literary output after 1923. He learned enough Gaelic to produce a volume of verse translations and three books of prose adapted from Gaelic myths and legends. His *Collected Poems* will probably outlive his other work. Between the two World Wars, Stephens made several lecture tours in the U.S. and spent much time in Paris, where James Joyce and he became close friends. Joyce believed, perhaps correctly, that they were both born on the same day, and wished Stephens to finish *Finnegans Wake* for him if he died or went blind. "Three Women Who Wept," from *Here Are Ladies*, represents Stephens

at his best, full of originality and humor. It also shows
the vein of sadism in his work and the tendency to mere
"cuteness" that weakens much of his writing. These
three linked anecdotes lie somewhere between the short
story proper and the prose poem.

Three Women Who Wept

I. He was one of those men who can call ladies by their
Christian names. One day he met twenty-four duchesses
walking on a red carpet, and he winked at them, and they
were all delighted. It was so at first he appeared to her.
Has a mere girl any protection against a man of that quality? and she was the very merest of girls—she knew it. It
was not that she was ignorant, for she had read widely
about men, and she had three brothers as to whom she
knew divers intimate things.

The girl who has been reared among brothers has few
defenses against other males. She has acquired two things
—a belief in the divine right of man, and a curiosity as to
what those men are like who are not her brothers. She may
love her brothers, but she cannot believe that they ade-
quately represent the other sex. Does not every girl wish to
marry the antithesis of her brother? The feeling is that one
should marry as far outside of the family as is possible, and
as far outside of one's self as may be; but love has become
subject to geography, and our choice is often bounded by
the tramline upon which we travel from our houses to our
businesses and back again.

While she loved and understood her brothers, she had
not in the least understood or believed in the stories she had
read, and so, when the Young Man out of a Book came to
her, she was delighted but perplexed.

It was difficult to live up to him worthily. It was difficult to know what he would do next, and it was exceedingly
difficult to keep out of his way; for, indeed, he seemed to
pervade the part of the world where she lived. He was as

ubiquitous as the air or the sky. If she went into a shop, he was pacing on the pavement when she came out. If she went for a walk he was standing at the place farther than which she had decided not to go. She had found him examining a waterfall on the Dodder, leaning over the bearpit in the Zoological Gardens, and kneeling beside her in the Chapel, and her sleep had been distressed by the reflection that maybe he was sitting on her windowsill like a sad sparrow drenched in the rain, all its feathers on end with the cold, and its eyes wide open staring at misery.

The first time they met he spoke to her. He plucked a handkerchief from somewhere and thrust it into her hand, saying—

"You have dropped this, I think"—and she had been too alarmed to disown it.

It was a mighty handkerchief. It was so big that it would scarcely fit into her muff.—"It is a tablecloth," said she, as she solemnly stuffed away its lengthy flaps. "It is his own," she thought a moment later, and she would have laughed like a mad woman, only that she had no time, for he was pacing delicately by her side, and talking in a low voice that was partly a whisper and partly a whistle, and was entirely and disturbingly delicious.

The next time they met very suddenly. Scarcely a dozen paces separated them. She could see him advancing towards her, and knew by his knitted brows that he was searching anxiously for something to say. When they drew together he lifted his hat and murmured—

"How is your handkerchief today?"

The query so astonished her that (the verb is her own) she simply bawled with laughter. From that moment he treated her with freedom, for if once you laugh with a person you admit him to equality, you have ranked him definitely as a vertebrate, your hand is his by right of species, scarcely can you withhold even your lips from his advances.

Another, a strange, a fascinating thing, was that he was afraid of her. It was inconceivable, it was mad, but it was true. He looked at her with disguised terror. His bravado was the slenderest mask. Every word he said was uttered tentatively, it was subject to her approval, and if she opposed a statement, he dropped it instantly and adopted her alternative as one adopts a gift. This astonished her, who had been prepared to be terrified. He kept a little distance between them as he walked, and when she looked at him he looked away. She had a vision of herself as an ogre—whiskers sprouted all over her face, her ears bulged and swaggled, her voice became a cavernous rumble, her conversation sounded like fee-faw-fum—and yet, her brothers were not afraid of her in the least; they pinched her and kicked her hat.

He spoke (but always without prejudice) of the loveliest things imaginable—matters about which brothers had no conception, and for which they would not have any reverence. He said one day that the sky was blue, and, on looking she found that it was so. The sky was amazingly blue. It had never struck her before, but there was a color in the firmament before which one might fall down and worship. Sunlight was not the hot glare which it had been: it was rich, generous, it was inexpressibly beautiful. The color and scent of flowers became more varied. The world emerged as from shrouds and cerements. It was tender and radiant, comeliness lived everywhere, and goodwill. Laughter! the very ground bubbled with it: the grasses waved their hands, the trees danced and curtsied to one another with gentle dignity, and the wind lurched down the path with its hat on the side of its head and its hands in its pockets, whistling like her younger brother.

And then he went away. She did not see him any more. He was not by the waterfall on the Dodder, nor hanging over the bear-pit in the Zoo. He was not in the Chapel, nor on the pavement when she came out of a shop. He was not anywhere. She searched, but he was not anywhere. And the sun became the hot pest it had always been: the heavens were stuffed with dirty clouds the way a secondhand shop is stuffed with dirty bundles: the trees were hulking corner-boys with muddy boots: the wind blew dust into her eye, and her brothers pulled her hair and kicked her hat; so that she went apart from all these. She sat before the mirror regarding herself with woeful amazement—

"He was afraid of me!" she said.

And she wept into his monstrous handkerchief.

II. When he came into the world he came howling, and he howled without ceasing for seven long years, except at the times when he happened to be partaking of nourishment, or was fast asleep, and, even then, he snored with a note of defiance and protest which proved that his humor was not for peace.

The time came when he ceased to howl and became fascinated by the problem of how to make other people howl. In this art he became an adept. When he and another child chanced to be left together there came, apparently from the uttermost ends of the earth, a pin, and the other child and the pin were soon in violent and lamentable conjunction.

So he grew.

"Be hanged if I know what to do with him," said his father as he rebuckled on his belt. "The devil's self hasn't got the shape or match of such an imp in all the length and breadth of his seven hells. I'm sick, sore, and sorry whacking him, so I am, and before long I'll be hung on the head of him. I'm saying that there's more deceit and devilment in his bit of a carcass than there is in a public house full of tinkers, so there is."

He turned to his wife—

"It's no credit at all the son you've bore me, ma'am, but a sorrow and a woe that'll be killing us in our old age and maybe damning our souls at the heel of it. Where he got his blackguardly ways from I'm not saying, but it wasn't from my side of the house anyway, so it wasn't, and that's a moral. Get out of my sight, you sniffling lout, and if ever I catch you at your practices again I'll lam you till you won't be able to wink without help, so I will."

"Musha," sobbed his wife, "don't be always talking out of you. Anyone would think that it was an old, criminal thief you were instructing, instead of a bit of a child that'll be growing out of his wildness in no time. Come across to me, child, come over to your mother, my lamb."

That night, when his father got into bed, he prodded his foot against something under the sheets. Investigation discovered a brown paper bag at the end of the bed. A further search revealed a wasp's nest, inside of which there was an hundred angry wasps blazing for combat. His father left the room with more expedition than decency. He did not stop to put on as much as his hat. He fled to the stream which ran through the meadow at the back of their house, and lay down in it, and in two seconds there was more bad language than water in the stream. Every time he lifted his head for air the wasps flew at him with their tails curled. They kept him there for half an hour, and in that time he laid in the seeds of more rheumatism than could be cured in two lifetimes.

When he returned home, he found his wife lying on the floor with a blanket wrapped about her head, groaning by instinct, for she was senseless.

Her face had disappeared. There was nothing where it had been but poisoned lumps. A few days later it was found that she was blind of one eye, and there was danger of erysipelas setting in.

The boy could not be found for some time, but a neighbor, observing a stone come from nowhere in particular and hit a cat, located the first cause in a ditch. He brought the boy home, and grabbed his father just in time to prevent murder being done.

It was soon found that the only thing which eased the restless moaning woman was the touch of her son. All her unmanageable, delirious thoughts centered on him—

"Sure he's only a boy; beating never did good to anything. Give him a chance now for wouldn't a child be a bit wild anyhow. You will be a good boy, won't you? Come to your mother, my lamb."

So the lad grew, from twelve to fifteen, from fifteen to twenty. Soon he attained to manhood. To his mother he seemed to have leaped in a day from the careless, prattling babe to the responsibly-whiskered miracle at whom mothers sit and laugh in secret delight. This towering, big-footed, hairy person! was he really the little boy who used to hide in her skirts when his father scowled? She had only to close her eyes and she could feel again a pair of little hands clawing at her breast, sore from the violent industry of soft, wee lips.

So he grew. Breeches that were big became small. Bony wrists were continually pushing out of coat cuffs. His feet would burst out of his boots. He grew out of everything but one. A man may outgrow his breeches, he cannot outgrow his nature: his body is never too big or too small to hold that.

Every living thing in the neighborhood knew him. When a cat saw him coming, it climbed a tree and tried to look as much like a lump of wood as it could. When a dog heard his step, it tucked its tail out of sight and sought for a hole in the hedge. The birds knew he carried stones in his pockets. No tree cast so black a shadow in the sunlight as he did. There were stories of a bottle of paraffin oil and a cat that screeched in flames. Folk told of a maltreated dog that pointed its nose to heaven and bayed a curse against humanity until a terrified man battered it to death with a shovel. No one knew who did it, but every one said there were only two living hearts capable of these iniquities—one belonged to the devil, the other to our young man, and they acquitted Satan of the deeds.

The owner of the dog swore by the beasts in the field and the stars in the sky that he would tear the throat of the man who had injured his beast.

The father drove his one-eyed wife from the house, and went with her to live elsewhere; but she left him and went back to her son, and her husband forswore the twain.

When women saw him in the road they got past him with their breath hissing through their teeth in fear. When men passed him they did it warily, with their fists clenched and their eyes alert. He was shunned by everyone. The strength of his arms also was a thing to be afraid of, and in the world there was but two welcomes for him, one from his mother, the other from an old, grey rat that slept in his breast—

"Sure, you're all against him," his mother would say. "Why don't you give the boy a chance? It's only the hot blood of youth that's working in him—and he never did it either. Look how kind he is to me! never the bad word or the hard look! Ye black hearts that blame my boy, look among yourselves for the villain. No matter who is against you, come to your mother, my lamb."

He was found one day at the foot of the cliff with his neck broken. Some said that he had slipped and fallen, some said he had committed suicide, other some pursed their lips tightly and said nothing. All were relieved that he was gone, saving his mother only, she mourned for her only son, and wept bitterly, refusing to be comforted until she died.

III. She had begun to get thin. Her face was growing sharp and peaked. The steady curve of her cheek had become a little indeterminate. Her chin had begun to sag and her eyes to look a little weary. But she had not observed these things, for we do not notice ourselves very much until some other person thinks we are worthy of observation and tells us so; and these changes are so gradual and tiny that we seldom observe them until we awaken for a moment or two in our middle age and then we get ready to fall asleep again.

When her uncle died, the solicitors who had administered his will handed her a small sum of money and intimated that from that date she must hew out her own path in life, and as she had most of the household furniture of her late uncle at her disposal, she decided to let lodgings. Setting about that end with all possible expedition she finished writing "Apartments to Let" on a square of pasteboard, and, having placed it prominently in a window, she folded her mittened hands and sat down with some trepidation to await the advent of a lodger.

He came in the night time with the stars and the moon. He was running like a youthful god, she thought, for her mind had not yet been weaned from certain vanities, and she could not see that a gigantic policeman was in his wake, tracking him with elephantine bounds, and now and again snatching a gasp from hurry to blow furious warnings on a whistle.

It was the sound of the whistle which opened her eyes through her ears. She went to the door and saw him coming framed in the moonlight, his arms pressed tightly to his sides, his head well up, and his feet kicking a mile a minute on the pavement. Behind him the whistle shrilled with angry alarm, and the thunder of monumental feet came near as the policeman sprinted in majesty.

As the lodger ran, she looked at him. He was a long-legged young man with a pleasant, clean-shaven face. His eyes met hers, and, although he grinned anxiously, she saw that he was frightened. That frightened smile gripped her and she panted noiselessly, "Oh, run, run!"

As he drew level he fixed his gaze on her, and, stopping suddenly, he ducked under her arm and was inside the house in a twinkling.

The poor lady's inside curled up in fear and had started to uncurl in screams when she felt a hand laid gently on her arm, and, "Don't make a noise, or I'm caught," said a voice, whereupon, and with exceeding difficulty, she closed her mouth while the scream went sizzling through her teeth in little gasps. But now the enemy appeared round the corner, tooting incessantly on his whistle, and whacking sparks from the cobblestones as he ran. Behind her she could hear the labored breathing of a spent runner. The lodger was kneeling at her skirts: he caught her hand and pressed his face against it entreatingly—

The policeman drew near—

"Did you see a fellow skedaddling along here, ma'am?" said he.

She hesitated for only a moment and then, pointing to a laneway opposite, replied—

"He went up there."

"Thank you, ma'am," said the policeman with a genial smile, and he sprinted up the laneway whistling cheerily.

She turned to the lodger—

"You had better go now," said she.

He looked at her ruefully and hesitated—

"If I go now," he replied, "I'll be caught and get a month. I'll have to eat skilly, you know, and pick oakum, and get my hair cut."

She looked at his hair—it was brown and wavy, just at his ears it crisped into tiny curls, and she thought it would be a great pity to cut it. He bore her scrutiny well, with just a trifle of embarrassment and a shyly humorous eye—

"You are the kindest woman I ever met," said he, "and I'll never forget you as long as I live. I'll go away now because I wouldn't like to get you into trouble for helping me."

"What did you do?" she faltered.

"I got into a fight with another man," he replied, "and while we were hammering each other, the policeman came up. He was going to arrest me, and, before I knew what I was doing, I knocked him down."

She shook her head—

"You should not have done that. That was very wrong, for he was only doing his duty."

"I know it," he admitted, "but, do you see, I didn't know what I was doing, and then, when I hit him, I got frightened and ran."

"You poor boy," said she tenderly.

"And somehow, when I saw you, I knew you wouldn't give me up: wasn't it queer?"

What a nice, gentlemanly young fellow he is, she thought.

"But, of course, I cannot be trespassing on your kindness any longer," he continued, "so I'll leave at once, and if ever I get the chance to repay your kindness to a stranger—"

"Perhaps," said she, "it might not be quite safe for you to go yet. Come inside and I will give you a cup of tea. You must be worn out with the excitement and the danger. Why, you are shaking all over: a cup of tea will steady your nerves and give him time to stop looking for you."

"Perhaps," said he, "if I turned my coat inside out and turned my trousers up, they wouldn't notice me."

"We will talk it over," she replied with a wise nod.

That was how the lodger came. He told her his name and his employment—he was a bookmaker's clerk. He brought his luggage, consisting mostly of neckties, to her house the following day from his former lodgings—

"Had a terrible time getting away from them," said he. "They rather liked me, you know, and couldn't make out why I wanted to leave."

"As if you weren't quite free to do as you wished," quoth his indignant new landlady.

"And then, when they found I would go, they made me pay two weeks' rent in lieu of notice—mean, wasn't it?"

"The low people," she replied. "I will not ask you to pay anything this week."

He put his bandbox on the ground, and shook hands with her—

"You are a brick," said he, "the last and the biggest of them. There isn't the like of you in this or any other world, and never was and never will be, world without end, amen."

"Oh, don't say that," said she shyly.

"I will," he replied, "for it's the truth. I'll hire a sand-wichman to stop people in the street and tell it to them. I'll get a week's engagement at the theatre and sing it from the stage. I'll make up a poem about your goodness. I don't know what to do to thank you. Do you see, if I had to pay you now I'd have to pawn something, and I really believe I have pawned everything they'd lend on to get the money for that two weeks' rent. I'm broke until Friday, that's my payday, but that night I'll come home with my wages piled up on a cart."

"I can lend you a few shillings until then," said she laughing.

"Oh, no," said he. "It's not fair. I couldn't do that," but he could.

Well the light of the world shone out of the lodger. He was like a sea breeze in a soap factory. When he awakened in the morning he whistled. When he came down to breakfast he sang. When he came home in the evening he danced. He had an amazing store of vitality: from the highest hair on the top of his head down to his heels he was alive. His average language was packed with jokes and wonderful curses. He was as chatty as a girl, as good-humored as a dog, unconscious as a kitten—and she knew nothing at all of men, except, perhaps, that they wore trou-

sers and were not girls. The only man with whom she had
ever come in contact was her uncle, and he might have
been described as a sniffy old man with a cold; a blend of
gruel and grunt, living in an atmosphere of ointment and
pills and patent medicine advertisements—and, behold, she
was living in unthinkable intimacy with the youngest of
young men; not an old, ache-ridden, cough-racked, corn-
footed septuagenarian, but a young, fresh-faced, babbling
rascal who laughed like the explosion of a blunderbuss,
roared songs as long as he was within earshot and danced
when he had nothing else to do. He used to show her how
to do hand-balances on the armchair, and while his boots
were cocked up in the air she would grow stiff with terror
for his safety and for that of the adjacent crockery.

The first morning she was giving him his breakfast, intending afterwards to have her own meal in the kitchen,
but he used language of such strangely attractive ferocity,
and glared at her with such a humorously mad eye that she
was compelled to breakfast with him.

At night, when he returned to his tea, he swore by this
and by that he would die of hunger unless she ate with him;
and then he told her all the doings of the day, the bets that
had been made and lost, and what sort of a man his boss
was, and he extolled the goodness of his friends, and lectured on the vast iniquity of his enemies.

So things went until she was as intimate with him as if
he had been her brother. One night he came home just a
trifle tipsy. She noted at last what was wrong with him, and
her heart yearned over the sinner. There were five or six
glasses inside of him, and each was the father of an antic.
He was an opera company, a gymnasium, and a menagerie
at once, all tinged with a certain hilarious unsteadiness
which was fascinating. But at last he got to his bed, which
was more than she did.

She sat through the remainder of the night listening to
the growth of her half-starved heart. Oh, but there was a
warmth there now—! Springtime and the moon in flood.
What new leaves are these which the trees put forth? Bird,
singing at the peep of morn, where gottest thou thy song?

Be still, be still, thou stranger, fluttering a wing at my breast—

At the end of a month the gods moved, and when the gods move, they trample mortals in the dust.

The lodger's employer left Dublin for London, taking his clerk with him.

"Good-bye," said he.

"Good-bye," she replied, "and a pleasant journey to you."

And she took the card with "Apartments to Let" written upon it and placed it carefully in the window, and then, folding her mittened hands, she sat down to await the coming of another lodger, and as she sat she wept bitterly.

JAMES JOYCE
1882–1941

In *A Portrait of the Artist as a Young Man*, James Joyce reworked in fictional form the story of his supposed break with his family, his church, and his country—three themes that supplied him subject matter the rest of his life. He left it to his biographers, Herbert Gorman and Richard Ellmann, to recount the later stages of his flight from convention: how he eloped to Europe with a hotel housemaid in 1904 and married her in 1931, after a quarter-century of intense and jealous fidelity, when their two children, to whom he was almost obsessively devoted, were grown up; how he supported them in Trieste as a language teacher and later, in Zurich and Paris, accepted subsidies from admirers rather than do hack writing or lecturing, yet spent vast amounts of time and energy promoting a favorable reception for his books; how he died in Switzerland, an exile from exile, fleeing the German invasion of France, anguished at separation from his insane daughter. Joyce never did anything twice, in literature at any rate. He wrote one volume of poems, *Chamber Music* (the later *Pomes Penyeach* is only a pamphlet); one volume of short stories, *Dubliners*; one autobiographical novel, *A Portrait*; one play, *Exiles*; one full-dress multicharacter novel, *Ulysses*; and finally one fantastic dream poem, *Finnegans Wake*—part novel, part world history, part apocalypse—for which he refashioned the English language. Of the fifteen short stories in *Dubliners*, the best (and longest) is "The Dead," much anthologized. "Clay," among the shortest, is a masterpiece too. The way Joyce reveals Maria from within and suggests with a few firm strokes not only her whole life but that of all her family is an object lesson to any writer. The title refers first of all to the clay into which Maria—face of a witch, heart of a peacemaker—puts her hand during the Hallowe'en game, foretelling her death within the year; it tells us also that Maria, like Adam, is made of clay—and so are we. Maria's song, from the opera *The Bohemian Girl*, by the Dublin composer Michael William Balfe, needs a little explanation: the first verse, which she sings twice by mistake, is incongruous enough in view of her poverty, but the second and last verse, omitted by her, begins, "I dreamt that suitors sought my hand . . ." Maria has apparently given up all hope of suitors

The brief passage from *A Portrait* is to show that Joyce could tell an anecdote in Irish country dialect as well as the next man. He could use the oral tradition or let it alone according to the need of the moment.

Clay

The matron had given her leave to go out as soon as the women's tea was over and Maria looked forward to her evening out. The kitchen was spick and span: the cook said you could see yourself in the big copper boilers. The fire was nice and bright and on one of the side-tables were four very big barmbracks.[1] These barmbracks seemed uncut; but if you went closer you would see that they had been cut into long thick even slices and were ready to be handed round at tea. Maria had cut them herself.

Maria was a very, very small person indeed but she had a very long nose and a very long chin. She talked a little through her nose, always soothingly: *"Yes, my dear,"* and *"No, my dear."* She was always sent for when the women quarrelled over their tubs and always succeeded in making peace. One day the matron had said to her:

[1] Spiced currant cakes eaten in Ireland at Hallowe'en. Gaelic *bairín breac* (speckled cake).

"Maria, you are a veritable peacemaker!"

And the sub-matron and two of the Board ladies had heard the compliment. And Ginger Mooney was always saying what she wouldn't do to the dummy who had charge of the irons if it wasn't for Maria. Everyone was so fond of Maria.

The women would have their tea at six o'clock and she would be able to get away before seven. From Ballsbridge to the Pillar, twenty minutes; from the Pillar to Drumcondra, twenty minutes; and twenty minutes to buy the things. She would be there before eight. She took out her purse with the silver clasps and read again the words *A Present from Belfast*. She was very fond of that purse because Joe had brought it to her five years before when he and Alphy had gone to Belfast on a Whit-Monday trip. In the purse were two half-crowns and some coppers. She would have five shillings clear after paying tram fare. What a nice evening they would have, all the children singing! Only she hoped that Joe wouldn't come in drunk. He was so different when he took any drink.

Often he had wanted her to go and live with them; but she would have felt herself in the way (though Joe's wife was ever so nice with her) and she had become accustomed to the life of the laundry. Joe was a good fellow. She had nursed him and Alphy too; and Joe used often say:

"Mamma is mamma but Maria is my proper mother."

After the break-up at home the boys had got her that position in the *Dublin by Lamplight* laundry, and she liked it. She used to have such a bad opinion of Protestants but now she thought they were very nice people, a little quiet and serious, but still very nice people to live with. Then she had her plants in the conservatory and she liked looking after them. She had lovely ferns and wax-plants and, whenever anyone came to visit her, she always gave the visitor one or two slips from her conservatory. There was one thing she didn't like and that was the tracts on the walks; but the matron was such a nice person to deal with, so genteel.

When the cook told her everything was ready she went into the women's room and began to pull the big bell. In a

few minutes the women began to come in by twos and
threes, wiping their steaming hands in their petticoats and
pulling down the sleeves of their blouses over their red
steaming arms. They settled down before their huge mugs
which the cook and the dummy filled up with hot tea, already mixed with milk and sugar in huge tin cans. Maria
superintended the distribution of the barmbrack and saw
that every woman got her four slices. There was a great
deal of laughing and joking during the meal. Lizzie Flem-
ing said Maria was sure to get the ring and, though Flem-
ing had said that for so many Hallow Eves, Maria had to
laugh and say she didn't want any ring or man either; and
when she laughed her grey-green eyes sparkled with disappointed shyness and the tip of her nose nearly met the tip
of her chin. Then Ginger Mooney lifted her mug of tea and
proposed Maria's health while all the other women clat-
tered with their mugs on the table, and said she was sorry
she hadn't a sup of porter to drink it in. And Maria laughed
again till the tip of her nose nearly met the tip of her chin
and till her minute body nearly shook itself asunder because she knew that Mooney meant well though, of course,
she had the notions of a common woman.

But wasn't Maria glad when the women had finished
their tea and the cook and the dummy had begun to clear
away the tea-things! She went into her little bedroom and,
remembering that the next morning was a mass morning,
changed the hand of the alarm from seven to six. Then she
took off her working skirt and her house-boots and laid her
best skirt out on the bed and her tiny dress-boots beside the
foot of the bed. She changed her blouse too and, as she
stood before the mirror, she thought of how she used to
dress for mass on Sunday morning when she was a young
girl; and she looked with quaint affection at the diminutive
body which she had so often adorned. In spite of its years
she found it a nice tidy little body.

When she got outside the streets were shining with rain
and she was glad of her old brown waterproof. The tram
was full and she had to sit on the little stool at the end of
the car, facing all the people, with her toes barely touching the floor. She arranged in her mind all she was going

to do and thought how much better it was to be independent and to have your own money in your pocket. She hoped they would have a nice evening. She was sure they would but she could not help thinking what a pity it was Alphy and Joe were not speaking. They were always falling out now but when they were boys together they used to be the best of friends: but such was life.

She got out of her tram at the Pillar and ferreted her way quickly among the crowds. She went into Downes's cake-shop but the shop was so full of people that it was a long time before she could get herself attended to. She bought a dozen of mixed penny cakes, and at last came out of the shop laden with a big bag. Then she thought what else would she buy: she wanted to buy something really nice. They would be sure to have plenty of apples and nuts. It was hard to know what to buy and all she could think of was cake. She decided to buy some plumcake but Downes's plumcake had not enough almond icing on top of it so she went over to a shop in Henry Street. Here she was a long time in suiting herself and the stylish young lady behind the counter, who was evidently a little annoyed by her, asked her was it wedding-cake she wanted to buy. That made Maria blush and smile at the young lady; but the young lady took it all very seriously and finally cut a thick slice of plumcake, parcelled it up and said:

"Two-and-four, please."

She thought she would have to stand in the Drumcondra tram because none of the young men seemed to notice her but an elderly gentleman made room for her. He was a stout gentleman and he wore a brown hard hat; he had a square red face and a greyish moustache. Maria thought he was a colonel-looking gentleman and she reflected how much more polite he was than the young men who simply stared straight before them. The gentleman began to chat with her about Hallow Eve and the rainy weather. He supposed the bag was full of good things for the little ones and said it was only right that the youngsters should enjoy themselves while they were young. Maria agreed with him and favored him with demure nods and hems. He was very nice with her, and when she was getting out at the Canal

Bridge she thanked him and bowed, and he bowed to her and raised his hat and smiled agreeably; and while she was going up along the terrace, bending her tiny head under the rain, she thought how easy it was to know a gentleman even when he has a drop taken.

Everybody said: *"O, here's Maria!"* when she came to Joe's house. Joe was there, having come home from business, and all the children had their Sunday dresses on. There were two big girls in from next door and games were going on. Maria gave the bag of cakes to the eldest boy, Alphy, to divide and Mrs. Donnelly said it was too good of her to bring such a big bag of cakes and made all the children say:

"Thanks, Maria."

But Maria said she had brought something special for papa and mamma, something they would be sure to like, and she began to look for her plumcake. She tried in Downes's bag and then in the pockets of her waterproof and then on the hall-stand but nowhere could she find it. Then she asked all the children had any of them eaten it— by mistake, of course—but the children all said no and looked as if they did not like to eat cakes if they were to be accused of stealing. Everybody had a solution for the mystery and Mrs. Donnelly said it was plain that Maria had left it behind her in the tram. Maria, remembering how confused the gentleman with the greyish moustache had made her, colored with shame and vexation and disappointment. At the thought of the failure of her little surprise and of the two and fourpence she had thrown away for nothing she nearly cried outright.

But Joe said it didn't matter and made her sit down by the fire. He was very nice with her. He told her all that went on in his office, repeating for her a smart answer which he had made to the manager. Maria did not understand why Joe laughed so much over the answer he had made but she said that the manager must have been a very overbearing person to deal with. Joe said he wasn't so bad when you knew how to take him, that he was a decent sort so long as you didn't rub him the wrong way. Mrs. Donnelly played the piano for the children and they danced and sang. Then the two next-door girls handed round the nuts. Nobody could find the nutcrackers and Joe was nearly getting cross over it and asked how did they expect Maria to crack nuts without a nutcracker. But Maria said she didn't like nuts and that they weren't to bother about her. Then Joe asked would she take a bottle of stout and Mrs. Donnelly said there was port wine too in the house if she would prefer that. Maria said she would rather they didn't ask her to take anything: but Joe insisted.

So Maria let him have his way and they sat by the fire talking over old times and Maria thought she would put in a good word for Alphy. But Joe cried that God might strike him stone dead if ever he spoke a word to his brother again and Maria said she was sorry she had mentioned the matter. Mrs. Donnelly told her husband it was a great shame for him to speak that way of his own flesh and blood but Joe said that Alphy was no brother of his and there was nearly being a row on the head of it. But Joe said he would not lose his temper on account of the night it was and asked his wife to open some more stout. The two next-door girls had arranged some Hallow Eve games and soon everything was merry again. Maria was delighted to see the children so merry and Joe and his wife in such good spirits. The next-door girls put some saucers on the table and then led the children up to the table, blindfold. One got the prayer-book and the other three got the water; and when one of the next-door girls got the ring Mrs. Donnelly shook her finger at the blushing girl as much as to say: O, *I know all about it!* They insisted then on blindfolding Maria and leading her up to the table to see what she would get; and, while they were putting on the bandage, Maria laughed and laughed again till the tip of her nose nearly met the tip of her chin.

They led her up to the table amid laughing and joking and she put her hand out in the air as she was told to do. She moved her hand about here and there in the air and descended on one of the saucers. She felt a soft wet substance with her fingers and was surprised that nobody spoke or took off her bandage. There was a pause for a few seconds; and then a great deal of scuffling and whispering. Somebody said something about the garden, and at last Mrs. Donnelly said something very cross to one of the next-door girls and told her to throw it out at once: that was no play. Maria understood that it was wrong that time and so she had to do it over again: and this time she got the prayer-book.

After that Mrs. Donnelly played Miss McCloud's Reel for the children and Joe made Maria take a glass of wine. Soon they were all quite merry again and Mrs. Donnelly said Maria would enter a convent before the year was out because she had got the prayer-book. Maria had never seen Joe so nice to her as he was that night, so full of pleasant talk and reminiscences. She said they were all very good to her.

At last the children grew tired and sleepy and Joe asked Maria would she not sing some little song before she went, one of the old songs. Mrs. Donnelly said *"Do, please, Maria!"* and so Maria had to get up and stand beside the piano. Mrs. Donnelly bade the children be quiet and listen to Maria's song. Then she played the prelude and said *"Now, Maria!"* and Maria, blushing very much, began to sing in a tiny quavering voice. She sang *I Dreamt that I Dwelt*, and when she came to the second verse she sang again:

> I dreamt that I dwelt in marble halls
> > With vassals and serfs at my side,
> And of all who assembled within those walls
> > That I was the hope and the pride.
> I had riches too great to count; could boast
> > Of a high ancestral name,
> But I also dreamt, which pleased me most,
> > That you loved me still the same.

But no one tried to show her her mistake; and when she had ended her song Joe was very much moved. He said that there was no time like the long ago and no music for him like poor old Balfe, whatever other people might say; and his eyes filled up so much with tears that he could not find what he was looking for and in the end he had to ask his wife to tell him where the corkscrew was.

Davin's Story

from *A Portrait of the Artist as a Young Man.*

—A thing happened to myself, Stevie, last autumn, coming on winter, and I never told it to a living soul and you are the first person now I ever told it to. I disremember if it was October or November. It was October because it was before I came up here to join the matriculation class.

Stephen had turned his smiling eyes towards his friend's face, flattered by his confidence and won over to sympathy by the speaker's simple accent.

—I was away all that day from my own place over in Buttevant—I don't know if you know where that is—at a hurling match between the Croke's Own Boys and the Fearless Thurles and by God, Stevie, that was the hard fight. My first cousin, Fonsy Davin, was stripped to his buff that day minding cool[1] for the Limericks but he was up with the forwards half the time and shouting like mad. I never will forget that day. One of the Crokes made a woeful wipe at him one time with his caman[2] and I declare to God he was within an aim's ace of getting it at the side of his temple. Oh, honest to God, if the crook of it caught him that time he was done for.

—I am glad he escaped, Stephen had said with a laugh, but surely that's not the strange thing that happened you?

—Well, I suppose that doesn't interest you but leastways there was such noise after the match that I missed the train home and I couldn't get any kind of a yoke to give me a lift for, as luck would have it, there was a mass meeting that same day over in Castletownroche and all the cars in the country were there. So there was nothing for it only to

---

[1] Gaelic *cúl,* "goal."

[2] Gaelic *camán,* "hurley."

stay the night or to foot it out. Well, I started to walk and on I went and it was coming on night when I got into the Ballyhoura hills; that's better than ten miles from Kilmallock and there's a long lonely road after that. You wouldn't see the sign of a christian house along the road or hear a sound. It was pitch dark almost. Once or twice I stopped by the way under a bush to redden my pipe and only for the dew was thick I'd have stretched out there and slept. At last, after a bend of the road, I spied a little cottage with a light in the window. I went up and knocked at the door. A voice asked who was there and I answered I was over at the match in Buttevant and was walking back and that I'd be thankful for a glass of water. After a while a young woman opened the door and brought me out a mug of milk. She was half undressed as if she was going to bed when I knocked and she had her hair hanging; and I thought by her figure and by something in the look of her eyes that she must be carrying a child. She kept me in talk a long while at the door and I thought it strange because her breast and her shoulders were bare. She asked me was I tired and would I like to stop the night there. She said she was all alone in the house and that her husband had gone that morning with his sister to see her off. And all the time she was talking, Stevie, she had her eyes fixed on my face and she stood so close to me I could hear her breathing. When I handed her back the mug at last she took my hand to draw me in over the threshold and said: *'Come in and stay the night here. You've no call to be frightened. There's no one in it but ourselves. . . .'* I didn't go in, Stevie. I thanked her and went on my way again, all in a fever. At the first bend of the road I looked back and she was standing at the door.

LENNOX ROBINSON
1886–1958

Esmé Stuart Lennox Robinson was born in County Cork, the youngest son of an Anglican clergyman. Educated privately and at Bandon Grammar School, he began to write early. His first play was produced at the Abbey Theatre in 1908. After another of his plays had been performed there, he was invited by W. B. Yeats to direct at the Abbey. Although this very shy, very tall young man knew nothing about the technical side of the theatre, he accepted the job. From 1910 to 1914, and again from 1919 to 1923, he directed plays at the Abbey. In 1923 he was appointed a member of the Board of Directors of the theatre, a position that he held until 1956, frequently directing, as well as teaching acting and direction. From 1912 on he often visited the United States to lecture or direct plays. He did not marry until 1931. Robinson eventually became the most skillful technician of all the Abbey dramatists and one of the most prolific among them. Lighthearted comedies like *The White-Headed Boy* (1918) and *Is Life Worth Living?* (1933), serious plays about the Irish political and social scene like *The Lost Leader* (1918) and *The Big House* (1926), a *tour de force* of Expressionism like *Church Street* (1934)—all his varied dramatic work has earned him a smaller reputation than he deserves. Robinson worked in almost every literary form except poetry, and even there he was joint editor of *The Oxford Book of Irish Verse*. He published only two volumes of short stories, *Dark Days* (1918) and *Eight Short Stories* (1919). "Education," from the latter volume, deals with a theme that is rare in Irish literature but not in Irish life—the pro-

vincial amateur confronted with "the big league."
Robinson may have drawn in part on his own feelings
during his first days at the Abbey, but he, unlike his
hero, persevered. Many Irish artists remain amateurs
all their lives without even realizing it: this unaware-
ness often gives their work an odd charm.

Education

He was more tired than he cared to own. He had borne
the journey to Dublin without conscious fatigue, had sat
on deck talking to Mrs. Conder after dinner and till they
reached Holyhead, but once stretched out in his sleeper,
fatigue had sprung on him like a beast unleashed, had
gripped him in every muscle, making sleep an impossibility.

Particularly, of course, it had settled itself in his leg and
back. There it was perfectly at home; it had lived there day
and night for more years than it was pleasant to remember,
and had learned long ago a thousand subtle ways of claim-
ing possession of him. It had never been more subtle than
at this moment, never more elusive, so that when he tried
to bring relief to his knee by changing his attitude, it immediately became obvious that the pain had all accumulated in his back, and when he turned his attention there it
fled away, throwing spears of pain as it fled, to settle somewhere else.

But his brain was too busy and excited to bother to pursue it. After half an hour's tossing and turning, he accepted the bodily fatigue with resignation as he had accepted it so often before, and accepted, too, the fact that
something was unleashed in his brain, was galloping and
racing. He gave it its head with a sigh and waited for what
it would show him.

At first there came a succession of inconsequent objects
which only he could piece together and make sense of.
Foremost among them was a worn sofa, a grand piano, and
himself endlessly progressing from the sofa to the piano
and back again. In the carpet which lay between, his feet

seemed to have worn a deep track during sixteen years, those sixteen years since that accident with the pony carriage, which had broken and bruised him but which had bruised his mother more deplorably, more intangibly, in her brain, in her nerves, making it an agony for her to lose sight for one moment of her boy, her only child. His father was in no picture of his brain, yet always ominous in the background, not dead but swallowed up years ago in some financial disaster, something dishonest and disgraceful that had for ever tarnished his reputation, and caused him to fly from Doon House, from Ireland, from the life of his wife and child. Gradually they had lived down the disgrace of that cowardly flight; it was difficult for anyone to deny sympathy to the pathetically nervous deserted wife, and more difficult to deny anything to the boy, so stricken in body, so sacrificed to his mother's broken nerves; impossible, finally, as the years went on to deny anything to his genius.

For it was not for nothing that the track had been worn between the sofa and the piano, not for nothing those hours of practice as long—and longer—than his strength would permit, not for nothing those weekly visits of a Professor, a real Doctor of Music, from the neighboring town. At sixteen young Martin was precocious, and at twenty he played the Professor off the piano and out of Doon House.

Life went by to a lilt of music, each hour of it set to a gay or sad air. Wasn't the train at this moment beating out the first subject of that dearly-loved Chopin sonata? As he hummed it, the rhythm altered and became a merciless, hurrying *motif* from the last movement of *Scheherazade* —extraordinary how the throb of the train fitted it, how it came down with a strong accent, a "rat-tat-tat" just where it was required. He wondered whether Mrs. Conder was awake and listening to it.

He owed her *Scheherazade* and Borodin and many others whose names had been unknown to him a month ago, as unknown as her name. Tom Conder had taken the Castle for a month's fishing and she came too to entertain her husband's guests, Colonels and Majors and Captains, a seemingly endless succession of them, all so alike to her and all so dull, but friends of dear old Tom's and for his sake gladly welcomed. It was fisherman's weather and she spent long wet days in the house reading and practicing her songs. Ten days of this found her bored, and when she was approached and asked to sing at a local concert in aid of some all-deserving charity, she gladly consented. But she must have an accompanist, and the schoolmistress who was recommended to her stared helplessly at the most simple of her songs and rose from the piano stool after ten minutes' labor, saying, "You'll have to get Mr. Martin, he's the only one here will be able to play that class of song. You've a gorgeous voice, only it's a pity you couldn't sing something more simple-like—more of an air to it—sure Doon won't know what to think of this. I'd like you to beat the Canon's niece; three encores she got the last time and such airs as she gives herself, though she hasn't much voice at all, only the way she sings, half playacting all the time."

Mrs. Conder enquired further. It seemed that Mr. Martin, too, gave himself "airs" but in this case he was entitled to do so. He wouldn't play accompaniments for everyone, and wouldn't play "that cheap music." But he made people like what he played; it was "like a miracle" what he could do with a piano, especially with his own piano, which was a big one, not like the one at the school with two notes dumb and another that always stuck down and was a great bother till you learned the knack of lifting it with your thumb. She'd send Mr. Martin over to the castle at once; the sooner the program was settled the better.

He came the next morning, driving over in a low pony carriage. He walked, even in the house, with the help of a stick and was at first very shy, but as soon as he had limped over to the piano, his shyness disappeared and they were soon deeply intent on the songs.

That morning came back to him now as the prelude to many other happy meetings. He had never before had a chance of playing with a good singer. He had played a good deal with a fiddle, but the bank clerk who played it so obviously preferred Braga's *Serenata* to a Mozart sonata (though he could play both) that their musical communion was limited. He had never before—not, at any rate, since the days of the Professor—met a musician so nearly his equal in taste. It was wonderful not to have to apologize for liking Brahms and Beethoven better than Braga, wonderful not to run the risk of being thought to have "airs."

But he had from the first, from the moment his Professor had left him, rather finely taken the risk of that. He would play anywhere and for anyone, but only the music he himself liked. And his rather haughty attitude justified itself. At first Doon sat restless or bored, then it gave grudging admiration to his playing; it ended by becoming immensely proud of him. His young handsome face, his limp, his wonderful playing combined to make him a personage. No town in the county possessed any person that could touch him for allure. A doctor's daughter who had been to school in Paris and who lost her heart at once to his dark hair and his white, magical fingers, called him "a great artist." Doon laughed when it heard the term, but in a week it had adopted it and whispered it at tea parties and in drawing rooms over shops; and the piano tuner was kept busy after the awful occasion (Mrs. O'Brien's evening party at the National Bank) when Martin, after playing a few bars, had begged to be excused until some future occasion when his hostess's piano might be less excruciatingly out of tune.

His final rehearsal with Mrs. Conder took place at his own house, and after tea he played to her for an hour and then sat with her over the fire and talked to her in the dusk. He told her his rather miserable story and asked for her advice. His mother was dead now, had died three months before; he was free at last, he could travel.

"Certainly you must travel," Mrs. Conder declared, "and you can't do better than begin by travelling back with us to London. Come with us when we go at the end of the month."

"What an idea!"

"It's a good one. You'll be more comfortable with us than at an hotel. Manchester Square is quite convenient. There is a little good music to be heard, some bad opera; you shall go to everything you want to hear."

"Bad or good, it's bound to be better than Doon music.

I hear nothing but what I make myself. I haven't been to London since I was twelve; when mother's nerve went she couldn't travel and, as I had always to be within call of her, I couldn't travel either."

"Then travel now to Manchester Square."

"No, no, you're—you're grand people. I'd be out of the picture. Why, I haven't even a presentable suit of dress clothes!"

"That doesn't matter nowadays."

He refused the invitation, but it was renewed several times during the weeks that followed, and Tom brought a good-natured pressure to bear on him. And now here he lay, bright and sleepless, travelling to London, with Tom snoring quite close to him and Mrs. Conder not far away. Travelling to London, to music, to life, with the wheels throbbing out that pitiless phrase from *Scheherazade*.

In the car from Euston as they travelled towards Manchester Square, looking at his pallor, she told him she didn't want to see him before dinner time nor even then unless he felt inclined. But by teatime he had had some sleep, and wandered downstairs and found her in the drawing room. She had expected "nobody," she said; but six or eight people were talking and drinking tea, and to them he was introduced in a comprehensive way. Mrs. Conder labelled him—as she labelled everyone; his tag read "Mr. Martin who has come over from Ireland with us to hear music," and on these terms he got on with the strangers very well. Most of them seemed musical and gossiped about who was "back," and who was coming, and a new girl who was a marvel, and an old man who was impossible but such a dear. All this was out of Martin's depth, and he could only listen, brightly interested. The Blüthner lay temptingly near, and he longed to play. After his night of pain and his deep sleep he felt full of inspiration, and to these people he could have expressed himself without fear of being misunderstood.

He had come to London to listen, and it was only now that it suddenly flashed upon him that here at least and for the first time in his life he would find an audience. Not, of course, a Queen's Hall audience, not a concert with advertisements and tickets and a printed program, but an audience now and then in this spacious room of chosen people, people like himself to whom music was a passion, who might differ from him, but who would understand him. Mrs. Conder would gather them there from time to time and he would play to them as he had often played to her; by pleasing her friends, he would repay a little of all he owed her.

It was intoxicating, this idea of at last finding an audience. At Doon everyone liked music, it was genteel to like music, but only one or two had really cared. The doctor's daughter was one of them but Martin had regretfully come to believe that the reasons why she "liked" so enthusiastically were not musical ones, that they had too much to do with the personality of the player. But here his personality would be a negligible quantity and he would be liked for his music alone.

There was nobody at dinner except a widowed sister of Mrs. Conder's, who was staying at Manchester Square. Tom had gone to the country to some friends, and would be away for a week. "Meanwhile," his wife declared, "we'll have an orgy. Where is the paper, what is there we can hear?"

Not so very much as it turned out. Tomorrow an orchestral concert, old classical stuff. "Let me off that, I've a committee, but you must go, you shall have the car," the next day nothing, the day after De Burgh and his fiddle, two days later the great, the incomparable Dremling.

"You'll love him, he's enormous in size and in his art, he's a dear old-fashioned thing. He'll begin with a Scarlatti, then some Bach, then a big, big Beethoven, a Chopin or two, some Brahms, and, to show he's quite up to date, he'll finish with something French and modern which he simply hasn't the remotest idea how to play. But we'll go away before he gets to that. Now play to me a little and then I'm going to send you to bed."

He played to her for an hour while she sat over the fire scribbling notes with great rapidity.

"You're in good form tonight," she told him. "No, I

won't sing but I'm asking a few people in tomorrow night, a cousin of mine who sings and her husband who plays the violin and a young man—the only man in London who can play Debussy."

"I hope he'll come," Martin said. "I'm like Dremling, I can't play that modern stuff. Will you sing those French songs I floundered so over; will he play with you?"

"Mr. Martin hasn't a word to say, Dremling has left him speechless. The dear man was in great form I admit. Play to us Hugo, please, Mr. Martin refuses to touch a note."

"Can you bear me after Dremling?" Hugo asked.

"I always like to hear you. You've no pretensions, you know you're not a pianist."

Martin lay on the sofa, his eyes closed. He said nothing. Mrs. Conder spurred Hugo on to one piece and then another until at midnight he got up to go.

Martin got up to bid him good night.

"You're not in good form tonight, I'm afraid," Hugo said kindly as they shook hands. "I want to hear you play, perhaps you will next time I come."

"I? Oh, I can't play the piano," the tired young man replied.

"You expect me to believe that?" Hugo laughed.

Mrs. Conder followed Hugo to the hall. When she returned to the drawing room, Martin was standing in front of the fire, his elbow on the mantelpiece, his back turned to her.

"Go to bed," she said kindly, laying her hand on his arm. He turned round.

"Good gracious, how tired you look!" she exclaimed.

"Why didn't you tell me?" he said.

"Tell you?—What?"

"That I'm no good, that I can't play."

"But you can play; you have given me a great deal of pleasure."

"You're always so kind," he said bitterly.

"Kind?"

"Thank you, at any rate, and most sincerely for not

gratifying my conceit by asking me to play to your friends here. The one consolation I have is to remember that, however much I may have made a fool of myself at Doon, no one but you has heard me play a note here."

"But—"

"You were so kind, you kept on sparing me—you always suggested I was tired. Thank you, thank you a thousand times."

"Why?—What?"

"And I dreamed I'd find an audience here, an audience worthy of listening to me. Worthy of *me!*"

"Mr. Martin, why—"

"I can't play the piano," he said squarely.

"That's because you've just heard Dremling. He takes the conceit out of us all."

"Dremling? Oh, it's not Dremling—he least of all! What I've learned in four days! The way you raised your eyebrows that afternoon I was so enthusiastic about the girl who accompanied you. 'Oh! she's not a pianist,' you said. The woman who played the Brahms sonata with your cousin, the boy who played Debussy, the magic, the poetry of it, the things he made the piano do, the girl who played the Beethoven concerto at the concert, Dremling this afternoon, and then Hugo."

"Hugo?"

"Hugo, worst of all."

"But Hugo can't play."

"That's it, that's it, he 'can't play'; you've said so yourself—and that girl who accompanied you 'can't play'; and that man who was at the piano for an hour yesterday afternoon 'can't play.' None of them can play, but they all play as well as I do—better."

"My dear man, you play much better than Hugo or Jerry."

"They don't pretend to be pianists—they never practice, they've not given their whole lives to it as I have. Why were you so kind to me at Doon? Why didn't you tell me the truth? Or did you think I wouldn't believe you, that it was better I should find out for myself in this dreadful way? Was that why you brought me to London?"

Poor Mrs. Conder turned away.

"My God, when I think of it I grow hot all over. Do they all know at Doon? Is it a kind conspiracy because I'm unfortunate, crippled? Are they sighing behind my back: 'Poor Mr. Martin, I suppose we must ask him to play. He thinks he can'?"

"I am sure they all think you play beautifully," she said gently.

"No, no, there'll be some who must see through me, someone like you, some stranger will come from time to time and listen and *know*. Oh, the things I've said, the attitude I've taken up!"

He put his hands over his face.

"I can never go back there. I can never face Doon again."

"What nonsense."

"They'll say 'like father like son'; both deceive, cheat, pretend, lie."

"You haven't lied, you've said nothing you didn't believe to be true, done nothing you didn't believe."

"They'll never believe that I didn't know. I'm losing the only thing I ever had or rather finding out that I never had it at all."

"You have it. Yes, it's in you. If you had been taught, if you had had a chance of hearing music, if your mother had let you travel."

"If, if, if," he mocked. "If I had never been born, if the pony had kicked my head in that time instead of only my back."

"You are cruel to yourself."

"I must pay myself out for all that secret complacency, that feeling of superiority. I despised them, I felt I was a great man."

"You are great compared with them."

"How do you know? They're so polite, *you* were so polite. You deceived me as entirely as they did. I can never play to them again."

"You can go back and tell them what you have learned here."

"They will pretend not to believe me, they will half-persuade me, I'll end by playing for them but always with the feeling that there may be one amongst them, like you, who knows, sees me for a conceited fraud, a pretentious amateur who gives himself airs. Anything, anything would be better than that."

"Then don't go back. Stay here, take lessons."

"And be in the end—what? Still third-rate, still an amateur. I haven't the physical strength to work hard. Whichever way I turn, I'm caught. But if only people would believe that I was innocent, that I didn't know."

"Think of all the pleasure you have given Doon. They have spoken about you to me often. Believe me, they think you great. There is no conspiracy to deceive you. You must go back to them, you must play for them again."

He shook his head.

"Never. You don't know my story—my father's story. I have always tried to be perfectly honest, never like him. I, a bigger deceiver than ever he was. I shall go back—but I shall never play again."

"Do you think you will be able to keep that vow?"

"I shall tell them I cannot play."

"They will force you to play."

"They can never force me to believe in myself again."

"But they will make you play."

Again he shook his head.

"Never. I shall prove to them that I can't play."

"That will be impossible."

"No, quite easy."

"What do you mean?"

"I shall maim myself, shoot off a finger."

She caught his hands.

"You are mad, you must never do that. It would be wicked. It is a sin even to speak of doing such a thing. You talk of truth, honesty—do you call that honest?"

"More honest to deceive them once and be done with lies for ever."

"You mustn't, you mustn't."

"I will."

She dropped his hands.

"Why did I bring you to London?" she moaned.

"Thank God you did. Thank God you taught me the truth."

She sank into a chair.

"It's horrible, you mustn't. Believe in yourself again, believe they believe, believe *I* believe!"

To that absurd appeal he made no reply and when she looked at him again a minute later, she found he was staring at his hands, stroking the fingers of his right hand gently as if he were bidding them farewell.

LIAM O'FLAHERTY

1897–1984

Liam O'Flaherty was born on the main island of the
Aran group just a year before Synge paid his first visit
there. Gaelic was O'Flaherty's native tongue, but he
soon learned English. Educated for the priesthood
by the Holy Ghost Fathers as a boarder at two of
their secondary schools—those attended by Pádraic
Ó Conaire—O'Flaherty entered the Dublin diocesan
seminary before deciding that he lacked a vocation.
After attending University College, Dublin, briefly he
joined the Irish Guards and fought in France. Shell-
shocked in 1917, he received a medical discharge from
the British Army. After knocking about the world for
two years in various jobs at sea and ashore, he returned
to the Aran Islands for a time. Next he went to Dublin
and played a brief part in the Civil War. Fearing arrest,
he escaped to London and there started to write. His
first novel, *Thy Neighbour's Wife*, was published in 1923.
With the encouragement of Edward Garnett, once D. H.
Lawrence's editor, O'Flaherty wrote two more novels
and two volumes of short stories in the next three years,
winning worldwide attention with *The Informer* (1926),
later made into a famous Hollywood movie by John
Ford. Like Lawrence, whose writing he sometimes
strove to emulate, O'Flaherty eloped with a professor's
wife whom he later married. He lived for long periods
in the U.S. and France, and visited Russia. Later he
spent most of his time in Ireland. O'Flaherty reached his
peak as a novelist with *Skerrett* (1932) and *Famine* (1937);
his fourteenth novel was published in 1951. He
continued to write short stories. In 1953 he published
his first volume of short stories in Gaelic, *Dúil* (Desire).
"The Blow" may have been written originally in Gaelic,
for it corresponds to the story "An Buille" in *Dúil*. It

shows the compassion of his later stories, as well as the extraordinary capacity to observe and identify with animals apparent even in his earliest work. "Lovers," not collected in any of his volumes, dates from 1931; it approaches human beings entirely from the outside, a viewpoint very common in his early work. One senses that O'Flaherty was still immature enough to want to shock his readers by callousness and cynicism, but I think the two "lovers" win our compassion nonetheless.

Lovers

It was extremely hot. Old Michael Doyle had been to the shop to get an ounce of tobacco. Now he found it difficult to make his way home. Leaning heavily on his stick, he walked slowly along under the shelter of a high wall that lined the road.

"I'm sorry now," he grumbled, "I didn't send one of the youngsters to fetch it."

About a minute later he halted, straightened himself, and added:

"But they might have kept the money. Aw! 't's terrible the way I'm treated in what used to be my own house. Aw! I had better sit down and have a smoke. God Almighty! Isn't it hot?"

He was seventy-seven years old. He had once been a man of great size, but now he was huddled together, an ungainly heap, as if all his limbs had been broken and disjointed and then stitched haphazard. His nose was a lump, his lower lip had drawn together in a bun, and his bleary eyes, through constant running, had made drains down his cheeks. His clothes were patched in an astonishing way. They did not fit, and had obviously been cast off by his son and grandchildren. One of his grandsons was thirty years of age.

With great difficulty he sat down under the shelter of the

wall. When he stretched out his legs and crossed his feet, the shadow of the wall reached halfway down his thighs. That was good. The upper part of his body was quite cool, and he sighed with content.

"Aye!" he said. "It's a mortal terror how strength leaves a person."

He fumbled in his pocket for his pipe. It had got entangled in his handkerchief, so that came out too, and with it everything that was in that pocket. He dropped the handkerchief beside him on the grass that grew under the wall. Then he got his knife out of the other pocket of his waistcoat. He spent more than two minutes trying to open it, and finally succeeded in doing so by placing the edge of the blade against the sharp corner of a stone in the wall.

"Hoick!" he said with pleasure. "I'm not dead yet. Wasn't that clever now?"

Then he began to clean the bowl of his pipe. He blew through the stem. It whistled. It was clear. Putting the pipe down beside him on the grass he searched in his pockets for the ounce of tobacco he had just bought. It was nowhere to be found. He took off his hat and looked into the crown, without success, even though he fumbled under the band and pawed all over. He opened his waistcoat and then his shirt. He searched about his chest. The tobacco was nowhere. Then he got excited and began to get to his feet, crying angrily:

"That robber didn't give it to me. She took money and kept the tobacco." As he was getting up, he put his hand on the handkerchief he had dropped. There was a hard lump under it. He cried: "Ha! Here it is. Who'd ever think of it?"

So he settled himself down again, but in the effort to do so he dislodged the tobacco and he sat on it. When he examined the handkerchief there was nothing in it.

"Oh! Well!" he said. "There's devilry in this."

He began to scratch his head and then again set about looking for the tobacco, prodding the grass with his stick and clawing with his hands.

An old woman called Mary Kane, passing in the opposite direction, halted to watch him. She was seventy years old, but quite brisk. Her face was withered, like an old apple, but she still retained all her faculties. She wore boots with very high heels. It was obvious that she had once very beautiful legs and her carriage was that of a woman who was once beautiful. She wore a cashmere shawl that trailed down her back, almost to the ground, in a triangle, with the apex at her heels. In spite of the heat, she wore the shawl right out over her head, almost hiding her face.

She halted in front of the old man and then, recognizing him, she threw back her shawl and made a dramatic gesture with her arms.

"Bless my soul!" she said. "If it isn't Michael Doyle. Ah! Musha, how are you, brother?"

The old man looked up slowly, shaded his eyes, and said:

"God and Mary to you. What village are you from?"

"Arrah! Don't you know me?" she said.

"Pooh!" said the old man. "I don't know a person these days. They do be making fun of me. What village did you say?"

"D'ye mean to say ye don't know Mary Kane?"

"Oho!" said the old man. "Is that who you are? Well now! And how is everybody belonging to you?"

"Aren't you the artful creature?" she said. "Don't you know well I live alone and that I have nobody belonging to me, God help us?"

"Oho!" said the old man. " 'Faith, I don't know you at all."

"Oh!" said the old woman, throwing out her arms. "Isn't he artful? And what are you looking for, may I ask?"

"Eh? What would I be looking for?"

"I saw you pawing about on the grass."

"Begob, strangers are curious. And what would you be watching me for?"

"You're a sour old devil, Michael Doyle."

"Why wouldn't I be sour when I just lost my tobacco?"

"Haw!" she said, jamming her arms against her hips and shaking herself with violence. "Sure I knew you had lost something, and that you were pawing about for it, like a newborn infant, God help you; it's back you're going to the cradle, you that were the pride of the parish."

"Begob," he said, "whoever you are, you have the gift of
the gab. But it's strange anyways. A minute ago I had it in
me hand. And now the devil has swallowed it."

"Let me search," she said.

"Search away," he said. "You won't find a grain of it."

The old woman peered about sharply on the grass.

"What's this?" she said, picking up a button. "Did it fall
off your waistcoat?"

He peered at it.

"It's a button," he said. "I found it and I'm keeping it
for a young fellow. They like buttons. I do keep buttons
and give them to the children. Then they go messages for
me. It's cheaper that way than pennies."

"It's nowhere to be seen," she said. "I declare to God,
but I bet you're sitting on it. Move your old bones."

She pushed him aside and found the tobacco, half buried
in the grass. She held it up before his eyes in triumph. He
grabbed it from her without a word of thanks. Having
found his knife, he began to pare off some of the tobacco
into the palm of his hand. She sat down beside him on her
heels. He paid no attention to her, but began to fill his pipe.
She watched him closely, with her lips drawn back from
her teeth and her eyes narrowed, after the manner of people who are in the habit of looking long distances out to
sea. Then she said:

"Now tell me on your soul, Michael, don't you know
me?"

He looked at her sourly and said:

"Begob, you're a great woman for arguing, so you are."

"I declare he doesn't know me," she said plaintively.
"Oh! Isn't this life cruel? It's five years since I saw you last,
Michael, and you knew me then, although you passed me
by with a sour nod of salutation, same as you always did
since my marriage. Even the misfortunes that I suffered
didn't soften you. And now your memory has gone completely. Like grass in a flooded field it's buried under the
weight of years. Ah! Sure it breaks my heart to see you so,
all withered like a rooted bush. And I that can remember
the day when you had golden curls on your head and your
eyes glittered like the sea with the sun full on it. Aye!

Death should come young to the unfortunate. They are foolish who weep over a young corpse. For it's an unholy sight you are, all crippled and not knowing me."

Unheeding, the old man cracked a match and put it to his pipe and sucked, making a great noise each time his hollowed cheeks expanded. Smoke belched from the pipe. When it was well lit he hurled away the match, spat and wiped his mouth on his sleeve. All his movements were uncomely. Yet the old woman watched him with a queer longing in her faded eyes.

"This is queer talk you have, woman," he said gloomily. "Who are you anyway? You're from a strange village, I'm thinking."

The old woman drew her shawl about her head once more and sniffed. She put a corner of her apron to her eyes. Taking his pipe out of his mouth, the old man looked at her closely. Then he spat, mumbled something, and pulled his hat further down over his eyes. The old woman began to rock gently.

"Not like you," she said, "my memory gets sharper with old age. Like a sick nerve it stabs me when I'm least expecting and then I go dreaming sadly through the years. Sure the first day I set eyes on you is as plain to me as the wall's black shadow on the road there. I was milking the cows when you came by on a horse in the evening. You blessed me and I looked up and then you stopped your horse and we began to talk, and I gave you warm milk to drink out of the can. Musha! There and then I belonged to you. Don't you remember that evening?"

"Oho!" said the old man. "What evening are you talking about?"

"Musha, don't you remember how we used to meet on the hill above my father's house, how I used to run up the little road after nightfall and you used to be waiting for me?"

"Pooh!" said the little man. "The devil a bit o' me remembers anything o' the kind. There now. Sure I hardly ever stir out of the house. Me waiting for ye!"

"Sure it's not today or yesterday I'm talking about," she said, "but this fifty-four years ago. I remember it well. I was sixteen, and you were just turned twenty-three. Poor man, it's all the drinking and fighting you did that brought you to this crippled state."

"Arrah! Be easy with you," he said. "What drinking did I do? A few pints now and again. An odd glass of whisky."

"God forgive you," she said. "You were four times in jail, not to mention the time you came with your relations and stole me out of the house with a strong hand, and you gave Ned Kane such a beating with a stick that he spent three months in hospital and you got six months in jail for it."

"Who? Me?" he said, taking his pipe out of his mouth and looking at her intently. "Me in jail? What for?"

"For nearly killing Ned Kane with a stick that night you took me."

The old man's face suddenly lit with a gleam of memory. He opened his mouth and then brought his right hand down heavily on his knee.

"Aw!" he said, with great emphasis. "Ned Kane. I remember the dirty scoundrel. Hah! Musha, the devil take him. If I hit him he deserved it. A dirty scoundrel from head to foot. Begob then, I did beat him and I beat him well."

He groped for his stick, clutched it, and said excitedly:

"By my soul! I don't care who's listening, but I'll say this much: There was a day when I could beat with my bare hands any man in this parish that ever sucked at his mother's breasts."

"But don't you remember the night you came to the house?"

"Eh?" said the old man.

He scratched his head and still looked at her intently with his rheumy eyes. But his face gradually grew vacant and he said:

"Well, now ye drove it all out of my head again with your talk. Ech! I get dizzy with this heat. They do be making fun of me about it. I put down my hat and I declare to God I can't find it a minute after."

"Ah! God help you, poor man," she said wearily. "But sure it's me that is to be pitied more. Maybe if I had you in our youth it wouldn't be. There'd be the care of children to soften the falling years. There it is. Every bit of it is plain to me, alive like a blister. You came then with your uncle and two men from your village to ask for me, and my father gave you the door. 'Is it to a drunkard that hasn't a shirt to his back I'd give my daughter?' said he. We had four cows then, and we were rich, and it was well-known that I had thirty acres of land and the stock and two hundred gold sovereigns for my portion. That's how it was. It was to Ned Kane he wanted to give me, and it was Ned I married in spite of everything."

"Tare an' ouns," said the old man crossly. "My pipe is gone out."

"Let it be," she said, "and listen to me. Though you don't remember, or pretend you don't, whichever it is, I'll tell you the truth now, for it's my first opportunity in all these years. When they wanted to marry me to Kane, I came and told you, and you said you'd take me, if the devil was sitting on my bed counter. So there it was. Ned Kane came with his people, and they were in the house making the match, when all of a sudden there was a clatter of horses outside, and you called out. It was dead of night. 'Come out, Ned Kane,' says you, 'or faith you'll come out a corpse.' Your uncle, Peter Timoney, was with you and Simon Grealish and Hugh Rody and more men, too. Then you burst in the door and laid out whatever was there. Such shouting was never heard before or after. Then you barged into the room where I was with my mother and the women. My mother marked you with a tongs, but nothing could stop you that night. And glad enough I was to go, too. Then you took me away behind you on the horse, but sure when the priest was awakened at the dawn, he refused to marry us. Then the police came and we hiding at your uncle's house, and every man was arrested. Back I was brought. Oh! That was the night. And d'ye mean to tell me, Michael Doyle, that you don't remember it?"

The old man paused, with a lighted match to the bowl of his pipe. He looked up at her and then, without speaking, he drew at the pipe, lit it, and threw away the match.

"People do have great talk of the fighting I done," he

said. "They're always casting it in my face. But I daresay I was no worse than others."

He began to grumble while the old woman continued her story.

"You went to jail then," she said, "and when Kane came out of hospital we were married. What could I do? Sure I had no hand or part in it. I'd have gone with you anywhere. I used to cry my eyes out then, but there was nothing to be done. And, God forgive you, it was me you blamed for it. It's been a long and lonely life of misery I had, with Kane drinking and routing whatever there was, all he could lay his hands on, until he died of sickness. Not a child blessed my hearth, and hardly a relation is left to me now. And that's the way it is. Nor you left to me either; nothing only a sad, sad memory of a love that was strangled in its cradle."

She sobbed and rocked herself, with her shawl far out over her eyes. The old man moved about restlessly, looking at her from time to time, mumbling to himself. At last he said:

"Poor woman, you have your sorrow."

"Aye," she said. "It's a load I carry with me always. This talking has made it heavier. I wish I passed you by."

She got to her feet, shook herself and straightened out her shawl. She dried her eyes with her apron. Then she threw back her shawl and looked at him. Her eyes were red and her lips twitched.

"Won't you say a gentle word to me," she said, "before I go my road?"

He looked up at her stupidly.

"God bless you!" he said.

"And you, Michael," she answered. "May you rest in peace!"

She turned and walked away, her shawl in a triangle, her high heels tipping the road sharply. He looked after her, pulling slowly at his pipe.

His withered countenance seemed to have lost all traces of human consciousness. It was apelike. His rheumy eyes, wrinkled like those of a gorilla, had no light in them.

"Pooh!" he said after a while. "What was that poor woman saying?"

He sat with his mouth wide open for another few minutes, as if trying to remember something. But his mind was a complete blank. Then he struggled to his feet and trudged homewards, walking on the grass by the wall in the shadow.

The Blow

When the car halted before the farmyard, his father told Neidin to open the big iron gate.

"Hurry up," the father shouted angrily at the little boy, who was getting out of the car timidly. "Why the devil can't you move yourself with energy, like an ambitious and eager young fellow? Honest to God! Anybody would think you are a little girl, by the way you set about doing a job."

The father was a big fat red-faced man called Eamonn O'Floinn. He owned quite a large hotel at a nearby seaside resort; to which a great number of English visitors had been coming since the war, owing to the continued rationing of food in their own country. He raised pigs on the leavings of those people. It was to buy piglets that he had come to this nursery-farm, with his young son at foot. By nature a greedy and rough-mannered fellow, without much intelligence or sensitivity, he had become quite unbalanced by the extraordinary amount of money he was earning of late. Indeed, the poor man had almost become a complete savage. He was dashing about from morning till night, like a beast gone mad with summer heat, trying to add more and more to his already considerable wealth.

"Look sharp," he cried out again, when the boy was approaching the gate. "Lord God! I often think that you are no child of mine. Stir yourself. We didn't come here for an outing, but to do a job of work."

All this shouting and abuse made the little boy numb with fear, instead of rousing him to speedy action. He approached the gate like a wounded beetle, dragging his feet along the ground and hesitating after each paltry step. Indeed, that was more or less his customary carriage; even when all was well with his sensitive being. One got the impression that he was always trying to make his way over extremely dangerous and uneven ground. He was eleven years old and reasonably tall for that age; but his undeveloped frame was very thin. There was hardly any flesh on his bare shins. He needed only a few inches of belt to hold his short grey pants in position about his waist. His bones showed through his blue jersey. The points of his elbows were quite as sharp as those of an old cow's hips. Even so, he looked attractive owing to the beauty of his countenance. His big blue eyes made manifest that his body was being starved by the rapid growth of his hungry intellect. There was far more depth of understanding in them already than in those of his father; understanding and wonder and suffering. A delicate tremor was passing along the edge of his refined mouth just then, owing to the intensity of his emotion; like the trembling of a flower when touched by a current of cold air.

He had pulled the heavy bolts and he was on the point of swinging back the left half of the gate, when he became aware that young birds were chattering excitedly in a nest above his head. In spite of his fear, he paused and looked up at a large clump of ivy that grew on the apex of a stone arch, high above the gate. The nest was in the ivy. A large rusty bell, from whose mouth a short piece of decayed rope was dangling, hung from the arch by a chain. The chain and the top of the bell, which had not been used for some time, were also covered with ivy.

"You little devil!" the father roared. "Now you stand watching birds, like a simpleton. What on earth am I to do with you? Open that gate."

The boy started and seized the left half of the gate with both hands. Then he pushed with all his strength. The iron was very heavy and it had not been oiled for a long time. Neidin found great difficulty in making it swing on its hinges.

"Lord God!" the father yelled. "Why can't you give it a good strong push? You've not got the strength of a flea in you."

The gate finally began to swing open. It made a melancholy sound on a high note, as if the movement gave it pain.

"Push hard," the father shouted. "Throw it right back. That's the way to do it. Keep going now. Don't slacken."

While Neidin was crossing over to open the second half, one of the old sparrows flew out of the nest with a loud noise after sharing a worm among its brood. The boy stood still once more and watched the bird fly swiftly towards the east, until his father began to beat upon the steering wheel of the car with clenched fists.

"I'll have your life," the father cried in a voice that was shrill with rage. "Oh! God Almighty! This must be a punishment for some unknown sin that I committed. You have me crucified. Crucified!"

This fresh outburst completely roused the boy and he opened the second half of the gate much more quickly. He had not quite pushed it back completely, however, when his father drove the car forward abruptly and he was forced to jump out of the way.

"There's not a single drop of my blood in you," the father yelled, as the car was going through the gateway. "You took after your mother, a miserable idler like yourself."

The boy trembled from head to foot and he wanted terribly to burst into tears, on hearing his mother insulted in this brutal fashion. He adored his mother; a gentle and affectionate person that took delight in his strange ideas and listened with rapt attention to the fantastic tales he was in the habit of telling her before going to sleep. His mother! She was his angel guardian and his heavenly queen. At that moment, his father was more loathsome to him than a devil from hell, for referring to her with such gross contempt. He had to bite hard into his lower lip before he managed to restrain his tears. His cheeks went pale and he felt cold down along his spine.

However, a child's memory of good or evil is very short-lived. He had barely gone through the gateway, in pursuit of the car, when the wonders of the farmyard banished his sorrow. This was his first visit to the place. It was long and narrow, with a lofty stone wall at each end and pigsties along both sides. The cement floor was smooth and neat.

A drinking trough, to which a pump was attached, stood in the center. Another large gate pierced the far wall. It stood ajar. Huge pigs were digging with their snouts in a mud-covered paddock that lay beyond.

"Oh! What a lovely place!" said Neidin to himself with delight, as he looked in all directions. "It's really beautiful."

The father halted the car before a sty in which a tall grey-haired man was taking soiled bedding off the floor with a pitchfork.

"Hello there, Peadar," he said to the grey-haired man.

"Hello, Eamonn," the grey-haired man said. "A warm day."

"Very warm," said Eamonn as he got out of the car. "I thought I'd come to have a look at your young pigs, to see if I could find six or seven that I'd care to buy."

The grey-haired man leaned his chest against the top of his pitchfork, spat and said with great force:

"Six or seven? Let me tell you, Eamonn, that I have over three score of the best young pigs you ever saw in your life."

"Good for you, Peadar," said Eamonn. "Where are they?"

"Just a moment," said Peadar. "I'm going to show you a litter of ten that are as handsome—"

"Ten would be too many," Eamonn interrupted. "I only want six or seven. That's my limit."

"When you lay eyes on this litter," said Peadar, as the two men crossed the yard, "your mouth is going to water for every single one of them. They're all lovely creatures."

"A man might want to have the sun," said Eamonn, "without his purse being well enough filled to let him make the purchase."

"Listen to who is talking about a purse not being well enough filled," said Peadar. "A man that's rotten with money."

"Are you referring to me?" cried Eamonn in pretended amazement. "A man that has no land? A man that has to pay for everything on the nail?"

"Never mind about that kind of talk," said Peadar. "I let it in one ear and out the other. The rich always pretend to be poor."

At that moment, a huge sow pig entered the yard
through the paddock gate. Her hide was daubed with mud
from head to tail. She had her snout to the ground and her
little sharp eyes stared angrily straight ahead, as if she were
bearing down on a deadly enemy. Her bristles were standing up straight on the nape of her neck and her tail was
twisted into a tight ball on her rump, with the tapering end
stiffly erect. As she twirled her haunches arrogantly with
each stride, the empty bag of her long udder swayed from
side to side of her slack belly and the shrunken teats kept
dancing to and from, like puppets being dangled on a multitude of strings. Her huge ears kept flapping rhythmically.

"Oh! Good heavens!" Neidin said to himself, as he stared
at the animal with delight. "She is nearly as tall as a donkey. Oh! See how long she is. She is surely longer than a
donkey. She's wonderful. Oh! Indeed, she is really the most
beautiful thing I have ever seen."

He followed the sow over to a corner, where his father
and the grey-haired man were leaning against the half-door
of a sty.

"Hurrais! Hurrais!" he whispered to her officiously, pretending that she belonged to him and that he was driving
her home from the paddock. "Get along now, old girl. Hurrais!"

The sow paid no attention whatsoever to the little boy
that was walking along beside her and patting her haunch
with his palm. She kept on her way resolutely, at a fierce
gait, until she reached the two men. She halted directly behind their heels with her snout to the ground.

"That fellow there," said the grey-haired man, as he
pointed a finger at the animal that occupied the sty, "is the
boar that sired the litter I'm going to sell you. There's a
beautiful boar for you. I'm ready to swear in a court of
law, before a judge, that you couldn't find in the whole of
this county a finer animal, or one that could—"

At that moment, the sow raised her snout and began to
call with great force, in a deep and harsh tone. Her voice
seemed to issue from the center of her being with the
majesty of thunder. Like bullets coming from a machine

gun, call followed call in unbroken measure, without making haste or slackening. The sound was mysterious and brutal; like the howling of a she-animal in a dark forest at the beginning of life, making known her urge towards motherhood. The boar answered the fifth call with a scream that had the intensity of madness. Then he attacked the heavy wooden door of the sty with his forefeet and his snout.

"Be off," said the grey-haired man, as he struck the sow in the side with his foot. "Get away. Hurrais!"

The sow went meekly up the yard, complaining in a low tone with her snout to the ground. The boar continued to scream and to beat upon the door, until the grey-haired man began to whack him about the head with a heavy stick. Then he became silent and took to gnawing the bottom of the door with his teeth, shivering with anger from head to tail.

"That fellow is a real devil," the grey-haired man said proudly to Neidin's father. "There's no end to his strength, or to his courage. He is not afraid of man or dog."

"He is a fine length," said Eamonn, "but he looks a bit too narrow in the loins. I'd say that his get would not have enough room to grow a good load of meat. Neither would they, in my opinion, be strong enough in the leg to—"

"That kind of talk is foolish," Peadar interrupted in an irritated tone. "I'm telling you that every single one of his get—"

"Look here," Eamonn interrupted. "I'm only saying that—"

"There is no sense at all," Peadar interrupted once more, "in casting aspersions on a litter that you have not seen. Come on over here until I show you a sight that will gladden your eyes."

When the two men had gone, Neidin put his two hands on top of the half-door and then rose up on his toes. He had just looked down into the sty at the enraged animal, when the latter grunted and stepped a short distance to the rear.

"Oh! You devil" said Neidin to himself excitedly. "This one is bigger still. There is no end to his length."

The boar spread his forelegs, lowered his snout, and then

charged at the door with all his strength. He struck it with his forehead like a bull, down near its base. It shook so violently that the little boy was almost knocked from his perch. If the wood had not been thick and tough, it would have been smashed to little pieces.

"Oh! You devil!" Neidin cried out loud in a delighted tone. "There was a blow for you."

The boar drew back again and settled himself to deliver a second blow. He changed his mind at the last moment and looked up at the little boy. There was bitter hatred in his eyes and foam dripped from his jaws. Yet the boy did not feel at all afraid of the savage boar. On the contrary, a lump came into his throat with pity for the enraged creature that was imprisoned in that foul-smelling little room and beaten by its jailers for trying to fulfill the passion of its nature. He also felt pity for the sow, and the mysterious sound of her voice kept ringing in his ears; just as he pitied the whispering of the wind that came through the window of his room on a stormy night; unintelligible secrets doomed to eternal wandering on the lonely air.

"Don't be angry with me," he whispered gently to the boar. "It's not my fault that you are shut up in this room. I'd let you out if I could. Indeed, I'd let you out at once."

Then he continued to stare at the boar intently. The enraged animal and the boy stood eye to eye, as if joined in a mysterious intimacy.

"Come on over here," the father shouted suddenly.

Neidin hurried over to a sty in which the two men were looking at a litter of half-grown pigs.

"Is it teaching him how to make a bargain you are?" the grey-haired man said when Neidin arrived. "If it is, he couldn't have a better teacher than yourself."

"Every sort of knowledge is useful to a boy," said Eamonn, who was examining the young pigs in expert fashion. "Listen to me, Peadar. I don't like to be finding fault, but two or three of these are very backward. I'd say that they would never be—"

"Never mind that," the grey-haired man interrupted. "They won't be long improving on a full belly."

"It wouldn't be worth my while," said Eamonn, "to carry those scrawny ones home. Let us put a price on the seven that are middling."

"I'm only the manager," said the grey-haired man. "Her ladyship told me to ask seven pounds a head for this litter, through and through."

"In that case," said Eamonn, as he jumped out into the yard over the half-door, "I'm only wasting my time here."

"Don't be so hasty," said the grey-haired man, as he followed Eamonn out into the yard. "I'm telling you that—"

"I only want the seven that are middling," Eamonn interrupted.

"All right, then," said the grey-haired man, as he went up the yard. "I don't mind going over to herself, in order to put in a good word for you. I'll tell her you only want the seven champions."

"Do that," said Eamonn casually, as he leaned over the half-door of a sty in which there was a sow with a large litter of very young piglets.

"I'll do my best," the grey-haired man shouted from a distance.

"Don't be long," Eamonn shouted in reply. "I have a lot to do."

"I won't be two minutes," said the grey-haired man.

"Come over here," the father said to Neidin. "Come and look at these."

Neidin went over slowly, stood beside his father and looked into the sty over the half-door.

"Pay attention to what you see there," the father said, "because you can learn a great deal from watching what there is to be seen."

The sow was lying on her side and the whole litter was trying to suck milk from her teats. Since the lower half of the udder was concealed beneath some straw that lay on the floor, there were not enough teats exposed to give the whole numerous brood access to the milk. So that the hungry piglets kept pushing against one another and whimpering in a forlorn tone. No sooner did one of them manage to grab a teat and begin to suck a mouthful of the warm fluid than it was pushed aside without ceremony by the others. Some were lifted up into the air. Others were knocked down and trodden underfoot. Two were much larger than their mates. They alone managed to stand their ground at teat and swallow a fair share of nourishment before being dispossessed. Away out in front, a tiny piglet was foolishly trying to suck milk from the sow's ear. The frail creature was trembling from head to tail and it moaned piteously, as its little snout darted hither and thither ineffectually, trying to establish contact with the fountain of its life.

"Do you see that?" said the father.

"I do," said Neidin gently.

"What do you see?" said the father.

"A sow giving suck to her litter," said Neidin.

"Is that all?" said the father.

"What else is there to see?" said Neidin.

"Do you see the tiny one, that's trying to suck milk from her ear like a fool?" said the father.

A lump again came into Neidin's throat through pity for the hapless creature that had lost its wits through panic and the weakness of extreme hunger.

"I do," he said almost inaudibly.

"When that little fellow was born," said the father, "he was just as big as the others. Look at him now. He hasn't grown an inch, because he is cowardly and lazy. He didn't have enough energy or strength to fight for his share of the milk. He was thrown aside every time he tried to seize a teat and drink his fill. Instead of fighting for his rights, he quit every time he was struck. Now he is paying for his cowardice, the miserable little wretch. Do you understand?"

"Yes, father," Neidin whispered.

The sow began to rise at that moment. As she tossed her head, the tiny piglet was struck in the side. It fell in a heap among some straw in the center of the floor.

"Did you see that?" said the father. "Even his mother has no respect for the miserable dwarf. She hit him."

The boy got violently angry and stamped on the floor with his left foot as hard as he could.

"She didn't hit him on purpose," he cried out in a shrill tone. "He got in her way when she was rising. It was an accident."

"I tell you she hit him on purpose," the father shouted.

"She didn't," said Neidin.

"She did," said the father, "and she was right. That's how it is in this world. There is neither pity nor mercy, among people as well as among animals, bad or good, for the weak and cowardly."

"That's not true," cried the boy, as tears began to come from his eyes. "I'm sorry for the little pig. I'm very sorry for him."

The father got furious and struck the boy in the cheek with the back of his hand.

"Shut up," he said through his clenched teeth.

The boy stood up stiffly on being struck, like a soldier at attention before an officer; with his clenched fists close to his sides and his chin thrust forward and his heels together. It seemed to him that his whole being had been frozen by the poisonous cold of the blow, which banished from his consciousness everything that pertained to the divinity of his nature; so that he was no longer capable of feeling either pity or mercy. Struck! It was just as if he had been struck by a demon from hell with a sledgehammer, which turned the marrow of his bones and the warm streams of his blood into ice; blood and marrow that had been pregnant until then with a godly love of life and that bore the suffering of compassion without relenting. Now his intellect stood alone, without contact with the loving heart by which its pride had hitherto been held in check; a cold devilish intellect, that no longer gave the heat of human passion to the wonders that entered his brain through the windows of his eyes.

"You are a shame and a disgrace," the father shouted in fury. "A disgrace! A boy of eleven crying like a baby! Crying!"

"Crying!" said the boy coldly, as he turned his head and looked at his father in a most haughty fashion. "I'm not crying."

That was quite true. The first two tears, drawn from his eyes by pity for the hapless little animal, had begun to fall when he was struck. Now they stood on the pinnacles of

his cheeks, like two pears, frozen in their flight by the
shock. Yet the eyes above them were clear and cold, like
the water of a rock-pool in the sunlight, showing only the
devilish pride of intellectual solitude; pride and contempt.

The father got frightened by the extraordinary manner
in which his son's character seemed to have changed as a
result of the blow. So that he regretted the disappearance
of the girlish timidity that had annoyed him so terribly until then. He himself almost burst into tears through shame
and remorse. His heart throbbed painfully with love for this
strange boy; the only child that had come from his loins.
Yet his nature was so harsh that he was unable to bow
down before his conscience. Neither was he able to admit
that he was at fault in striking the blow.

"You're not crying," he said in a flustered tone. "Indeed, you are not; but you are doing something that is far
worse. You are looking at your father bitterly. If I touched
you, it was only for your own good, trying to put sense
into your silly head. You are spoiled by your mother. She
has made a pet of you, letting you do whatever you please
and setting you against your father. I'm alone in the house.
The two of you have no more respect for me than you
would have for a mad dog. Oh! Lord God! I'm crucified
by the two of you. Crucified! Crucified!"

He turned suddenly and marched up the yard, wringing
his hands behind his back and complaining angrily.

"Crucified!" he continued. "I had better take to the roads
as a tramp, following my face, before I lose my mind.
What's the good of working and earning money for people
that hate me? I'd be better off breaking stones on the road."

All that abusive talk had absolutely no effect whatsoever
on the boy. Indeed, he scarcely understood the words. Neither was he influenced in the least by the misery of the tiny
piglet, even though he was staring at it intently. The hapless little creature had now retired to a corner of the sty,
where it stood with its head concealed beneath a few wisps
of straw, completely cut off from its mother and the rest
of the litter. Defeated and isolated! Now its miserable body
was shivering in fear of its solitude and of imminent death
through hunger. The boy, on the other hand, felt strong

and arrogant in this cold world that was bereft of pity.

He remained transfixed in that devilish trance until the sow began to call in a loud and urgent tone. She was now erect and the whole brood was sucking at her teats, except the little one that had been struck. The little one raised its head on hearing its mother's voice. Then it ran towards her, lurching unsteadily from side to side and tripping over wisps of straw. Now it was able to find a place at the udder. It took a teat into its mouth and began to drink. Although the boy watched the sow carefully from the moment she began to call, he was not aware that she took any notice of the little one's approach. Yet she ceased calling at the moment it began to drink.

"She called him," he whispered excitedly. "She did, indeed. She called him. That proves that she didn't hit him on purpose. She is fond of him. She is gentle and kind."

His heart softened while he spoke and he began to quiver with joy, because love had returned to the world. His throat filled up to its brink with a wave of tenderness, that was warm like new milk. Tears began to flow from his eyes in a steady stream and he felt a burning desire to run to his father, in order to say that he no longer felt hurt by the blow.

"No, father," he said to himself fervently. "I don't feel hurt at all. I'm very fond of you. Oh! I'm terribly fond of you."

The grey-haired man returned at that moment and spoke to Eamonn near the water trough.

"She is satisfied," he said. "You may have the seven big ones for seven pounds ten a head."

"Seven pounds ten!" cried Eamonn in an outraged tone. "Has she taken leave of her senses?"

"She has not," said the grey-haired man. "Indeed, she is only asking half the proper price of those champions. Look here. Those fellows are almost reared. You'd only have to give them a few bags of bran—"

"A few bags of bran?" Eamonn shouted. "Don't disgust me with that kind of nonsense. Seven pounds ten a head is highway robbery."

"Enough of that now," Peadar shouted. "If you mean

business, buy the pigs; if not, run along home before I lose my temper with you. I never heard such scandalous talk in all my life."

Eamonn raised his hand up to his shoulder and said:

"Stick it out, Peadar."

The grey-haired man thrust forth his open right palm, which Eamonn struck with his own palm.

"Seven pounds a head," Eamonn shouted, "and devil a penny more. Are you satisfied?"

Peadar put his hands behind his back and said:

"Seven pounds ten. That's her last word. Take it or leave it."

"I'll leave it," Eamonn shouted, as he made for his car in great haste. "I'll waste no more of my time. Good day to you."

"Safe journey," Peadar muttered, as he walked away in the opposite direction. "We live and learn. Such abuse! Lord God! I never heard the like of it from an honest man."

"Come on, Neidin," Eamonn shouted, as he got into his car. "We are going home now."

The little boy wiped his eyes hurriedly and came over to the car. Although his head was downcast and his clenched hands were held close to his sides, after the manner of a nervous child, he no longer felt afraid of his father. Indeed, he was possessed by a great wave of joy that ran madly through his veins and sang in his heart.

"Come on now," said the father. "Jump into the car. There is no sense at all in our staying any longer here."

"Hold on, Eamonn," Peadar shouted from a distance, when the engine was running. "Are you ready to split the difference?"

"Seven pounds five a head?" said Eamonn.

"Seven pounds five," said Peadar.

"I'm satisfied," said Eamonn in a gloomy tone, "although it's throwing good money away. Indeed, it's a mortal sin to pay that price for middling creatures like them."

"You are practically getting them for nothing," Peadar shouted in an equally melancholy tone. "Seven lovely creatures—"

Neidin felt terribly proud when he realized that his father had won the battle of wits.

"You got the better of him, father," he whispered excitedly.

The father looked at his son in astonishment. Then he smiled and his red face flushed with joy. It was the first time that his son had made a friendly approach of this sort; a gesture of comradeship and intimacy. It was manifest to him that the blow had been forgiven. He was beside himself with rapture.

"Don't say a word," he whispered through the side of his mouth, with one eye closed. "Pretend it was us that were robbed."

While he ran the car over to the sty to fetch the bought piglets, he had a strange feeling of having escaped miraculously from imminent destruction.

"Never again," he said to himself fervently. "I'll never lay a hand on him again."

When the seven piglets had been put into the back of the van, he paid the grey-haired man and drove away.

"Good luck to you," the grey-haired man said, as the car was going out the gate, "and may God spare your health."

Eamonn burst out laughing when the car reached the main road. He really laughed because he had finally managed to get on intimate terms with his son, but he pretended to be gloating over the good bargain he had made.

"I got the better of him right enough," he shouted boastfully. "I may tell you that every single one of them is worth fifteen shillings more than I paid."

"He got afraid," Neidin cried out delightedly, "when you pretended that you were going without them."

The father was thrilled by the tenderness in the voice of the strange young being, who had hitherto been as remote and unfathomable as the sea. His only son! He devoutly thanked God for the heavenly gift of his son's comradeship.

"That was only a trick," he shouted gaily at the top of his voice. "I had no intention of going away."

"He thought you did," said Neidin.

"He did," said the father, "because he doesn't know his

business. If he were smart enough, he'd know well that no man in his sober senses would leave lovely creatures like those behind for the sake of a few miserable shillings. Listen, son. I never in all my life laid eyes on such lovely young pigs. They are huge and every one of them is as healthy as a mountain trout. Look at their skins and their eyes and the fineness of their hair. For God's sake, Neidin, take a look at them and tell me whether you ever saw their equals."

The little boy turned on his seat and looked back at the seven young creatures, that stood facing him in a compact group. All seven of them stared with intent interest at the little boy; motionless except for the inquisitive quivering of their circular snouts.

"Oh! They are lovely, father," the boy said earnestly. "They really are lovely."

The father continued to boast in a loud ecstatic tone about his cleverness in having made such a splendid bargain. Now his voice was respectful instead of being harsh, as if he understood that he would henceforth merely be the faithful servant and guardian of this son, whom he had failed to dominate by brute force.

"How lovely they are!" Neidin said to himself, as he looked at the little pigs. "The insides of their ears are quite pink and transparent. Oh! What pretty little nostrils! They are as round as buttons. See that? These little ones are not a bit afraid of me. They are just wondering who I am and what I'm doing here. Oh! I'm going to be very fond of them."

He stretched out his hand gently towards the little pigs. They all shuddered at once, drew back slightly, and stared at the moving hand. Then the boy halted the movement of his hand and smiled. The animals lost their fear and became motionless once more; except for their quivering nostrils, that were smelling the hand.

They did not shudder when the hand moved forward gently again and touched the forehead of the one that stood in the center of the group. Instead of being afraid, all the others sniffed and-jerked their heads slightly, begging to be touched gently.

SEAN O' FAOLAIN
1900——

Born in Dublin, the son of a policeman, Sean O'Faolain
grew up in Cork City, where he became a member of
Daniel Corkery's dramatic society, learned Gaelic, and
took part in the Irish Civil War, taking the Republican
side. After graduating from University College, Cork,
O'Faolain taught in a school for a while, then went to
Harvard in 1926 on a fellowship and earned an M.A.
there. After teaching in the U.S., England, and Ireland,
he became a full-time writer. His first book, *Midsummer
Night Madness* (1932), was a volume of short stories—the
first of four, not counting a collected volume, *The Finest
Stories of Sean O'Faolain* (1957). He has also published
four novels, three travel books, four biographies, an
autobiography, two volumes of literary criticism, a play,
and a volume of poems translated from the Gaelic.
During World War II he edited a fine "little magazine",
The Bell, in Dublin. A leading figure in the Irish cultural
world, he has fought hard for civil liberties and for the
right of workers in the creative and performing arts to
earn a decent living. His wife, Eileen, was also a writer
and his daughter, Julia O'Faolain, has written novels
and short stories. He has frequently lectured and held
visiting professorships in the U.S. O'Faolain is a shrewd
observer of the rise and fall of social classes, as "The Fur
Coat" suggests. He also has a strong feeling for exiles,
whether they be Americans in Ireland, Irish in America,
or just Irish in Ireland. "Two of a Kind", from his
volume of stories *I Remember! I Remember!* (1961), is
reminiscent of his novel *Come Back to Erin* (1940), which
also treats the theme of exile. At his best, O'Faolain
envelops his characters in Christian charity while
avoiding sentimentality.

The Fur Coat

When Maguire became Parliamentary Secretary to the Minister for Roads and Railways, his wife wound her arms around his neck, lifted herself on her toes, gazed into his eyes, and said, adoringly:

"Now, Paddy, I must have a fur coat."

"Of course, of course, me dear," Maguire cried, holding her out from him admiringly; for she was a handsome little woman still, in spite of the graying hair and the first hint of a stoop. "Get two fur coats! Switzers's will give us any amount of tick from now on."

Molly sat back into her chair with her fingers clasped between her knees and said, chidingly:

"You think I'm extravagant!"

"Indeed, then, I do not. We've had some thin times together and it's about time we had a bit of comfort in our old age. I'd like to see my wife in a fur coat. I'd love to see my wife take a shine out of some of those straps in Grafton Street—painted jades that never lifted a finger for God or man, not to as much as mention the word *Ireland*. By all means get a fur coat. Go down to Switzer's tomorrow morning," he cried with all the innocence of a warmhearted, inexperienced man, "and order the best fur coat that money can buy."

Molly Maguire looked at him with affection and irritation. The years had polished her hard—politics, revolution, husband in and out of prison, children reared with the help of relatives and Prisoners' Dependents' funds. You could see the years on her fingertips, too pink, too coarse, and in her diamond-bright eyes.

"Paddy, you big fool, do you know what you'd pay for a mink coat? Not to mention a sable? And not as much as to whisper the word broadtail?"

"Say a hundred quid," said Paddy, manfully. "What's a hundred quid? I'll be handling millions of public money from now on. I have to think big."

She replied in her warm Limerick singsong; sedately and proudly as befitted a woman who had often, in her father's country store, handled thousands of pound notes.

"Do you know, Paddy Maguire, what a really bang-up fur coat could cost you? It could cost you a thousand guineas, and more."

"One thousand guineas? For a coat? Sure, that's a whole year's salary."

"It is."

Paddy drew into himself. "And," he said, in a cautious voice, "is that the kind of coat you had in mind?"

She laughed, satisfied at having taken him off his perch.

"Yerrah, not at all. I thought I might pick up a nice little coat for, maybe, thirty or forty or, at the outside, fifty quid. Would that be too much?"

"Go down to Switzer's in the morning and bring it home on your back."

But, even there, she thought she detected a touch of the bravo, as if he was still feeling himself a great fellow. She let it pass. She said she might have a look around. There was no hurry. She did not bring up the matter again for quite fifteen minutes.

"Paddy! About that fur coat. I sincerely hope you don't think I'm being *vulgar?*"

"How could you be vulgar?"

"Oh, sort of *nouveau riche.* I don't want a fur coat for show-off." She leaned forward eagerly. "Do you know the reason why I want a fur coat?"

"To keep you warm. What else?"

"Oh, well, that too, I suppose, yes," she agreed shortly. "But you must realize that from this on we'll be getting asked out to parties and receptions and so forth. And—well —I haven't a rag to wear!"

"I see," Paddy agreed; but she knew that he did not see.

"Look," she explained, "what I want is something I can wear any old time. I don't want a fur coat for grandeur." (This very scornfully.) "I want to be able to throw it on and go off and be as well dressed as anybody. You see, you can wear any old thing under a fur coat."

"That sounds a good idea." He considered the matter as

judiciously as if he were considering a memorandum for a projected bypass. She leaned back, contented, with the air of a woman who has successfully laid her conscience to rest.

Then he spoiled it all by asking, "But, tell me, what do all the women do who haven't fur coats?"

"They dress."

"Dress? Don't ye all dress?"

"Paddy, don't be silly. They think of nothing else but dress. I have no time for dressing. I'm a busy housewife and, anyway, dressing costs a lot of money." (Here she caught a flicker in his eye which obviously meant that forty quid isn't to be sniffed at either.) "I mean they have costumes that cost twenty-five pounds. Half a dozen of 'em. They spend a lot of time and thought over it. They live for it. If you were married to one of 'em, you'd soon know what it means to dress. The beauty of a fur coat is that you can just throw it on and you're as good as the best of them."

"Well, that's fine! Get the ould coat."

He was evidently no longer enthusiastic. A fur coat, he had learned, is not a grand thing—it is just a useful thing. He drew his briefcase towards him. There was that pier down in Kerry to be looked at. "Mind you," he added, "it'd be nice and warm, too. Keep you from getting a cold."

"Oh, grand, yes, naturally, cozy, yes, all that, yes, yes!"

And she crashed out and banged the door after her and put the children to bed as if she were throwing sacks of turf into a cellar. When she came back he was pouring over maps and specifications. She began to patch one of the boy's pyjamas. After a while she held it up and looked at it in despair. She let it sink into her lap and looked at the pile of mending beside her.

"I suppose when I'm dead and gone, they'll invent plastic pyjamas that you can wash with a dishcloth and mend with a lump of glue. "

"She looked into the heart of the turf fire. A dozen pyjamas—underwear for the whole house—

"Paddy!"

"Huh?"

"The last thing that I want anybody to start thinking is that I, by any possible chance, could be getting grand notions."

She watched him hopefully. He was lost in his plans.

"I can assure you, Paddy, that I loathe—I simply loathe all this modern show-off."

"That's right."

"Those wives that think they haven't climbed the social ladder until they've got a fur coat!"

He grunted at the map of the pier.

"Because I don't care what you or anybody else says, Paddy, there *is something* vulgar about a fur coat. There's no shape to them. Especially musquash. What I was thinking of was black Indian lamb. Of course, the real thing would be ocelot. But they're much too dear. The real ones. And I wouldn't be seen dead in an imitation ocelot."

He glanced sideways from the table. "You seem to know a lot about fur." He leaned back and smiled benevolently. "I never knew you were hankering all this time after a fur coat."

"Who said I'm hankering! I am *not*. What do you mean? Don't be silly. I just want something decent to wear when we go out to a show, or to wear over a dance frock, that's all. What do you mean—hankering?"

"Well, what's wrong with that thing you have with the fur on the sleeves? The shiny thing with the what-do-you-call-'ems—sequins, is it?"

"*That!* Do you mean *that?* For heaven's sake, don't be talking about what you don't know anything about. I've had *that* for fourteen years. It's like something me grandmother wore at her own funeral."

He laughed. "You used to like it."

"Of course, I liked it when I got it. Honestly, Paddy Maguire, there are times when—"

"Sorry, sorry, sorry. I was only trying to be helpful. How much is an ocelot?"

"Eighty-five or ninety—at the least."

"Well, why not?"

"Paddy, tell me honestly. Honestly, now! Do you seriously think that I could put eighty-five pounds on my back?"

With his pencil Maguire frugally drew a line on the map, reducing the pier by five yards, and wondered would the county surveyor let him get away with it.

"Well, the question is: will you be satisfied with the Indian lamb? What colour did you say it is? Black? That's a very queer lamb."

Irritably he rubbed out the line. The wretched thing would be too shallow at low water if he cut five yards off it.

"It's dyed. You could get it brown, too," she cried. "You could get all sorts of lamb. Broadtail is the fur of unborn Persian lambs."

That woke him up: the good farmer stock in him was shocked.

"Unborn lambs!" he cried. "Do you mean to say that they—"

"Yes, isn't it awful? Honest to Heaven, Paddy, anyone that'd wear broadtail ought to be put in prison. Paddy, I've made up my mind. I just couldn't buy a fur coat. I just won't buy it. That's the end of it."

She picked up the pyjamas again and looked at them with moist eyes. He turned to devote his full attention to her problem.

"Molly, darling, I'm afraid I don't understand what you're after. I mean, do you or do you not want a fur coat? I mean, supposing you didn't buy a fur coat, what else could you do?"

"Just exactly what do you mean?"—very coldly.

"I mean, it isn't apparently necessary that you should buy a fur coat. I mean, not if you don't really want to. There must be some other way of dressing besides fur coats? If you have a scunner against fur coats, why not buy something else just as good? There's hundreds of millions of other women in the world and they all haven't fur coats."

"I've told you before that they dress! And I've no time to dress. I've explained all that to you."

Maguire got up. He put his back to the fire, his hands behind him, a judicial look on him. He addressed the room.

"All the other women in the world can't all have time to dress. There must be some way out of it. For example, next month there'll be a garden party up at the President's house. How many of all these women will be wearing fur coats?" He addressed the armchair. "Has Mrs. de Valera time to dress?" He turned and leaned over the turf basket. "Has Mrs. General Mulcahy time to dress? There's ways and means of doing everything." (He shot a quick glance at the map of the pier; you could always knock a couple of feet off the width of it.) "After all, you've told me your-self that you could purchase a black costume for twenty-five guineas. Is that or is that not a fact? Very well then," triumphantly, "why not buy a black costume for twenty-five guineas?"

"Because, you big fathead, I'd have to have shoes and a blouse and hat and gloves and a fur and a purse and every-thing to match it, and I'd spend far more in the heel of the hunt, and I haven't time for that sort of thing and I'd have to have two or three costumes—Heaven above, I can't ap-pear day after day in the same old rig, can I?"

"Good! Good! That's settled. Now, the question is: shall we or shall we not purchase a fur coat? Now! What is to be said for a fur coat?" He marked off the points on his fin-gers. "Number one: it is warm. Number two: it will keep you from getting cold. Number three—"

Molly jumped up, let a scream out of her, and hurled the basket of mending at him.

"Stop it! I told you I don't want a fur coat! And you don't want me to get a fur coat! You're too mean, that's what it is! And, like all the Irish, you have the peasant streak in you. You're all alike, every bloody wan of ye. Keep your rotten fur coat. I never wanted it—"

And she ran from the room sobbing with fury and dis-appointment.

"Mean?" gasped Maguire to himself. "To think that any-body could say that I—Mean!"

She burst open the door to sob:

"I'll go to the garden party in a mackintosh. And I hope that'll satisfy you!" and ran out again.

He sat miserably at his table, cold with anger. He murmured the hateful word over and over, and wondered could there be any truth in it. He added ten yards to the pier. He reduced the ten to five, and then, seeing what he had done, swept the whole thing off the table.

It took them three days to make it up. She had hit him below the belt and they both knew it. On the fourth morning she found a check for a hundred and fifty pounds on her dressing table. For a moment her heart leaped. The next moment it died in her. She went down and put her arms about his neck and laid the check, torn in four, into his hand.

"I'm sorry, Paddy," she begged, crying like a kid. "You're not mean. You never were. It's me that's mean."

"You! Mean?" he said, fondly holding her in his arms.

"No, I'm not mean. It's not that. I just haven't the heart, Paddy. It was knocked out of me donkeys' years ago." He looked at her sadly. "You know what I'm trying to say?"

He nodded. But she saw that he didn't. She was not sure that she knew herself. He took a deep, resolving breath, held her out from him by the shoulders, and looked her straight in the eyes. "Molly, tell me the truth. You want this coat?"

"I do. O God, I do!"

"Then go out and buy it."

"I couldn't, Paddy. I just couldn't."

He looked at her for a long time. Then he asked:
"Why?"

She looked straight at him and, shaking her head sadly, she said in a little sobbing voice:
"I don't know."

Two of a Kind

Maxer Creedon was not drunk, but he was melancholy-drunk, and he knew it and he was afraid of it.

At first he had loved being there in the jammed streets, with everybody who passed him carrying parcels wrapped in green or gold, tied with big red ribbons and fixed with berried holly sprigs. Whenever he bumped into someone, parcels toppled and they both cried "Ooops!" or "Sorree!" and laughed at one another. A star of snow sank nestling into a woman's hair. He smelled pine and balsam. He saw twelve golden angels blaring silently from twelve golden trumpets in Rockefeller Plaza. He pointed out to a cop that when the traffic lights down Park Avenue changed from red to green the row of white Christmas trees away down the line changed color by reflection. The cop was very grateful to him. The haze of light on the tops of the buildings made a halo over Fifth Avenue. It was all just the way he knew it would be, and he slopping down from Halifax in that damned old tanker. Then, suddenly, he swung his right arm in a wild arc of disgust.

"To hell with'em! To hell with everybody!"

"Ooops! Hoho, there! Sorree!"

He refused to laugh back.

"Poor Creedon!" he said to himself. "All alone in New York, on Christmas-bloody-well-Eve, with nobody to talk to, and nowhere to go only back to the bloody old ship. New York all lit up. Everybody all lit up. Except poor old Creedon."

He began to cry for poor old Creedon. Crying, he reeled through the passing feet. The next thing he knew he was sitting up at the counter of an Eighth Avenue drugstore sucking black coffee, with one eye screwed up to look out at the changing traffic lights, chuckling happily over a yarn his mother used to tell him long ago about a place called Ballyroche. He had been there only once, nine years ago, for her funeral. Beaming into his coffee cup, or looking out at the changing traffic lights, he went through his favorite yarn about Poor Lily:

"Ah, wisha! Poor Lily! I wonder where is she atall, atall now. Or is she dead or alive. It all happened through an Italian who used to be going from one farm to another selling painted statues. Bandello his name was, a handsome black divil o' hell! I never in all my born days saw a more handsome divil. Well, one wet, wild, windy October morning what did she do but creep out of her bed and we all sound asleep and go off with him. Often and often I heard my father say that the last seen of her was standing under the big tree at Ballyroche Cross, sheltering from the rain, at about eight o'clock in the morning. It was Mikey Clancy the postman saw her. 'Yerrah, Lily girl,' says he, 'what are you doing here at this hour of the morning?' 'I'm waiting,' says she, 'for to go into Fareens on the milk cart.' And from that day to this not a sight nor a sound of her no more than if the earth had swallowed her. Except for the one letter from a priest in America to say she was happily married in Brooklyn, New York."

Maxer chuckled again. The yarn always ended up with the count of the years. The last time he heard it, the count had reached forty-one. By this year it would have been fifty.

Maxer put down his cup. For the first time in his life it came to him that the yarn was a true story about a real woman. For as long as four traffic-light changes he fumbled with this fact. Then, like a man hearing a fog signal come again and again from an approaching ship, and at last hearing it close at hand, and then seeing an actual if dim shape wrapped in a cocoon of haze, the great idea revealed itself.

He lumbered down from his stool and went over to the telephones. His lumpish finger began to trace its way down the gray pages among the Brooklyn *Ban's*. His finger stopped. He read the name aloud. *Bandello, Mrs. Lily*. He found a dime, tinkled it home, and dialed the number slowly. On the third ring he heard an old woman's voice. Knowing that she would be very old and might be deaf, he said very loudly and with the extra-meticulous enunciations of all drunks:

"My name is Matthew Creedon. Only my friends all call me Maxer. I come from Limerick, Ireland. My mother came from the townland of Ballyroche. Are you by any chance my Auntie Lily?"

Her reply was a bark:

"What do you want?"

"Nothing at all! Only I thought, if you are the lady in question, that we might have a bit of an ould gosther. I'm a sailor. Docked this morning in the Hudson."

The voice was still hard and cold:

"Did somebody tell you to call me?"

He began to get cross with her.

"Naw! Just by a fluke I happened to look up your name in the directory. I often heard my mother talking about you. I just felt I'd like to talk to somebody. Being Christmas and all to that. And knowing nobody in New York. But if you don't like the idea, it's okay with me. I don't want to butt in on anybody. Good-by."

"Wait! You're sure nobody sent you?"

"Inspiration sent me! Father Christmas sent me!" (She could take that any way she bloody-well liked!) "Look! It seems to me I'm buttin' in. Let's skip it."

"No. Why don't you come over and see me?"

Suspiciously he said:

"This minute?"

"Right away!"

At the sudden welcome of her voice all his annoyance vanished.

"Sure, Auntie Lily! I'll be right over. But, listen, I sincerely hope you're not thinking I'm buttin' in. Because if you are—"

"It was very nice of you to call me, Matty, very nice indeed. I'll be glad to see you."

He hung up, grinning. She was just like his mother—the same old Limerick accent. After fifty years. And the same bossy voice. If she was a day she'd be seventy. She'd be tall, and thin, and handsome, and the real lawdy-daw, doing the grand lady, and under it all she'd be as soft as mountain moss. She'd be tidying the house now like a divil. And giving jaw to ould Bandello. If he was still alive.

He got lost on the subway, so that when he came up it was dark. He paused to have another black coffee. Then he paused to buy a bottle of Jamaica rum as a present for her. And then he had to walk five blocks before he found the house where she lived. The automobiles parked under the lights were all snow-covered. She lived in a brownstone house with high steps. Six other families also had rooms in it.

The minute he saw her on top of the not brightly lit

landing, looking down at him, he saw something he had completely forgotten. She had his mother's height, and slimness, and her wide mouth, but he had forgotten the pale, liquid blue of the eyes and they stopped him dead on the stairs, his hand tight on the banister. At the sight of them he heard the soft wind sighing over the level Limerick plain and his whole body shivered. For miles and miles not a sound but that soughing wind that makes the meadows and the wheat fields flow like water. All over that plain, where a crossroads is an event, where a little, sleepy lake is an excitement. Where their streams are rivers to them. Where their villages are towns. The resting cows look at you out of owls' eyes over the greasy tips of the buttercups. The meadow grass is up to their bellies. Those two pale eyes looking down at him were bits of the pale albino sky stretched tightly over the Shannon plain.

Slowly he climbed up to meet her, but even when they stood side by side she was still able to look down at him, searching his face with her pallid eyes. He knew what she was looking for, and he knew she had found it when she threw her bony arms around his neck and broke into a low, soft wailing just like that Shannon wind.

"Auntie! You're the living image of her!"

On the click of a finger she became bossy and cross with him, hauling him by his two hands into her room:

"You've been drinking! And what delayed you? And I suppose not a scrap of solid food in your stomach since morning?"

He smiled humbly.

"I'm sorry, Auntie. 'Twas just on account of being all alone, you know. And everybody else making whoopee." He hauled out the peace offering of the rum. "Let's have a drink!"

She was fussing all over him immediately.

"You gotta eat something first. Drinking like that all day, I'm ashamed of you! Sit down, boy. Take off your jacket. I got coffee, and cookies, and hamburgers, and a pie, I always lay in a stock for Christmas. All of the neighbors visit me. Everybody knows that Lily Bandello keeps an open house for Christmas, nobody is ever going to say

Lily Bandello didn't have a welcome for all her friends and relations at Christmastime—"

She bustled in and out of the kitchenette, talking back to him without stop.

It was a big, dusky room, himself looking at himself out of a tall, mirrored wardrobe piled on top with cardboard boxes. There was a divan in one corner as high as a bed, and he guessed that there was a washbasin behind the old peacock-screen. A single bulb hung in the center of the ceiling, in a fluted glass bell with pink frilly edges. The pope over the bed was Leo XIII. The snowflakes kept touching the bare windowpanes like kittens' paws trying to get in. When she began on the questions, he wished he had not come.

"How's Bid?" she called out from the kitchen.

"Bid? My mother? Oh, well, of course, I mean to say— My mother? Oh, she's grand, Auntie! Never better. For her age, of course, that is. Fine, fine out! Just like yourself. Only for the touch of the old rheumatism now and again."

"Go on, tell me about all of them. How's Uncle Matty? And how's Cis? When were you down in Ballyroche last? But, sure, it's all changed now I suppose, with electric light and everything up to date? And I suppose the old pony and trap is gone years ago? It was only last night I was thinking of Mikey Clancy the postman." She came in, planking down the plates, an iced Christmas cake, the coffeepot. "Go on! You're telling me nothing."

She stood over him, waiting, her pale eyes wide, her mouth stretched. He said:

"My Uncle Matty? Oh well, of course, now, he's not as young as he was. But I saw him there last year. He was looking fine. Fine out. I'd be inclined to say he'd be a bit stooped. But in great form. For his age, that is."

"Sit in. Eat up. Eat up. Don't mind me. He has a big family now, no doubt?"

"A family? Naturally! There's Tom. And there's Kitty, that's my Aunt Kitty, it is Kitty, isn't it, yes, my Auntie Kitty. And—God, I can't remember the half of them."

She shoved the hamburgers towards him. She made him pour the coffee and tell her if he liked it. She told him he was a bad reporter.

"Tell me all about the old place!"

He stuffed his mouth to give him time to think.

"They have twenty-one cows. Holsteins. The black and white chaps. And a red barn. And a shelter belt of pines. 'Tis lovely there now to see the wind in the trees, and when the night falls, the way the lighthouse starts winking at you, and—"

"What lighthouse?" She glared at him. She drew back from him. "Are ye daft? What are you dreaming about? Is it a lighthouse in the middle of the County Limerick?"

"There is a lighthouse! I saw it in the harbor!"

But he suddenly remembered that where he had seen it was in a toyshop on Eighth Avenue, with a farm beyond it and a red barn and small cows, and a train going round and round it all.

"Harbor, Matty? Are ye out of your senses?"

"I saw it with my own two eyes."

Her eyes were like marbles. Suddenly she leaned over like a willow—just the way his mother used to lean over —and laughed and laughed.

"I know what you're talking about now. The lighthouse on the Shannon! Lord save us, how many times did I see it at night from the hill of Ballingarry! But there's no harbor, Matty."

"There's the harbor at Foynes!"

"Oh, for God's sake!" she cried. "That's miles and miles and miles away. 'Tis and twenty miles away! And where could you see any train, day or night, from anywhere at all near Ballyroche?"

They argued it hither and over until she suddenly found that the coffee was gone cold and rushed away with the pot to the kitchen. Even there she kept up the argument, calling out that certainly, you could see Moneygay Castle, and the turn of the River Deel on a fine day, but no train, and then she went on about the stepping-stones over the river, and came back babbling about Normoyle's bull that chased them across the dry river, one hot summer's day—

He said:

"Auntie! Why the hell did you never write home?"

"Not even once?" she said, with a crooked smile like a bold child.

"Not a sight nor a sound of you from the day you left Ballyroche, as my mother used to say, no more than if the earth swallowed you. You're a nice one!"

"Eat up!" she commanded him, with a little laugh and a tap on his wrist.

"Did you always live here, Auntie Lily?"

She sat down and put her face between her palms with her elbows on the table and looked at him.

"Here? Well, no—That is to say, no! My husband and me had a house of our very own over in East Fifty-eighth. He did very well for himself. He was quite a rich man when he died. A big jeweler. When he was killed in an airplane crash five years ago, he left me very well off. But sure I didn't need a house of my own and I had lots of friends in Brooklyn, so I came to live here."

"Fine! What more do you want, that is for a lone woman! No family?"

"I have my son. But he's married, to a Pole, they'll be over here first thing tomorrow morning to take me off to spend Christmas with them. They have an apartment on Riverside Drive. He is the manager of a big department store, Macy's on Flatbush Avenue. But tell me about Bid's children. You must have lots of brothers and sisters. Where are you going from here? Back to Ireland? To Limerick? To Ballyroche?"

He laughed.

"Where else would I go? Our next trip we hit the port of London. I'll be back like an arrow to Ballyroche. They'll be delighted to hear I met you. They'll be asking me all sorts of questions about you. Tell me more about your son, Auntie. Has he a family?"

"My son? Well, my son's name is Thomas. His wife's name is Catherine. She is very beautiful. She has means of her own. They are very happy. He is very well off. He's in charge of a big store, Sears Roebuck on Bedford Avenue. Oh, a fine boy. Fine out! As you say. Fine out. He has three children. There's Cissy, and Matty. And—"

Her voice faltered. When she closed her eyes, he saw

how old she was. She rose and from the bottom drawer of a chest of drawers she pulled out a photograph album. She laid it in front of him and sat back opposite him.

"That is my boy."

When he said he was like her, she said he was very like his father. Maxer said that he often heard that her husband was a most handsome man.

"Have you a picture of him?"

She drew the picture of her son towards her and looked down at it.

"Tell me more about Ballyroche," she cried.

As he started into a long description of a harvest home he saw her eyes close again, and her breath came more heavily and he felt that she was not hearing a word he said. Then, suddenly, her palm slapped down on the picture of the young man, and he knew that she was not heeding him any more than if he wasn't there. Her fingers closed on the pasteboard. She shied it wildly across the room, where it struck the glass of the window flat on, hesitated, and slid to the ground. Maxer saw snowflakes melting as often as they touched the pane. When he looked back at her she was leaning across the table, one white lock down over one eye, her yellow teeth bared.

"You spy!" she spat at him. "You came from *them!* To spy on me!"

"I came from friendliness."

"Or was it for a ha'porth of look-about? Well, you can go back to Ballyroche and tell 'em whatever you like. Tell 'em I'm starving if that'll please 'em, the mean, miserable, lousy set that never gave a damn about me from the day I left 'em. For forty years my own sister, your mother, never wrote one line to say—"

"You know damn well she'd have done anything for you if she only knew where you were. Her heart was stuck in you. The two of you were inside one another's pockets. My God, she was forever talking and talking about you. Morning, noon, and night—"

She shouted at him across the table.

"I wrote six letters—"

"She never got them."

"I registered two of them."

"Nobody ever got a line from you, or about you, only for the one letter from the priest that married you to say you were well and happy."

"What he wrote was that I was down and out. I saw the letter. I let him send it. That Wop left me flat in this city with my baby. I wrote to every body—my mother, my father, to Bid after she was your mother and had a home of her own. I had to work every day of my life. I worked today. I'll work tomorrow. If you want to know what I do, I clean out offices. I worked to bring up my son, and what did he do? Walked out on me with that Polack of his and that was the last I saw of him, or her, or any human being belonging to me until I saw you. Tell them every word of it. They'll love it!"

Maxer got up and went over slowly to the bed for his jacket. As he buttoned it, he looked at her glaring at him across the table. Then he looked away from her at the snowflakes feeling the windowpane and dying there. He said, quietly:

"They're all dead. As for Limerick—I haven't been back to Ireland for eight years. When my mum died, my father got married again. I ran away to sea when I was sixteen."

He took his cap. When he was at the door he heard a chair fall and then she was at his side, holding his arm, whispering gently to him:

"Don't go away, Matty." Her pallid eyes were flooded. "For God's sake, don't leave me alone with *them* on Christmas Eve!"

Maxer stared at her. Her lips were wavering as if a wind were blowing over them. She had the face of a frightened girl. He threw his cap on the bed and went over and sat down beside it. While he sat there like a big baboon, with his hands between his knees, looking at the snowflakes, she raced into the kitchen to put on the kettle for rum punch. It was a long while before she brought in the two big glasses of punch, with orange sliced in them, and brown sugar like drowned sand at the base of them. When she held them out to him he looked first at them, and then at her, so timid, so pleading, and he began to laugh and laugh—a laugh that he choked by covering his eyes with his hands.

"Damn ye!" he groaned into his hands. "I was better off drunk."

She sat beside him on the bed. He looked up. He took one of the glasses and touched hers with it.

"Here's to poor Lily!" he smiled.

She fondled his free hand.

"Lovie, tell me this one thing and tell me true. Did she really and truly talk about me? Or was that all lies too?"

"She'd be crying rain down when she'd be talking about you. She was always and ever talking about you. She was mad about you."

She sighed a long sigh.

"For years I couldn't understand it. But when my boy left me for that Polack, I understood it. I guess Bid had a tough time bringing you all up. And there's no one more hard in all the world than a mother when she's thinking of her own. I'm glad she talked about me. It's better than nothing."

They sat there on the bed talking and talking. She made more punch, and then more, and in the end they finished the bottle between them, talking about everybody either of them had known in or within miles of the County Limerick. They fixed to spend Christmas Day together, and have Christmas dinner downtown, and maybe go to a picture, and then come back and talk some more.

Every time Maxer comes to New York he rings her number. He can hardly breathe until he hears her voice saying, "Hello, Matty." They go on the town then and have dinner, always at some place with an Irish name, or a green neon shamrock above the door, and then they go to a movie or a show, and then come back to her room to have a drink and a talk about his last voyage, or the picture postcards he sent her, his latest bits and scraps of news about the Shannon shore. They always get first-class service in restaurants, although Maxer never noticed it until the night a waiter said, "And what's mom having?" at which she gave him a slow wink out of her pale Limerick eyes and a slow, wide, lover's smile.

FRANK O'CONNOR

1903–1966

Frank O'Connor, born Michael O'Donovan in the city of
Cork, has told of his early life in *An Only Child* (1961)
with a humor and pathos that cannot be recaptured in a
summary. His mother was a domestic servant and his
father an intermittently alcoholic laborer. The family of
three often approached the edge of destitution, but
mutual love held them together. His elementary-school
education was made unusual only by his encountering
Daniel Corkery as a teacher. Corkery interested him in
learning Gaelic and kept an eye on him. Leaving school
at the mandatory age of fourteen, O'Connor took a
series of blind-alley jobs until the Irish Civil War. He
joined the Republican forces against the new Free State
government and was captured. Many fellow prisoners
were college graduates, who helped him to complete his
education so satisfactorily that he won a national
competition with an essay on Turgenev written in
Gaelic. Later, he became a professional librarian in
Dublin, where "AE" published his early writing in *The
Irish Statesman*. Yeats had him appointed to the Board of
Directors of the Abbey Theatre, a position he held until
1939. O'Connor has paid long visits to England and the
U.S., his first wife being English and his second
American. He taught at Harvard and elsewhere, and
made some remarkable broadcasts and recordings of his
own and others' writings, being blessed with a magnifi-
cent speaking voice. Regarded as the Old Master of the
Irish short story, he was published in a wide variety of
magazines, but in the end *The New Yorker* tended to
monopolize his output. His first book of short stories,
Guests of the Nation (1931) was followed by five more,

besides the collections, *The Stories of Frank O'Connor* (1952) and *More Stories* (1954). *A Set of Variations*, a final volume of stories, was published posthumously. O'Connor also published two novels, travel books, literary criticism, original poetry and translations from Gaelic poetry in *Kings, Lords and Commons* (1959) and *The Little Monasteries* (1963). Although the essence of O'Connor cannot be captured in but two stories, I have chosen an early and a late one: "Peasants" from *Bones of Contention* (1936), and "The Man of the World" from *Domestic Relations* (1957).

Peasants

When Michael John Cronin stole the funds of the Carricknabreena Hurling, Football and Temperance Association, commonly called the Club, everyone said: "Devil's cure to him!" "'Tis the price of him!" "Kind father for him!" "What did I tell you?" and the rest of the things people say when an acquaintance has got what is coming to him.

And not only Michael John but the whole Cronin family, seed, breed, and generation, came in for it; there wasn't one of them for twenty miles round or a hundred years back but his deeds and sayings were remembered and examined by the light of this fresh scandal. Michael John's father (the heavens be his bed!) was a drunkard who beat his wife, and his father before him a land-grabber. Then there was an uncle or grand-uncle who had been a policeman and taken a hand in the bloody work at Mitchelstown long ago, and an unmarried sister of the same whose good name it would by all accounts have needed a regiment of husbands to restore. It was a grand shaking-up the Cronins got altogether, and anyone who had a grudge in for them, even if it was no more than a thirty-third cousin, had rare sport, dropping a friendly word about it and saying how sorry he was for the poor mother till he had the blood lighting in the Cronin eyes.

There was only one thing for them to do with Michael

John; that was to send him to America and let the thing
blow over, and that, no doubt, is what they would have
done but for a certain unpleasant and extraordinary incident.

Father Crowley, the parish priest, was chairman of the
committee. He was a remarkable man, even in appearance;
tall, powerfully built, but very stooped, with shrewd, love-
less eyes that rarely softened to anyone except two or three
old people. He was a strange man, well on in years, noted
for his strong political views, which never happened to co-
incide with those of any party, and as obstinate as the
devil himself. Now what should Father Crowley do but try
to force the committee to prosecute Michael John?

The committee were all religious men who up to this had
never as much as dared to question the judgments of a man
of God: yes, faith, and if the priest had been a bully, which
to give him his due he wasn't, he might have danced a jig
on their backs and they wouldn't have complained. But a
man has principles, and the like of this had never been
heard of in the parish before. What? Put the police on a
boy and he in trouble?

One by one the committee spoke up and said so. "But
he did wrong," said Father Crowley, thumping the table.
"He did wrong and he should be punished."

"Maybe so, Father," said Con Norton, the vice-chair-
man, who acted as spokesman. "Maybe you're right, but
you wouldn't say his poor mother should be punished too
and she a widow-woman?"

"True for you!" chorused the others.

"Serve his mother right!" said the priest shortly. "There's
none of you but knows better than I do the way that young
man was brought up. He's a rogue and his mother is a fool.
Why didn't she beat Christian principles into him when she
had him on her knee?"

"That might be, too," Morton agreed mildly. "I wouldn't
say but you're right, but is that any reason his Uncle Peter
should be punished?"

"Or his Uncle Dan?" asked another.

"Or his Uncle James?" asked a third.

"Or his cousins, the Dwyers, that keep the little shop in

Lissnacarriga, as decent a living family as there is in County Cork?" asked a fourth.

"No, Father," said Norton, "the argument is against you."

"Is it indeed?" exclaimed the priest, growing cross. "Is it so? What the devil has it to do with his Uncle Dan or his Uncle James? What are ye talking about? What punishment is it to them, will ye tell me that? Ye'll be telling me next 'tis a punishment to me and I a child of Adam like himself."

"Wisha now, Father," asked Norton incredulously, "do you mean 'tis no punishment to them having one of their own blood made a public show? Is it mad you think we are? Maybe 'tis a thing you'd like done to yourself?"

"There was none of my family ever a thief," replied Father Crowley shortly.

"Begor, we don't know whether there was or not," snapped a little man called Daly, a hot-tempered character from the hills.

"Easy, now! Easy, Phil!" said Norton warningly.

"What do you mean by that?" asked Father Crowley, rising and grabbing his hat and stick.

"What I mean," said Daly, blazing up, "is that I won't sit here and listen to insinuations about my native place from any foreigner. There are as many rogues and thieves and vagabonds and liars in Cullough as ever there were in Carricknabreena—ay, begod, and more, and bigger! That's what I mean."

"No, no, no, no," Norton said soothingly. "That's not what he means at all, Father. We don't want any bad blood between Cullough and Carricknabreena. What he means is that the Crowleys may be a fine substantial family in their own country, but that's fifteen long miles away, and this isn't their country, and the Cronins are neighbors of ours since the dawn of history and time, and 'twould be a very queer thing if at this hour we handed one of them over to the police. . . . And now, listen to me, Father," he went on, forgetting his role of pacificator and hitting the table as hard as the rest, "if a cow of mine got sick in the morning, 'tisn't a Cremin or a Crowley I'd be asking for help, and

damn the bit of use 'twould be to me if I did. And everyone knows I'm no enemy of the Church but a respectable
farmer that pays his dues and goes to his duties regularly."

"True for you! True for you!" agreed the committee.

"I don't give a snap of my finger what you are," retorted
the priest. "And now listen to me, Con Norton. I bear
young Cronin no grudge, which is more than some of you
can say, but I know my duty and I'll do it in spite of the
lot of you."

He stood at the door and looked back. They were gazing
blankly at one another, not knowing what to say to such
an impossible man. He shook his fist at them.

"Ye all know me," he said. "Ye know that all my life
I'm fighting the long-tailed families. Now, with the help of
God, I'll shorten the tail of one of them."

Father Crowley's threat frightened them. They knew he
was an obstinate man and had spent his time attacking
what he called the "corruption" of councils and commit-
tees, which was all very well as long as it happened outside
your own parish. They dared not oppose him openly because he knew too much about all of them and, in public
at least, had a lacerating tongue. The solution they favored
was a tactful one. They formed themselves into a Michael
John Cronin Fund Committee and canvassed the parish-
ioners for subscriptions to pay off what Michael John had
stolen. Regretfully they decided that Father Crowley
would hardly countenance a football match for the purpose.

Then with the defaulting treasurer, who wore a suitably
contrite air, they marched up to the presbytery. Father
Crowley was at his dinner but he told the housekeeper to
show them in. He looked up in astonishment as his dining
room filled with the seven committeemen, pushing before
them the cowed Michael John.

"Who the blazes are ye?" he asked, glaring at them over
the lamp.

"We're the Club Committee, Father," replied Norton.

"Oh, are ye?"

"And this is the treasurer—the ex-treasurer, I should
say."

"I won't pretend I'm glad to see him," said Father Crowley grimly.

"He came to say he's sorry, Father," went on Norton. "He is sorry, and that's as true as God, and I'll tell you no lie—" Norton made two steps forward and in a dramatic silence laid a heap of notes and silver on the table.

"What's that?" asked Father Crowley.

"The money, Father. 'Tis all paid back now and there's nothing more between us. Any little crossness there was, we'll say no more about it, in the name of God."

The priest looked at the money and then at Norton.

"Con," he said, "you'd better keep the soft word for the judge. Maybe he'll think more of it than I do."

"The judge, Father?"

"Ay, Con, the judge."

There was a long silence. The committee stood with open mouths, unable to believe it.

"And is that what you're doing to us, Father?" asked Norton in a trembling voice. "After all the years, and all we done for you, is it you're going to show us up before the whole country as a lot of robbers?"

"Ah, ye idiots, I'm not showing ye up."

"You are then, Father, and you're showing up every man, woman, and child in the parish," said Norton. "And mark my words, 'twon't be forgotten for you."

The following Sunday Father Crowley spoke of the matter from the altar. He spoke for a full half hour without a trace of emotion on his grim old face, but his sermon was one long, venomous denunciation of the "long-tailed families" who, according to him, were the ruination of the country and made a mockery of truth, justice, and charity. He was, as his congregation agreed, a shockingly obstinate old man who never knew when he was in the wrong.

After Mass he was visited in his sacristy by the committee. He gave Norton a terrible look from under his shaggy eyebrows, which made that respectable farmer flinch.

"Father," Norton said appealingly, "we only want one word with you. One word and then we'll go. You're a hard character, and you said some bitter things to us this morning; things we never deserved from you. But we're quiet, peaceable poor men and we don't want to cross you."

Father Crowley made a sound like a snort.

"We came to make a bargain with you, Father," said Norton, beginning to smile.

"A bargain?"

"We'll say no more about the whole business if you'll do one little thing—just one little thing—to oblige us."

"The bargain!" the priest said impatiently. "What's the bargain?"

"We'll leave the matter drop for good and all if you'll give the boy a character."

"Yes, Father," cried the committee in chorus. "Give him a character! Give him a character!"

"Give him a what?" cried the priest.

"Give him a character, Father, for the love of God," said Norton emotionally. "If you speak up for him, the judge will leave him off and there'll be no stain on the parish."

"Is it out of your minds you are, you half-witted anga-shores?" asked Father Crowley, his face suffused with blood, his head trembling. "Here am I all these years preaching to ye about decency and justice and truth and ye no more understand me than that wall there. Is it the way ye want me to perjure myself? Is it the way ye want me to tell a damned lie with the name of Almighty God on my lips? Answer me, is it?"

"Ah, what perjure!" Norton replied wearily. "Sure, can't you say a few words for the boy? No one is asking you to say much. What harm will it do you to tell the judge he's an honest, good-living, upright lad, and that he took the money without meaning any harm?"

"My God!" muttered the priest, running his hands distractedly through his grey hair. "There's no talking to ye, no talking to ye, ye lot of sheep."

When he was gone the committeemen turned and looked at one another in bewilderment.

"That man is a terrible trial," said one.

"He's a tyrant," said Daly vindictively.

"He is, indeed," sighed Norton, scratching his head. "But

in God's holy name, boys, before we do anything, we'll give
him one more chance."

That evening when he was at his tea, the committeemen
called again. This time they looked very spruce, business-
like, and independent. Father Crowley glared at them.

"Are ye back?" he asked bitterly. "I was thinking ye
would be. I declare to my goodness, I'm sick of ye and yeer
old committee."

"Oh, we're not the committee, Father," said Norton
stiffly.

"Ye're not?"

"We're not."

"All I can say is, ye look mighty like it. And, if I'm not
being impertinent, who the deuce are ye?"

"We're a deputation, Father."

"Oh, a deputation! Fancy that, now. And a deputation
from what?"

"A deputation from the parish, Father. Now, maybe
you'll listen to us."

"Oh, go on! I'm listening, I'm listening."

"Well, now, 'tis like this, Father," said Norton, dropping
his airs and graces and leaning against the table. "'Tis
about that little business this morning. Now, Father, maybe you don't understand us and we don't understand you.
There's a lot of misunderstanding in the world today, Father. But we're quiet simple poor men that want to do the
best we can for everybody, and a few words or a few
pounds wouldn't stand in our way. Now, do you follow
me?"

"I declare," said Father Crowley, resting his elbows on
the table, "I don't know whether I do or not."

"Well, 'tis like this, Father. We don't want any blame on
the parish or on the Cronins, and you're the one man that
can save us. Now all we ask of you is to give the boy a
character—"

"Yes, Father," interrupted the chorus, "give him a character! Give him a character!"

"Give him a character, Father, and you won't be troubled by him again. Don't say no to me now till you hear
what I have to say. We won't ask you to go next, nigh or

near the court. You have pen and ink beside you and one couple of lines is all you need write. When 'tis over you can hand Michael John his ticket to America and tell him not to show his face in Carricknabreena again. There's the price of his ticket, Father," he added, clapping a bundle of notes on the table. "The Cronins themselves made it up, and we have his mother's word and his own word that he'll clear out the minute 'tis all over."

"He can go to pot!" retorted the priest. "What is it to me where he goes?"

"Now, Father, can't you be patient?" Norton asked reproachfully. "Can't you let me finish what I'm saying? We know 'tis no advantage to you, and that's the very thing we came to talk about. Now, supposing—just supposing for the sake of argument—that you do what we say, there's a few of us here, and between us, we'd raise whatever little contribution to the parish fund you'd think would be reasonable to cover the expense and trouble to yourself. Now do you follow me?"

"Con Norton," said Father Crowley, rising and holding the edge of the table, "I follow you. This morning it was perjury, and now 'tis bribery, and the Lord knows what 'twill be next. I see I've been wasting my breath. . . . And I see too," he added savagely, leaning across the table towards them, "a pedigree bull would be more use to ye than a priest."

"What do you mean by that, Father?" asked Norton in a low voice.

"What I say."

"And that's a saying that will be remembered for you the longest day you live," hissed Norton, leaning towards him till they were glaring at one another over the table.

"A bull," gasped Father Crowley. "Not a priest."

" 'Twill be remembered."

"Will it? Then remember this too. I'm an old man now. I'm forty years a priest, and I'm not a priest for the money or power or glory of it, like others I know. I gave the best that was in me—maybe 'twasn't much but 'twas more than many a better man would give, and at the end of my days—" lowering his voice to a whisper he searched them with his terrible eyes, "—at the end of my days, if I did a wrong thing, or a bad thing, or an unjust thing, there isn't man or woman in this parish that would brave me to my face and call me a villain. And isn't that a poor story for an old man that tried to be a good priest?" His voice changed again and he raised his head defiantly. "Now get out before I kick you out!"

And true to his word and character not one word did he say in Michael John's favor the day of the trial, no more than if he was a black. Three months Michael John got and by all accounts he got off light.

He was a changed man when he came out of jail, downcast and dark in himself. Everyone was sorry for him, and people who had never spoken to him before spoke to him then. To all of them he said modestly: "I'm very grateful to you, friend, for overlooking my misfortune." As he wouldn't go to America, the committee made another whip-round and between what they had collected before and what the Cronins had made up to send him to America, he found himself with enough to open a small shop. Then he got a job in the County Council, and an agency for some shipping company, till at last he was able to buy a public house.

As for Father Crowley, till he was shifted twelve months later, he never did a day's good in the parish. The dues went down and the presents went down, and people with money to spend on Masses took it fifty miles away sooner than leave it to him. They said it broke his heart.

He has left unpleasant memories behind him. Only for him, people say, Michael John would be in America now. Only for him he would never have married a girl with money, or had it to lend to poor people in the hard times, or ever sucked the blood of Christians. For, as an old man said to me of him: "A robber he is and was, and a grabber like his grandfather before him, and an enemy of the people like his uncle, the policeman; and though some say he'll dip his hand where he dipped it before, for myself I have no hope unless the mercy of God would send us another Moses or Brian Boru to cast him down and hammer him in the dust."

The Man of the World

When I was a kid there were no such things as holidays for me and my likes, and I have no feeling of grievance about it because, in the way of kids, I simply invented them, which was much more satisfactory. One year, my summer holiday was a couple of nights I spent at the house of a friend called Jimmy Leary, who lived at the other side of the road from us. His parents sometimes went away for a couple of days to visit a sick relative in Bantry, and he was given permission to have a friend in to keep him company. I took my holiday with the greatest seriousness, insisted on the loan of Father's old travelling bag and dragged it myself down our lane past the neighbors standing at their doors.

"Are you off somewhere, Larry?" asked one.

"Yes, Mrs. Rooney," I said with great pride. "Off for my holidays to the Learys'."

"Wisha, aren't you very lucky?" she said with amusement.

"Lucky" seemed an absurd description of my good fortune. The Learys' house was a big one with a high flight of steps up to the front door, which was always kept shut. They had a piano in the front room, a pair of binoculars on a table near the window, and a toilet on the stairs that seemed to me to be the last word in elegance and immodesty. We brought the binoculars up to the bedroom with us. From the window you could see the whole road up and down, from the quarry at its foot with the tiny houses perched on top of it to the open fields at the other end, where the last gas lamp rose against the sky. Each morning I was up with the first light, leaning out the window in my nightshirt and watching through the glasses all the mysterious figures you never saw from our lane: policemen, railwaymen, and farmers on their way to market.

I admired Jimmy almost as much as I admired his house, and for much the same reasons. He was a year older than I, was well-mannered and well-dressed, and would not as-

sociate with most of the kids on the road at all. He had a
way when any of them joined us of resting against a wall
with his hands in his trousers pockets and listening to them
with a sort of well-bred smile, a knowing smile that seemed
to me the height of elegance. And it was not that he was a
softy, because he was an excellent boxer and wrestler and
could easily have held his own with them any time, but he
did not wish to. He was superior to them. He was—there
is only one word that still describes it for me—sophisticated.

I attributed his sophistication to the piano, the binoculars, and the indoor john, and felt that if only I had the
same advantages I could have been sophisticated, too. I
knew I wasn't, because I was always being deceived by
the world of appearances. I would take a sudden violent
liking to some boy, and when I went to his house, my admiration would spread to his parents and sisters, and I
would think how wonderful it must be to have such a home;
but when I told Jimmy he would smile in that knowing way
of his and say quietly: "I believe they had the bailiffs in a
few weeks ago," and, even though I didn't know what bailiffs were, bang would go the whole world of appearances,
and I would realize that once again I had been deceived.

It was the same with fellows and girls. Seeing some bigger chap we knew walking out with a girl for the first time,
Jimmy would say casually: "He'd better mind himself: that
one is dynamite." And, even though I knew as little of girls
who were dynamite as I did of bailiffs, his tone would be
sufficient to indicate that I had been taken in by sweet
voices and broad-brimmed hats, gaslight and evening
smells from gardens.

Forty years later I can still measure the extent of my
obsession, for, though my own handwriting is almost illegi-
ble, I sometimes find myself scribbling idly on a pad in a
small, stiff, perfectly legible hand that I recognize with
amusement as a reasonably good forgery of Jimmy's. My
admiration still lies there somewhere, a fossil in my memory, but Jimmy's knowing smile is something I have never
managed to acquire.

And it all goes back to my curiosity about fellows and

girls. As I say, I only imagined things about them, but Jimmy knew. I was excluded from knowledge by the world of appearances that blinded and deafened me with emotion. The least thing could excite or depress me: the trees in the morning when I went to early Mass, the stained-glass windows in the church, the blue hilly streets at evening with the green flare of the gas lamps, the smells of cooking and perfume—even the smell of a cigarette packet that I had picked up from the gutter and crushed to my nose— all kept me at this side of the world of appearances, while Jimmy, by right of birth or breeding, was always at the other. I wanted him to tell me what it was like, but he didn't seem to be able.

Then one evening he was listening to me talk while he leant against the pillar of his gate, his pale neat hair framing his pale, good-humored face. My excitability seemed to rouse in him a mixture of amusement and pity.

"Why don't you come over some night the family is away and I'll show you a few things?" he asked lightly.

"What'll you show me, Jimmy?" I asked eagerly.

"Noticed the new couple that's come to live next door?" he asked with a nod in the direction of the house above his own.

"No," I admitted in disappointment. It wasn't only that I never knew anything, but I never noticed anything either. And when he described the new family that was lodging there, I realized with chagrin that I didn't even know Mrs. MacCarthy, who owned the house.

"Oh, they're just a newly married couple," he said. "They don't know that they can be seen from our house."

"But how, Jimmy?"

"Don't look up now," he said with a dreamy smile while his eyes strayed over my shoulder in the direction of the lane. "Wait till you're going away. Their end wall is only a couple of feet from ours. You can see right into the bedroom from our attic."

"And what do they do, Jimmy?"

"Oh," he said with a pleasant laugh, "everything. You really should come."

"You bet I'll come," I said, trying to sound tougher than

I felt. It wasn't that I saw anything wrong in it. It was rather that, for all my desire to become like Jimmy, I was afraid of what it might do to me.

But it wasn't enough for me to get behind the world of appearances. I had to study the appearances themselves, and for three evenings I stood under the gas lamp at the foot of our lane, across the road from the MacCarthys', till I had identified the new lodgers. The husband was the first I spotted, because he came from his work at a regular hour. He was tall, with stiff jet-black hair and a big black guardsman's moustache that somehow failed to conceal the youthfulness and ingenuousness of his face, which was long and lean. Usually, he came accompanied by an older man, and stood chatting for a few minutes outside his door—a black-coated, bowler-hatted figure who made large, sweeping gestures with his evening paper and sometimes doubled up in an explosion of loud laughter.

On the third evening I saw his wife—for she had obviously been waiting for him, looking from behind the parlor curtains, and when she saw him she scurried down the steps to join in the conversation. She had thrown an old jacket about her shoulders and stood there, her arms folded as though to protect herself further from the cold wind that blew down the hill from the open country, while her husband rested one hand fondly on her shoulder.

For the first time, I began to feel qualms about what I proposed to do. It was one thing to do it to people you didn't know or care about, but, for me, even to recognize people was to adopt an emotional attitude towards them, and my attitude to this pair was already one of approval. They looked like people who might approve of me, too. That night I remained awake, thinking out the terms of an anonymous letter that would put them on their guard, till I had worked myself up into a fever of eloquence and indignation.

But I knew only too well that they would recognize the villain of the letter and that the villain would recognize me, so I did not write it. Instead, I gave way to fits of anger and moodiness against my parents. Yet even these were unreal, because on Saturday night when Mother made a parcel of my nightshirt—I had now become sufficiently self-conscious not to take a bag—I nearly broke down. There was something about my own house that night that upset me all over again. Father, with his cap over his eyes, was sitting under the wall lamp, reading the paper, and Mother, a shawl about her shoulders, was crouched over the fire from her little wickerwork chair, listening; and I realized that they, too, were part of the world of appearances I was planning to destroy, and as I said good-night, I almost felt that I was saying good-bye to them as well.

But once inside Jimmy's house I did not care so much. It always had that effect on me, of blowing me up to twice the size, as though I were expanding to greet the piano, the binoculars, and the indoor toilet. I tried to pick out a tune on the piano with one hand, and Jimmy, having listened with amusement for some time, sat down and played it himself as I felt it should be played, and this, too, seemed to be part of his superiority.

"I suppose we'd better put in an appearance of going to bed," he said disdainfully. "Someone across the road might notice and tell. *They*'re in town, so I don't suppose they'll be back till late."

We had a glass of milk in the kitchen, went upstairs, undressed, and lay down, though we put our overcoats beside the bed. Jimmy had a packet of sweets but insisted on keeping them till later. "We may need these before we're done," he said with his knowing smile, and again I admired his orderliness and restraint. We talked in bed for a quarter of an hour; then put out the light, got up again, donned our overcoats and socks, and tiptoed upstairs to the attic. Jimmy led the way with an electric torch. He was a fellow who thought of everything. The attic had been arranged for our vigil. Two trunks had been drawn up to the little window to act as seats, and there were even cushions on them. Looking out, you could at first see nothing but an expanse of blank wall topped with chimney stacks, but gradually you could make out the outline of a single window, eight or ten feet below. Jimmy sat beside me and opened his packet of sweets, which he laid between us.

"Of course, we could have stayed in bed till we heard

them come in," he whispered. "Usually you can hear them at the front door, but they might have come in quietly or we might have fallen asleep. It's always best to make sure."

"But why don't they draw the blind?" I asked as my heart began to beat uncomfortably.

"Because there isn't a blind," he said with a quiet chuckle. "Old Mrs. MacCarthy never had one, and she's not going to put one in for lodgers who may be gone tomorrow. People like that never rest till they get a house of their own."

I envied him his nonchalance as he sat back with his legs crossed, sucking a sweet just as though he were waiting in the cinema for the show to begin. I was scared by the darkness and the mystery, and by the sounds that came to us from the road with such extraordinary clarity. Besides, of course, it wasn't my house and I didn't feel at home there. At any moment I expected the front door to open and his parents to come in and catch us.

We must have been waiting for half an hour before we heard voices in the roadway, the sound of a key in the latch and, then, of a door opening and closing softly. Jimmy reached out and touched my arm lightly. "This is probably our pair," he whispered. "We'd better not speak any more in case they might hear us." I nodded, wishing I had never come. At that moment a faint light became visible in the great expanse of black wall, a faint, yellow stairlight that was just sufficient to silhouette the window frame beneath us. Suddenly the whole room lit up. The man I had seen in the street stood by the doorway, his hand still on the switch. I could see it all plainly now, an ordinary small, suburban bedroom with flowery wallpaper, a colored picture of the Sacred Heart over the double bed with the big brass knobs, a wardrobe, and a dressing table.

The man stood there till the woman came in, removing her hat in a single wide gesture and tossing it from her into a corner of the room. He still stood by the door, taking off his tie. Then he struggled with the collar, his head raised and his face set in an agonized expression. His wife kicked off her shoes, sat on a chair by the bed, and began to take off her stockings. All the time she seemed to be talking because her head was raised, looking at him, though you couldn't hear a word she said. I glanced at Jimmy. The light from the window below softly illumined his face as he sucked with tranquil enjoyment.

The woman rose as her husband sat on the bed with his back to us and began to take off his shoes and socks in the same slow, agonized way. At one point he held up his left foot and looked at it with what might have been concern. His wife looked at it, too, for a moment and then swung halfway round as she unbuttoned her skirt. She undressed in swift, jerky movements, twisting and turning and apparently talking all the time. At one moment she looked into the mirror on the dressing table and touched her cheek lightly. She crouched as she took off her slip, and then pulled her nightdress over her head and finished her undressing beneath it. As she removed her underclothes she seemed to throw them anywhere at all, and I had a strong impression that there was something haphazard and disorderly about her. Her husband was different. Everything he removed seemed to be removed in order and then put carefully where he could find it most readily in the morning. I watched him take out his watch, look at it carefully, wind it, and then hang it neatly over the bed.

Then, to my surprise, she knelt by the bed, facing towards the window, glanced up at the picture of the Sacred Heart, made a large hasty Sign of the Cross, and, covering her face with her hands, buried her head in the bedclothes. I looked at Jimmy in dismay, but he did not seem to be embarrassed by the sight. The husband, his folded trousers in his hand, moved about the room slowly and carefully, as though he did not wish to disturb his wife's devotions, and when he pulled on the trousers of his pyjamas he turned away. After that he put on his pyjama jacket, buttoned it carefully, and knelt beside her. He, too, glanced respectfully at the picture and crossed himself slowly and reverently, but he did not bury his face and head as she had done. He knelt upright with nothing of the abandonment suggested by her pose, and with an expression that combined reverence and self-respect. It was the expression of an employee who, while admitting that he might have a few little weaknesses like the rest of the staff, prided himself on having deserved well of the management. Women, his slightly complacent air seemed to indicate, had to adopt these emotional attitudes, but he spoke to God as one man to another. He finished his prayers before his wife; again he crossed himself slowly, rose, and climbed into bed, glancing again at his watch as he did so.

Several minutes passed before she put her hands out before her on the bed, blessed herself in her wide, sweeping way, and rose. She crossed the room in a swift movement that almost escaped me, and next moment the light went out—it was as if the window through which we had watched the scene had disappeared with it by magic, till nothing was left but a blank black wall mounting to the chimney pots.

Jimmy rose slowly and pointed the way out to me with his flashlight. When we got downstairs we put on the bedroom light, and I saw on his face the virtuous and sophisticated air of a collector who has shown you all his treasures in the best possible light. Faced with that look, I could not bring myself to mention the woman at prayer, though I felt her image would be impressed on my memory till the day I died. I could not have explained to him how at that moment everything had changed for me, how, beyond us watching the young married couple from ambush, I had felt someone else watching us, so that at once we ceased to be the observers and became the observed. And the observed in such a humiliating position that nothing I could imagine our victims doing would have been so degrading.

I wanted to pray myself but found I couldn't. Instead, I lay in bed in the darkness, covering my eyes with my hand, and I think that even then I knew that I should never be sophisticated like Jimmy, never be able to put on a knowing smile, because always beyond the world of appearances I would see only eternity watching.

"Sometimes, of course, it's better than that," Jimmy's drowsy voice said from the darkness. "You shouldn't judge it by tonight."

SAMUEL BECKETT
1906-1989

Samuel Barclay Beckett grew up in Foxrock, one of the few well-to-do commuting suburbs of Dublin. His father was a quantity surveyor, and the Becketts in general were Protestants and members of the professions. Beckett was educated at a small private day school in Dublin and then sent as a boarder to Portora Royal School, Enniskillen, Oscar Wilde's alma mater. Unlike Wilde, he was an outstanding athlete at school and the captain of the cricket team. In 1923 he entered Trinity College, Dublin, where after a slow start he took first place at the B.A. examination for Honors students in Modern Literature, 1927. After teaching English at the École Normale Supérieure in Paris and French at Trinity College, he traveled and wrote in England, France, and Germany for four years, settling in Paris in 1937. Except for two years in the Unoccupied Zone during World War II and a year working at the Irish Red Cross Hospital at St. Lô, 1945–46, he made his home in Paris. Beckett admired James Joyce and contributed an essay to the famous *Exagmination* (1929) of the "work in progress" that ultimately became *Finnegans Wake.* He wrote other works in English before and during World War II, including two novels, poems, an essay on Proust, and *More Pricks Than Kicks* (1934), his first book of short stories. After the war he began to publish novels in French, but did not attain worldwide fame until the French version of his play *Waiting for Godot* was staged in Paris in January, 1953. After that, anything that he wrote in French or English—most of the latter work being translated from his own French—was received with excitement by the *avant-garde* public all over the world. His second and last volume of short fiction, *Nouvelles et Textes pour rien* (1955), has never been fully translated into English. "Dante and the Lobster" from *More Pricks Than Kicks* shows us a Beckett "hero" who is better off materially than the later layabouts and cripples but, like them, seeks to live as much as possible in a world of his own manufacture. Unfortunately, the horrors of "real" life keep breaking into that world with macabre humor: McCabe's execution, the boiling alive of the lobster, Dante's harsh vision, which is intensified by "rare movements of compassion." Whether Beckett, too, is moved by compassion the reader will have to decide for himself.

Dante and the Lobster

It was morning and Belacqua was stuck in the first of the canti in the moon. He was so bogged that he could move neither backward nor forward. Blissful Beatrice was there, Dante also, and she explained the spots on the moon to him. She shewed him in the first place where he was at fault, then she put up her own explanation. She had it from God, therefore he could rely on its being accurate in every particular. All he had to do was to follow her step by step. Part one, the refutation, was plain sailing. She made her point clearly, she said what she had to say without fuss or loss of time. But part two, the demonstration, was so dense that Belacqua could not make head or tail of it. The disproof, the reproof, that was patent. But then came the proof, a rapid shorthand of the real facts, and Belacqua was bogged indeed. Bored also, impatient to get on to Piccarda. Still he pored over the enigma, he would not concede himself conquered, he would understand at least the meanings of the words, the order in which they were spoken and the nature of the satisfaction that they conferred on the misinformed poet, so that when they were ended he was refreshed and could raise his heavy head, intending to return thanks and make formal retraction of his old opinion.

He was still running his brain against this impenetrable passage when he heard midday strike. At once he switched his mind off its task. He scooped his fingers under the book and shovelled it back till it lay wholly on his palms. *The Divine Comedy* face upward on the lectern of his palms. Thus disposed he raised it under his nose and there he slammed it shut. He held it aloft for a time, squinting at it angrily, pressing the boards inwards with the heels of his hands. Then he laid it aside.

He leaned back in his chair to feel his mind subside and the itch of this mean quodlibet die down. Nothing could be done until his mind got better and was still, which gradually it did. Then he ventured to consider what he had to do next. There was always something that one had to do next. Three large obligations presented themselves. First lunch, then the lobster, then the Italian lesson. That would do to be going on with. After the Italian lesson he had no very clear idea. No doubt some niggling curriculum had been drawn up by someone for the late afternoon and evening, but he did not know what. In any case it did not matter. What did matter was: one, lunch; two, the lobster; three, the Italian lesson. That was more than enough to be going on with.

Lunch, to come off at all, was a very nice affair. If his lunch was to be enjoyable, and it could be very enjoyable indeed, he must be left in absolute tranquility to prepare it. But if he were disturbed now, if some brisk tattler were to come bouncing in now big with a big idea or a petition, he might just as well not eat at all, for the food would turn to bitterness on his palate, or, worse again, taste of nothing. He must be left strictly alone, he must have complete quiet and privacy to prepare the food for his lunch.

The first thing to do was to lock the door. Now nobody could come at him. He deployed an old *Herald* and smoothed it out on the table. The rather handsome face of McCabe the assassin stared up at him. Then he lit the gas-ring and unhooked the square flat toaster, asbestos grill, from its nail and set it precisely on the flame. He found he had to lower the flame. Toast must not on any account be done too rapidly. For bread to be toasted as it ought, through and through, it must be done on a mild steady flame. Otherwise you only charred the outsides and left the pith as sodden as before. If there was one thing he abominated more than another it was to feel his teeth meet in a bathos of pith and dough. And it was so easy to do the thing properly. So, he thought, having regulated the flow and adjusted the grill, by the time I have the bread cut that will be just right. Now the long barrel-loaf came out of its biscuit tin and had its end evened off on the face of McCabe. Two inexorable drives with the bread-saw and a pair of neat rounds of raw bread, the main elements of his meal, lay before him, awaiting his pleasure. The stump of the loaf went back into prison, the crumbs, as though there were no such thing as a sparrow in the wide world, were swept in a fever away, and the slices snatched up and carried to the grill. All these preliminaries were very hasty and impersonal.

It was now that real skill began to be required, it was at this point that the average person began to make a hash of the entire proceedings. He laid his cheek against the soft of the bread, it was spongy and warm, alive. But he would very soon take that plush feel off it, by God but he would very quickly take that fat white look off its face. He lowered the gas a suspicion and plaqued one flabby slab down on the glowing fabric, but very pat and precise, so that the whole resembled the Japanese flag. Then on top, there not being room for the two to do evenly side by side, and if you did not do them evenly you might just as well save yourself the trouble of doing them at all, the other round was set to warm. When the first candidate was done, which was only when it was black through and through, it changed places with its comrade, so that now it in its turn lay on top, done to a dead end, black and smoking, waiting till as much could be said of the other.

For the tiller of the field the thing was simple, he had it from his mother. The spots were Cain with his truss of thorns, dispossessed, cursed from the earth, fugitive and vagabond. The moon was that countenance fallen and branded, seared with the first stigma of God's pity, that an outcast might not die quickly. It was a mix-up in the mind of the tiller, but that did not matter. It had been good enough for his mother, it was good enough for him.

Belacqua on his knees before the flame, poring over the grill, controlled every phase of the broiling. It took time, but if a thing was worth doing at all it was worth doing well, that was a true saying. Long before the end the room was full of smoke and the reek of burning. He switched off the gas, when all that human care and skill could do had been done, and restored the toaster to its nail. This was an act of dilapidation, for it seared a great weal in the paper. This was hooliganism pure and simple. What the hell did he care? Was it his wall? The same hopeless paper had been there fifty years. It was livid with age. It could not be dis-improved.

Next a thick paste of Savora, salt, and Cayenne on each round, well worked in while the pores were still open with the heat. No butter, God forbid, just a good foment of mustard and salt and pepper on each round. Butter was a blunder, it made the toast soggy. Buttered toast was all right for Senior Fellows and Salvationists, for such as had nothing but false teeth in their heads. It was no good at all to a fairly strong young rose like Belacqua. This meal that he was at such pains to make ready, he would devour it with a sense of rapture and victory, it would be like smiting the sledded Polacks on the ice. He would snap at it with closed eyes, he would gnash it into a pulp, he would van-quish it utterly with his fangs. Then the anguish of pun-gency, the pang of the spices, as each mouthful died, scorching his palate, bringing tears.

But he was not yet all set, there was yet much to be done. He had burnt his offering, he had not fully dressed it. Yes, he had put the horse behind the tumbrel.

He clapped the toasted rounds together, he brought them smartly together like cymbals, they clave the one to the other on the viscid salve of Savora. Then he wrapped them up for the time being in any old sheet of paper. Then he made himself ready for the road.

Now the great thing was to avoid being accosted. To be stopped at this stage and have conversational nuisance committed all over him would be a disaster. His whole being was straining forward towards the joy in store. If he were accosted now he might just as well fling his lunch into the gutter and walk straight back home. Sometimes his hunger, more of mind, I need scarcely say, than of body, for this meal amounted to such a frenzy that he would not have hesitated to strike any man rash enough to buttonhole and baulk him, he would have shouldered him out of his path without ceremony. Woe betide the meddler who crossed him when his mind was really set on this meal.

He threaded his way rapidly, his head bowed, through a familiar labyrinth of lanes and suddenly dived into a little family grocery. In the shop they were not surprised. Most days, about this hour, he shot in off the street in this way.

The slab of cheese was prepared. Separated since morning from the piece, it was only waiting for Belacqua to call and take it. Gorgonzola cheese. He knew a man who came from Gorgonzola, his name was Angelo. He had been born in Nice but all his youth had been spent in Gorgonzola. He knew where to look for it. Everyday it was there, in the same corner, waiting to be called for. They were very decent obliging people.

He looked sceptically at the cut of cheese. He turned it over on its back to see was the other side any better. The other side was worse. They had laid it better side up, they had practised that little deception. Who shall blame them? He rubbed it. It was sweating. That was something. He stooped and smelt it. A faint fragrance of corruption. What good was that? He didn't want fragrance, he wasn't a bloody gourmet, he wanted a good stench. What he wanted was a good green stenching rotten lump of Gorgonzola cheese, alive, and by God he would have it.

He looked fiercely at the grocer.

"What's that?" he demanded.

The grocer writhed.

"Well?" demanded Belacqua, he was without fear when roused, "is that the best you can do?"

"In the length and breadth of Dublin" said the grocer "you won't find a rottener bit this minute."

Belacqua was furious. The impudent dogsbody, for two pins he would assault him.

"It won't do" he cried, "do you hear me, it won't do at all. I won't have it." He ground his teeth.

The grocer, instead of simply washing his hands like Pilate, flung out his arms in a wild crucified gesture of supplication. Sullenly Belacqua undid his packet and slipped the cadaverous tablet of cheese between the hard cold black boards of the toast. He stumped to the door where he whirled round however.

"You heard me?" he cried.

"Sir" said the grocer. This was not a question, nor yet an expression of acquiescence. The tone in which it was let fall made it quite impossible to know what was in the man's mind. It was a most ingenious riposte.

"I tell you" said Belacqua with great heat "this won't do at all. If you can't do better than this" he raised the hand that held the packet "I shall be obliged to go for my cheese elsewhere. Do you mark me?"

"Sir" said the grocer.

He came to the threshold of his store and watched the indignant customer hobble away. Belacqua had a spavined gait, his feet were in ruins, he suffered with them almost continuously. Even in the night they took no rest, or next to none. For then the cramps took over from the corns and hammer-toes, and carried on. So that he would press the fringes of his feet desperately against the end-rail of the bed or, better again, reach down with his hand and drag them up and back towards the instep. Skill and patience could disperse the pain, but there it was, complicating his night's rest.

The grocer, without closing his eyes or taking them off the receding figure, blew his nose in the skirt of his apron. Being a warmhearted human man he felt sympathy and pity for this queer customer who always looked ill and dejected. But at the same time he was a small tradesman, don't forget that, with a small tradesman's sense of per-

sonal dignity and what was what. Thruppence, he cast it
up, thruppence worth of cheese per day, one and a tanner
per week. No, he would fawn on no man for that, no, not
on the best in the land. He had his pride.

Stumbling along by devious ways towards the lowly public where he was expected, in the sense that the entry of his
grotesque person would provoke no comment or laughter,
Belacqua gradually got the upper hand of his choler. Now
that lunch was as good as a *fait accompli*, because the in-
continent bosthoons of his own class, itching to pass on a
big idea or inflict an appointment, were seldom at large in
this shabby quarter of the city, he was free to consider
items two and three, the lobster and the lesson, in closer
detail.

At a quarter to three he was due at the School. Say five
to three. The public closed, the fishmonger reopened, at
half-past two. Assuming then that his lousy old bitch of an
aunt had given her order in good time that morning, with
strict injunctions that it should be ready and waiting so that
her blackguard boy should on no account be delayed when
he called for it first thing in the afternoon, it would be time
enough if he left the public as it closed, he could remain on
till the last moment. Benissimo. He had half-a-crown. That
was two pints of draught anyway and perhaps a bottle to
wind up with. Their bottled stout was particularly excellent
and well up. And he would still be left with enough coppers
to buy a *Herald* and take a tram if he felt tired or was
pinched for time. Always assuming, of course, that the lobster was all ready to be handed over. God damn these
tradesmen, he thought, you can never rely on them. He had
not done an exercise but that did not matter. His Profes-
soressa was so charming and remarkable. Signorina Adriana Ottolenghi! He did not believe it possible for a woman
to be more intelligent or better informed than the little Ottolenghi. So he had set her on a pedestal in his mind, apart
from other women. She had said last day that they would
read *Il Cinque Maggio* together. But she would not mind
if he told her, as he proposed to, in Italian, he would frame
a shining phrase on his way from the public, that he would

prefer to postpone the *Cinque Maggio* to another occasion. Manzoni was an old woman, Napoleon was another. *Napoleone di mezza calzetta, fa l'amore a Giacominetta.* Why did he think of Manzoni as an old woman? Why did he do him that injustice? Pellico was another. They were all old maids, suffragettes. He must ask his Signorina where he could have received that impression, that the 19th century in Italy was full of old hens trying to cluck like Pindar. Carducci was another. Also about the spots on the moon. If she could not tell him there and then she would make it up, only too gladly, against the next time. Everything was all set now and in order. Bating, of course, the lobster, which had to remain an incalculable factor. He must just hope for the best. And expect the worst, he thought gaily, diving into the public, as usual.

Belacqua drew near to the school, quite happy, for all had gone swimmingly. The lunch had been a notable success, it would abide as a standard in his mind. Indeed he could not imagine its ever being superseded. And such a pale soapy piece of cheese to prove so strong! He must only conclude that he had been abusing himself all these years in relating the strength of cheese directly to its greenness. We live and learn, that was a true saying. Also his teeth and jaws had been in heaven, splinters of vanquished toast spraying forth at each gnash. It was like eating glass. His mouth burned and ached with the exploit. Then the food had been further spiced by the intelligence, transmitted in a low tragic voice across the counter by Oliver the improver, that the Malahide murderer's petition for mercy, signed by half the land, having been rejected, the man must swing at dawn in Mountjoy and nothing could save him. Ellis the hangman was even now on his way. Belacqua, tearing at the sandwich and swilling the precious stout, pondered on McCabe in his cell.

The lobster was ready after all, the man handed it over instanter, and with such a pleasant smile. Really a little bit of courtesy and goodwill went a long way in this world. A smile and a cheerful word from a common working-man and the face of the world was brightened. And it was so easy, a mere question of muscular control.

"Lepping" he said cheerfully, handing it over.

"Lepping?" said Belacqua. What on earth was that?

"Lepping fresh, sir" said the man, "fresh in this morning."

Now Belacqua, on the analogy of mackerel and other fish that he had heard described as lapping fresh when they had been taken but an hour or two previously, supposed the man to mean that the lobster had very recently been killed.

Signorina Adriana Ottolenghi was waiting in the little front room off the hall, which Belacqua was naturally inclined to think of rather as the vestibule. That was her room, the Italian room. On the same side, but at the back, was the French room. God knows where the German room was. Who cared about the German room anyway?

He hung up his coat and hat, laid the long knobby brown-paper parcel on the hall table, and went prestly in to the Ottolenghi.

After about half an hour of this and that obiter, she complimented him on his grasp of the language.

"You make rapid progress" she said in her ruined voice.

There subsisted as much of the Ottolenghi as might be expected to of the person of a lady of a certain age who had found being young and beautiful and pure more of a bore than anything else.

Belacqua, dissembling his great pleasure, laid open the moon enigma.

"Yes" she said "I know the passage. It is a famous teaser. Offhand I cannot tell you, but I will look it up when I get home."

The sweet creature! She would look it up in her big Dante when she got home. What a woman!

"It occurred to me" she said "apropos of I don't know what, that you might do worse than make up Dante's rare movements of compassion in Hell. That used to be" her past tenses were always sorrowful "a favorite question."

He assumed an expression of profundity.

"In that connexion" he said "I recall one superb pun anyway: *'qui vive la pietà quando è ben morta . . .'* "[1]

She said nothing.

"Is it not a great phrase?" he gushed.

She said nothing.

"Now" he said like a fool "I wonder how you could translate that?"

Still she said nothing. Then:

"Do you think" she murmured "it is absolutely necessary to translate it?"

Sounds as of conflict were borne in from the hall. Then silence. A knuckle tambourined on the door, it flew open and lo it was Mlle. Glain, the French instructress, clutching her cat, her eyes out on stalks, in a state of the greatest agitation.

"Oh" she gasped "forgive me. I intrude, but what was in the bag?"

"The bag?" said the Ottolenghi.

Mlle. Glain took a French step forward.

"The parcel" she buried her face in the cat "the parcel in the hall."

Belacqua spoke up composedly.

"Mine" he said, "a fish."

He did not know the French for lobster. Fish would do very well. Fish had been good enough for Jesus Christ, Son of God, Savior. It was good enough for Mlle. Glain.

"Oh" said Mlle. Glain, inexpressibly relieved, "I caught him in the nick of time." She administered a tap to the cat. "He would have tore it to flitters."

Belacqua began to feel a little anxious.

"Did he actually get at it?" he said.

"No no" said Mlle. Glain "I caught him just in time. But I did not know" with a bluestocking snigger "what it might be, so I thought I had better come and ask."

Base prying bitch.

The Ottolenghi was faintly amused.

[1] *Inferno*, XX; 28. "Here pity lives when it is rightly dead." (Laurence Binyon translation).

"Puisqu'il n'y a pas de mal . . ." she said with great fatigue and elegance.

"Heureusement" it was clear at once that Mlle. Glain was devout *"heureusement."*

Chastening the cat with little skelps she took herself off. The grey hairs of her maidenhead screamed at Belacqua. A virginal bluestocking, honing after a penny's worth of scandal.

"Where were we?" said Belacqua.

But Neapolitan patience has its limits.

"Where are we ever?" cried the Ottolenghi, "where we were, as we were."

Belacqua drew near to the house of his aunt. Let us call it winter, that dusk may fall now and a moon rise. At the corner of the street a horse was down and a man sat on his head. I know, thought Belacqua, that that is considered the right thing to do. But why? A lamplighter flew by on his bike, tilting with his pole at the standards, jousting a little yellow light into the evening. A poorly dressed couple stood in the bay of a pretentious gateway, she sagging against the railings, her head lowered, he standing facing her. He stood up close to her, his hands dangled by his sides. Where we were, thought Belacqua, as we were. He walked on, gripping his parcel. Why not piety and pity both, even down below? Why not mercy and Godliness together? A little mercy in the stress of sacrifice, a little mercy to rejoice against judgment. He thought of Jonah and the gourd and the pity of a jealous God on Nineveh. And poor McCabe, he would get it in the neck at dawn. What was he doing now, how was he feeling? He would relish one more meal, one more night.

His aunt was in the garden, tending whatever flowers die at that time of year. She embraced him and together they went down into the bowels of the earth, into the kitchen in the basement. She took the parcel and undid it and abruptly the lobster was on the table, on the oilcloth, discovered.

"They assured me it was fresh" said Belacqua.

Suddenly he saw the creature move, this neuter creature. Definitely it changed its position. His hand flew to his mouth.

"Christ!" he said "it's alive."

His aunt looked at the lobster. It moved again. It made a faint nervous act of life on the oilcloth. They stood above it, looking down on it, exposed cruciform on the oilcloth. It shuddered again. Belacqua felt he would be sick.

"My God" he whined "it's alive, what'll we do?"

The aunt simply had to laugh. She bustled off to the pantry to fetch her smart apron, leaving him goggling down at the lobster, and came back with it on and her sleeves rolled up, all business.

"Well" she said "it is to be hoped so, indeed."

"All this time" muttered Belacqua. Then, suddenly aware of her hideous equipment: "What are you going to do?" he cried.

"Boil the beast" she said, "what else?"

"But it's not dead" protested Belacqua "you can't boil it like that."

She looked at him in astonishment. Had he taken leave of his senses?

"Have sense" she said sharply, "lobsters are always boiled alive. They must be." She caught up the lobster and laid it on its back. It trembled. "They feel nothing" she said.

In the depths of the sea it had crept into the cruel pot. For hours, in the midst of its enemies, it had breathed secretly. It had survived the Frenchwoman's cat and his witless clutch. Now it was going alive into scalding water. It had to. Take into the air my quiet breath.

Belacqua looked at the old parchment of her face, grey in the dim kitchen.

"You make a fuss" she said angrily "and upset me and then lash into it for your dinner."

She lifted the lobster clear of the table. It had about thirty seconds to live.

Well, thought Belacqua, it's a quick death, God help us all.

It is not.

MICHAEL McLAVERTY

1907——

A Catholic who lives in predominantly Protestant Northern Ireland, Michael McLavery was born in the inland county of Monaghan but as a child moved to the city of Belfast with his parents. This move from country to city recurs as a theme in his work; he also shows familiarity with life on the rugged northern coast of Ireland, having spent part of his boyhood on Rathlin Island. Educated at St. Malachy's College and Queen's University, Belfast, he obtained a Master of Science degree in 1933. Afterwards he taught in Belfast. McLaverty's first short story was published in 1933, his first novel, *Call My Brother Back*, in 1939. Seven other novels have been published since, as well as three volumes of short stories and *Collected Short Stories* (1978). It was hard to choose just one story since so many of them reach a high standard. "Pigeons", from *The Game Cock and Other Stories*, which touches on the underground struggle of the Irish Republican Army against the Government of Northern Ireland, runs the risk of degenerating into mere propaganda, but the innocence of its boy narrator and the central symbol of the pigeons help keep the story's implications universal.

Pigeons

Our Johnny kept pigeons, three white ones and a brown one that could tumble in the air like a leaf. They were nice pigeons, but they dirtied the slates and cooed so early in the morning that my Daddy said that someday he would wring their bloody necks. That is a long while ago now, for we still have the pigeons, but Johnny is dead; he died for Ireland.

Whenever I think of our Johnny I always think of Saturday. Nearly every Saturday night he had something for me, maybe sweets, a toy train, a whistle, or glass marbles with rainbows inside them. I would be in bed when he'd come home; I always tried to keep awake, but my eyes wouldn't let me—they always closed tight when I wasn't thinking. We both slept together in the wee back room, and when Johnny came up to bed he always lit the gas, the gas that had no mantle. If he had something for me, he would shake me and say: "Frankie, Frankie, are you asleep?" My eyes would be very gluey and I would rub them with my fists until they would open in the gaslight. For a long while I would see gold needles sticking out of the flame, then they would melt away and the gas become like a pansy leaf with a blue heart. Johnny would be standing beside the bed and I would smile all blinky at him. Maybe he'd stick a sweet in my mouth, but if I hadn't said my prayers he'd lift me out on to the cold, cold floor. When I would be jumping in again in my shirt tails, he would play whack at me and laugh if he got me. Soon he would climb into bed and tell me about the ice-cream shops, and the bird shop that had funny pigeons and rabbits and mice in the window. Someday he was going to bring me down the town and buy me a black and white mouse, and a custard bun full of ice cream. But he'll never do it now because he died for Ireland.

On Saturdays, too, I watched for him at the backdoor when he was coming from work. He always came over the waste ground, because it was the shortest. His dungarees would be all shiny, but they hadn't a nice smell. I would pull them off him, and he would lift me on to his shoulder, and swing me round and round until my head got light and the things in the kitchen went up and down. My Mammie said he had me spoilt. He always gave me pennies on Saturday, two pennies, and I bought a licorice pipe with one penny and kept the other for Sunday. Then he would go into the cold scullery to wash his black hands and face; he would stand at the sink, scrubbing and scrubbing and singing "The Old Rusty Bridge by the Mill," but if you went near him he'd squirt soap in your eye. After he had washed

himself, we would get our Saturday dinner, the dinner with
the sausages because it was payday. Johnny used to give me
a bit of his sausages, but if my Mammie saw me she'd slap
me for taking the bite out of his mouth. It was a long, long
wait before we went out to the yard to the pigeons.

The pigeon shed was on the slates above the closet.
There was a ladder up to it, but Johnny wouldn't let me
climb for fear I'd break my neck. But I used to climb up
when he wasn't looking. There was a great flutter and flapping of wings when Johnny would open the trapdoor to let
them out. They would fly out in a line, brownie first and
the white ones last. We would lie on the waste ground at
the back of our street watching them fly. They would fly
round and round, rising higher and higher each time. Then
they would fly so high we would blink our eyes and lose
them in the blue sky. But Johnny always found them first.
"I can see them, Frankie," he would say. "Yonder they
are. Look! above the brickyard chimney." He would put
his arm around my neck, pointing with his outstretched
hand. I would strain my eyes, and at last I would see them,
their wings flashing in the sun as they turned towards home.
They were great fliers. But brownie would get tired and he
would tumble head over heels like you'd think he was going to fall. The white ones always flew down to him, and
Johnny would go wild. "He's a good tumbler, but he won't
let the others fly high. I think I'll sell him. " He would look
at me, plucking at the grass, afraid to look up. "Ah,
Frankie," he would say, "I won't sell him. Sure I'm only
codding." All day we would sit, if the weather was good,
watching our pigeons flying, and brownie doing somer-
saults. When they were tired they would light on the blue
slates, and Johnny would throw corn up to them. Saturday
was a great day for us and for our pigeons, but it was on
Saturday that Johnny died for Ireland.

We were lying, as usual, at the back, while the pigeons
were let out for a fly round. It was a lovely sunny day. Every house had clothes out on the lines, and the clothes were
fluttering in the breeze. Some of the neighbors were sitting
at their backdoors, nursing babies or darning socks. They
weren't nice neighbors for they told the rent man about the

shed on the slates, and he made us pay a penny a week for it. But we didn't talk much to them, for we loved our pigeons, and on that lovely day we were splitting our sides laughing at the way brownie was tumbling, when a strange man in a black hat and burberry coat came near us. Johnny jumped up and went to meet him. I saw them talking, with their heads bent towards the ground, and then the strange man went away. Johnny looked very sad and he didn't laugh at brownie any more. He gave me the things out of his pockets, a penknife, a key, and a little blue notebook with its edges all curled. "Don't say anything to Mammie. Look after the pigeons, Frankie, until I come back. I won't be long." He gave my hand a tight squeeze, then he walked away without turning round to wave at me.

All that day I lay out watching the pigeons, and when I got tired I opened the notebook. It had a smell of fags and there was fag dust inside it. I could read what he had written down:

Corn 2-6d
Club 6d
3 Pkts. Woodbine 6d
Frankie 2d

He had the same thing written down on a whole lot of pages; if he had been at school he would have got slapped for wasting the good paper. I put the notebook in my pocket when my Mammie called me for my tea. She asked me about Johnny and I told her he wouldn't be long until he was back. Then it got late. The pigeons flew off the slates and into the shed, and still Johnny didn't come back.

It came on night. My sisters were sent out to look for him. My daddy came home from work. We were all in now, my two sisters and Mammy and Daddy, everyone except Johnny. Daddy took out his pipe with the tin lid, but he didn't light it. We were all quiet, but my mother's hands would move from her lap to her chin, and she was sighing. The kettle began humming and shuffling the lid about, and my Daddy lifted it off the fire and placed it on the warm hob. The clock on the mantelpiece chimed eleven and my sisters blessed themselves—it got a soul out of Purgatory when you did that. They forgot all about my bedtime and I was let stay up though my eyes felt full of sand. The rain was falling. We could hear it slapping in the yard and trindling down the grate. It was a blowy night, for someone's back door was banging, making the dogs bark. The newspapers that lay on the scullery floor to keep it clean began to crackle up and down with the wind till you'd have thought there was a mouse under them. A bicycle bell rang in the street outside our kitchen window and it made Mammie jump. Then a motor rattled down, shaking the house and the vases on the shelf. My Daddy opened the scullery door and went into the yard. The gas blinked and a coughing smell of a chimney burning came into the kitchen. I'm sure it was Mrs. Ryan's. She always burned hers on a wet night. If the peelers caught her she'd be locked in jail, for you weren't allowed to burn your own chimney.

I wished Daddy would burn ours. It was nice to see him putting the bunch of lighted papers on the yard-brush and sticking them up the wide chimney. The chimney would roar, and if you went outside you'd see lines of sparks like hot wires coming out and the smoke bubbling over like lemonade in a bottle. But he wouldn't burn it tonight, because we were waiting on Johnny.

"Is there any sign of him?" said Mammie, when Daddy came in again.

"None yet; but he'll be all right; he'll be all right. We'll say the prayers, and he'll be in before we're finished."

We were just ready to kneel when a knock came to the back door. It was a very dim knock and we all sat still, listening. "That's him, now," said Daddy, and I saw my mother's face brightening. Daddy went into the yard and I heard the stiff bar on the door opening and feet shuffling. "Easy now: Easy now," said someone. Then Daddy came in, his face as white as a sheet. He said something to Mammie. "Mother of God it isn't true—it isn't!" she said. Daddy turned and sent me up to bed.

Up in the wee room I could see down into the yard. The light from the kitchen shone into it and I saw men with black hats and the rain falling on them like little needles, but I couldn't see our Johnny. I looked up at the shed on the slates, the rain was melting down its sides, and the wet felt was shining like new boots. When I looked into the yard again, Daddy was bending over something. I got frightened and went into my sisters' room. They were crying and I cried, too, while I sat shivering in my shirt and my teeth chattering. "What's wrong?" I asked. But they only cried and said: "Nothing, son. Nothing. Go to sleep, Frankie, like a good little boy." My big sister put me into her bed, and put the clothes around me and stroked my head. Then she lay on the top of the bed beside me, and I could feel her breathing heavily on my back. Outside it was still blowy for the wind was kicking an empty salmon tin which rattled along the street. For a long time I listened to the noises the wind made, and then I slept.

In the morning when I opened my eyes I wondered at finding myself in my sisters' room. It was very still: the blinds were down and the room was full of yellow light. I listened for the sound of plates, a brush scrubbing, or my big sister singing. But I heard nothing, neither inside the house nor outside it. I remembered about last night, my sisters crying because our Johnny didn't come home. I sat up in bed; I felt afraid because the house was strange, and I got out and went into the wee back room.

The door was open and there was yellow light in it, too, and the back of the bed had white cloth and I couldn't see over it. Then I saw my Mammie in the room sitting on a chair. She stretched out her arms and I ran across and knelt beside her, burying my face in her lap. She had on a smooth, black dress, and I could smell the camphor balls off it, the smell that kills the moths, the funny things with no blood and no bones that eat holes in your jersey. There were no holes in Mammie's dress. She rubbed my head with her hands and said: "You're the only boy I have now." I could hear her heart thumping very hard, and then she cried, and I cried and cried, with my head down on her lap. "What's wrong, Mammie?" I asked, looking up at her wet eyes. "Nothing, darling: nothing, pet. He died for Ireland." I turned my head and looked at the bed. Johnny was lying on the white bed in a brown dress. His hands were pale and they were joined around his rosary beads, and a big crucifix between them. There was a big lump of wadding at the side of his head and wee pieces up his nose. I cried more and more, and then my Mammie made me put on my clothes, and go downstairs for my breakfast.

All that day my Mammie stayed in the room to talk to the people that came to see our Johnny. And all the women shook hands with Mammie and they all said the same thing: "I'm sorry for your trouble, but he died for his country." They knelt beside the white bed and prayed, and then sat for awhile looking at Johnny, and speaking in low whispers. My sisters brought them wine and biscuits, and some of them cried when they were taking it, dabbing their eyes with their handkerchiefs or the tails of their shawls. Mrs. McCann came and she got wine, too, though she had told the rent man about the shed on the slates and we had to pay a penny a week. I was in the wee room when she came, and I saw her looking at the lighted candles and the flowers on the table, and up at the gas that had no mantle. But she couldn't see it because my big sister had put white paper over it, and she had done the same with the four brass knobs on the bed. She began to sniff and sniff and my Mammie opened the window without saying anything. The blind began to snuffle in and out, the lighted candles to waggle, and the flowers to smell. We could hear the pigeons cooing and flapping in the shed, and I could see at the back of my eyes, their necks fattening and their feathers bristling like a dog going to fight. It's well Daddy didn't hear them or he might have wrung their necks.

At night the kitchen was crammed with men and women, and many had to sit in the cold scullery. Mrs. Ryan, next door, lent us her chairs for the people to sit on. There was lemonade and biscuits and tea and porter. Some of the men, who drank black porter, gave me pennies, and they smoked and talked all night. The kitchen was full of smoke and it made your eyes sting. One man told my Daddy he should be a proud man, because Johnny had died for the Republic. My Daddy blinked his eyes when he heard this, and he got up and went into the yard for a long time.

The next day was the funeral. Black shiny horses with

their mouths all suds, and silver buckles on their straps, came trotting into the street. All the wee lads were looking at themselves in the glossy backs of the cabs where you could see yourself all fat and funny like a dwarf. I didn't play because Johnny was dead and I had on a new, dark suit. Jack Byrne was out playing and he told me that we had only two cabs and that there were three cabs at his Daddy's funeral. There were crowds of peelers in the street, some of them talking to tall, red-faced men with overcoats and walking sticks.

Three men along with my Daddy carried the yellow coffin down the stairs. There was a green, white, and gold flag over it. But a thin policeman, with a black walking stick and black leggins, pulled the flag off the coffin when it went into the street. Then a girl snatched the flag out of the peeler's hands and he turned all pale. At the end of our street there were more peelers and every one wore a harp with a crown on his cap. Brother Gabriel used to fairly wallop us in school if we drew harps with crowns on them. One day we told him the peelers wore them on their caps. "Huh!" he said, "The police! the police! They don't love their country. They serve England. England, my boys! The England that chased our people to live in the damp bogs! The England that starved our ancestors till they had to eat grass and nettles by the roadside. And our poor priests had to say Mass out on the cold mountains! No, my dear boys, never draw a harp with a crown on it!" And then he got us to write in our books:

"Next to God I love thee
Dear Ireland, my native land!"

"It's a glorious thing," he said, "to die for Ireland, to die for Ireland!" His voice got very shaky when he said this and he turned his back and looked into the press. But Brother Gabriel is not in the school now; if he was he'd be good to me, because our Johnny died for Ireland.

The road to the cemetery was lined with people. Little boys that were at my school lifted a fringe of hair when the coffin passed. The trams were stopped in a big, long line—

it was nice to see so many at one look. Outside the gates of the graveyard there was an armored car with no one peeping his head out. Inside it was very still and warm with the sun shining. With my Daddy I walked behind the carried coffin and it smelt like the new seats in the chapel. The crowds of people were quiet. You could hear the cinders on the path squanching as we walked over them, and now and again the horses snorting.

I began to cry when I saw the deep hole in the ground and the big castles of red clay at the side of it. A priest, with a purple sash round his neck, shovelled a taste of clay on the coffin and it made a hard rattle that made me cry sore. Daddy had his head bowed and there were tears in his eyes, but they didn't run down his cheeks like mine did. The priest began to pray, and I knew I'd never see Johnny again, never, never, until I'd die and go to Heaven if I kept good and didn't say bad words and obeyed my Mammie and my Daddy. But I wouldn't like Daddy to tell me to give away the pigeons. When the prayers were over a tall man with no hat and a wee moustache stood beside the grave and began to talk. He talked about our Johnny being a soldier of the Republic, and, now and then, he pointed with his finger at the grave. As soon as he stopped talking we said the Rosary, and all the people went away. I got a ride back in a black cab with my Daddy and Uncle Pat and Uncle Joe. We stopped at "The Bee Hive" and they bought lemonade for me and porter for the cab driver. And then we went home.

I still have the pigeons and big Tom Duffy helps me to clean the shed and let them out to fly. Near night I give them plenty of corn so that they'll sleep long and not waken Daddy in the morning. When I see them fattening their necks and cooing I clod them off the slates.

Yesterday I was lying on the waste ground watching the pigeons and Daddy came walking towards me smoking his pipe with the tin lid. I tried to show him the pigeons flying through the clouds. He only looked at them for a minute and turned away without speaking, and now I'm hoping he won't wring their necks.

BRYAN MacMAHON

1909——

Bryan MacMahon was born in Listowel, County Kerry, where he was a schoolmaster until his retirement in 1974. During World War II he worked in a factory in the North Midlands of England, an experience he reported brilliantly in "The Plain People of England" for Sean O'Faolain's magazine, *The Bell.* He wrote a number of short stories for the same magazine during the 1940's, but did not publish his first book, *The Lion-Tamer and Other Stories,* until 1948. The response of American critics and readers to the U.S. edition (1949) necessitated three printings of the book within two months, an unusual sale for short stories by even an established writer. Naturally, a number of American magazines, from *Partisan Review* to *Mademoiselle,* showed interest in his subsequent work. He has since published a novel, *Children of the Rainbow* (1952), and several books of short stories including *The Red Petticoat* (1955). He is married and has a large family. MacMahon's stories are often sentimental or too florid in their vocabulary, but the one here, from *The Red Petticoat,* has a tartness that makes it palatable. It is a bit like the sloes that the parish clerk is eating at the end of it: these bitter little wild plums taste odd, but one can't help eating them, just the same.

The Sound of the Bell

Sunday Mass was over, and the priest was removing his vestments when there was a rap on the heavy sacristy door. Maurice Fitz, the old parish clerk, opened it. Outside he saw a cluster of men, mostly middle-aged and old. The clerk's eyes narrowed. "Oh, the little dabchicks," he said, "the little dabchicks from Boherbeg."

"We want to see the parish priest," said one of the men, a tall hook-nosed fellow; wearing riding breeches and leggings.

"If you do, Mister Gravel Pit, you'll have to wait till he's finished his thanksgiving."

"We'll wait!"

The clerk closed the door slowly, narrowly eyeing the men as he did so. He was dressed in greeny-black cloth. Jutting into the nape of his stiff collar were the icicles of his poor grey hair. When he was left with but a small aperture through which to peer, he said: "Riddle-me-riddle-me-ree! Boots and breeding brought them here." His astonishingly sensible face redeemed the eccentricity of this statement.

The ten or eleven men waited under the damp inhospitable stone of the church. Every man, except the man with the riding breeches, had his right shoulder higher than his left. This was from constant use of spade and slawn. One man stood a little to the rear. He was dumpy and his face was dyed purple by the cold. A drop of water at the end of his long nose made him look extremely disconsolate. His attitude indicated a vague desire to be disassociated from the others. The man with the riding breeches thrust his hands deep into his fob pockets and looked around in order to stiffen the loyalty of the others. The man with the purple face glanced at him and said timidly: "Maybe 'twould be better to call to see him in the house tomorrow, Richie?"

"We'll see him here and now!" said the other stoutly.

Just then the door opened—seemingly of its own volition —and the men trooped in.

Father Fennel was drying his hands on a linen towel. He was less a tiny man than a large man shrunken. He seemed frail and defenseless. He had a habit of blinking. As he dried his hands he looked down at the big boots moving across the polished parquetry. The men had now formed a solid ring around him. The clerk slammed the door with unnecessary loudness and scampered around the periphery of the ring until he was near the priest. He took a brass candlestick from a table. His movements implied a distrust of the men's honesty.

"Good day, men," said the priest.

"Good day, Father Fennell," chorused the men.

The man with the purple face was now in front. "Hard weather for this time of year, Father . . ."

"Is that you, Johnny Mahoon? Well? Any word from Jim?"

Johnny Mahoon inflated. "Next time he'll come home he'll have the collar, Father."

"With the help of God, Johnny!" said the priest.

"With the help of God, Father," said Johnny with meekness and pride.

There was a lull. The clerk opened a wardrobe door and discommoded some of the deputation. He thrust his head in among the bright vestments and began to sing: *"Who'll hang the ringer on the black cat's neck? Who'll hang the ringer on black cat's neck?"*

The heavy boots stirred uneasily.

The priest balled up the towel and dropped it on a small table. "Well, men, what brought ye?" he asked.

The men looked at Richie MacNamara of the gravel pit. Out of his fob pockets Richie's hands seemed unsure and nervous. Nevertheless, he began: "We came, Father, about the bell!"

"The bell?"

"Ay! the new bell!"

"What about it? A little high-pitched in tone, but just the same everybody says 'tis a grand bell."

A deep voice came from among the men: "It's a fine bell for them that are living in the shadow of the steeple."

"Wax!" said the parish clerk.

"I don't quite follow ye," said Father Fennell.

Richie MacNamara had become brave: "You put a shilling a cow on us to pay for that bell. At Donovan's station —you remember, Father?"

"I remember. And ye paid it like good Christian men."

"Wax!" said the parish clerk.

"Father," Richie enquired, "did any man from Boherbeg ever default in his station money?"

"Not in my time!"

"No, Father! Nor in Father Gibson's time! Nor in Father Prendiville's time! Nor in Father Danny O'Shea's time! Nor in the time of any parish priest that came before you. And another thing, Father, did we ever deny you your lawful christmas dues?"

"Ye did not!"

"And did we ever leave you short of the winter's firing?"

"Never! That goes without saying."

"And we paid our part for the new bell, didn't we?"

"Ye did. Ye did. Ye did."

The clerk was opening and slamming drawers. *"Around the world for sport,"* he sang: *"around the world for sport."*

Richie MacNamara turned. "We were talking to the parish priest," he said, "and not to the parish clerk." He made the word clerk sound like an obscenity.

The old man straightened himself. He swivelled deliberately, wet his lips with a meditative tongue, narrowed his eyes and said: "Richie MacNamara, I remember the morning you were christened. An ugly little scaldie with ropes of black hair on you and the bubble in your skull moving in and out." He snorted. "They must ha' been damn fond o' children when they r'ared you."

Richie MacNamara reddened. The priest raised a pacifying hand. Johnny Mahoon stepped into the breach. Since his son was going for the Church, he reckoned that he had a leg in both worlds.

"Father, about that bell! We gave it a fair trial. We tested it from all angles and airts and in all winds and weathers. And it's our contention that the bell can't be heard beyond Teerfeeney Cross."

The clerk stopped folding a maniple to snort: "It can be heard in Moinveenagh and in Derrigo. It can even be heard in Clounassig with a hill between. 'Tis a queer state of affairs that it should skip the holy hollow of Boherbeg."

Johnny Mahoon refused to be deflected. "We couldn't fault th' ould bell, Father. We set our clocks to it. We began and ended work to it. The wimmin put down the praties to it and we came back from the bog to it. If it was a thing it was a dead bell we said a Lord-ha'-mercy on the soul of the faithful departed. If 'twas a Mass bell we took care to be in good time. And if it was a thing it rang out in the heart of the night, we knew that something terrible had happened—that there was a fire, or—"

"—that the parish priest had died," said the sepulchral voice somewhere in the deputation.

"God spoke first!" said the clerk sharply, implying that Father Fennell might bury the lot of them.

Richie MacNamara brought his face close to the priest's. "We never went ag'in a parish priest yet!" he half threatened.

The clerk guffawed and slammed home a drawer. "Oho, ye did not!" he said. "Except the time of the pews! And the time of the wran-dance! And the time of the raffle for the half-a-cow!"

"Bridle your tongue, man!" Father Fennell ordered his clerk.

The clerk took a conical candle extinguisher from the wall and opened the door leading to the sanctuary. He turned. "What did Father Gibson call ye? The pagans of the parish, with yeer eggs in one another's haywynds and yeer knots for ripping calves' guts and yeer three drops of cock's blood on the ace of hearts."

The clerk clutched the extinguisher as if it were a lance. He raised his voice a full tone: "And ye were never crowned till Father Prendiville called Boherbeg the boondoon of Ireland. Riddle-me-riddle-me-ree! Ye never wint ag'in a parish priest! What about the battle of the Red Gullet when the wounded shoemaker was cured with Ippo wine and squills?"

He slammed the door with a great hollow sound. The priest turned to the men. "When he isn't a duke, he's a weasel. Ye haven't to put up with him the round of the year like I have. May God look down on me! I was a happy man in Ballytarv." The deputation made belligerent noises of commiseration.

"About the bell," continued the priest evenly: "it was put there to be heard."

"You took the word out of my mouth, Father," said Johnny Mahoon.

"I'll tell ye what! I'll ramble up there one of these days to hear the midday Angelus. Wouldn't that be the best thing I could do?"

"That'll suit us gallant, Father," chorused the men. "Any day you name, Father. 'Tis a slack time o' the year."

"Well, we'll say Tuesday; that is if his lordship will consent to drive the pony to Boherbeg."

Johnny Mahoon was alert to change the subject. " 'Twill go to the rain, Father," he observed.

Judiciously: "I wouldn't agree with you, Johnny."

With sham concern: "Wouldn't you now, Father?"

"No, John. The glass is steady. I'd say 'twould keep hammering away at the frost."

"Maybe you have the right of it, Father. I won't cross your opinion."

The big boots clumped awkwardly out of the sacristy. As they went down the road the bell of the church began to peal loudly behind them. "Bling, bling," it went. One of the men took out his watch and looked at it puzzledly. He could find no reason for the bell's ringing. The plodding men glowered at the unwelcome sound.

When the pony and trap came to the humped bridge of Boherbeg, the priest and the clerk saw the men standing in a resolute lump. For the most part each man was wearing a navy blue Sunday suit, with a gleaming stud in the neckband of his white shirt. One old fellow wore a clawhammer coat with two black buttons in the back. They all stood there looking at the priest and the clerk with stone-dead eyes. Beside them flowed a dark chocolate-colored stream, widening into a pool, on the surface of which seesawed three or four ducks as pretty as decoys. The boreen, rutted and battered by cartwheels, stretched away for a mile on the side of the stream. The thatched cabins crouched among the trees on the roadside. The black ridge of the bog bank rose behind the crouching houses.

The men of Boherbeg had a saddle horse ready for the priest. Father Fennell eyed the animal mistrustfully. The clerk descended and, taking the pony's head, led it forward through the people. They made way with a certain amount of studied indolence. Then the priest came gingerly out of the trap. After a few words an able-bodied man came forward and tossed the priest into the saddle. Father Fennell seemed out of breath. The people closed in around him and tried to mesh him in their conversation. Johnny Mahoon took the horse's head. The procession began. After the clerk had tied the pony to a gatepost, he sauntered after.

The womenfolk and the children came to the doorways of the cabins. They, too, were dressed in their Sunday best. Catching the priest's eye, they beamed and bobbed in his direction. When they came to Mahoon's, Johnny proudly brought the procession to a halt. His wife, Maria, dressed in a yellow blouse and black gabardine skirt, was standing at the gatepost. She was a great cudgel of a woman. As the priest approached, she kept smoothing her hips with movements indicative of welcome for the royalty that someday would be invested in her son. Under her arm was a large cerise cushion.

"I'm hearing great accounts of Jim, Maria."

"He's a good boy, Father, God bless him."

"Tell him to call up to me when he comes home."

"I will indeed, Father," said Maria Mahoon.

The priest made as if to rein away, but at that moment a girl came from behind the woman's dress. The child was carrying a linen-covered tray on which stood a tall glass of milk. "A glass of milk, Father!" said Maria Mahoon, proudly.

The clerk was leaning on a low wall of clipped evergreens. He looked truculently at Mahoon's trim cabin. "To hell with thatch!" he said loudly. In the silence that followed he began a kind of tuneless whistling.

The priest smiled at the child and, taking the milk, drank it delicately. Instinctively the people pressed forward to watch his mouth and throat working.

Johnny Mahoon took the cerise cushion from his wife and imprisoned it in his free armpit. He led the animal forward over the soft torn road. The procession moved across a little bridge made of sods laid on straight boughs, thence along a passage up to the bogland. The turf of the cutaway was resilient and dry; the strength of the bog breeze sent the priest into a bout of coughing. Children straggled behind the men; among these children moved the clerk, still at his reedy whistling.

The crowd came to a halt beside a chair set near a fence. The chair had a tall back and armrests. The fence behind was padded with the paper of stunted oak leaves and the fiber of coarse hay rakings so that scarcely a puff of the northern breeze sneaked through it. Johnny Mahoon placed the cushion on the chair. The priest was helped down from the horse. He took his seat without comment. At first he thought he was on a throne, but glancing around at the great ring of people he realized that he was in a dock. His eyes fell. He began to gather his breath. When again he looked up, there was a gap in the people so that from the rising ground he could look down in the direction of the village.

There came a blundering and tearing in the fence behind the seated priest; suddenly from out the oak leaves crashed an old man with a greeny coat. He stood on the top of the fence and glared down at the priest and the people. "The country is creeping with druids!" said the clerk. The observation had an unmistakable grotesque pertinence.

"Who have you ringing the bell, Father?" came a voice from the ring.

"Donal Sullivan."

"A dependable man!" It was impossible to say whether this was said sarcastically or not. The clerk ceased his whistling.

"Great timing!" said Johnny Mahoon bluffly, taking out his watch and looking at it steadfastly.

" 'Tis, indeed!" said the priest, looking at *his* watch. Over the heads of the people he could see the children on the fences silhouetted against the sky.

Priest and people fell silent as each man's ear aimed the east. They had no need to look. Every man could have put his elongated hand backward and away downhill over the mushrooming rods of the ash trees and pressed his index finger hard down on the unseen button of the village. A gull whitened in the northern sky. Over their heads a crow slowly clapped his black hands.

There was now little or no noise. The horse was tearing at the grass; the people's ears examined the rhythm of this noise and learned to anticipate it. Once, behind the priest's back, a man made so bold as to crack a match and redden his pipe. But he allowed the pipe to go out after a few puffs that he suddenly realized were resented by the others. Deep somewhere in a slit, bogwater chuckled.

Twice the priest threw out flimsy beginnings of conversation, but the whispered replies from the men disconcerted him. Eventually he scored a sterling point by looking steadfastly at the turf-ricks, changing his position on the cerise cushion and corrugating his forehead thoughtfully. Johnny Mahoon was forced to say: "As soon as the passages become reliable we'll draw out the turf. Then you'll be the first decade in our bead."

"How's the enemy now, Father?" queried the man with the deep voice, who was suddenly discovered to be a little gnarled man with a fumed-oak face.

The priest took out his watch and looked at it. He kept the face of the watch masked with his thumb.

"In or around, Denis!"

"In or around, is it, Father?" said Denis slyly. He went back into the ring, hawked and spat on the grass behind him.

Once again the ears probed the east—fruitlessly.

"I'd say 'tis the louvers are at fault!" said one man, who had the reputation of being a chimney maker.

"Or the scope of the swing!" said another, who had been a hurler in his youth.

"Or the temper of the metal!" said a third, who hoped to inherit a forge.

The clerk was chanting: "Oh, I was early idle in that vast barbaric land."

Then a shot—and a second shot—ambushed their western and heedless ears. The sounds came from over the immediate horizon of the bogland. The priest popped up out of his coat. His head had the precise movements of a ventriloquist's doll. Watches flashed in and out among the old men to offset this distraction. Already the children were deserting. Richie MacNamara of the gravel pit came forward.

"I'd say it has the hour well spoiled now, Father," he said severely.

Glowing with pleasure, the priest was watching a pointer fanning strongly on the upper ridge. "Ha, ha!" he said, "there's a game I served my time to."

The dog, moving in his well-loved element, came down toward the people. Then the fowler broke the skyline. He stood for a little space and looked down at the scene below him. When the priest had risen from the chair, the fowler saw the cushion blaze up among the dark press of bodies. He made as if to move away but the cautious movements of his dog attracted him and he came gingerly onward. He was a tall man with a free stride. The pointer leaped from the turf bank and nosed in the low ground. The people watched it working forward. The fowler descended through a gap in the bank.

Then the people of Boherbeg discovered that their priest had escaped.

The fowler stood waiting for Father Fennell, who was now approaching him with the stride of a boy. The dog slowed before a clump of rushes, then froze in dead set and gently raised its right paw. The priest took the gun from the fowler and stole up on the dog. Turn and turn about the dog was taut and quivering. The priest stooped and raised the gun to his shoulder. In this attitude he wasn't as big as a hatching hen. The ring of people prepared to receive the shot in their western ears.

Then from the east came the sound of the bell. "Pling! Pling! Pling!" it went unmistakably. The priest wearily lowered the gun from his shoulder and turned a shrewd affectionate face on the people. The dog broke discipline and moved in on the game. The snipe rose and flung itself deftly at the air. With rusty squeakings it was exalted in the sky where it mimicked the blinkings of a skylark.

The clerk popped something into his mouth, grimaced wryly and said: "This is a noble locality for sloes."

MARY LAVIN
1912——

Born in East Walpole, Massachusetts, of Irish parents, Mary Lavin first went to school there. When her family moved back to Ireland, she bitterly resented it and long felt homesick for New England. Nevertheless, she found herself in a beautiful setting in Ireland, an estate belonging to Bective House, County Meath. The Boyne River runs alongside; a ruined Cistercian abbey, founded in 1146, stands nearby. Young Mary Lavin wandered alone through the estate, absorbing everything. She received her secondary education at Loreto Convent, Dublin, and earned a B.A. and an M.A. from University College, Dublin. Jane Austen was the subject for her Master's thesis; she had begun a Ph.D. thesis on Virginia Woolf when her first short story came to her. From that moment, she writes, "I have never written a single paragraph that has not had its source in the imagination." Mary Lavin married a Dublin solicitor, William Walsh, and they had three daughters. After his death she supported her family by farming as well as writing. If she gave up the former entirely for the latter, she would lose her grip on real life, she feels. Miss Lavin's first volume of short stories, *Tales from Bective Bridge*, appeared in 1942 with a preface by Lord Dunsany, a County Meath neighbor. She has since published two novels and seven volumes of short stories, including the important *Selected Stories* (1959), *The Great Wave and Other Stories* (1961), *Happiness* (1969) and *Collected Stories* (1985). From Mary Lavin's many stories focusing on a lifelong struggle between husband and wife over some relatively trivial yet insoluble problem, "Brigid," from *Selected Stories*, is the most condensed and incisive. But condensation and incisiveness are not typical Lavin qualities; a longer, more meditative story like "The Nun's Mother," from *At Sallygap and Other Stories* (1947), is more characteristic. Measured by Joyce's standard, this interior monologue has its weak points, but its subject appears unique in Irish literature. Frank O'Connor wisely said of Mary Lavin, "She fascinates me more than any other of the Irish writers of my generation because, more than any of them, her work reveals the fact that she has not said all she has to say."

Brigid

The rain came sifting through the air, and settled like a bloom on the fields. But under the trees it fell between the leaves in single heavy drops, noisily, like cabbage water running through the large holes of a colander.

The house was in the middle of the trees.

"Listen to that rain!" said the woman to her husband. "Will it never stop?"

"What harm is a sup of rain?" said the man.

"That's you all over again," she said. "What harm is anything, as long as it doesn't affect yourself?"

"How do you mean, when it doesn't affect me? Look at my feet. They're sopping; and look at my hat, it's soused." He took it off, and shook the rain off it on to the spitting bars of the fire grate.

"Quit that," said the woman. "Can't you see you're raising ashes?"

"What harm is the ashes doing?"

"I'll show you what harm," she said, taking down a dish of cabbage and potato from the shelf over the fire, "there's your dinner destroyed with them." The yellow cabbage was slightly sprayed with ash.

"Ashes are healthy, I often heard it said. Put it here!" and he sat down at the table, taking up his knife and fork, and indicating where the plate was to be put by patting the table with the handles of the cutlery. "Is there no bit of meat?" he asked, prodding the potato critically.

"There's plenty in the town, I suppose."

"In the town? And why didn't somebody go to the town, might I ask?"

"Who was there to go? You know as well as I do there's no one here to be traipsing in and out everytime there's something wanted from the town."

"I suppose one of our fine daughters would think it the end of the world if she was asked to go for a bit of a message? Let me tell you they'd get men for themselves quicker if they were seen doing a bit of work once in a while."

"Who said anything about getting men for them?" said their mother. "They're time enough getting married."

"Is that the way?" said Owen. "Mind you now, anyone would think that you were anxious to get them off your hands with the way every penny that comes into the house goes on bits of silks and ribbons for them."

"I'm not going to let them be without their bit of fun just because you have other uses for your money than spending it on your own children!"

"What other uses have I? Do I smoke? Do I drink? Do I play cards?"

"You know what I mean."

"I suppose I do." The man was silent. He left down his fork. "I suppose you're hinting at poor Brigid again?" he said. "But I told you forty times, if she was put into a home she'd be just as much of an expense to us as she is above in the little house there." He pointed out of the window with his fork.

"I see there's no use in talking about it," said the woman, "but all I can say is God help the girls, and you, their own father, putting a drag on them so that no man will have anything to do with them after hearing about Brigid."

"What do you mean by that? This is something new. I thought it was only the bit of bread and tea she got that you grudged the poor thing. This is something new. What is this?"

"You oughtn't to need to be told, a man like you that

saw the world, a man that was in England and London, a man that traveled like you did."

"I don't know what you're talking about." He took up his hat and felt it to see if the side he had placed near the fire was dry. He turned the other side toward the fire. "What are you trying to say?" he said. "Speak plain!"

"Is any man going to marry a girl when he hears her own aunt is a poor half-witted creature, soft in the head, and living in a poke of a hut, doing nothing all day but sitting looking into the fire?"

"What has that got to do with anybody but the poor creature herself? Isn't it her own trouble?"

"Men don't like marrying into a family that has the like of her in it."

"Is that so? I didn't notice that you were put out much by marrying me, and you knew all about poor Brigid. You used to bring her bunches of primroses, and I remember you pulling the flowers off your hat one day and giving them to her when she started crying over nothing. You used to say she was a harmless poor thing. You used to say you'd look after her."

"And didn't I? Nobody can say I didn't look after her. Didn't I do my best to have her taken into a Home where she'd get proper care? You can't deny that."

"I'm not denying anything. You never gave me peace or ease since the day we were married. But I wouldn't give in. I wouldn't give in, and what is more I won't give in now, either. I won't let it be said that I had hand or part in letting my own sister be put away."

"But it's for her own good—" said the woman, and this time her voice was softer and she went over and turned the wet hat again on the fender. "It's nearly dry," she said, and then she went back to the table and took up the plate from which he had eaten and began to wash it in a basin of water that was at the other end of the table. "It's for her own good. I'm surprised you can't see that; you, a sensible man, with two grown-up daughters. You'll be sorry one of these days when she's found dead in the chair—the Lord between us and all harm—or when she falls in the fire and gets scorched to death—God preserve us from the like! I was reading, only the other day, in a paper that came round something from the shop, that there was a case like that up in the Midlands."

"I don't want to hear about it," said the man, shuffling his feet. "This hat is dry, I think," he said, and he put it on his head and stood up.

"That's the way you always go on," said the woman. "You don't want to listen to anything unpleasant. You don't want to listen to anything that's right. You don't want to listen because you know what I'm saying is true and you know you'd have no answer to put against what I'd say!"

"You make me tired," said the man; "it's always the one story in this house. Why don't you get something else to talk about for a change?"

The woman ran to the door and blocked his way out.

"Is that the last you have to say?" she said. "You won't give in?"

"I won't give in. Poor Brigid. Didn't my mother make me promise her that I'd never have hand or part in putting the poor creature away? 'Leave her alone,' my mother used to say, 'she's doing no harm to anyone.'"

"She's doing harm to our daughters," said the woman, "and you know that. Don't you?" She caught his coat and stared at him. "You know the way Matty Monaghan gave up Rosie after dancing with her all night at the dance in the Town Hall last year. Why did he do that, do you suppose? It's little you know about it at all! You don't see Mamie crying her eyes out some nights after coming in from a walk with the girls and hearing little bits of talk from this one and that one, and putting two and two together, and finding out for herself the talk that goes on among the young men about girls and the kind of homes they come from!"

"There'd be a lot more talk if the poor creature was put away. Let me tell you that, if you don't know it for yourself! It's one thing to have a poor creature, doing no one any harm, living quiet, all by herself, up at the end of a boreen where seldom or never anyone gets a chance of seeing her, and it's another thing altogether to have her taken away in a car and everyone running to the window to see the car pass and talking about her and telling stories from one to another till it would be no time at all they'd be letting on she was twice as bad as she is, and the stories about her would be getting so swollen that none of us could go down the streets without being stared at as if we were all queer!"

"You won't give in?" said his wife once more.

"I won't give in."

"Poor Mamie. Poor Rosie," said their mother, and she put the plates up on the dresser.

Owen shuffled his feet. "If you didn't let it be seen so plain that you wanted to get them off, they might have a better chance. I don't know what they want getting married for in any case. They'd be better off to be interested in the place, and raise a few hens, and make a bit of money for themselves, so that they could be independent and look people up and down and outstare the boldest!"

"It's little you know about anything, that's all I have to say," said the woman.

Owen moved to the door.

"Where are you going now?" said the woman.

"There's no use in my telling you and drawing down another stream of abuse on myself, when I mention the poor creature's name."

The woman sighed and then stood up and walked over to a press in the corner.

"If that's where you're going you might as well take over these clean sheets." She took down a pair of sheets from where they were airing on the shelf over the fire. "You can't say but that I look after her, no matter what," she said.

"If you remembered her the way I do," said the man, "when she was only a little bit of a child, and I was growing up and going to school, you'd know what it feels like to hear talk about putting her in a home. She used to have lovely hair. It was like the flossy heads of the dandelions when they are gone past their best. No one knew she was going to be a bit soft until she was toddling around and beginning to talk, and even then they thought she was only slow, that she'd grow out of it."

"I know how you feel," said the woman. "I could cry sometimes myself when I think of her. But she'd be so happy in a home! We could visit her any time we wanted. We could hire a car and drive over there, all of us, on a fine Sunday now and again. It would be some place to go. And it wouldn't cost no more than it costs to keep her as it is."

She didn't know whether he heard the end of the sentence because he was gone down the path, and was cutting across through the field, with the ash plant in his hand.

"He was cutting across the field with the ash plant in his hand, when I was coming up the road," said Rosie, when she came in to her supper, and her mother asked her if she had seen her father out in the yard.

"He was going to your Aunt Brigid then," said her mother. "Did you not see him after that?"

"That was three hours ago," said Mamie. "He wouldn't be over there all this time." Mamie was sitting down taking her supper.

"The tea is spoiled," said their mother. "I may spill it out. There'll have to be a fresh pot of tea made when he comes in."

"I suppose he's mending a chair or a table for Aunt Brigid," said Rosie. "He wouldn't be just sitting over there all this time."

"You wouldn't know what he'd be doing," said the mother, and the girls looked at each other. They knew then that there had been words between their father and mother while they were out.

"Maybe one of you ought to run over and see what's keeping him?" said their mother.

"Oh, let him alone. If he wants to stay over there, let him stay. He'll have to be home soon to put in the calves anyway. It's nearly dark."

It was quite dark, and the calves were still out. It was beginning to rain, and the girls had gone out again to a dance, when Owen's wife went across the field herself, and up the boreen to the hut where the poor soft creature lived all alone.

How can she sit there in the dark? thought Owen's wife, when she didn't see a light in the window, but as she got nearer she saw there was a faint light from the flames of the fire on the hearth. She felt sure that Owen wasn't there. He wouldn't be there without lighting a lamp, or a bit of a candle! There was no need to go in. She was going to turn back from the middle of the yard, but it seemed an unnatural thing not to call to the door and see if the poor creature was all right.

She was the same as ever, sitting by the fire with a silly smile, and not looking up till she was called three or four times.

"Brigid, did you see Owen?"

Brigid looked up. "Owen is a queer man," she said, and that was all the answer she gave.

"So he was here! What time did he leave?"

Brigid grumbled something.

"What are you saying?" said Owen's wife.

"He wouldn't go home," said Brigid. "I told him it was time to go home for his tea, but he wouldn't answer me. 'Go home,' I said, but he wouldn't say anything."

"When he did go, at last, what time was it? Did you notice?"

Brigid was difficult sometimes. Was she going to be difficult now?

"He wouldn't speak to me," said Brigid, suddenly.

Suddenly Owen's wife saw his ash plant lying on the table.

"Is he still here?" she said, sharply, and she glanced back at the door. "Is he out in the yard? I didn't see him! I didn't hear him!"

"He wouldn't speak to me," said Brigid again.

The other woman couldn't see her in the dark. The fire was flickering too irregularly to see by its light.

"But where is he? Is he in the yard? Is there anything the matter with him?" She ran to the door and she called out into the dark, but there was no answer. She stood there trying to think, and then she heard Brigid talking to herself again, but she didn't trouble to listen. She might as well go home. Wherever he was, he wasn't here. "If he comes back, tell him I was here looking for him," she said. "I'll go home through the other field."

Brigid said something then, that made her turn sharply and look at her.

"What did you say?" she said.

"Tell him yourself," said Brigid, and then she seemed to be talking to herself again.

Owen's wife looked at her. She was worse than she ever was before.

Brigid was leaning down in the dark before the fire.

"Why don't you talk?" she was saying. "Why don't you talk?"

Urgently, Owen's wife began to pull out the old settle bed that was in front of the fire without knowing why she did it, but she could feel the blood beating in her ears and behind her eyes.

"He fell down there and he wouldn't get up!" said Brigid. "I told him to get up. I told him that his head was getting scorched. But he wouldn't listen to me. He wouldn't get up. He wouldn't do anything."

Owen's wife closed her eyes. She was all of a sudden afraid to look. But when she opened her eyes and looked down, Owen's eyes stared up at her, wide open, from where he lay on his back on the floor.

"Owen!" she screamed—and she tried to pull him up.

His shoulders were stiff and heavy. She caught his hands. They were stiff and cold. Was he dead? She felt his face. But his face was so hot, she couldn't put her hand on it. If he was dead he'd be cold. She wanted to scream and scream and to run out of the house, but first she tried to drag him as far as she could from the ashy hearth. Then suddenly feeling the living eyes watching her from behind, and seeing the dead eyes staring up at her from the blistered red face, she sprang upright, knocking over a chair, and ran out of the house, and ran down the boreen.

Her screams brought people running out from their doors, the light streaming out each side of them. She couldn't speak, but she pointed up the hill.

It was dark down at the pump. And she could hear the feet running in the way she had pointed. Then they had reached the cottage, and there were no more feet, but great talk and shouting. She sat down on the side of the pump, but there was a smell of burning in the air, and when she saw that it came from her own hands she wanted to scream again. There was burnt hair stuck to her hands. Desperately she bent forward and began to wash them in the water, while all the time a pain gathered in her heart, not yet the pain of loss, but the pain of having failed, failed in some terrible way.

I failed him always, she thought, from the start. I never loved him like he loved me; not even then, long ago, the time I took the flowers off my hat. It wasn't for Brigid, like he thought. I was only making myself out to be what he thought I was—what he thought I was. I didn't know enough about loving to change myself for love. I didn't even know enough about it to keep him loving me, either. He had to give it in the end, to Brigid.

He gave it all to Brigid; to a poor daft thing that didn't know enough to pull him up, or call someone, when he fell down in a stroke. If it was anyone else was with him, he might have had a chance.

Oh, how had it happened? How could love be wasted, and go to loss like that?

It was like the way the tossy balls of cowslips that they used to make as children were forgotten and left behind in the fields, till they were trodden into the muck by the cattle and sheep.

Suddenly she thought of the heavy feet of the neighbors tramping the boards of the cottage up in the fields behind her, and rising up almost swifter than her thoughts, she suddenly ran back to them.

"Oh, you poor woman," said someone near the door, seeing her thrust past the children at the threshold.

They began to make way for her to where, on the settle bed, they had laid her husband. But she tried instead to part her own way through them to the door of the room off the kitchen.

"It's Brigid I'm thinking about," she said.

They knew her mind better than she credited them, because one of them plucked her sleeve.

"Something will have to be done about her now."

"It will that," she said, decisively, and her voice was as true as a bell. "It'll leave a mark on her, poor thing. And the worst of it was to have to leave him lying there and not be able to stir him."

She went over to the door of the room.

"That's what I want to tell you," she said, looking around her defiantly, falsifying their meaning. "She'll need proper minding. To think she hadn't the strength to run for help, or pull him back a bit from the heat. Where is she? Where are you, Brigid?"

Then she saw her, sitting on the side of the bed, in the other room.

"Get your hat and coat, Brigid," she said crossly. "You're coming home with me."

The Nun's Mother

Well, it was all over now, anyway. Mrs. Latimer closed her eyes and laid her head back against the horsehair cushions in the taxi. It was all over now, anyway, and she was certainly glad of that much. She kept her eyes closed as they drove down the convent avenue. And what is more, she decided childishly, she would keep them closed, keep them closed at any rate until they reached the gate lodge. In the main road she might perhaps open them. But then, would she know when that was: when they were in the main road, she meant; of course she would, the taxi would go up with a little bump and then down with a little bump. Inside Luke and herself would joggle about no matter how hard they clung to the leather straps. Their elbows would come together and, like corks on a wave-wash, their feet would lift a little from the rubber flooring and fall into place again. Her hair would catch on the loose threads of the cushions, or on one of the uncovered buttons. It would hurt for a second. Cat hairs. Only cat hairs. Her plaited bun kept the rest of her hair too taut to drag. Although, indeed, it would not matter a terrible lot if any of it got pulled. She could get Luke to free them. Or jerk her head and free them herself. What harm if they broke. Her hair was thick enough to stand it. And since it got gray there was no sense in being too particular.

It wasn't so very gray, of course, considering her age and that. Indeed, most people thought she was the youngest of her family, instead of the eldest. She was much younger-looking than Luke. (She opened her eyes a little and looked at him.) This last week had told on him too. Worn him out. But it had taken more effect on herself all the same. Until lately her underneath hairs had been as brown as when she was a girl, but only this morning she had seen a fleck or two of gray reflected in the mirror when the brush sprayed out her hair upon her shoulder. It had been a great strain, a great strain for both of them.

Poor Luke. His hand was on her knee now. They must be coming to the gate lodge. Up with a little bump. Down with a little bump. Out over the paving stones into the main road. They joggled together. He steadied himself with his hand on her knee, and when they wheeled into the tar road he left it on her knee. That was for sympathy. Sympathy with her sorrow. He was waiting for her to open her eyes until he told her how badly he felt for her.

Oh, so that was it! She had not realized. That was why she had hesitated to open them. Instinct. She had hesitated to shock Luke by letting him see her eyes empty of hurt, empty of sorrow. Empty, that was to say, of all appropriate expression. For she felt, at the moment, absolutely nothing. Nothing but relief that it was all over.

She certainly was not suffering. No matter how unnatural it might seem, it was nevertheless true that she was not suffering a bit. And Luke, poor Luke, he was not only hurt, but frightened and perplexed. Men had such an irrational horror of the cloister, the very word they used—"nunnery" —was so medieval. Really and truly she quite believed that Luke had been more hurt and repulsed by what Angela had done than he would have been had she got into some serious scrape or other. Yes, even *that* kind of scrape. If anything like *that* had happened he would have been shocked and grieved, angered and worried, but he would, underneath it all, have been infinitely gentle and understanding. For that would have been something within the orbit of his instincts. This, on the other hand, was completely alien to his nature. This was treasonable. This was abnormal.

A woman felt different. Women had a curious streak of chastity in them, no matter how long they were married, or how ardently they loved. And so, for most women, when they heard that a young girl was entering a convent, there was a strange triumph in their hearts at once; and during the day, as they moved around the house, they felt a temporary hostility to their husbands, towards the things of his household, towards his tables and chairs; yes, indeed, down even to his dishes and dishcloths. They flicked the dishcloths from them, from time to time, sending fans of filigree spray into the warm kitchen air, and all the time their minds were filled with conquering visions of glad young girls (who might have been themselves) going garlanded with lilies down a cool green cloisteral arch ivied over by the centuries; and, what was more, those glad young girls were going without once looking back at the blazing lawns, lit with brightly burning sun and hotly flaming flowers where lovers with lutes were lying. Yes, that was undoubtedly how most women felt. Or how else could one account for the success of novels like *The White Sister* that were always appearing in the shop windows? But *she* didn't feel like that. Of course, she could understand the feeling. She would admit that much: she could understand it. And Luke's grief, that too, she could understand. She could even imagine just how the pain of grief would have felt had it seized her, too, and dug into her with its claws. She could summon the feeling at once as if it were real and sincere. She could bare her breast and draw down the stroke of the pitiless beak. If she wished. But she didn't. Hadn't she always been sincere?

If asked, in all sincerity, how the loss of Angela affected her, she would have to answer truthfully and say that it meant no more fun out shopping, no more flippancies, no more visits to the Small Women shops (matrons and outsize now forever), no more angling to get new young men for parties (bridge and sandwiches now forever), no more need to lay aside linen, no more need to be on the lookout for bargains in silver spoons and forks (even when they were going for a song). No need, in short, to remain young.

Now, no longer, need she dream of riding down the years and passing under the arch of age, with a prancing two-in-hand. It would be a single gallop from now on. And one that would get faster with the years. Faster and faster she would go from now on, throwing up choking dust in the air and crazed by the cries from the wayside, cries of weary, childless women calling out after her: "Well for you, Mrs. Latimer, well for you, with a daughter a nun to pray for you."

A nun to pray for her. That meant the prayers of her daughter Angela. She had faith, of course. She believed in prayer to a certain extent, prayers of praise and prayers of remorse. Not what they meant—petition-prayers to find a ten-shilling note that was lost, prayers that it would not rain on the day of the tennis tournament. That was not real prayer. That she discounted. But real prayer, for her soul's salvation, from Angela, it was absurd! Her daughter Angela!—with plaits down her back until last spring and always sitting so immodestly with her bare thighs showing—it was, as she said at first, absurd.

There now. That was the truth. That was what she really felt about it. Not grief or sorrow in her loss, and not pride and joy either in the fact that the Lord had chosen the fruit of her tree. To be quite honest, she didn't believe He *had* chosen Angela. Angela had *gone*. But why? There was the mystery. Angela had made her choice and gone away without thinking of them, without caring how they felt, it seemed. And now there was Luke with tears in his eyes. And there was she herself—a nun's mother.

It was quite a title. A nun's mother. "Mrs. Latimer has a daughter a nun." "Meet Mrs. Latimer, who has a daughter in the convent." She would be quite an exhibit at church bazaars and charity whist drives. She might even have to assume an attitude. Would she, perhaps, have to dress in black? to smoke only in a cupboard, to put up holy pictures, even in the downstairs rooms, to write S.A.G. on the back of her envelopes, to—to—what else do the mothers of nuns have to do?—to donate settees to the convent parlor? It was enough to give anyone mixed emotions. All very well for Luke. There was no notoriety attached to being the father of a nun. And when he went to visit her he would be treated quite normally. Angela would not criticize him nor blush if his tie was rather bright. She would talk to him gladly and freely and not be afraid that Reverend Mother would come into the room and notice this, or speak afterwards about that, or comment, even ever so lightly, on the other. It was all very well for him. When he got used to the idea he would quite like going up to Mount St. Joseph and walking around with his cool, stately daughter in black-pleated gabardine with a high, firm virgin bust. He'd grow to love it, and gradually give up going to the club, give up wanting to go abroad for the summers—But she must not allow her resentment to include him too, because this resignation was yet a long way from him, might, indeed, never come to him, for how could she tell? She must be understanding with him. But it was very difficult when she did not know exactly how he felt. He was so silent.

He was always so silent when he was hurt. When she had first told him about Angela he had hardly said a word. Certainly nothing important or memorable. Had he said anything at all? She couldn't remember. Quite possible that he had not. Or perhaps he had just said "Angela?" like that, with a question in the word and a swift lift of his head to the light. "Angela?"—like that. As if they had half a dozen daughters, and that she had possibly mixed the names. He could be most irritating. There was no doubt about it. Most irritating. Look at him now straining back to see if he could catch another glimpse of the convent through the trees. His eyes were probably still filled with tears. She must shut her own eyes quickly before he turned around. It would be unspeakably annoying to think he was crying. There was his hand on her knee again, saying as clearly as words, "Just a little while longer, Maud, silence and sympathy just a little while longer, the length of the drive home, and then we will talk." About other things, of course. Not about Angela. That would be understood.

It was odd that he never could talk about Angela without great difficulty. And his efforts to do so during the last month had been unbearably irritating. Heavily, from time to time he would gulpingly ask a question about her.

"Are you sure she knows her own mind?"

He had asked that at least six nights running, coming into their bedroom without mentioning a name. Through sheer annoyance and strain she had said, "Who are you talking about?" Just to hurt him because he was so clumsy and helpless. The fact that he was so pathetic had made her torment him deliberately. Why, she did not know. Unless perhaps that she felt impatient that he could not take up where she had failed and find out why their lovely Angela was going away from them for ever and ever. He had made such desperate attempts to find out from her, without ever once thinking of going directly to Angela. "Does she know what she is giving up?" He would ask that at the oddest times. She knew what he meant, of course, what any man would have meant, and what any but Luke would have put so much more clearly. "Oh, yes," she had heard herself answer always, moving a chair, or twitching across a curtain. "Her mind is quite made up, I assure you." Why had she not gone to him and caught at the lapels of his coat and said, "I don't know, I don't know.—I'm afraid to ask her."

For that had been so. Hadn't it? She had been impatient with Luke only because she saw that he was suffering as she was, and that, what was worse, he was depending on her to ease his suffering. Why had she done nothing? Why?

It was queer that she who was so extraordinarily free with her tongue talking to most people should have been afraid to ask her own daughter one simple question. One small fact was all they both wanted to find out, and yet she could not rouse herself to ask outright, nor calm herself to employ the subtlety of trivial questions whose answers would weave together into the information she was seeking. In either case, Angela might give her a rebuff. If it had been a son instead of a daughter it would have been easier, she felt sure. But then, if it had been a son it would all have been out of her hands, anyway. Luke would have been so efficient then. Men were so straight with each other. No nonsense. "Look here, boy—" and "Tell me frankly, son—" and "Have you thought about this, my boy—" The "this" would be sex and love and the bodies of men and women. It would all be spoken of lightly, easily, even, indeed, with a slight flavor of humor, and the question would be settled once and for all. The boy would go ahead with his own idea, or he would think over what had been said. In either case they would know that he was equipped with knowledge enough to make an adult choice. But was Angela so equipped? Should she have spoken to her, straight out, about her body and the bodies of men?

It was so hard for women to be frank with each other. With men it was easy. With each other impossible. Or so she had found. Always. At school even. Women were so covert and sly when they were alone, so prudish, so guarded. All that awful, lumpy shuffling and protruding of elbows that went on under slips and nightdresses in order to dress or undress. No simplicity, no grace. And that was what it was to be a modest woman, to shuffle and clutch at straps and buttons.—Men were so much more normal. Why! they'd think nothing of walking around with nothing on. And if they were given any encouragement they'd never wear bathing suits. A bit startling perhaps at first, when you thought it would have been the other way round. Women's bodies were so much more graceful; molded so secretively, so subtly. In art it actually was the other way round, as if women were the franker sex. If only they were, how handy everything would be; no falsity; no clutching at sheets when the door knob rattled; no "turn around for a minute, dear"; no nonsense. But most of all, none of the terrible reticence about the body between mothers and daughters, a reticence based on revulsion, and not, as with mothers and sons, upon respect and mystery. She was conscious of this revulsion every time she was alone with her daughter during the last month. It seemed to her sometimes that Angela assumed a defiance every time they were together as much as to say, "Speak now, if you dare, about me and my private affairs—" It could have been only imagination, of course, but it kept her lips closed as surely as if the words had been really spoken. Luke knew nothing of all this. She would have to give him credit for that much. She could have thrown something at him when he inquired every night as they undressed, "Well, dear? Did you have a word with her?"

A word with her! It was in irony she had first said that she had. "A nice long chat," she had said sneeringly. But he had been bending down taking off his slippers and he had heard the words and missed the sneer. His face had lit up with such relief and she had been so repentant of her unkindness that she did not tell him she had been sarcastic. After that he had somehow relied on her to talk to Angela. He had lost his uneasy look and stopped asking clumsy questions. Instead, he got the more irritating habit of throwing them together at every possible moment. "Wouldn't you like to run along. I'll be after you in a few minutes." And if by any chance he came into a room when they were talking (about getting the poodle's hair cut or putting more sugar in the rhubarb) he would scuttle out again with apologies, like a visitor who got up too early, saying, "Don't let me disturb you." It was a wonder she had not run after him and beat at him with a newspaper. She had wanted so badly to be cruel or crude or vulgar. Poor Luke. She loved him so much but why, *oh why*, had he not kept his nose out of this.

Poor Luke. That was unfair. He was more sincere than she was, that was all. And he had been so worried about Angela. He was certain they had had a long talk and that Angela had assured her that she knew exactly what she was doing. That accounted for the strange way he treated the girl towards the end, as if she were a bit frightening, somebody not quite real, a little too unworldly, too precious, to be treated like a daughter. Because, of course, there was only one real difference for Luke between the cloister and the world—the difference of the flesh and the flesh denied. Poverty and obedience didn't matter a rap to him. He said as much twenty times a day.

"Poverty? Haven't the nuns more money than anyone in

the country? Haven't they bought up all the fine castles and demesnes there are? Isn't there always a good smell of meat boiling in a convent no matter what hour you may call? And central heating? Poverty did you say? Nonsense!" She wanted to say "Nonsense yourself" when she saw Angela giving away her little blue velvet toque to one of her friends and telling the chambermaid she could take all her pictures of film stars. For a girl like Angela who stored up such rubbish, ribbons and programs and postcards and letters and goodness knows how much other stuff, the poverty of community possessions would be terrible. But of course she hadn't wanted to add to Luke's sorrow, and so she let him talk away as much as he wanted. He had a few words about obedience too.

"You'd have to be a lot more obedient in an office," he would assure her, "and no roses in heaven after it either." But about chastity Luke had had nothing to say. That was what floored him. That a daughter of his should choose a life of chastity—a daughter of his—the child of his own delight. It was beyond his power to comprehend how such a choice existed for a woman. Poor Luke. He had looked at her sometimes as she sat brushing her hair, for all the world as if he were longing to ask, "Would you have done it?— Would you have given it all up?" But of course he never said anything of the kind.

Mrs. Latimer felt panic rise in her again. What would he say if he knew that she had not said one word to Angela about what she was giving up?

Men were so complacent. What could she have said? Yes! What could she have said to her own daughter that would not have been sickeningly embarrassing for them both.

It would have been no use saying anything. No matter what she had said, she would be as much in doubt as she was at this minute about Angela's knowledge of life. Of course, she had not said a word to her. And it was all over now, anyway. She must remember that. From now on it was no use worrying. She must tell Luke that too. For better or worse it was all over now.

What an unfortunate choice of phrase—for better or

worse. . . . And yet marriage, after all, was more worse than better, more of a cross than a crown. She herself had not found it so. Far from it . . . dear Luke . . . but so most of her married friends told her. They didn't even need to tell her, she could see for herself. In fact, when she thought about them, she felt relieved that Angela had taken the veil. It was only when she thought about herself and Luke that she felt sorry. Sorry? Yes, so sorry she could cry with pity.

Angela was going to miss it all; the heavy weight of the hard male breast, the terror, the pain, the soft delirium seeping through. She clutched the hand strap tightly. Better not to remember those far-back years. She must forget them if she was to assume a role. And assume a role she must. She must singe the edges of the past and its dear delight with a religious remorse. She must seal the memories of her love into a casket of stern taciturnity. She must let her fate fall into its natural folds, and she must act and think like a nun's mother. For Luke's sake. She must be able to turn to him and smile and press his hand, tell him that the Lord had been good to them, had chosen them above others, had sent them a cross of sweet lebanon wood embossed with flowers and foliage. Yes. That was the way she should feel. She would discipline herself to feel so. She would make her brazen soul seek shame in the joys of its past. She would search into the dimmest hours of the days and nights gone by, hours most misted over by the languors of love, and find some memory to blush her cheeks.

But she could find nothing. She had no shame for herself. Wait a minute. Perhaps there was a moment when she had reddened for Luke's shame? Perhaps by thinking of him she could see some foolishness in their love.

She thought of him, as she had often seen him, with his head bent back, eyes heavy and breath unsure, answering her questions reluctantly and incoherently, a vein in his forehead throbbing. Then she turned deliberately and stared at him where he sat beside her in the taxi. She looked at him sitting bolt upright on the edge of the taxi seat, his hands folded firmly and an umbrella across his knees.

Now, was she not repulsed? Now, did she not feel compunction, to think that she had reduced this nattiness in a bowler hat to the small indignity of a dressing gown and urgently feeling fingers? No; she did not.

It was better to be honest to the end. She felt instead a pride and potency that made her press her shoulder blades into the horsehair cushioned seat while her breast rose high and firm, carrying a coral cameo brooch up from the depths of sepia lace and down again to its hollows. None of all the women she knew had lived with love as long and as intimately as she had done. No one knew what love was as well as she.

And now her own daughter would have her hair shorn and hide her body with twenty-five yards of black. Her daughter would never know anything about it. Should she have told her?

But with what words? She would have no words different from those the sisters had used to draw her into the cloister. She could hear their gentle voices saying with St. Paul that love was the fulfilling of the law, and speaking too of the greater love that no man hath than he. . . . What chance had a few words from her against the power of quotations a thousand years old? Anything she could say would sound weak. "What do you know, Angela, of the love of a man for a woman?" Just suppose that Angela had listened and answered that she knew nothing. Supposing she had been gentle and trusting and said, "Tell me, Mother." It was extremely unlikely, but just suppose, for a moment, that it had happened. What would she have said love was? Not generous. Not kind. Not gentle. Not dignified. Not humble. Not to be described, in short, by any adjective that would appeal to a young girl straight from school. There were no words to describe it. Those who had tried were exiled and their books were burned on the quayside. It couldn't be described. And yet Luke had asked if she had "had a word with her." How irritating. Such a lack of understanding. Why didn't he try himself. Mrs. Latimer kicked the car rug.

Even if she could have described the peace and beauty of marriage, perhaps she would not have done so. For why, after all, should she take the responsibility of interfering with a vocation. Just because she didn't put a lot of faith in the idea of a personal call was no reason, when she came to think of it, for interfering with the life of someone who did. Wasn't there a girl in her own mother's town who wanted to be a nun? And, when her parents interfered, she went up on the roof one night in a nightdress, with a crucifix in her hand and her hair all down her back. The poor girl was saved, if she had intended jumping down, but her mind had gone. Interference was dangerous. It was not right to accept the responsibility of another soul.

Nonsense. There she was again trying to delude herself. She had accepted that responsibility twenty years ago when she brought her daughter into the world. Even at the time she had been aware of it. She had lain in her darkened room and tried to gaze down the widening wedge of the years ahead. She had seen her child and her child's children, and their children's children, wandering wider and wider over the world as year followed year; strange, terrifying people; lawyers, doctors, soldiers, nurses, deans with rolled parchments, drunkards, men of business, cheats, liars . . . along they trudged over the land while she lay in her grave, and from time to time they turned back with frightened faces, and each face had the cast of hers; her features, her skin, her hair, her eyes. They all seemed to stream out from her as she had often seen people stream out of a cinema, coming singly through the doors, joining into pairs, going on to the pavements and walking there in threes and fours, then five, then six abreast. On, on, widening out into twenties, fifties, hundreds, thousands, as they spread like a ray over the city.

A great weariness came over her at this thought of the future in which she had played so short but so significant a part. She became panic-stricken and it seemed to her that all those people were aware of her part in their birth, even those who were generations away in the hidden years, and that they called a vision of her face to mind and reproached her and said, "If only you . . . if only you . . . You alone could have saved us from life." For the lives they led had suddenly seemed evil in every case. Some were prising open drawers and looking over their shoulders. Some were stealthily crossing the "t's" of letters that were forged.

Some were creeping down dark stairs and waiting in hall-
ways for a silent, empty street before they ventured out
with turned-up collars. All were better never born. All were
born because she had shaken a bough and let down the
fertile pollen of life over flowers she would never see bloom
—wicked dark blossoms that were better left unbudded.
Why had she done it? Why had she not gone away one
summer afternoon like her daughter Angela, in black gabardine, with no nail varnish and a clean face washed with
soap?

Angela would never have such responsibility. She would
never be an old woman sitting in a taxi dreading the
pointed finger of the unborn. With Angela life would end
like a bud blown onto the river and carried away in its
beauty. Life would end? End with Angela? But she had
forgotten, she had been inattentive, she had been so de-
pressed . . . why had she not realized what Angela's going would mean? Up through her body into her eyes flew
the blue bird of happiness that had cowered afraid and out
with a flutter of smiles it flew from her lips. How had she
been so stupid? Why had she not thought of it sooner? It
seemed so obvious now. Angela had freed her from the future. Angela had cut them both adrift from the shore of the
menacing future. There would be no people branching out
into armies of evil in the years beyond control. There would
be no pointing fingers. She had received some grace. Her
flower had shed its seed and the seed had flowered to beauty, but beyond that beauty it had not blown. Down into
the dark clay both petals, hers and Angela's, would fall together. Suddenly she felt happy again, happy and carefree.
Angela had freed her from her only fear.

Had she perhaps been conscious of this freedom somewhere in the pools of her thought without having brought
it up to the light? Had the feeling of happiness lurked in
her eyes the day her daughter had come to her and told
her of her decision? For if it had (though she certainly had
not been conscious of it), that would account for the
strange antagonism in Angela's eyes as she held out a paper and said:—

"Here's a list of what I've to get."

The list had made everything seem so certain, so definite, that even then, even before Luke began to worry, she had felt it was too late to do anything. The list had filled the weeks, crowding out everything else. It was hard to believe it was written on a half sheet of note paper. It took up the whole day every day. It took away the leisure they had always had downtown for a cup of coffee or tea. It made it impossible to stop, even for ten minutes, and run into a news theater. Such peculiar things as it called for! Her feet ached walking, and Angela was irritable and cross. White corsets, for instance! Where would you go for them? *She* hadn't known. They tried about twenty places before they got them. The sales girl had thought it so odd. "I don't know where you would get them, madam. Pink are all we are ever asked for." They spoke as if *she* wanted them. As if *she* wore them. Good Lord, did they think she looked like someone who wore white corsets? She had been furious. Poor Angela. But it had been intensely irritating. "It's outlandish," she had said to the poor girl every other ten minutes. And Angela had not answered, had pretended not to hear, but her cheeks had burned up red. And no wonder. It was enough to make anyone blush. White seemed so immodest, like something you'd see on the seashore, sticking out from under a bathing sheet while a fat woman got ready for a dip; a silly woman who would hold hands and flop up and down in the water edge without wetting her top. White corsets—disgusting! Once as they came through the swing doors of the twelfth shop into a blazing city sun, Angela had ventured to say in a quiet voice that the list said white *or* black. "Black?" she had screamed (the people had turned and stared at them). "Black?" Out of the question. Bad enough to be taken for a fool, without being taken for a prostitute as well.

Yes. She had said prostitute. What if Angela had been shocked, she was going far enough from the world where such words were said. And in any case she probably did not know what the word meant. She was going into a sanctuary of lisle stockings and flannel petticoats three deep.

They had to have a dressmaker fix up the petticoats. There was no use trying the shops for them. "And you'll have to tell her what you want them for, too," she had said to the reluctant Angela, "or else she will think you are mad." That had been unkind. Everything she said those days seemed sharp and bitter. But every hour brought a fresh annoyance. Even the old dressmaker had become a pest. She had showered them with leaflets and medals and medallions. She had given them memorial cards of fathers and aunts and cousins and sisters, all of whom had looked most alive in their pictures, with waxed whiskers or tight buns and their shoulders stiffened as if to say, "I'm not dead. She just thinks I am." And she had asked them to pray for this and for that, and promised her own prayers in return. Then, worst of all, there was the dreadful day that she had come back with the petticoats while Benny Trench was visiting them and had started all that shocking nonsense about the bandages and the statue. She would never forget it. Poor Angela reddening and Benny getting ready to go so that he could spread the story all over the city. He would probably pretend that it was Angela who had told the story. Or she herself. Well, he would hardly go that far. No one would believe him. He would say it was Angela who told it—Angela, who was always so reserved and sceptical, always, even there on the convent steps.

That last week had been one of constant humiliation; tactless remarks every other minute; presents arriving by every post. And such presents, holy pictures, holy water fonts, prayer books, quartz angels, rosary beads—and, of course, the thought that came first to mind as you watched her untie the parcels was that the poor child should have been getting wedding presents; finger bowls and glass decanters, boudoir cushions and silver salvers. Did Angela never think that, at times, herself? Did she never have regrets? You could not tell by her face.

What in the world had come over her? It was, of course, sheer nonsense to say that she did not know what she was giving up. Hadn't she read books? Hadn't she been to the cinema often enough? Hadn't she gone to parties? And hadn't they, surely, surely, hadn't they played postman's knock at any of those parties? And, whether they did or not, there were countless ways that girls became accustomed to life and learned its implications. How was this she herself had got the first inklings? She couldn't remember exactly.

There was one very clear memory of gay Cousin Charlie that might have been important. He had kissed her the night she came home from school as she was going through the kitchen door with a tray of coffee in her hands. She hadn't been able to do anything to stop him. "On your way now, Crybaby," he had said to her, "and tell your ma." But she hadn't told her ma. She had gone up to her room instead and sat in the dusk thinking of him until it was time to light the lamps. And before she had gone to bed that night she had carefully set up stitches in canary-colored wool to knit him a sweater. Poor Cousin Charlie. He had gone to America before she had the front finished, and it wasn't a year until she was engaged to Luke and starting to knit the jumper again, beginning the back, to give it to him. Poor Charlie. Who knows what would have happened to her had it not been for him? She could not remember much about those early days before she put her hair up, but she had vague memories of being rather a prude, and her sisters had some joke or other, that they kept up to this day, about the way she looked at Papa when he spoke about the heifer. . . . She didn't know what it was even now, but it proved what a ridiculous girl she must have seemed to them. Poor Charlie, he had done more harm than good with his kisses, but not in her case.

Had nobody ever kissed Angela? Angela who was as pretty as a cool, wet flower. What flower did she always remind you of? Not a summer one, but some spring chalice flower. What one? Perhaps no one had ever dared kiss her, she looked so inaccessible, like a water lily, still and pale and beautiful, but cool and clear and remote as well.

Should they have given more parties for her, or sent her away on holidays with a girl friend? Yet all around them were people who had been bitterly sorry for giving their girls too much liberty. It was hard to know just what to do. Even if no one had ever kissed her she had her imagination, hadn't she? Although the other was far the simplest way to learn, still, when it came to a fine point one could justly ask what nice girl, brought up in a convent, had any experience of boys. Yet that did not prevent them from having a healthy curiosity. Could there be anything, after all, in the idea of a Personal Call, a Divine Choice? It was so hard not to be sceptical when you had traveled a bit and read a lot. But how else could you account for a lovely girl like Angela going away like that so suddenly? If she were plain, or delicate, or even aggressive about women's rights, she would not have worried. But a girl as fitted for love as Angela, decked out with petals, you would think, to attract and to draw men towards her. She was so beautifully balanced and reasonable for a girl, so normal and so calm, that the shock of this sudden fanaticism (what else was it?) overcame you completely.

Never had a child been as normal. Right up to this very summer her room had been hung all over with pictures of film stars. And, as a child, no one ever needed to tell her to pull up her socks or wash her hands. She kept herself pretty and neat by instinct to please and attract. She was always in trouble with her nurse for looking around in church to smile at the boys in the choir, and as for frizzing her hair with her fingers, nothing would stop her. People told her since (thank God she had not known at the time) that when the child was six or seven she used to spend hours at the foot of the drive holding up her dress and calling to the bread men and messenger boys to look at her lovely new dress with bloomers to match.

What had changed her? Why had she turned aside from such a simple and happy vanity? Whatever it was that made her change, it was not religion. That might be a terrible thing for a Catholic woman to say, but wasn't it clear to be seen? When had Angela ever been pious? No beads at Mass, no prayer book, looking around her all the time, yawning during the sermon and pushing going out of the door, as if she were coming out from a football match. Since she had made up her mind to go away she had been worse than ever. She wouldn't come near the house if she saw the curate's car at the door, and she had lost her temper completely with Luke the day he asked her to go to twelve o'clock mass with Aunt Helen in case she got dizzy in the heated atmosphere. "Haven't I been to mass already?" she asked as irritably as if no one were ever known to go twice, much less three or four times, like some people.

At moments like that it seemed that there was some queer reason at the back of her idea. But then at other times she seemed anxious enough to go, and eager for the time to come.

Well, it had come, and there was no use worrying now. While there had been times she had lain awake for nights and thought about nothing else till dawn. All to no good. Angela was gone. Now she must reconcile herself to the inevitable and help Luke to form new dreams. How proud he would become of her again in a new and reverent way as she came towards him across the polished floors, swinging her beads and swaying her skirts, tall, aloof and proud, with the firm, high bust of a virgin.

There had been no mention of brassieres on the list. She only remembered that now. Yet all the nuns had the same young line of bosom, even the oldest of them. No strain of bearing children probably, and an erect carriage at all times. And then those stiff old-fashioned corsets. She would never forget them. She would never get the simple pleasure that Luke would get from looking at Angela in her habit. She would be filled with petty feelings of disgust and irritation about some trivial thing like a corset. But perhaps after a time she would not care. As long as Angela herself did not care. . . .

But that was the mystery. Did Angela care? Flannel nightdresses with ruffles around the neck and long sleeves for a girl like a cool water lily. How did she bear it? Why did she go through with it? Things like that were the real test, not the big things like leaving home and obeying a superior. Flannel next your skin and wearing a bathing suit in the bath, things like that were the test. Why had she gone through with it? What had given her the idea in the first place?

"Luke?" (She must ask him that, whether or not he guessed that she had not spoken to Angela about it.)

"Luke?"

"Just a minute, dear." He was leaning back and looking

out the little window at the back of the car. Not at the convent still, she hoped; that would be insincere and theatrical. He turned round with a frown.

"Did you see that man at the lamppost?" he asked.

(How like a man to switch from one thing to another.)

"No, I didn't notice."

"Well, I did, and what is more I've seen him before, off and on since Easter. Up to no good I should say; a bit off. I think I'll give the police a ring and have them watch him. He might give someone a nasty fright, school children or the like, not properly dressed and that kind of thing—"

The taxi drew up at the house. Luke began to pay the driver in the light of the headlamps. Suddenly she felt weary. And she went wearily up the steps. But the weariness was all in her heart. It was hard to be a mother. Hard to be vigilant night and day and at the end of it not to know whether you had failed or triumphed. She looked down the dark green avenue and thought with fear of the maniac a few yards down the road. His face, that she had not seen, came clear before her frightened eyes. He was bending down among rushes on a river bank and reaching out with cruel fingers to pluck at a floating lily, a water lily, cool, clear and remote, whose petals folded up with the rancidness of his breath. But whether he reached it or not she didn't have time to see in her dream, because the door was flung open by Hetty, who hurried her into the lighted hall.

"The tea is wet, ma'am. I heard the car on the drive."

Hetty spoke with a wonderful gentleness. The fire was piled with logs. The silver shone. Her slippers, as well as Luke's, were warming on the fender. There was some change in the atmosphere. Hetty was so kindly and like an old friend. What was it? And then she knew with a sinking of heart and another vision of fear. Everyone would be kind to her now and treat her with high respect as well. For she had proved herself. She was the mother of a nun.

JAMES PLUNKETT

1920——

James Plunkett Kelly was born in the Dublin suburb of
Sandymount (as was Yeats) and received his secondary
education from the Irish Christian Brothers at their
Synge Street schools. He also studied violin and viola at
the Dublin Municipal School of Music, on occasions
playing the viola professionally. After clerking for the
Dublin Gas Company, Mr. Plunkett became an official
of the Workers' Union of Ireland in 1945. The head of
the union until his death in 1947 was the famous Jim
Larkin, once imprisoned in the U.S. for his I.W.W.
activities. In 1955 Plunkett paid a visit to the Soviet
Union. During World War II he contributed in his
spare time to the Irish humor magazine *Barrack Variety*.
Later he published short stories in *The Bell* and *Irish
Writing* and wrote radio plays, including one about Jim
Larkin. He has also written plays for the Abbey Theatre
and three novels, one of which, *Strumpet City*, was filmed
for television. His first volume of stories, *The Trusting
and the Maimed* (1955), was published first in the United
States rather than in Great Britain or Ireland. In the
title story and in one or two others Plunkett seems to be
chafing against the limitations of this form: he wants
more than one setting, more than one group of
characters. His less ambitious stories, like "Weep for
Our Pride" and the one here, succeed better. Their
setting and low-keyed style, and their scrupulous
realism, are reminiscent of Joyce's *Dubliners*.

The Half-Crown

The man in the bookshop was suspicious. He had his hands
in the pockets of his grey overall and he looked at you in a

sharp knowing way which made you feel guilty.

"A *Hall and Knight's Algebra*," Michael, embarrassed, said.

The eyes, cold and commercial, looked from the book to Michael. "Hocking it. Slipping it out of the house to flog it for cigarettes and the pictures," said the eyes. The hand took the book.

"A shilling," the man said, and sucked his tooth.

"That's not enough," Michael said, "it's worth more than that. It's worth three bob at least." The man turned the book over, pretending to examine it. He saw that Michael's sports jacket was too small for him and the ends of his flannel trousers were turned down in an attempt to conceal their shortness.

"Name and address?" he asked, as though absentmindedly. That was written inside the cover. But if they really inquired and they got to know at home?

"What's that necessary for?" Michael countered. "You don't think I stole it?"

"I'm entitled to ask that," the man said. "Lots of books is pinched this time of the year. Besides," he added, "maybe your mammy doesn't know you're selling it." He used the word "mammy" very deliberately as an insult to Michael's self-esteem. "Well," he said, "how about one and sixpence?"

"It's worth more than one and six," Michael persisted doggedly. The man handed it back. "There you are," he said without interest, "take it or leave it." That was that.

The previous evening he had been so certain of getting at least half a crown that he had told Anne Fox he would meet her at the station. He had been out swimming with Mark, her brother, at Sandycove and when they came back she stood on the steps to talk to them. He had leaned over the borrowed bicycle with the togs and towel wrapped about the handlebars, enticed by her dark eyes, her slim bare knees, and moved by the cool and salty odor of his own body. He would risk a lot to be with her. Getting half a crown had seemed a small enough task. He thought she was very beautiful. At one point the thought so absorbed him that she said to him smiling, "A penny for them, Michael." But he had no words as yet for graciousness.

It had been the first thought to come into his mind when he was wakened too early that morning by his mother's hand stirring his shoulder. She was taking the child to the dispensary and wanted to be down early to be well placed in the queue.

"Michael son," she said at a quarter to eight. "Michael!" But the sun even at that hour was so strong in the bedroom he found it difficult to open his eyes. Without any intention of moving, he said he was coming. At half past eight she again called him. "Your father has gone ages ago. You promised me you'd get up early," she said. But he pulled his shoulder away to show her how he hated her to touch him. Gradually over the past year he had felt hatred of her growing in him.

"I'm coming," he said angrily, "go and leave me alone." And when she had closed the door, he turned over deliberately on his side. She had to be shown that shaking him would get her nowhere. But after a while, his anxiety to ask her for money had overcome his anger and he got up. She had fried bread for breakfast because it would save the butter, and when he sat down at table, she served him with her hat and coat on. She had the baby in the pram. The rest of the children were with her married sister in the country. He said to her:

"We're going on an outing today. I want to know if you can give me half a crown."

"Half a crown," she said unhappily. "You got your pocket money on Saturday."

"You don't call one-and-sixpence pocket money."

That rebuffed her for a moment. She made another effort.

"Can't you borrow a bicycle somewhere?"

"We're going to Bray," he said. "The rest are going on the three o'clock train."

"Couldn't you arrange to meet them out there?"

Meet them out there? Tell them he had finished with school and could find no work and he couldn't help it if it meant being short of cash? He flung fried bread across the table.

"Keep your lousy half-crown," he had said, rising to go into the bathroom.

"Michael," she called after him, "you know if I had it I'd give it to you." He refused to answer. Then in a hurt tone she called to him, "I gave you two shillings last week." But he banged the door loudly. Later he had heard her take the pram down the steps by herself.

He stuffed the book back in his pocket. The sun, high over the tall buildings and the summer crowds, beat down on his bare head. Even under the striped awnings outside the shops in Grafton Street it was intolerably hot. There was an aroma of coffee in the air to stir his appetite, and flowers blazed yellow and red in vendor's baskets. Near the Green two girls on bicycles looked at him with interest. One was a tidy piece but she wasn't as nice as Anne Fox. He wouldn't think of Anne Fox in that way. None of the girls was as nice as Anne Fox. She was different. She wouldn't do that—no—she wouldn't let you—no. But if he couldn't go to Bray, maybe Dorgan would see her home. He got on easily with girls and when he knew Michael was soft on Anne, he would make sure to cut in on him. Dorgan loved to do that. He would invent stories for the rest of the gang, which he could tell in a way that made it hard not to believe them. If he did he would break his bloody neck. Then of course the rest would think it was sour grapes, but it wasn't that at all. Anne wouldn't let you do that; she was a nice girl but she was soft on him too. He knew by the way she looked at him last night on the steps, and the way she leaned her head back a little so that he could see her soft warm shapely throat and the way she laughed at what he said to show she liked him to talk to her. So nice it had been last night on the high steps under the green-gold, cloud-crossed evening sky to ask her; and now it was all being bagged-up because of a lousy half-crown.

His father and mother were both at table. He walked through quietly to sneak the book back on the shelf. The baby was asleep in the pram. It had blobs of white ointment on its face. Bits of bun lay on its dress and coverlet. He took his place and his mother rose immediately to fetch his meal for him. The tassels of a faded green cover hung down beneath the tablecloth. There was a hole worn in the center when the tablecloth was not on but you covered it with a fern pot and that was more or less all right. He looked at his father slyly with the idea of putting out a hint for some money but his father's face was not a good-humored one—in fact—no—it wasn't. His father's face was moist and flabby. Though it was so warm, he wore a dark suit and a butterfly collar which was respectable because of his calling. He was a clerk in the office of Joshua Bright & Son, Timber Merchants. In good humor he told stories which always ended in Mr. Bright saying, "Kavanagh, you're a man after my own heart. How on earth did you fix it? I'm certainly indebted," or words to that effect. It always made you want to kick both of them in the fanny. But Bright was not on the menu today. There was something else.

"If I've told you once," began his father, "I've told you a dozen times that a razor should be dried and cleaned when you've finished with it. No one with manners a cut above those of a pig would leave a razor in the condition mine was left in. I've never objected to you using it—though what in God's name you have to shave is beyond me—all I ask is that you dry it after you."

He remembered he had not dried it. He had left it down to put water in his hair in the absence of hair dressing and of course he forgot—well, he didn't exactly forget but he was in a bad humour over his mother.

"Razor?" he lied, pointlessly and brazenly. "I never touched your razor."

His father turned to his mother. "There's your rearing for you now," he said; "the lie springs easy to his lips. If he's going to sit there—"

His mother immediately tried to conciliate them. Too quickly, in her desire to placate them his mother said, "You might have left it yourself, you were in such a hurry this morning."

"That's right," his father shouted, and let the knife and fork fall with a clatter on the plate, "stick up for him. Encourage him to deceive and defy his own father. I'll be a bloody lunatic before long between the pair of you."

"You can think what you like," Michael persisted. "It wasn't me."

"Michael," put in his mother.

"Then I suppose it was the cat," his father said with childish sarcasm, "or maybe it walked out of the case by itself. But I'll tell you one thing, you'll use it no more. You can get a razor of your own."

"I suppose you'll tell me how."

"Buy one. Do a little study to fit yourself for earning your keep."

"You must have studied a bit yourself in your day." Michael sneered. "You earn such a hell of a lot now."

He left the table. As he entered the next room, a cup flew past his ear and shattered against the wall. It was unexpected and he jumped.

"You impertinent brat," his father yelled after him. He locked the door hastily.

He came out when he was certain his father had gone. His mother took his meal from the oven where she had put it to keep it hot. She had been crying. That sort of thing had never happened before.

"Have your meal, child," she said. "I don't know what's to become of us."

"I don't want it."

"It isn't right to answer your father like that; you should respect him. He works hard for what he gets."

"He knows how to hold on to it too."

She was silent. Then she said, "You know you'd get the half-crown if we had it. What were you ever denied that we had to give?"

"You can buy that baby in there sweet cake."

"A little penny bun. I'm ashamed of you, Michael."

That, unaccountably, slipped under his guard and stung him.

"You mind your own bloody business," he lashed back.

In St. Stephen's Green, children, their nurses watching them, were feeding the ducks from paper bags. And at the pond with the artificial sprays which spurted threads of pearly-bright water into the thirsty air, children were sailing a boat. Michael lounged with his hands in his pockets. They were catching the train now.

"Michael Kavanagh is awful to be late like this," the girls were saying with angry little jerks of their heads, and the fellows were saying, "Oh, he'll come, don't bother, let's get a carriage." They were going to Bray to swim and after to lie in the bracken. They were going to eat ice cream and drink lemonade which the boys would buy for the girls, and eat sandwiches and make tea which the girls would bring for the boys. Anne would lie in the bracken. For the length of his own afternoon he could watch the people sleeping with newspapers over their faces and look at the flowers which blazed with a barren and uncommunicative joyousness. The sculptured face of Mangan brought some lines to his mind. "I could scale the blue air. I could walk—climb —I could—" How the hell did it go? That was school. You knew these things when you sat for Leaving Cert, and then after a while you wondered how the hell did it go. You left school and watched the advertisements.

"Junior clerk reqd. rep. firm Hons. Leaving Cert. Knowledge book-keeping asset. 15/ weekly to start. Good prospects."

Queue with the rest; don't stammer—oh—don't stutter —think, oh, think. Cool—be cool and smile respectfully. Self-possession is nine-tenths of the law.

Your mother had pressed your suit and sat up into the small hours ironing and darning. She had already begun a Novena to Saint Anthony. (O please, Saint Anthony, send him work: O please. O sweet and good Saint Anthony, intercede for my boy.) Your father gave you advice. He told you, take off your hat and smile easily and pleasantly. Don't fidget or sit on the edge of the chair, which wasn't to say, of course, that you were to put your feet on the desk. He had had a word with Gussy Gallagher who was said to have tons of influence since he hit it lucky in the auctioneering business. He was reputed to be a brigadier-general or something in the Knights of Columbanus. Now and then your mother looked across.

"Pay attention to what your father is telling you," she would say. When she ironed late at night like that her hair fell in straggles over her face, her breath caught her now and then, her forehead so white showed moistly in the steamy light.

As you sat waiting to be interviewed you kept saying like an idiot over and over again something silly—like:

"When Richelieu attained to office he was faced with the task of building a French navy."

Like when you were a child you went to the shop repeating in case you might forget: A pint of milk—a tin of beans— a duck loaf—and a half-pound of margarine and say the margarine is for baking. (That was a lie, but it was only a little white lie if your mother told you to tell it.)

But in the end someone else, like Harte or Joe Andrews, always got the job. Joe Andrews didn't know much about Richelieu, but he knew someone on the selection board with a bit more pull than Gussy Gallagher or Saint Anthony.

Knowledge weakened with winter, sickened with spring, withered and died in the hot July sun, giving place to new growths, to the contemplation of women, to long vacant hours, to quick greeds and slow lusts and jealous incessant neediness.

He sat down on one of the benches which were placed at secluded intervals along the quiet path. His mother was a silly bitch and his father a skinflint. His mother went out with his father to the pictures once a week and this was the night. It was the only night they went out but they could stay at home tonight because the other children were away and he was damned if he was going to stay in to mind the baby. That would be one way of getting his own back. The whole set-up was a bloody cod.

There was a thin white line running down the right side of his face, from his nose to the corner of his lips. He tried to relieve the tautness from time to time by rubbing his face with his hands, but failed because it welled up from inside him. Over him hung a wealth of almond blossom and opposite to him was a laburnum tree. It showered with perfect grace of movement to the tips of its trailing branches. Near it sat an old man and a child. He was a white-haired, serene-faced old man, whose ample waistcoat was crossed by two golden chains. On one end of the chain hung a watch. The little child was playing with it. She put it to her ear, listened, laughed. "Tick tock, tick tock," the old man said, making an attempt to imitate the sound. Frequently he bent down to chuck her under the chin or smile at her. Growing tired of the watch, she put her hand in his pocket to pull out a pair of glasses, a white handkerchief and a silver coin. The glasses and handkerchief were discarded, but she kept the coin. When she threw it, it flashed in the sun; when it fell, it rang musically on the path and rolled round and round. It staggered in circles before flopping down. The old man, whom you knew to be old more by the stringy looseness of the neck behind his white butterfly collar than by any sign of age in the bright face, smiled an invitation to Michael to enjoy the antics of the child. But Michael only hated the child. He hated the child because a foolish and indulgent old man allowed it to play carelessly with a precious piece of silver. The milled edges of a half-crown were strong and comforting. You could stand a girl's fare and buy her ice cream, or buy cigarettes to smoke after a swim, and fish and chips to eat from a paper bag on the way home with the lads at night. The coin went up and down and he followed it greedily with his eyes. Sometimes it fell, a bright though tiny star, out of the child's reach, and the child would toddle across innocently to retrieve it. Sometimes when it fell, it staggered clumsily towards Michael. When the game had gone on for some time the old man lost interest and began to nod. Michael looked up and down the path. A keeper was examining a flower bed some distance away. There was nobody near. But to rise, take up the coin and walk away quickly—that would be too obvious. The child might cry, or the old man open his eyes at the wrong moment. With half-closed eyes he followed the course of the coin.

To steal a half-crown could be mortal or venial. Three

conditions were required for mortal sin and these were: (1) grave matter; (2) perfect knowledge; (3) full consent. It would be mortal to steal it from a poor man, but venial to steal it from a rich man, because it was dependent on the gravity of the injustice done. Not that he cared whether it was mortal or venial because he had committed sins of impurity which were always mortal and killed the soul, and it was eight months since his last confession. Automatically he almost said, "and I accuse myself of my sins." When the slide went click in the darkness, the priest didn't say a penny for them he said well my child and with tongue stuck to roof and sweat of shame you had to tell. If you were caught you were a (not-nice-word) thief.

The coin fell and rolled towards him. He watched it. It curved, glittering, towards his left. Gingerly he reached out his foot and stopped it. Then he looked sharply at the old man, whose eyes were still closed. He bent and picked it up.

"Go on," he whispered to the child when she came near him, "hump off." The face upturned to him was tiny and questioning. He could have raised his boot and crushed it without caring. But her bewilderment frightened him. When she began to cry he jumped up and said to her: "Here—we'll look for it in the grass."

He was earnestly searching along the verge when the old man stood beside him.

"Poor little pet," he said, "what's the matter now?"

"She lost her half-crown. I think it rolled in here."

They hunted for a considerable time. Michael kept his face averted. His heart thumped. He was afraid the old man might see it there thumping against his ribs, pulsing in his neck, calling out thief, thief, so loudly that it must surely be heard. But the child began to sob and the old man comforted her by promising to bring her off to buy ice cream. After some time he told Michael he would have to leave it for the sweeper. "Finders keepers," he said regretfully but pleasantly as he was going.

Waiting impatiently while the old man and the child went off, Michael sat down again. He had no notion of the time. He should have asked the old fool before he went. They had gone in the direction of the station, but he would not dare to go that way lest they should meet again. The old man would want to chat. Where did he live? Was he still at school? What were his intentions? Suitable openings were hard to find for a young man standing on the threshold of life. A grunt, a stammer. There were no other answers to these things, none that he had found. They were simple expressions of amiability which always made the machinery of his mind lumber and clank, defeated and chaotic. He could never find responses. He was afraid if the old man spoke to him, he would blurt out, "I took the half-crown and I'm sticking to it. You can do what you like about it." So he sat for half an hour and then went off in the opposite direction, taking a roundabout way to the station. He passed the university where Mark would soon begin to study to be a doctor. He always had money. Mark would never need to put his foot on a half-crown dropped by a child in a public park.

The street was so quiet he could hear his own footsteps echoing, and the building itself seemed peacefully asleep. There was a smell of dust and a sunlit silence. He thought of cool waters, of Anne Fox in her red bathing costume raising her round arms to let cool water fall from them glitteringly. She would climb Bray Head in her light cotton frock, slim knees bending, a sea-fragrance about her. It would not be easy to find them. She might go anywhere about the Head to lie in the bracken. She might lie in the bracken with Dorgan. He would have to search and search.

He hastened up the steps to the station, as though by hastening he could persuade the train to leave any earlier, or be with her any sooner. But when he reached the top he stood still. Just turning away from the booking office, holding the child by the hand, was the old man. The child wanted to carry the tickets. On the steps, an impassable barrier, stood guilt and terror. Instinctively and immediately he moved away.

At the corner of the Green, leaning against one of the pillars which had held the ornamental chains that one time bordered the pavement, he remained for a long time. He knew it was after six o'clock because people were passing in clusters on bicycles, and the hunger pains in his belly

were worse. He should have taken his dinner. He was staring at the sky, golden and tranquil behind barred clouds,
when his mother stopped beside him. She had been shopping and was pushing the pram with the baby in it. He
knew it was she but barely moved to acknowledge her. Let
her see him miserable. Let her see that he had only a corner to stand at and a sky to stare into. It would hurt her
and that was something to know. Once he had loved them.
When he was young, before the other children came along,
he and his mother had often waited for his father at that
very corner with a flask of tea and sandwiches and hot currant buns. They used to go into the Green to sit on the
grass and have a picnic. But now he hated them. He had
nothing to say to them. He had hated them for a long time
now but they refused to recognize it. His mother waited.
Then she said, "A penny for them, Michael."
    Anne Fox had said that too, and now she was lying in
the bracken with Dorgan. He made a sullen mask of his
face and refused to answer. After a while, this time more
urgently, she said, "Michael."
    He grunted and shrugged.
    "The baby isn't well," she began, once again placating
him, trying to soften him, to bring him back to her. "I
think I'll stay in tonight. You can go to the pictures instead. Make it up with your father at tea and then the pair
of you can go off together."
    "What is there to make up?" he asked. "You make me
sick."
    Hesitantly she suggested: "You weren't very nice to him
at dinner."
    "He wasn't very nice to me—was he?"
    He looked around as he asked and was shocked to see
tears in her eyes. But she averted her head and began to
walk. He lagged behind, refusing to walk beside her. He
saw in hunger and misery the squat steeple of the Method-
ist church, and over it the sky crossed regularly with clouds
—a painted sea. Girls in the sea were slim and lovely. Girls
in the sea had straight slim shapely legs. He looked at his
mother's legs. They were very thin. They were encased in
cheap unfashionable stockings, woolly, yellow in color,

wrinkled above the calves, much darned and dragged at the ankles. Her skirt was uneven as it swung about them. He watched the effort of her short step-by-step movement. He could not remember ever having looked at his mother's legs before. Now it stabbed him like a sword. His throat contracted. He searched for something brutal to say, something to protect himself against this fresh and unexpected onslaught of pain. She walked with her thin back towards him, her hands guiding the pram.

"We'll have to hurry home," she said brightly; "your poor father will be ages waiting."

He hoped to God she had wiped her eyes. He did not want people to see her. She quickened her pace and panted with the initial push.

"I have an egg for your tea," she added.

The brutality in him subsided. An egg for his tea. It made him want to laugh. But it also made him want to stretch out his hand to her, to touch her, to tell her he was sorry. But there were no words. He cast around for words. But when he even tried to think of them the grinding and turmoil in his head only became worse. Then his fingers touched the stolen half-crown. A flush of shame and unworthiness crept sullenly into his cheeks. It was suddenly without value. It could not buy what he wanted. Because he hardly knew what he wanted. He struggled with his own tears. He watched her now with immense tenderness, sorry for her, aching with love for her. But still something, his pride or his great shyness, would not permit him to speak to her or even to walk beside her.

In that way they went home; she walking ahead and unwitting, and he, who had no words for anything except churlishness or anger, followed silently.

BRIAN FRIEL
1929——

Brian Friel was born a member of the Catholic minority in Northern Ireland. Having qualified as a teacher, he spent ten years working in various Northern Ireland schools. In 1960 he resigned in order to devote his time entirely to writing. He is married and has two children. He now lives in County Donegal, of which he says, "It is the wildest, most beautiful, and most barren part of Ireland, and the people are almost completely untouched by present-day hysteria and hypocrisy." Much of the area is Gaelic-speaking. The name Friel or O'Friel, incidentally, is common in County Donegal. He has published two volumes of short stories, *The Saucer of Larks* (1962) and *The Gold in the Sea*, and a number of plays which were performed at the Abbey Theatre in Dublin as well as in London and New York. Many of his stories have been published in *The New Yorker*. Although Friel's stories deal exclusively with rural or small-town life, they give an impression of variety; he has, however, in no sense broken away from the traditional short story. What impresses one most about "Foundry House," aside from its controlled but powerful emotion, is the fact that Friel refuses, like his protagonist, Joe Brennan, to accept a trite pattern of disillusion. The Hogans are still "A great family. A grand family," in spite of all the erosion that time has inflicted upon them and their home. Joe phrases his veneration for them in the old words because he knows no others, but these words have subtly altered in meaning, and his respect now rests on a more solid foundation.

Foundry House

When his father and mother died, Joe Brennan applied for their house, his old home, the gate lodge to Foundry House. He wrote direct to Mr. Bernard (as Mr. Hogan was known locally), pointing out that he was a radio-and-television mechanic in the Music Shop; that although he had never worked for Mr. Hogan, his father had been an employee in the foundry for over fifty years; and that he himself had been born and reared in the gate lodge. Rita, his wife, who was more practical than he, insisted that he mention their nine children and the fact that they were living in three rooms above a launderette.

"That should influence him," she said. "Aren't they supposed to be one of the best Catholic families in the North of Ireland?" So, against his wishes, he added a paragraph about his family and their inadequate accommodation, and sent off his application. Two days later, he received a reply from Mrs. Hogan, written on mauve scented notepaper with fluted edges. Of course she remembered him, she said. He was the small, round-faced boy with the brown curls who used to play with her Declan. And to think that he now had nine babies of his own! Where did time go? He could collect the keys from the agent and move in as soon as he wished. There were no longer any duties attached to the position of gatekeeper, she added—not since wartime, when the authorities had taken away the great iron gates that sealed the mouth of the avenue.

"Brown curls!" Rita squealed with delight when Joe read her the letter. "Brown curls! She mustn't have seen you for twenty years or more!"

"That's all right, now," was all Joe could say. He was moved with relief and an odd sense of humility at his unworthiness. "That's all right. That's all right."

They moved into their new house at the end of summer.

It was a low-set, solid stone building with a steep roof and exaggerated eaves that gave it the appearance of a gnome's house in a fairy tale. The main Derry-Belfast road ran parallel to the house, and on the other side the ground rose rapidly in a tangle of shrubs and wild rhododendron and decaying trees, through which the avenue crawled up to Foundry House at the top of the hill. The residence was not visible from the road or from any part of the town; one could only guess at its location somewhere in the green patch that lay between the new housing estate and the brassiere factory. But Joe remembered from his childhood that if one stood at the door of Foundry House on a clear morning, before the smoke from the red-brick factories clouded the air, one could see through the trees and the undergrowth, past the gate lodge and the busy main road, and right down to the river below, from which the sun drew a million momentary flashes of light that danced and died in the vegetation.

For Joe, moving into the gate lodge was a homecoming; for Rita and the children, it was a changeover to a new life. There were many improvements to be made—there was no indoor toilet and no running water, the house was lit by gas only, and the windows, each made up of a score of small, diamond-shaped pieces of glass, gave little light—and Joe accepted that they were inevitable. But he found himself putting them off from day to day and from week to week. He did not have much time when he came home from work, because the evenings were getting so short. Also, he had applied to the urban council for a money grant, and they were sending along an architect soon. And he had to keep an eye on the children, who looked on the grounds as their own private park and climbed trees and lit fires in the undergrowth and played their shrieking games of hide-and-seek or cowboys-and-Indians right up to the very front of the big house itself.

"Come back here! Come back!" Joe would call after them in an urgent undertone. "Why can't you play down below near your own house? Get away down at once with you!"

"We want to play up here, Daddy," some of them would

plead. "There are better hiding places up here."

"The old man, he'll soon scatter you!" Joe would say. "Or he'll put the big dog on you. God help you then!"

"But there is no old man. Only the old woman and the maid. And there is no dog, either."

"No Mr. Bernard? Huh! Just let him catch you, and you'll know all about it. No Mr. Bernard! The dog may be gone, but Mr. Bernard's not. Come on now! Play around your own door or else come into the house altogether."

No Mr. Bernard! Mr. Bernard always had been, Joe thought to himself, and always would be—a large, stern-faced man with a long white beard and a heavy step and a walking stick, the same ever since he remembered him. And beside him the Great Dane, who copied his master as best he could in expression and gait—a dour, sullen animal as big as a calf and as savage as a tiger, according to the men in the foundry. And Mrs. Hogan? He supposed she could be called an old woman now, too. Well over sixty, because Declan and he were of an age, and he was thirty-three himself. Yes, an old woman, or at least elderly, even though she was twenty years younger than her husband. And not Declan now, or even Master Declan, but Father Declan, a Jesuit. And then there was Claire, Miss Claire, the girl, younger than Declan by a year. Fat, blue-eyed Claire, who had blushed every time she passed the gate lodge because she knew some of the Brennans were sure to be peering out through the diamond windows. She had walked with her head to one side, as if she were listening for something, and used to trail her fingers along the box-wood that fringed both sides of the avenue. "Such a lovely girl," Joe's mother used to say. "So simple and so sweet. Not like the things I see running about this town. There's something good before that child. Something very good." And she was right. Miss Claire was now Sister Claire of the Annunciation Nuns and was out in Africa. Nor would she ever be home again. Never. Sister Claire and Father Declan—just the two of them, and both of them in religion, and the big house up above going to pieces, and no one to take over the foundry when the time would come. Everything they could want in the world, anything that money could buy, and they turned their backs on it all. Strange, Joe thought. Strange. But right, because they were the Hogans.

They were a month in the house and were seated at their tea, all eleven of them, when Mrs. Hogan called on them. It was now October and there were no evenings to speak of; the rich, warm days ended abruptly in a dusk that was uneasy with cold breezes. Rita was relieved at the change in the weather, because now the children, still unsure of the impenetrable dark and the nervous movements in the undergrowth, were content to finish their games when daylight failed, and she had no difficulty in gathering them for their evening meal. Joe answered the knock at the door.

"I'm so sorry to disturb you, Mr. Brennan. But I wonder could you do me a favor?"

She was a tall, ungraceful woman, with a man's shoulders and a wasted body and long, thin feet. When she spoke, her mouth and lips worked in excessive movement.

Rita was at Joe's elbow. "Did you not ask the woman in?" she reproved him. "Come on inside, Mrs. Hogan."

"I'm sorry," Joe stammered. "I thought—I was about to—" How could he say he didn't dare?

"Thank you all the same," Mrs. Hogan said. "But I oughtn't to have left Bernard at all. What brought me down was this. Mary—our maid, you know—she tells me that you have a tape-recording machine. She says you're in that business. I wonder could we borrow it for an afternoon? Next Sunday?"

"Certainly, Mrs. Hogan. Certainly," said Rita. "Take it with you now. We never use it. Do we, Joe?"

"If Sunday suits you, I would like to have it then when Father Declan comes," Mrs. Hogan said. "You see, my daughter, Claire, has sent us a tape recording of her voice —these nuns nowadays, they're so modern—and we were hoping to have Father Declan with us when we play it. You know, a sort of family reunion, on Sunday."

"Any time at all," said Rita. "Take it with you now. Go and get it, Joe, and carry it up."

"No, no. Really. Sunday will do—Sunday afternoon. Besides, neither Bernard nor I know how to work the machine. We'll be depending on you to operate it for us, Mr. Brennan."

"And why wouldn't he?" said Rita. "He does nothing on a Sunday afternoon, anyway. Certainly he will."

Now that her request had been made and granted, Mrs. Hogan stood irresolutely between the white gaslight in the hall and the blackness outside. Her mouth and lips still worked, although no sound came.

"Sunday then," she said at last. "A reunion."

"Sunday afternoon," said Rita. "I'll send him up as soon as he has his dinner in him."

"Thank you," said Mrs. Hogan. "Thank you." Her mouth formed an "O," and she drew in her breath. But she snapped it shut again and turned and strode off up the avenue.

Rita closed the door and leaned against it. She doubled up with laughter. "Lord, if you could only see your face!" she gasped between bursts.

"What do you mean, my face?"

"All scared-looking, like a child caught stealing!"

"What are you raving about?" he asked irritably.

"And she was as scared-looking as yourself." She held her hand to her side. "She must have been looking for the brown curls and the round face! And not a word out of you! Like a big, scared dummy!"

"Shut up," he mumbled gruffly. "Shut up, will you?"

Joe had never been inside Foundry House, had never spoken to Mr. Bernard, and had not seen Declan since his ordination. And now, as he stood before the hall door and the evil face on the leering knocker, the only introductory remark his mind would supply him was one from his childhood: "My daddy says here are the keys to the workshop and that he put out the fire in the office before he left." He was still struggling to suppress this senseless memory when Father Declan opened the door.

"Ah, Joe, Joe, Joe! Come inside. Come inside. We are waiting for you. And you have the machine with you? Good man! Good man! Great! Great!"

Father Declan was fair and slight, and his gestures fluttering and birdlike. The black suit accentuated the whiteness of his hair and skin and hands.

"Straight ahead, Joe. First door to the right. You know
—the breakfast room. They live there now, Father and
Mother. Convenient to the kitchen, and all. And Mother
tells me you are married and have a large family?"

"That's right, Father."

"Good man! Good man! Marvelous, too. No, no, not
that door, Joe; the next one. No, they don't use the drawing room any more. Too large and too expensive to heat.
That's it, yes. No, no, don't knock. Just go right in. That's
it. Good man! Good man!"

One minute he was behind Joe, steering him through the
hallway, and the next he had sped past him and was standing in the middle of the floor of the breakfast room, his
glasses flashing, his arms extended in reception. "Good
man. Here we are. Joe Brennan, Mother, with the tape recorder."

"So kind of you, Joe," said Mrs. Hogan, emerging from
behind the door. "It's going to be quite a reunion, isn't it?"

"How many young Brennans are there?" asked Father
Declan.

"Nine, Father."

"Good! Good! Great! Great!"

"Such healthy children, too," said Mrs. Hogan. "I've seen
them playing on the avenue. And so—so healthy."

"Have a seat, Joe. Just leave the recorder there. Anywhere at all. Good man. That's it. Fine!"

"You've had your lunch, Mr. Brennan?"

"Yes, thanks, Mrs. Hogan. Thank you all the same."

"What I mean is, you didn't rush off without it?"

"Lucky for you, Joe," the priest broke in. "Because these
people, I discover, live on snacks now. Milk and bananas
—that sort of thing."

"You'll find the room cold, I'm afraid, Mr. Brennan."

"If you have a power plug. I'll get this thing—"

"A power plug. A power plug. A power plug. A power
plug." The priest cracked his fingers each time he said the
words and frowned in concentration.

"What about that thing there?" asked Mrs. Hogan, pointing to the side of the mantelpiece.

"That's a gas bracket, Mother. No. Electric. Electric."
One white finger rested on his chin. "An electric power
plug. There must be one somewhere in the—ah! Here we
are!" He dropped on his knees below the window and
looked back exultantly over his shoulder. "I just thought so.
Here we are. I knew there must be one somewhere."

"Did you find one?" asked Mrs. Hogan.

"Yes, we did, didn't we, Joe? Will this do? Does your
machine fit this?"

"That's grand, Father."

"Good! Good! Then I'll go and bring Father down. He's
in bed resting. Where is the tape, Mother?"

"Tape? Oh, the tape! Yes, there on the sideboard."

"Fine! Fine! That's everything, then. Father and I will
be down in a minute. Good! Good!"

"Logs," said Mrs. Hogan to herself. Then, remembering
Joe, she said to him, "We burn our own fuel. For econo-
my." She smiled bleakly at him and followed her son from
the room.

Joe busied himself with rigging up the machine and putting the new tape in position. When he was working in
someone's house, it was part of his routine to examine the
pictures and photographs around the walls, to open drawers and presses, to finger ornaments and bric-a-brac. But,
here in Foundry House, a modesty, a shyness, a vague def-
erence to something long ago did not allow his eyes even
to roam from the work he was engaged in. Yet he was
conscious of certain aspects of the room; the ceiling was
high, perhaps as high as the roof of his own house, the fireplace was of black marble, the door handle was of cut
glass, and the door itself did not close properly. Above his
head was a print of horses galloping across open fields;
the corner of the carpet was nibbled away. His work gave
him assurance.

"There you are now, Mrs. Hogan," he said when she returned with a big basket of logs. "All you have to do is turn
this knob and away she goes."

She ignored his stiff movement to help her with her load
of logs, and knelt at the fireplace until she had built up the
fire. Then, rubbing her hands down her skirt, she came and

stood beside him.

"What was that, Mr. Brennan?"

"I was saying that all you have to do is to turn this knob here to start it going, and turn it back to stop it. Nothing at all to it."

"Yes?" she said, thrusting her lips forward, her mind a blank.

"That's all," said Joe. "Right to start, left to stop. A child could work it." He tugged at the lapels of his jacket to indicate that he was ready to leave.

"No difficulty at all," she repeated dreamily. Then suddenly alert again, "Here they come. You sit there, Mr. Brennan, on this side of the fire, Father Declan will sit here, and I will sit beside the table. A real family circle."

"You'll want to listen to this by yourselves, Mrs. Hogan. So if you don't mind—"

"Don't leave, Mr. Brennan. You will stay, won't you? You remember Claire, our lovely Claire. You remember her, don't you? She's out in Africa, you know, and she'll never be home again. Never. Not even for a death. You'll stay, and hear her talking to us, won't you? Of course you will." Her fingertips touched the tops of her ears. "Claire's voice again. Talking to us. And you'll want to hear it too, won't you?"

Before he could answer, the door burst open. Mr. Bernard had come down.

It took them five minutes to get from the door to the leather armchair beside the fire, and Joe was reminded of a baby being taught to walk. Father Declan came in first, backward, crouching slightly, his eyes on his father's feet and his arms outstretched and beckoning. "Slow-ly. Slow-ly," he said in a hypnotist's voice. "Slow-ly. Slow-ly." Then his father appeared. First a stick, then a hand, an arm, the curve of his stomach, then the beard, yellow and untidy, then the whole man. Since his return to the gate lodge, Joe had not thought of Mr. Bernard beyond the fact that he was there. In his mind there was a twenty-year-old image that had never been adjusted, a picture which was so familiar to him that he had long since ceased to look at it. But this was not the image, this giant who had grown in height and swollen in girth instead of shrinking, this huge, monolithic figure that inched its way across the faded carpet, one mechanical step after the other, in response to a word from the black, weaving figure before him. Joe looked at his face, fleshy, trembling, colored in dead purple and gray-black, and at the eyes, wide and staring and quick with the terror of stumbling or of falling or even of missing a syllable of the instructions from the priest. "Lift again. Lift it. Lift it. Good. Good. Now down, down. And the right, up and up and up—yes—and now down." The old man wore an overcoat streaked down the front with food stains, and the hands, one clutching the head of the stick, the other limp and lifeless by his side, were so big they had no contour. His breathing was a succession of rapid sighs.

Until the journey from door to armchair was completed, Mrs. Hogan made fussy jobs for herself and addressed herself to no one in particular. "The leaves are terrible this year. Simply terrible. I must get a man to sweep them up and do something with the rockery, too, because it has got out of hand altogether—"

"Slow-ly. Slow-ly. Left. Left. That's it—up yet. Yes. And down again. Down."

"I never saw such a year for leaves. And the worst of it is the wind just blows them straight up against the hall door. Only this morning, I was saying to Mary we must make a pile of them and burn them before they smother us altogether. A bonfire—that's what we'll make."

"Now turn. Turn. Turn. That's it. Right round. Round. Round. Now back. Good. Good."

"Your children would enjoy a bonfire, wouldn't they, Mr. Brennan? Such lively children they are, too and so healthy, so full of life. I see them, you know, from my bedroom window. Running all over the place. So lively and full of spirits."

A crunch, a heavy thud, and Mr. Bernard was seated, not upright but sideways over the arm of the chair, as he had dropped. His eyes blinked in relief at having missed disaster once more.

"Now," said Mrs. Hogan briskly, "I think we're ready to

begin, aren't we? This is Mr. Brennan of the gate lodge, Daddy. He has given us the loan of his tape-recording machine and is going to work it for us. Isn't that kind of him?"

"How are you, Mr. Hogan?" said Joe.

The old man did not answer, but looked across at him. Was it a sly, reproving look, Joe wondered, or was it the awkward angle of the old man's head that made it appear sly?

"Which of these knobs is it?" asked Father Declan, his fingers playing arpeggios over the recorder. " 'On.' This is it, isn't it? Yes. This is it."

"The second one is for volume, Father," said Joe.

"Volume. Yes. I see. Well, all set?"

"Ready," said Mrs. Hogan.

"Ready, Daddy?" asked Father Declan.

"Daddy's ready," said Mrs. Hogan.

"Joe?"

"Ready," said Joe, because that was what Mrs. Hogan had said.

"Here goes then," said Father Declan. "Come in, Claire. We're waiting."

The recorder purred. The soft sound of the revolving spools spread up and out until it was as heavy as the noise of distant seas. Mrs. Hogan sat at the edge of her chair; Mr. Bernard remained slumped as he had fallen. Father Declan stood poised as a ballet dancer before the fire. The spools gathered speed and the purring was a pounding of blood in the ears.

"It often takes a few seconds—" Joe began.

"Quiet!" snapped Mrs. Hogan. "Quiet, boy! Quiet!"

Then the voice came and all other sound died.

"Hello, Mammy and Daddy and Father Declan. This is Sister Claire speaking to the three of you from St. Joseph's Mission, Kaluga, Northern Rhodesia. I hope you are all together when this is being played back, because I am imagining you all sitting before a great big fire in the drawing room at this minute, Daddy spread out and taking his well-earned relaxation on one side, and you, Mammy, sitting on the other side, and Declan between you both. How are you all? I wish to talk to each of you in turn—to Declan first, then to you, Mammy, and last, but by no means least, to my dear Daddy. Later in the recording, Reverend Mother, who is here beside me, will say a few words to you, and after that you will hear my school choir singing some Irish songs that I have taught them and some native songs they have taught me. I hope you will enjoy them."

Joe tried to remember the voice. Then he realized that he probably had never heard Claire speak. This sounded more like reading than speaking, he thought—like a teacher reading a story to a class of infants, making her voice go up and down in pretended interest.

She addressed the priest first, and Joe looked at him—eyes closed, hands joined at the left shoulder, head to the side, feet crossed, his whole body limp and graceful as if in repose. She asked him for his prayers and thanked him for his letter last Christmas. She said that every day she got her children to pray both for him and for the success of his work, and asked him to send her the collection of Irish melodies—a blue-backed book, she said, which he would find either in the piano stool or in the glass bookcase beside the drawing-room window.

"And now you, Mammy. You did not mention your lumbago in your last letter, so I take it you are not suffering so much from it. And I hope you have found a good maid at last, because the house is much too big for you to manage all by yourself. There are many young girls around the mission here who would willingly give you a hand, but then they are too far away, aren't they? However, please God, you are now fixed up."

She went on to ask about the gardens and the summer crop of flowers, and told of the garden she had beside the convent and of the flowers she was growing. While her daughter spoke to her, Mrs. Hogan worked her mouth and lips furiously, and Joe wondered what she was saying to herself.

"And now I come to my own daddy. How are you, Daddy? I am sure you were very sorry when Prince had to be shot, you had him so long. And then the Prince before that —how long did you have him? I was telling Sister Monica here about him the other day, about the first Prince, and when I said he lived to be nineteen and a half, she just laughed in my face and said she was sure I was mistaken. But he was nineteen and a half, wasn't he? You got him on my sixth birthday, I remember, and although I never saw the second Prince—you got him after I had entered—I am quite sure he was as lovely as the first. Now, why don't you get yourself a third, Daddy? He would be company for you when you go on your rambles, and it would be nice for *you* to have him lying beside you on the office floor, the way the first Prince used to lie."

Joe watched the old man. Mr. Bernard could not move himself to face the recorder, but his eyes were on it, the large, startled eyes of a horse.

"And now, Daddy, before I talk any more to you, I am going to play a tune for you on my violin. I hope you like it. It is the 'Gartan Mother's Lullaby.' Do you remember it?"

She began to play. The music was tuneful but no more. The lean, tinny notes found a weakness in the tape or in the machine, because when she played the higher part of the melody, the only sound reproduced was a shrieking monotone. Joe sprang to his feet and worked at the controls but he could do nothing. The sound adjusted itself when she came to the initial melody again, and he went back to his seat.

It was then, as he turned to go back to the fire, that he noticed the old man. He had moved somehow in his armchair and was facing the recorder, staring at it. His one good hand pressed down on the sides of his chair and his body rocked backward and forward. His expression, too, had changed. The dead purple of his cheeks was now a living scarlet, and the mouth was open. Then, even as Joe watched, he suddenly levered himself upright in the chair, his face pulsating with uncontrollable emotion, the veins in his neck dilating, the mouth shaping in preparation for speech. He leaned forward, half pointing toward the recorder with one huge hand.

"*Claire!*"

The terrible cry—hoarse, breathy, almost lost in his asthmatic snortings—released Father Declan and Mrs.

Hogan from their concentration on the tape. They ran to him as he fell back into the chair.

Darkness had fallen by the time Joe left Foundry House. He had helped Father Declan to carry the old man upstairs to his bedroom and helped to undress him and put him to bed. He suggested a doctor, but neither the priest nor Mrs. Hogan answered him. Then he came downstairs alone and switched off the humming machine. He waited for almost an hour for the others to come down—he felt awkward about leaving without making some sort of farewell—but when neither of them came, he tiptoed out through the hall and pulled the door after him. He left the recorder behind.

The kitchen at home was chaotic. The baby was in a zinc bath before the fire, three younger children were wrestling in their pyjamas, and the five elder were eating at the table. Rita, her hair in a turban and her sleeves rolled up, stood in the middle of the floor and shouted unheeded instructions above the din. Joe's arrival drew her temper to him.

"So you came home at last! Did you have a nice afternoon with your fancy friends?"

He picked his steps between the wrestlers and sat in the corner below the humming gas jet.

"I'm speaking to you! Are you deaf?"

"I heard you," he said. "Yes, I had a nice afternoon."

She sat resolutely on the opposite side of the fireplace, to show that she had done her share of the work; it was now his turn to give a hand.

"Well?" She took a cigarette from her apron pocket and lit it. The chaos around her was forgotten.

"Well, what?" he asked.

"You went up with the recorder, and what happened?"

"They were all there—the three of them."

"Then what?"

"We played the tape through."

"What's the house like inside?"

"It's very nice," Joe said slowly. "Very nice."

She waited for him to continue. When he did not, she said, "Did the grandeur up there frighten you, or what?"

"I was just thinking about them, that's all," he said.

"The old man, what's he like?"

"Mr. Bernard? Oh, Mr. Bernard—he's the same as ever. Older, of course, but the same Mr. Bernard."

"And Father Declan?"

"A fine man. A fine priest. Yes, very fine."

"Huh!" said Rita. "It's not worth your while going out, for all the news you bring home."

"The tape was lovely," said Joe quickly. "She spoke to all of them in turn—to Father Declan and then to her mother and then to Mr. Bernard himself. And she played a tune on the violin for him, too."

"Did they like it?"

"They loved it, loved it. It was a lovely recording."

"Did she offer you anything?"

"Forced me to have tea with them, but I said no, I had to leave."

"What room were they in?"

"The breakfast room. The drawing room was always drafty."

"A nice room?"

"The breakfast room? Oh, lovely, lovely—Glass handle on the door and a beautiful carpet and beautiful pictures— everything. Just lovely."

"So that's Foundry House," said Rita, knowing that she was going to hear no gossipy details.

"That's Foundry House," Joe echoed. "The same as ever —no different."

She put out her cigarette and stuck the butt behind her ear.

"They're a great family, Rita," he said. "A great, grand family."

"So they are," she said casually, stooping to lift the baby out of its bath. Its wet hands patterned her thin blouse. "Here, Joe! A job for you. Dress this divil for bed."

She set the baby on his knee and went to separate the wrestlers. Joe caught the child, closed his eyes, and rubbed his cheek against the infant's soft, damp skin. "The same as ever," he crooned into the child's ear. "A great family. A grand family."

A Selective Bibliography

Note: As far as possible I have tried to avoid including stories already available in the following anthologies:

ANTHOLOGIES:

Irish Folk Stories and Fairy Tales. ed. W. B. Yeats. Universal Library.
Irish Stories and Tales. ed. Devin A. Garrity. Washington Square Press.
The Irish Genius. ed. Devin A. Garrity. Signet Books.
The Portable Irish Reader. ed. Diarmuid Russell. Viking.
1000 Years of Irish Prose: Part 1, The Literary Revival. ed. V. Mercier and D. H. Greene. Universal Library.

WORKS BY INDIVIDUALS:

Bowen, Elizabeth. *Stories.* Vintage Books.
Higgins, Aidan. *Killachter Meadow.* Evergreen Books.
Joyce, James. *Dubliners.* Compass Books.
O'Casey, Sean. *The Green Crow.* Universal Library.
O'Faolain, Sean. *The Finest Stories of Sean O'Faolain.* Bantam Books.
O'Flaherty, Liam. *Selected Stories.* ed. Devin A. Garrity. Signet Books.
Stephens, James. *A James Stephens Reader.* ed. Lloyd Frankenberg. Macmillan Paperbacks.
Stephens, James. *Irish Fairy Tales.* Collier Books.
Synge, John M. *The Aran Islands and Other Writings.* ed. Robert Tracy. Vintage Books.
Yeats, W. B. *The Celtic Twilight and a Selection of Early Poems.* ed. Walter Starkie. Signet Classics.

CRITICAL AND HISTORICAL WORKS: (Not in paperback)

Boyd, Ernest A. *Ireland's Literary Renaissance.* A. A. Knopf, 1922.
Carney, James. *Studies in Irish Literature and History.* Dublin Institute for Advanced Studies, 1955.
Delargy, James H. *The Gaelic Story-Teller.* (The Sir John Rhys Memorial Lecture). British Academy, 1945.

Dillon, Myles. *Early Irish Literature*. University of Chicago Press, 1948.

Flanagan, Thomas. *The Irish Novelists, 1800–1850*. Columbia University Press, 1959.

Kiely, Benedict. *Modern Irish Fiction—A Critique*. Golden Eagle Books, 1950.

Murphy, Gerard. *Saga and Myth in Ancient Ireland*. Colm Ó Lochlainn, 1955.

O'Connor, Frank. *The Lonely Voice: A Study of the Short Story*. World Publishing Co., 1963.

O'Faolain, Sean. *The Short Story*. Devin-Adair Co., 1951.

Acknowledgments

"Children" by Daniel Corkery. Reprinted by permission of The Devin-Adair Company from THE WAGER AND OTHER STORIES. Copyright 1950 by The Devin-Adair Co.

"The Shoemaker" by Seumas O'Kelly. Reprinted by permission of Alphonsus Sweeney from WAYSIDERS by Seumas O'Kelly. Copyright 1917 by The Talbot Press, Dublin.

"The Woman on Whom God Laid His Hand" by Pádraic O'Conaire. Translation by Séamus O Néill, reprinted with his permission. Copyright 1955 by IRISH WRITING.

"Three Women Who Wept" by James Stephens. Reprinted with permission of The Macmillan Company and the literary representatives of the Estate of the late James Stephens from HERE ARE LADIES by James Stephens. Copyright 1913 by The Macmillan Company, renewed 1941 by James Stephens.

"Clay" by James Joyce. Reprinted by permission of The Viking Press, Inc. from DUBLINERS by James Joyce. Originally published by B. W. Huebsch, Inc. in 1916.

"Davin's Story" by James Joyce. Reprinted by permission of The Viking Press, Inc. from A PORTRAIT OF THE ARTIST AS A YOUNG MAN by James Joyce. Copyright 1916 by B. W. Huebsch, Inc. 1944 by Nora Joyce.

"Education" by Lennox Robinson. Reprinted by permission of the author's estate. Copyright 1919 by Lennox Robinson.

"The Blow" by Liam O'Flaherty. Reprinted by permission of The Devin-Adair Company from THE STORIES OF LIAM O'FLAHERTY. Copyright 1956 by The Devin-Adair Co.

"Lovers" by Liam O'Flaherty. Reprinted by permission of Jacques Chambrun, Inc. Copyright 1932 by the author.

"The Fur Coat" by Sean O'Faolain. Reprinted by permission of The Devin-Adair Company from THE MAN WHO INVENTED SIN AND OTHER STORIES. Copyright 1948 by The Devin-Adair Co.

"Two of a Kind" by Sean O'Faolain. Reprinted by permission of Little, Brown and Company from I REMEMBER! I REMEMBER! by Sean O'Faolain. Copyright © 1960 by the author.

"Peasants" by Frank O'Connor. Reprinted by permission of Alfred A. Knopf, Inc. and Harold Matson Company, Inc. from THE STORIES OF FRANK O'CONNOR. Copyright 1936 by Frank O'Connor.

"The Man of the World" by Frank O'Connor. Reprinted by permission of Alfred A. Knopf, Inc. from DOMESTIC RELATIONS by Frank O'Connor. "The Man of the World" first appeared in *The New Yorker*. Copyright © 1957 by Frank O'Connor.

"Dante and the Lobster" by Samuel Beckett. Reprinted by permission of the Grove Press, Inc. Originally published in the United States in *Evergreen Review*, Vol. 1, No. 1. Copyright 1957 by Grove Press, Inc.